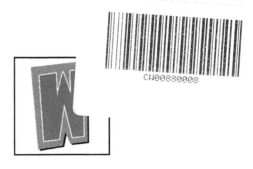

CW00880008

Special thanks to the following people for helping breathe life into the Godsverse:

Adam Goldstein, Alejandro Lee, Anna Carlson, Azia MacManus, Becky Fuller, Ben Coleman, Beth C, Brian Pickering, Bugz, Caledonia, Carl Bradley, Chad Bowden, Chris B, Chris Call, Daniel Groves, Dave Baxter, Deaven Shade, Dustin Cissell, Ed Vreeburg, Edward Nycz Jr., Emerson Kasak, Eva M., Gary Phillips, Harry Van den Brink, Hollie Buchanan II, Jake Schroeder, Janice Jurgens, Jason Crase, Jeff Lewis, Jennifer & Charlie Geer, Johnny Britt, Jonathan, Joshua Bowers, Journee Gautz, Jude M, Kenny Endlich, Logan Waterman, Louise Mc, Luis Bermudez, Matt Selter, Matthew Johnson, Michael Bishop, Moana McAdams, Nari Muhammad, Nick Smith, Celeste, Brian, and Niobe Cornish, Paul Nygard, Rhel ná DecVandé, Richard A Williams, Rick Parker, Rob MacAndrew, Robert Williams, Ronald, Rosalie Louey, Ruth, Stacy Shuda, Talinda Willard, Tamara Slaten, Tony Carson, tvest, Viannah E. Duncan, Victoria Nohelty, Walter Weiss, and Zachary.

GODSVERSE PLANETS

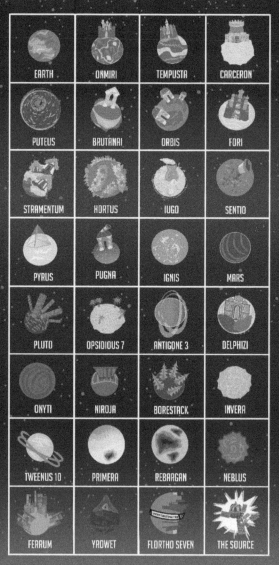

EARTH	ONMIRI	TEMPUSTA	CARCERON
PUTEUS	BRUTANAI	ORBIS	FORI
STRAMENTUM	HORTUS	IUGO	SENTIO
PYRUS	PUGNA	IGNIS	MARS
PLUTO	OPSIDIOUS 7	ANTIGONE 3	DELPHIZI
ONYTI	NIROJA	BORESTACK	INVERA
TWEENUS 10	PRIMERA	REBARGAN	NEBLUS
FERRUM	YROWET	FLORTHO SEVEN	THE SOURCE

1000 BC — BETRAYED (HELL PT 1)
/PIXIE DUST

500 BC — FALLEN (HELL PT 2)

200 BC — HELLFIRE (HELL PT 3)

1974 AD — MYSTERY SPOT (RUIN PT 1)

1976 AD — INTO HELL (RUIN PT 2)

1984 AD — LAST STAND (RUIN PT 3)

1985 AD — CHANGE

1985 AD — MAGIC/BLACK MARKET HEROINE

1985 AD — EVIL

1989 AD — DEATH'S KISS
(DARKNESS PT 1)

2000 AD — TIME

2015 AD — HEAVEN

2018 AD — DEATH'S RETURN (DARKNESS PT 2)

2020 AD — KATRINA HATES THE DEAD
(DEATH PT 1)

2176 AD — CONQUEST

2177 AD — DEATH'S KISS
(DARKNESS PT 3)

12,018 AD — KATRINA HATES THE GODS
(DEATH PT 2)

12,028 AD — KATRINA HATES THE UNIVERSE
(DEATH PT 3)

12,046 AD — EVERY PLANET HAS A GODSCHURCH
(DOOM PT 1)

12,047 AD — THERE'S EVERY REASON TO FEAR
(DOOM PT. 2)

12,049 AD — THE END TASTES LIKE PANCAKES
(DOOM PT 3)

12,176 AD — CHAOS

CHAOS

Book 11 of The Godsverse Chronicles

By:
Russell Nohelty

Edited by:
Leah Lederman

Proofread by:
Katrina Roets & Toni Cox

Cover by:
Psycat Covers

Planet chart and timeline design by:
Andrea Rosales

BOOK 1

CHAPTER 1

Kimberly

Location: Opsidious 7

Ten thousand years ago, I became Death.

Or, well, an incarnation of Death.

This day, I was summoned to a job which had stumped a half dozen of my best reapers, of which I had thousands, across the universe, doing my bidding. Honestly, it made me more a bureaucrat than anything these days. Every pantheon had its own version and its own claim on the universe, but I became Death for my Earth and a million Earths like it, which made me a busy celestial being.

"Where is she?" I asked a black-robed fairy waiting for me when I finally landed on the white sand beach of Opsidious Seven. I had trained Muriel myself a millennia ago. She wasn't one of my best reapers, even after a thousand years of experience, but she was competent enough that when she asked for my help specifically, I took a personal interest in this soul.

She pointed down the coastline. "She washed up last week, but she refuses to leave her body. We've tried everything, and she's injured three of us already. Even in death, she's too powerful for us to—"

"I got it." I rolled my eyes beneath the hood of my robe. "Thanks."

I walked down the sandy beach toward the point where Muriel had directed me before she vanished off for another case. I could only be at one place at one time. Even an immortal being had to account for time and space, which was why I assigned reapers across the endless cosmos, so I wouldn't have to do it all myself.

Opsidious Seven was far from my office on the far side of the galaxy from where I once lived on Earth. It was in a small pocket quadrant protected by the Greek Gods, sandwiched between a galaxy protected by the Hindu Gods and the Norse ones. Of course, they didn't call themselves that, but it was easier for me to think of them that way, the way I'd learned of them when I was still on Earth. They called themselves by the name of their most powerful gods, the Brahman line and the Odin line, respectively.

In the distance, I saw the body of a young woman, the tide lapping against it. It amazed me how similar each habitable world was, and they had made millions, though there were trillions more which had no life on them—or at least no life that was touched by the gods. The banal similarities of every Earth showed an innate lack of imagination on the part of the creators.

My job was to deliver to the underworld those who clung too tightly to their mortal coil. Most souls left their bodies willingly and without incident but sometimes, every thousand or so deaths, a soul clung to the last vestiges of their lives. That's when they called me in, the arbiter between the land of the living and land of the dead. It was not glamorous work, more akin to a counselor than any other role I'd taken on in the thousands of years since I became a god.

The sun shone on my face as I pulled back the black robe from my face and let the sand fill my sandals. The robe was part and parcel of my look. It was bestowed on me when I became the god of Death, and I forced the other grim reapers to wear it for camaraderie and consistency, even if the robe was a bit on the nose. Everybody needed a brand. The black robe distinguished us from other gods and bestowed us with a sense of austerity.

I approached the woman's body, bloated and waterlogged, near an outcropping of palm trees. Next to the body, a blue, shimmering apparition sat looking out at the water, holding the corpse's hand. She looked over at me with hollow eyes.

"I'm not going," the apparition said to me flatly. "I shouldn't be dead. This is all a mistake."

I nodded. "They all say that."

"You don't understand," the apparition said. "I'm—you know what, I've tried to explain this to every one of you, and I'm not going to do it again."

"I get it," I replied. "You were a god, and you think the rules don't apply to you. You wanted to speak to a manager, right?"

Her eyes narrowed. "Are you a manager?"

"In a way, I guess. I am Death incarnate. My name is Kimberly. Who are you?"

She chuckled. "You expect me to believe you are the god of Death, and your name is Kimberly."

"Can I sit?" I asked. She shrugged. "Frankly, I don't care if you believe me, but I am the god of Death. I don't consider myself much of a god, though. I'm more of a bureaucrat than anything."

She looked over at me, squinting under the beating sun. "If you are the god of Death, then how did you get your powers?"

"Do you know of the Four Horsemen?" I asked.

She nodded. "Conquest, Famine, Death, and War, chosen to protect the end of the universe from Surt, the demon god."

"That's right. Well, they were called forth about ten thousand years ago, but they had turned against the universe, so I killed them—every one of them, including Death—to stop Ragnarök. And for my troubles, I was left with this burden to carry for the rest of my days."

"So you kill gods, then?" she asked, acerbic.

"Not as a rule," I replied. "But when the need arises, sometimes a god needs to die. We should all have the option to die."

"Gods aren't supposed to die," she said, looking out at the water.

"No, they aren't, but they do. Now more than ever."

"Yes, I know that," she said. "And I did, didn't I? Die, I mean."

There was no way for a mortal to deny one of my reapers. Each of them was endowed with a bit of my spark, making them as close to a god as one could get without being gods themselves. I didn't generally get calls like this about a deity, though. They required a more delicate touch.

"You did," I said softly. "What was your charge when you were alive?"

"They once called me a siren, but I soured on that name once humanity bastardized it and made us villains. Imagine acting as if a group of women protecting themselves were the bad guys."

"I don't have to imagine it," I said. "I've seen it too many times."

"I just wanted a simple life, to live out the end of time."

"How did you die?" I asked.

"My three sisters and I were attacked. They threw a bright blue ball at us, and when it exploded…my sisters took the brunt of the explosion and vanished instantly. It still killed me. My body didn't vanish, nor did my soul, like theirs, but I died all the same. My soul drifted across the ocean, tethered to my body until I wound up here."

"That's horrible," I said. I'd become pretty good at commiserating with souls over the last few thousand years. Being Death meant being dispassionate about any deaths while empathizing enough to bond with the people you must shepherd. "And what were you called?"

The siren turned to me. "Molpe."

I held out my hand. "Nice to meet you. I'm Kimberly, again."

"It's horrible to meet you." She didn't take my outstretched hand, instead dropping her haunting eyes to the ground. "There's nothing you can do to put me back in my body, is there?"

I shook my head. "Even if I could, your body is gone, bloated and waterlogged. I would not wish my worst enemy to live in that body."

"Where will I go?" Molpe asked.

I shrugged. "Frankly, this doesn't happen every day. I would like to take you to my boss, who has been around since the beginning. Perhaps she will know, and if not, then the Godschurch, I suppose."

"Piffle," Molpe said. "A group of ineffective and incompetent dolts."

"I don't disagree with you," I said. "But they also protect gods, and if you have died, then they will want to know and hopefully be able to figure out what to do with you."

"I don't know why," Molpe said after a few silent moments, "but I trust you."

"Well, I am very trustworthy." I held my hand out to her. "Will you take my hand? It's okay. You can touch it."

"You won't abandon me?" Molpe said.

I shook my head. "I would never do that. My job is to shepherd you to the end, and I take my job very seriously."

Molpe nodded and placed her hand in mine. It was cold, and I squeezed it to warm it. "Would you like to stay here for another moment, or are you ready to go?"

"Can you ever be ready?" she asked.

In ten thousand years, I had never met a person who was truly ready to leave. Even the most stoic and ready to die still clung to at least one aspect of their lives. "No, but you can look forward to the next thing. Those who are most content think of the end as a new beginning, with new challenges. I imagine that, like most gods, you haven't had a challenge in a long time."

"I have not," she said, letting go of her body. "A new challenge sounds nice."

I pushed up to my feet. "Then let us go, Molpe."

"Yes," she said, rising to join me. "Let us go."

CHAPTER 2

Rebecca

Location: Antigone Three

It felt good to be out in the field on an assignment again instead of stuck behind a desk, even if the circumstances weren't ideal. Training new recruits shouldn't be the purview of the director of the Godschurch, but there weren't enough senior agents to go around since losing 90 percent of our people to the Godless. I had to step up.

"Julia!" I shouted as she strafed down the hallway across from me. "Eyes forward."

"I know, Director," she replied. "I've only done this a couple thousand times before."

"Yeah," I said. "But never with the Godschurch."

Julia Freeman was one of Katrina's recruits. After the Godless destroyed the Godschurch and thinned our agents to almost nothing, Katrina and the other gods gave me lists of their best people to train. While the recruits made decent clay, they had a long way before they were molded into something worthy of the Godschurch. The gods under our protection had dwindled, and if we had any hope of getting more pantheons to join the cause, then we needed highly-trained agents.

"You go around back in case they run out that way. I'll go in hard and flush them out to you, okay?"

Julia nodded. "Got it."

We were on the tail of a terrorist selling old Horde weaponry to the highest bidder. We had done a decent job of snuffing out the remaining Godless cells in the decade since the Battle of the Obelisk, an epic confrontation between Dolos and his people and the Godschurch joined together with the gods.

Of course, in the old movies, that's where the story ended—with a glorious victory. I was living in the aftershock of the destruction wrought by the Godless. We destroyed their infrastructure, but they destroyed ours in kind, and we'd never truly recovered.

On top of that, the Horde were still out there, and their tech could still kill a god. Every time we snuffed out one of their cells on one planet, another would pop up again. They used different names in different galaxies and with different cells. This one went by Projekt Kaos. With over a hundred thousand planets to govern and a fraction of our previous might, it meant that at any one time, thousands of planets were left unprotected.

I pressed my shoulder up to the door of an old, run-down house, gripping my pistol tightly in my hand. We'd tracked a group of arms dealers selling Horde tech to this house three days ago, and with any luck, they were still there. Our thermal heat maps showed two people inside, and nobody had come or gone in the past day. The odds were good. Even if they were inside, though, they would likely be heavily armed.

Godless tech was unstable. It could explode randomly in even the most careful hands, and most arms dealers weren't very careful. One side benefit of this was that often, Godless cells blew themselves up. We couldn't always wait for that. Every cell we took down was another story to help us earn the gods' confidence.

I tapped the bug in my ear. "You ready?"

I heard the crackle in my ear from Julia, on the other side of the house. "In position."

We really needed this operation to go well, so the gods would hire us back to protect them. At one time, we had over 2,000 dues-paying gods, but that had dwindled to less than a hundred. It didn't help that by the time the Battle of the Obelisk was over, almost all our dues-paying members had been killed, which didn't instill much confidence with other gods that we could protect them.

We tried to explain that they died defeating Cronus, the biggest threat to our universe in a million years, but nobody wanted to hear it. Many asked for refunds. Some sued. In the end, we could barely survive.

I took a deep breath at the door. "Please go well."

I raised my leg and kicked the lock off the door before sliding inside the house. Two young men wearing cloth face masks sat on a dirty couch watching cartoons. Heaps of Godless tech glowed green underneath them.

"FREEZE!" I shouted. "Hands up!"

They both hopped up and rushed toward the back of the house. Of course, they did. They always ran, even though they rarely escaped. I chased them down a narrow hallway, flushing them toward Julia at the back door. One of the boys opened the back door and rushed outside.

"Now!"

A forearm came out of nowhere and clotheslined the perp, sending him to the ground. There was a flash and then a purple cloud of smoke. Julia appeared behind the other man, and she pulled him over her shoulder, flipping him onto the ground.

Both of the terrorists writhed on the floor in pain.

"I told you I could do it," Julia smiled at me. "I don't need training. Just let me loose."

One of the men pulled a handgun from a holster on his leg.

"GUN!" I shouted.

Julia dove away from the door, and I disappeared, using the fairy blood coursing through my veins to jump forward. When I appeared in a flash of my own purple smoke, I was in front of the door, aiming my pistol right at the man's head. "Don't do it."

His finger twitched for the trigger, and I fired two bullets, sending blood and brains splattering through the grass in the backyard. I whirled on Julia. "You don't need more training? Really? You almost died right there and put me in danger on top of that," I said. "That was sloppy. You can't just fall back on your pixie powers all the time, Julia."

"You did," Julia replied.

"That's different," I replied. "I was very careful to use them—"

"Listen, I appreciate what you're saying." Julia cut me off. "But I'm over 10,000 years old, and I think I know how to use my powers better than you know how to use yours."

I scoffed. "Then prove it next time."

"I don't know why you're complaining." Julia walked over to the other man. "We still got one. Was there any tech out front?"

"A bunch of it," I said.

She nodded. "Then we got that, too. Pretty good for a first mission, I think."

My eyes narrowed. "Don't get cocky. Pick him up, and let's call it in. It'll take hours for Zalnir to open a portal for us."

I was satisfied with the new prospect. Julia could handle her own. She had an attitude of superiority, even though she was brand new to the Godschurch. And she was infuriatingly flippant. Of course, what else did I expect from a Katrina recommendation, the single most cocky being I've ever met in my life?

CHAPTER 3

Katrina

Location: Delphizi

I hated diplomatic missions. They were always far from home and forced me to eat crow in front of gods that wanted nothing more than to show how much more powerful they were than everyone else and how much control they had over their people. It was an exercise in self-restraint to sit respectfully without beating them senseless.

Saraswati was nicer than most gods, but there was still a smugness about her like there was with every god I had ever met. I shouldn't have even been on these diplomatic missions, but after the gods learned that I had personally killed both Hera and Zeus, along with fighting Cronus on multiple occasions, I had become somewhat of a celebrity—the human who became a Devil, worked her way up to being a god, and fought a Titan.

My reputation preceded me, which meant that I had some amount of clout, and since I paid the Godschurch for protection, I became their best spokesperson. If I needed protection, then perhaps other gods did as well. After all, very few of them had ever defeated a Titan or even another god for that matter. Most gods, save for the power they held, were pussies.

Saraswati had been playing her veena, plucking it carefully for the past thirty minutes, lulling me to sleep. She smiled as she played. I fought the urge to nap and smiled back at her. Gods were always assessing your worth, so it was impossible to know if her torturously long song was a sign of respect or some kind of test. Either way, I needed it to stop before I fell into a deep sleep or a fit of rage.

Just as I opened my mouth to ask her to stop playing, she did so of her own accord. She placed her veena next to her and laid her hands in the lap of her white and red floral sari. She blinked at me several times as if she wanted me to start speaking. When I didn't, she opened her mouth to start herself. I tried never to speak first with the gods, for they were all tricky and vain, and speaking first put you at a natural disadvantage.

"I know why you have come, Katrina," Saraswati said.

"Of course you do," I said. "I sent my emissary ahead to speak to you, and she is nothing if not clear about my intentions."

I turned back to Akta, my personal bodyguard for most of the past ten thousand years. She was supposed to guard the queen of Hell, the Devil—which, at the moment, was my old friend from Earth, Connie. But Akta had always been a loyal soldier, and after Velaska released her from her obligation to the Devil's throne, I asked if she could be reassigned. Her mouth was locked in a sneer across her dark face, and her bright green eyes stared daggers back at me. She did not like being called an emissary, and she hated diplomatic missions more than I did. She wanted to hunt, and fight, and drink, and visits like this one to Saraswati allowed for none of those things.

"I find your position very odd," Saraswati said. "You have such a high reputation. Why would you need the protection of the Godschurch?"

I cleared my throat. I had rehearsed this speech a hundred times on a hundred planets for a hundred different gods. "It is specifically because of what I've seen that I know how valuable the Godschurch is. They protect me, and all gods from the challenges we don't even know are there. Despite my power, I can still only be in one place at a time, same as you, and there are gaps in my knowledge big enough to drive a steamboat through."

"I am the goddess of knowledge. There is very little I don't know about, my friend."

"That's hubris." I tsked. "Which I understand. We are very powerful, but we are not all-powerful. There are millions of habitable planets and tens of millions of threats. We cannot possibly hope to catch every one before they rise up to destroy us. By pooling our resources, the Godschurch is able to protect us better than any one of us could ever do on our own."

Saraswati sniffed. "But they don't seem to be doing a very good job. In fact, it seems like every god under their protection has either died or been in a life-threatening situation in the not-so-distant past."

"No doubt," I said with a nod. "That part is true, but it's only because of the Godschurch that we don't have the Mad Titan Cronus and his bride Rhea storming around the universe."

"No," Saraswati said. "But they did not kill them, either. They rest near the Source, do they not?"

The Godschurch base was positioned in geosynchronous orbit around the Source at the center of the cosmos, with hundreds of god-killing weapons trained on our most famous prisoners, Cronus and Rhea. "That's right, and we're running out of funds to protect the universe from them. If you don't want to see Cronus and Rhea rampage across the universe, then we need your support."

That was a slight lie. Since we beat them in the Battle of the Obelisk, they hadn't shown any aggression, and I wasn't sure what would happen if we disarmed the weapons trained at them. I didn't want to find out.

"I am unconvinced," Saraswati said. "Even if the Mad Titan wanted to destroy everything in the universe, this galaxy is so remote it would take eons for him to reach us."

I raised an eyebrow. "Don't be so sure. His ability to destroy is legendary. All I'm asking is that you bring this information to your pantheon. I'd like to speak to them."

"There is an air of desperation in your voice," Saraswati said. "It is unbecoming."

I swallowed. Akta took a step forward, but I held up my hand, and she stopped. "There is more than a hint of desperation in my body. That only an air of it reached my lips is a testament to the hard work I've done to control my emotions." I glared at her. "But I am still very bad at it." I pushed myself to my feet to stand. "Diplomacy does not suit me, but I am here, doing the bidding of the Godschurch because I believe in their mission, and I believe that we are better together than we are apart. I am part of a pantheon that is notoriously individualistic, and you saw what happened to us. We were cut in half and barely held on to our power. Since we've come together, we are stronger than ever. If you joined us, we could be stronger together...but I will not beg."

Saraswati nodded thoughtfully. "I appreciate your candor. I will take this to my pantheon." She turned behind her and turned back to me with a sack. "Meanwhile, this, I believe, is the down payment for my part of the Godschurch protection this year. Let me know if it is not enough."

I grabbed the sack from Saraswati and saw it filled with the god's gold, the only currency that the Godschurch accepted. "Holy shit, really?"

She nodded. "Yes, I have been separated from my brothers and sisters in your pantheon for too long. I look forward to joining with you again, and I hope to convince the other gods in my family to do the same. Until then, at least I will have your protection."

I nodded to her. "Thank you."

"Of course," Saraswati said. She picked up her veena and began to pluck it again. "Now, if you'll excuse me—"

As she began to play, I saw a flash of purple pop in front of me. Akta, with reflexes so fast even I could barely see them, pulled the veena from Saraswati's hand and threw it across the room.

"Excuse me!" Saraswati shouted. "How dare you—"

I spun around to grab the veena, but as I did, it began to glow blue, a shade of blue like I hadn't seen in many generations. I felt a hand yank me back behind the throne, where Saraswati screamed in panic.

"Bomb!" Akta said.

The room went up in a burst of blue light just as Akta smashed some of her pixie dust on the ground, and we vanished from sight.

CHAPTER 4

Akta

Location: Delphizi

The air was acrid when we had first walked into the room, but it wasn't until Katrina said "thank you" that I caught the faint blue hue coming from Saraswati's veena. Katrina always reminded me not to move and not to interrupt, but she also told me to protect her and Saraswati above everything else, so I had to act.

If I were wrong, then I would get a tongue lashing, but if I were right, I would be saving two lives and hopefully solidifying the necessity of the Godschurch in the process.

"Move!" I screamed as I rushed forward and grabbed the veena. I pushed Saraswati behind the throne she knelt on and pulled Katrina behind it as well, just as the veena began to pulsate a bright blue. If I was right, we were too close to the soul bomb to survive.

"What's—" Katrina started to say, but I grabbed her hand, slammed a handful of the pixie dust on the ground, and pulled Saraswati close as we vanished. We reappeared in front of the castle just in time to watch the explosion send wood and glass flying dozens of feet in every direction and leaving a black hole in the bottom left side of the castle. Most of the windows on the building were smashed as well.

"What just happened?" Saraswati asked.

"I'm sorry, your majesty," I said. "I had an instinct that there was a bomb inside your veena, and unfortunately, I was right."

"You had an instinct!" Katrina shouted, grabbing and pulling at her hair in frustration. "That is one hell of an instinct. Do you know what kind of bomb it was?"

"Yes, ma'am," I said. "Unfortunately, I've seen it before. We've seen it before, many generations ago. Do you remember the soul bombs Asmodeus used during Ragnarök?"

"Please…" Katrina said, releasing her hair and staring up at me. "Please tell me that it wasn't."

"I believe it was the same kind of soul bomb, ma'am."

"Gods-damn it," Katrina muttered. "I haven't seen one in thousands of years. I thought we destroyed that tech."

"We did," I said. "But somebody figured it out again. A billion systems with millions of planets across thousands of years, it's surprising it took so long."

"Excuse me," Saraswati said, visibly upset but clearly trying to maintain a sense of dignity and decorum. "What is…a soul bomb?"

"It's an insidious weapon made from the remains of a dead soul concentrated into a tiny package until it's ready to burst. It's strong enough to vaporize everything in its path, including a god." I choked back my anger. "We haven't seen one since I tracked down the original plans after Ragnarök."

"We burned those plans and killed anyone associated with their construction." Katrina was pacing and stammering, barely in control of her wits. "So, if they're all dead, then who did this?"

"I don't know, ma'am," I said. "But I intend to find out."

"See that you do," Katrina fumed before turning to Saraswati. She softened. "Are you okay?"

"Of course." Saraswati smiled. "It was only a veena, and I can make another castle. But my life—well, you have proven yourself, and the Godschurch, on this day."

"Thank you," Katrina replied, but she was frowning. "The question is, why did we even have to save you?"

"If I may, ma'am," I said. "I think we should not rule out the possibility that the bomb was not meant for her but you."

Katrina flung a hand in the air dismissively. "That's preposterous. Nobody knew I was here."

"Is that true?" I turned to Saraswati. "Do you have someone who keeps your schedule, or perhaps the schedule of the staff, who would know that Katrina was coming?"

Saraswati nodded. "Of course, my deva manages my affairs."

"Can you tell me where to find them?" I asked.

"Yes," Saraswati replied. "Lakshmi works in the front office."

I eyeballed the smoking remnants of the castle. "Let me guess, on the other side of the castle, far from the throne room."

"That's right."

Of course, she would be free and clear of the bomb if she was responsible for setting it off. "Not surprising."

***

Angels. Valkyries. Devas. They were all from the same lineage but with different names. A rose by any other name. They were equally brutal, ruthless, and controlling. They served at the right hand of a god and were usually the ones sent to wipe out insurrection.

I had been in the control of the Devil, and eventually Katrina, for 13,000 years, and in that time, I had met all sorts of angelic creatures. All of them underestimated me, which I used to my advantage. Let them think a pixie cannot be as good at deciphering the truth as the immortals were at deception. They saw my lack of godly heritage as a handicap, but it was my greatest strength. Assuming I was a dullard, they'd let their guard down just enough for me to suss out the reality from the fallacy.

Lakshmi wasn't in her office when I stalked into it. A small, blue girl with several arms carrying many plates down the hallway stopped when I hailed her. "Excuse me. Have you seen Lakshmi, the deva?"

The girl nodded. "She ran upstairs to the throne room after the explosion. She's probably still up there."

I climbed the wooden stairs of the castle and floated into the air over the wreckage. I found the deva surveying the damage and landed on the ground in front of her. "She's fine," I said.

"Excuse me," Lakshmi said, flustered. Her wings were extended behind her, and a dark red ruby rested on the middle of her tanned forehead. Otherwise, her dark, rich hair was the only thing that would have separated her from any other angel or Valkyrie I ever met.

"Both of them," I said. "Katrina and Saraswati are both safe."

She swallowed loudly. "That's good. Where are they?"

I shook my head. "You must think I'm quite the rube if you think I'm going to tell you that."

"Don't take that tone with me." She sneered at me. "I need to know where my god is so that I may protect her."

"If you're protecting her, then tell me, how did the soul bomb get into the veena? I've been here all day, and I haven't seen anyone else come or go from the throne room…except for you."

"Soul bomb?" she said, confused. "What is a soul bomb?"

"Don't play stupid. It is one of the few objects that can kill a god, vaporize them completely, and the number of people who know how to make them is vanishingly small."

"Is this more Godless tech?"

I shook my head. "They wish they could make something so powerful. The Godless once tried to pursue the tech, but it was too hard to steal souls from the underworld, so they moved to Horde tech. The result is the same if you want a dead god, which obviously you do."

"Preposterous," she grunted. "I love Saraswati. I chose this charge to be near her."

I stepped toward her. "Then you will have no problem coming with me to the Godschurch to answer some questions."

"I absolutely will not," she said, folding her arms across her chest. "I have to protect my god."

"Didn't you hear? She's under the protection of the Godschurch now. Less than a day, and we've already saved her life once. Now please, come quietly. If you are innocent, then you have nothing to fear."

"You would say that. I've never known any who are taken by the Godschurch and lived to tell about it."

"I swear on my life I will not let harm come to you," I said, a serious timber in my voice.

"Do it," I heard behind me. I spun to see Saraswati. "If you are innocent, then you will be home by nightfall."

I bowed my head. "I would like you to come with us, too. We can protect you better in the church than here."

"I don't want to go. I have work to do." Saraswati yawned. "And I need to rest."

"I know you do, but there can be no rest, not really until we uncover the plot on your life."

"Very well." She nodded, turning to Katrina, who walked in behind her. "I'm afraid our tete-a-tete will have to wait."

"Your safety will do more to help our cause, and yours, than any amount of words. Besides, we can arrange a meeting with your pantheon on base. Come with us, and find out why I love the Godschurch and why I gladly pay them for my protection."

Saraswati placed her hand on Katrina's and smiled. "Let us away."

CHAPTER 5

Julia

Location: Antigone Three

I did not like being treated like a child. While I had only been a member of the Godschurch for a few months, I had tracked monsters and worked in law enforcement for the underworld since I was newly dead over 10,000 years ago and had been responsible for solving thousands of cases long before Rebecca Lobdell was a twinkle in her mother's eye.

"Ow!" The perp we'd captured on Antigone Three winced as I dug my nails into his arm. My anger at Rebecca and her condescending tone was clouding my judgment and hurting the mission, which was to bring the perp to the Godschurch for interrogation. Behind me, Rebecca watched disapprovingly.

"Ease up," she said.

I loosened my fingers on the perp's arm. "Yes, Director."

Rebecca sighed. "What's taking them so long?"

She stood next to a palette of Godless tech that we had gathered from the terrorist's house. We were behind a rundown church on the outskirts of Lorti, the fifth biggest city on Antigone Three. It was hard to tell most human-built cities apart from each other. They were combinations of enormous skyscrapers reaching into the sky and the ramshackle houses that speckled their shadows. Hover cars sped overhead while rust buckets sputtered along the streets, a true testament between the haves and the have nots, and our terrorist was one of the latter.

"Where are they?" Rebecca grumbled under her breath and walked toward the doors, which were locked. Every planet touched by the gods had a Godschurch, which we used to travel between worlds. It was faster than space travel, after all, and we could jump thousands of light-years in a matter of seconds. As Rebecca pounded the door, a bright white light appeared behind it, and it swung open for us. "About time. Let's go."

She held up her fingers and beckoned the palette forward. Four booster rockets helped it rise into the air and move through the doorway. Rebecca followed, and when she was gone through the white light, I pushed the suspect forward.

"I ain't going in there!" he shouted, driving against me.

"I don't have time for this today," I said, pressing him harder until he stumbled through the glowing doorway. I followed behind him carefully. I knew that I would end up inside the Godschurch when I walked into the light, but it was no less alarming to do so. Akta told me it gets easier with time. She had been a member of the Godschurch for longer than I had and even worked with them over the centuries since before Connie's reign of Hell.

She'd brought me along on missions a couple of times, which was how I even got onto the Godschurch's radar when they were recruiting. A kind word from Katrina sealed the deal. It's not that I didn't like working for Connie or the Underworld, but the Godschurch put me in contact with way more interesting worlds. After tens of thousands of years, I had tired of the oppressive heat and craterous terrain of Hell.

My foot disappeared through the whiteness first. I shifted my weight forward, and my face followed. With one more step, I was through the door and into the Godschurch. The door slammed closed behind me, and I looked up at the marvelous cathedral in front of me, as grand as anything on Earth or in Hell.

Hundreds of columns lined the pews and seemed to carry on forever. Inlaid vines encrusted with jewels spiraled around every column and bloomed on the ceiling, where thousands of gem flowers made up a garden. Along each wall were stained glass reliefs of different gods from different pantheons, from Zeus and Hera to Odin and Brahma. There was even a relief of Katrina snarling down at us, which always made me chuckle.

"Get a move on," Rebecca said, her words echoing through the church. She was already halfway down the pews toward the altar. I grabbed the suspect and moved down the aisle, every step I took reverberating through the empty church.

Well, nearly empty. A burly man with seven arms wearing a red cloak and pointed hat sat behind a set of controls in an upper vestibule, high above us, controlling the Godschurch teleporters.

"This place is nice," the suspect said. "Too bad we're gonna blow it up soon."

My hand slipped, and I elbowed him in the back. "Sorry."

"No, you're not," he replied, winded.

I smiled. "Prove it."

Rebecca reached the altar. Above an elevated podium with five empty, gilded thrones sat the logo of the Godschurch, an all-seeing eye encrusted with jewels. It looked out upon the church and the doors that led to planets around the universe.

"Take the stairs," Rebecca said. "I'll use the elevator."

"Not fair," I said.

"No, it's not." She smiled wryly. There was a bit of humanity buried deep down under the stone-faced façade she'd built around herself. "That's the advantage of being the director. I'll meet you down there."

Rebecca turned left and hit an elevator button hidden in the oak walls. I turned right and walked toward a small wooden door next to the altar, nestled at the end of three ornate confessionals. I pushed open the door to the poorly lit, spiral staircase that descended further than I could see. The room was cool, lined with gray brick, and exceptionally plain, except for the portraits that hung on the walls.

"Dangerous, isn't it," the man said, "to have me in here, alone, with you?"

I chuckled. "Maybe for you, but I'm not scared of you. I've dealt with thousands like you in my time, which is longer than you could imagine."

"It's not going to matter for long," he snarled confidently.

"You keep saying that, but I don't think you understand that I have you in custody. There is no way out of the Godschurch except through those doors, which you can't access without Zalnir's help."

The suspect descended the stairs slowly. "No, I understand that. I just don't think you understand what is coming for you."

I smirked. "And what is coming for me?"

"Not just you, but all of you, and those you protect. The time of the gods is over. Kaos will awaken and end you all."

"Kid," I said with a sigh, "I've heard that before. And in ten thousand years, nobody has delivered, no matter how many have tried."

He chuckled. "That's all about to change. It only takes once."

"We'll see."

CHAPTER 6

Rebecca

Location: Godschurch Base

The contrast in smell from the natural oaken scene of the Godschurch to the antiseptic odor of the underground Godschurch base never failed to surprise me, even after I'd spent decades moving between them.

The doors of the elevator slid open, and I stepped out into the base. A young officer came to greet me, wearing the black and gray jumpsuit all recruits were forced to wear when they were not on a mission. Her holographic badge said "Sanders," with an all-seeing eye watermarked beneath it. They all looked the same to me, baby-faced and unfamiliar, without any of the lines on their faces from confronting the horrors of the world.

"Welcome back, Director," Sanders said with a toothy smile. I hated when they smiled. It was a sign of weakness in most of the animal kingdom, and it meant she hadn't seen enough of the world to put on a righteous scowl. She would learn. We would break her, eventually. The universe would break her before long.

"Thank you," I grunted, pointing back to the palette of Godless tech. "That all needs to be cataloged. We've got to pinpoint where it was procured."

"Absolutely," she said. "It would be my pleasure."

There was no way it would be her pleasure, but some amount of sucking up to the boss was par for the course. I walked through the corridor that led to the command center. On my left, a massive window looked out on the Source, which contained every fragment of creation energy that could be used to build or repair the universe. Few could tap into the power of creation. Zeus, Odin, and Brahma, along with a couple of others, including Cronus, who stared back at me and waved from his position in front of the Source.

The glass was one-way, which meant neither he nor his wife Rhea should have known I was back, and yet, he always seemed to know—either that, or he randomly waved at the Godschurch just hoping I was watching. I hated that Katrina made a deal with him to live near the Source so we could both protect and guard him. She might trust him, but I had every bit of confiscated Godless tech trained on him, along with some of our own tech, ready to fire at a moment's notice. If we fired even a fraction of it, both Titans would die instantly.

"You're back."

I spun around to find Akta looking at me. She wore a green shirt and long skirt that fell loosely at her knees. Both matched her emerald green eyes. She kept a gun on her hip to humor me but never used it, preferring the daggers she kept in her belt and the throwing knives she had strapped around her leg and arm. "How did it go?"

I looked over at Julia, who walked out of the stairwell and snaked her way through the computer terminals toward the jail cells situated behind the bullpen of the command center. Around the bullpen, a cadre of analysts worked to pinpoint problems around the universe and make sure we were able to respond as quickly as possible.

"It was fine." I knew she meant how did Julia do. "She was fine."

Julia was a descendant of Akta, and Akta had taught me how to use my own powers when she came to the Godschurch and found out I had fae blood. Julia was a natural fit, but she was not as pliable as Akta, who seemed to fit into the culture of the Godschurch like a snug glove.

"She will learn more in time," Akta said. "But she is a fine warrior and a good addition to your cause, especially in times like these."

"I'm sure she'll be fine." I nodded. "What about you? Were you able to get Saraswati?"

"Yes," Akta said. "Katrina secured her, and then, moments later, there was an attempt on her life."

"I don't like the sound of that," I said. "Is everyone okay?"

"Perfectly fine besides some property damage. It certainly showed our value quickly. Saraswati is working on bringing the other gods in her pantheon here for a meeting."

"Wonderful," I said. "Will you help Julia with the interrogation? I have a feeling your special brand of justice and knowledge of the attack could help track down whoever was trying to get at Saraswati."

"Of course, but I don't think it was just an attempt on Saraswati. I brought in Saraswati's deva for questioning just in case." Akta hesitated. "I think this was as much about an attack on Katrina as anything."

"That makes some sense," I said. "She does have a way of collecting enemies wherever she travels."

"She does." Akta couldn't help but chuckle, a rarity, before her face returned to its usual stoic expression. "Perhaps you can talk to the deva, Lakshmi. She has no respect for me, but she might speak to the director."

"I'll take care of it. Have you seen Katrina?"

"I know I'm her protection, but I can't keep track of her every minute of every day." She walked away from me, calling over her shoulder. "Last time I saw her, she was headed to an airlock to speak to Cronus."

"I hate when she does that. Do you think she knows that?"

"She knows," Akta said as she slid through an open door. "She just doesn't care."

***

I found it hard to believe that a deva would betray their charge or try to kill them, given that they were bred for service, but I had seen crazier things in this life. A disillusioned deva was a dangerous thing.

I made my way through the command center bullpen, checking in on each galaxy as I went. We had a small crew, which meant millions of planets went unmonitored every day, a fact that didn't go unnoticed by criminals throughout the universe.

I reached the back of the Godschurch base, where the medical bay and jail cells were located. As a dignitary of the Brahman line, Lakshmi wasn't confined to a cell. We were careful not to disrespect them unnecessarily. I found her in an interrogation room, scribbling on a sheet of paper. When I entered, she cocked her head.

"Good afternoon," I said. "My agent told me you wanted to speak with the director. Usually, we don't fulfill orders from suspects, but, given your position, I am willing to make an exception."

"Then you are the leader here?" Lakshmi asked.

"I am the director of the Godschurch."

"Good, because I do not want to say this twice." She ripped off a sheet of paper and handed it to me. "I am not responsible for this act, but I know what is."

I raised my eyebrows. "I'm all ears."

She took a long pause. "Have you ever heard of Projekt Kaos?"

The suspect that Julia and I captured had been a part of Projekt Kaos, one of the many new names for a faction of the Godless. I wasn't about to reveal that information. "No."

"Interesting," she said. "Are you sure you are the director of the Godschurch? It is my understanding that all directors are sworn in on the omega-level threats to the Godschurch."

I stared at her, unblinking.

Finally, she said, "Projekt Kaos is the only explanation for what has been happening to us."

"Us?"

Lakshmi nodded. "There have been other attempts on our gods. Two are dead. That is why I asked Saraswati to meet with you at all. She thought you were a joke, but I believe that hiring even a joke for protection is better than no protection at all."

"Thank you for your confidence," I grumbled. "What makes you think this is the work of Projekt Kaos?"

"The gods that were targeted, besides Saraswati." Lakshmi leaned forward. "Prithvi, god of the Earth, and Kama, god of love, along with Yama, god of the underworld, whom we managed to save. Unfortunately, we were not so lucky with the other two."

"What does that have to do with Projekt Kaos?"

"There is an old saying—a koan really, that I have heard on a whisper of the breeze. Earth, Love, Death, and the Night—lovers since the beginning—will return to Kaos, from whence they came. I have been intrigued by this koan for a long time, and every time I tracked down a clue, it led me back to Projekt Kaos and the Godschurch."

"Why us? Do you think the Godschurch is involved somehow?"

She took a deep breath, gathering her energy. "It is my understanding the Godschurch was specifically started to prevent Projekt Kaos from coming to pass, for it is older than the church itself. So old, only a small number know of its true nature. I hoped one of those people was you. Not knowing what it is does not change the fact that you must find out how to stop it, or all of our lives will be in danger. Perhaps the whole universe is in danger."

"I'll look into it." I bit my tongue before I said anything else, but it sounded like the ravings of a madwoman, perhaps one with a reason for vengeance against her boss.

"I do not expect you to believe me." Lakshmi rested her hands gently on the table. "Distrust and verify. I will stay here, willingly, until my innocence is proven." She smiled. "Could you bring me some tea? Two sugars and honey, please."

I smiled politely. "I'll see what I can do."

CHAPTER 7

Katrina

Location: Godschurch Base

I was the only person in the Godschurch who could talk to Cronus and Rhea. Or, to be more precise, I was the only person in the Godschurch they would talk to instead of vaporizing. Others tried blasting their voices from the command center, or even taking a spacesuit and walking out to them, but they just ignored them all, even Rebecca, and if somebody came close…well, zappy zappy, except for me.

"Are you really going out there again?" I heard behind me as I placed my hand on the airlock. I turned around to see Rebecca staring at me, arms folded across her chest.

"I need answers," I said.

"About what?" Rebecca said. "He hasn't moved for years except to scratch his balls. What answers could he provide?"

"I need to know who would try to kill me."

"I can tell you the answer to that," Rebecca replied. "Everybody! You are not very likable."

I chuckled despite myself. "Maybe, but he knows something about the attack today. I can feel it in my bones. Besides, if he doesn't, it's just my time that I've wasted, and I have an eternity of it left."

"What do you think he's going to say that he hasn't said before, and why would you believe anything he says?" Rebecca asked. "He's playing games with you."

"Nobody's tried to kill me before."

"Lots of people have tried to kill you."

"Not since the Battle of the Obelisk," I said. "Look, are you just here to get under my skin? Because mission accomplished."

"I'm trying to keep you safe. You pay dues just like the other gods, so you are my charge. You all are, and I can't protect you if you make stupid choices. Every time you do, you're taking your life into your own hands."

"Better my hands than somebody else's," I said.

Rebecca sighed. "Since I can't stop you, maybe you can help me."

"I can try," I said. "But no promises."

Rebecca lowered her voice. "That deva you and Akta brought here said that the assassination attempt was for something called Projekt Kaos."

"Why does that sound so familiar?"

"It's what the Godless have been calling themselves since the Battle of the Obelisk. Lakshmi says it goes further back than the Godless, to the origins of the universe, and the founding of the Godschurch itself."

"You think the Godless are working with the Godschurch now?"

Rebecca shook her head. "I don't know what to think, but I know that there's no such thing as coincidence. Either they have something in common, or the universe is playing a wicked trick on me."

"The universe is playing a wicked trick on all of us," I said and stepped into the airlock. "I'll ask him. Can you hit whatever button closes this thing?"

Rebecca pressed her hand against the lock, and the door slid closed. Once I slammed my hand on the red button that opened the airlock, the air slid out of the room with me along with it.

I flew toward the Source, toward Cronus and Rhea. It wasn't much of a home, as it didn't have walls or furniture, or even windows. I could have snapped my fingers and gotten there, but that might have alerted the command center something was different and sounded the alarm. The Godschurch had itchy trigger fingers. I didn't want to give them a reason to shoot me or the Titans. Besides, if there was something a god had on their side, it was time. We had eternity to make our way around the universe, which was equally frustrating and comforting.

Cronus and Rhea never learned how to put on clothes, or maybe they just didn't care for it. Cronus was at least covered in a thick layer of hair and a long beard which enveloped him down to his naval, but Rhea was bare, her large breasts drooping onto either side of her as she sprawled across space, fanning herself with a little fan like she was a Botticelli painting.

"Ah," Cronus said, seeing me. "If it isn't my favorite god."

"That's not saying much," I said. "You hate the gods. Being at the top of your heap is not a big accomplishment."

"Just think of it this way. If I ever got the chance to kill all the gods, you would be last. In that way, it's quite an honor."

Eons ago, Rhea had been banished to another universe, and Cronus was bound to a cave on a prison planet by Zeus. When I set him free, he ripped a hole in our universe to find Rhea. We were all nearly destroyed in the process before Apollo, Urania, and I bound him and Rhea to that other universe…for a time, at least until the Godless brought them back.

"See, saying things like that is the reason why the Godschurch has every piece of Godless tech they've ever confiscated aimed at you. If you played ball even a little bit, maybe they would loosen up."

Rhea laughed. "They will never loosen up, but that is the price of life, isn't it?"

"Well, for now," Cronus said.

"What does that mean?"

He shrugged. "I dunno. Just, in the scope of the universe, this time being held prisoner by the Godschurch has been a very small blip."

The Godless were originally controlled by Dolos, the son of Cronus and Rhea. His goal was to bring his parents back from that other dimension, which he did during the Battle of the Obelisk. A final confrontation ensued, and Rebecca was swallowed by the Mad Titan, only to slit open his belly and spill his blood, forcing their surrender. It was that end that allowed the uneasy peace we found ourselves in between the Titans and the Godschurch.

"Somebody tried to kill me today," I said, cutting to the chase.

"And let me guess, you think I had a part to play in it."

"I don't know what to think, but you still have the best motive, and the Godless are the reason you're back in this universe. Dollar to donuts, they are behind this assassination attempt. And since you both hate this universe, and the gods especially…it kinda makes sense, doesn't it?"

"Yes, until you remember that I stopped the destruction of this universe as well, didn't I?"

He wasn't wrong. However, he also set in motion the destruction of the universe, which meant he both tried to destroy the universe and saved it, which is like pointing a gun at somebody and then not firing at them and expecting a cookie for it.

"You did, but that doesn't mean your seething anger isn't bubbling up or that you aren't ready to try it again."

"And how would we even communicate with the Godless, darling?" Rhea said, dropping her fan into her lap. "As you mentioned, we are stuck here, bathing in the warmth of the Source, with every gun at your disposal aimed at us."

"I don't claim to know how the gods work, or how you as Titans go through the universe, or how you could get messages to each other. I just know that I really don't like people trying to kill me, and I'm not going to rest until I figure out what happened."

"My dear," Cronus said, stroking his long beard. "As I mentioned, you are my favorite god, so why would I want to kill you?"

"You don't need a reason. I guess I just don't believe you."

"You should."

"Says you," I replied. I waited for Cronus to continue, but when all he did was stare at me disapprovingly, I changed tactics. "Okay, let's say I believe you."

"As you have every reason to do," Rhea said, stretching out her large body. "For the record."

"Who else would want to kill me?"

"So many people," Cronus said.

"Other Titans?"

"Titans. Gods. Primordials. Angels. Devas. Valkyries." He counted on his fingers. "It's an extensive list."

"Interesting you say devas since we happen to have one in our custody. Do you know anything about Projekt Kaos?"

Cronus's eyes went wide. When he looked over at Rhea, she looked visibly shaken. "What do you know of those words?"

"Nothing," I said. "That's why I'm asking. The deva we arrested said it was the reason gods were being hunted, and the Godless now use it as their moniker, and since we battled them to stop you from coming back to this universe...Are you starting to see how it could all be interconnected?"

"If that's true, and this is all connected to Projekt Kaos..." Cronus said, nearly breathless, "then the universe is in trouble."

"Why?" I asked. "What is Projekt Kaos?"

"We don't know," Rhea said. "Not specifically. It was a plan put in place when the universe was young before even we were born. We just know it's bad."

"I thought you created all of this?" I said. "That's what you always told me."

"And I lied," Cronus said with a deep, guttural laugh. "I am a liar. But long before me, there were others that birthed me, who thought nothing of the universe. Those who were stoic, unyielding primordial. They created plans, for the end, for the beginning, for every scenario, and the worst of them all was Projekt Kaos, or as they called it then, Kaos."

"They spoke of it in hushed tones," Rhea added. "When they heard us coming, they would stop their talk. We heard the word Kaos many times on the wind of the universe before we fell out with our creators."

"But you don't know what it's about?"

"Only that if Projekt Kaos is what's behind this, then you must be cautious and speedy in equal measure. The very fabric of the universe rests in the balance."

"Fabulous," I said, pressing my fingers into the bridge of my nose. "That's just great. Can't I get one century where the whole universe isn't falling apart?"

Rhea smiled. "Apparently not. That is the way with leaders. There is always some other fire to put out. I much prefer sitting back and watching you do the work."

"If the universe is in trouble, that involves you, too," I said.

"I know," Rhea said. "And yet, I am not concerned. Either it will be solved, or it will not be, and I will return to the great beyond to be reborn again. Maybe as a kitty this time."

"You don't fool me," I said. "I saw how scared you were when I brought up Projekt Kaos. It fills you with fear, too, deep down in your bowels."

"Perhaps," she said, shooing me away. "But you seem to be on it, for now. Go now; you bore me."

"There's nothing you can tell me?" I said, throwing up my hands. "This is bull!"

"I can give you a name," Cronus said. "If it will shut you up."

"...Yes, please."

"You really shouldn't tell her," Rhea said, rolling her eyes.

"Oh, let the girl have her fun," Cronus said. "Indra."

"Is that a person, a place, a thing, or an idea?"

"Figure it out," Cronus said, lying on his wife's bulging stomach. "You have made me tired and reminded me of times I would rather forget. You are no longer welcome here today."

I spun around and headed back to the Godschurch. I knew better than to talk with them when they were done talking. I did not want to be eaten, and I had work to do now that I knew the universe was in trouble—yet again.

CHAPTER 8

Akta

Location: Godschurch Base

"Where did you get the tech?" Julia slammed her hands on the metal table in the interrogation room. When I opened the door, she wheeled on me. "Come to check on me?"

"Whoa," I said, holding up my hands. "I come in peace. Rebecca thought I could help."

"Whatever. I am not a child."

I furrowed my brow. "Can I please talk to you outside?"

"Ooooooh," the suspect said. "You're in trouble."

"Shut it," Julia grumbled before storming out of the room. I followed, locking the door behind me. When I turned to her, she was tapping her feet rapidly on the ground. "What do you want?"

I stepped forward until my nose was almost touching hers. I was her superior, after all, and her elder. "Your emotions are getting the better of you. You never undermine a colleague in front of a suspect."

Her face contorted in a grimace, and her hands clenched, along with her jaw. She wanted a fight, but after a moment, her anger broke, and she took a deep breath. "I know. I'm sorry. It's just—I'm sick of being treated like a rookie."

I laughed. "You are a rookie."

"No, I'm not!" she shouted. "I've been doing this for ten millennia."

"Not for this place. The Godschurch has its own rules, as you know. You're a great investigator, but this is a whole different level. We're not tracking down soul jumpers or quelling disputes in the colonies here. We're protecting gods, the gods who control the very fabric of the universe. It's a big deal, and Rebecca has taken you under her wing because she believes in you."

"Because of you," Julia mumbled.

"Maybe, but she still did it. I believe in you, too. Do you think she goes on missions with every recruit? Don't answer that. I'll do it for you. She doesn't. She's doing it because she sees promise in you, but you've always been rough around the edges."

"Hey—"

I touched her cheek. "I love that about you, but if you want to play in this game, you've gotta sand down those edges and deal with authority."

She turned away from me. "I hate authority."

"I know. You don't have to be here if you don't want to." I took a long pause. "Do you want to be here?"

Julia nodded without looking at me. "I do. I really do. I'm sick of chasing soul jumpers and handling local disputes for Connie."

I smiled. "Then you have to play the game, no matter how much you hate it."

Julia tilted her head to the ceiling. "Okay…but I really hate it."

"I know." I nodded toward the door. "Now, how far have you gotten with this suspect?"

She sighed, leaning against the wall, staring at the floor. "Nowhere, really. At least, nowhere I care to go. He's leading me down paths I've already been down."

I rubbed my hands together thoughtfully. "Well, I have new information relevant to this case. Maybe he'll break for me. Mind if I take a crack at it?"

Julia didn't look up but beckoned me to go inside the room. "Be my guest."

"What's his name?"

"Hanzel. Hanzel Yin."

"Wait here," I said, pushing open the door and walking into the interrogation room with the deepest scowl I could muster. "Sorry about that, Hanzel."

"You the big bad guy then?" he asked.

"Nothing like that," I said. "I'm just perturbed by something, and I thought you could help me."

"And why would I do that?"

I sat down across from him. "I almost died today...from a bomb that called to me from the past. One I haven't seen in a long time. It was much like Godless tech in that it killed gods, but it didn't glow green. It glowed blue, like a soul."

"I ain't never seen anything like that," Hanzel said.

"Oh, I'm sure you haven't. You're a very low-level weapons runner. This would have to be above your pay grade."

He slammed his hands on the metal table. "You don't know me, asshole. I'm the best smuggler in ten systems."

"Being the best smuggler in your pitiful systems is like being the best with numbers in preschool. It's cute, but it doesn't mean anything in the grand scheme. So, you're right. I shouldn't ask you. Any other gun runner would be more connected than you are and more likely to bring what I need." I stood up. "I'm sorry to have bothered you. It's a shame you can't help me. The Godschurch tends to go easy on people who help us."

"Dude, I ain't scared of you. We all gotta die."

I laughed. "Oh, death would be a great respite, but when you die, a soul goes to the underworld for torture. We don't want that. We want to torture you ourselves." I grabbed the suspect's nose and pulled it toward me. "We pull your soul out through your nose and send it through endless rounds of our own special brand of torture, designed by the gods for maximum pain." I slammed his head down on the table. "How does that sound?"

"You're lying."

I was lying, but that didn't matter. I had become good at it in 13,000 years, even though the words tasted foul on my tongue. "That's up to you to decide. Ask yourself, though, if I'm lying…I'm a very good liar, aren't I?" I looked deep into his eyes and watched the fear turn his stomach. "Now, if you help us, maybe I could arrange you to die on your own terms and take your chances with whatever underworld will have you. Who knows? Maybe I can get you into one where you get a respite from torture once a generation. But that's only if you can help me." I turned away. "And I know you can't help me find a smuggler that isn't a chump like you and might have the answers I need."

I walked toward the door slowly, waiting for Hanzel's inevitable cracking under pressure. "Wait!"

I spun on my heels and turned to him. "I'm very busy. Can you help me or not?"

"Were you telling the truth about that stuff?" He stumbled over every word, tears filling his eyes. "Will they really do that to me?"

"It's not pleasant."

"Okay." Hanzel's whole body shook with fear. "Look, I know who's peddling it cuz I've seen it before. They call it the Blue."

I set my hands on the table and leaned towards him. "Where can I find it?"

"There's a dealer on Onyti, Tyber sector. I made a deal with them a couple of months ago for some Horde bombs, and I saw some of that blue glowing stuff in his stash. I asked about it, but they told me they already had a buyer. Besides, it was way out of my price range."

"The Tyber sector is controlled by Odin's people. Are you sure that's the place?"

"Positive."

"If you're wrong—" I slammed my hand on the table, and Hanzel jumped, "you know what will happen."

"I'm not. I'm not. His name is Qeuntis. Go to a bar called the Elysium in a dead city called Flizquaria. Find the weirdest bartender working the place, and they'll bring you to him. Hey, if they find out you're a cop, they'll kill you."

I pushed up and turned back to the door. "They can try."

"Wait!" he screamed again. "Is that enough? Is that enough to save my soul?"

I shrugged. "That depends on whether your intel pans out."

I exited the interrogation room with a smile on my face. Julia was waiting for me. "Well?"

My smile broke into a chuckle. "Sung like a small child."

"Like a baby, you mean?"

"Babies can't sing." I walked down the hall. "Come on. We've got an arms dealer to track down."

"I'm coming?" Julia asked.

I turned to her. "Unless you want to be left behind."

"Rebecca won't like it."

"No, she won't, but I'm a senior agent, and I say you're coming."

Rebecca certainly wouldn't like it, but I cared more about getting a win for Julia than I did about getting in trouble with Rebecca. Besides, what is the point of living the straight and narrow if you couldn't bend it to your advantage every once and a while?

CHAPTER 9

Kimberly

Location: The Darkness

"Where are we going?" Molpe asked as we walked together. There was nothing except the Darkness as far as even a god's eyes could see. "Why is it so dark?"

"My boss prefers the dark," I replied. "So, we walk in darkness."

"Boss?" Molpe said. "Even you have a boss?"

I nodded. "Nyx. She is a mistress of the Darkness, the afterlife, and the gateway to the underworld. She is as old as the Darkness itself. She presides over all matters in the afterlife as well, as she is the mother of the first Death. I took over for him eons ago."

"You are not the original Death?" Molpe asked.

"I mean, I am Death," I said. "But only because I killed my predecessor, her child. It took a long time for Nyx to forgive me for killing him. Since then, I've been able to take my rightful place at her side, working with her to decide the fate of the dead."

"What is my fate?" Molpe asked, looking down at her feet.

"I don't know," I said. "Gods have died before, but in my time they all evaporated into the nothingness. You are the first I have seen with a soul, and frankly, I don't know what I should do with you."

It wasn't my job to bring every soul to the underworld. That would be too much, even with a near-infinite number of reapers working under me. My job was to bring those who didn't naturally want to leave their bodies or who did not go willingly into their abyss. The rules of the afterlife were confusing and complex. With a million billion stars and nearly as many pantheons of gods, everyone had their own form of the afterlife, and it was my job to make sure everybody got where they were supposed to go, whether they wanted to or not.

All souls go to their death dirty to some degree, and the underworld's job was to cleanse the souls and lead them back to the Source so they could be reused for creation. Hades, Anubis, Connie, Yama, and every other god that controlled their respective underworld were meant to cleanse souls and lead them back to the Source. The Source was pure light energy and creation. In balance with that, Nyx controlled the night and the Darkness. Yin and Yang, but not good and evil. Both were necessary for creation. The light from the Source powered all life, and death refilled the Source, allowing it to continue creating life.

"I smell death," a froggy voice croaked. Nyx was all-consuming, as much darkness as the Source was light.

"Hello, Nyx," I said, coming to a stop. I grabbed Molpe's hand as she stood shaking next to me. "Don't worry. I have you."

"You bring one to me whom I have never seen before." Nyx's voice wafted through my ears. "I smell death on you. What has happened to you, child?"

Molpe looked at me, fear in her eyes, before clearing her throat. "I…was murdered."

"Murder of a god?" Nyx said. A gust of wind encircled us. "Nasty business, killing a god."

"I don't know what to do with her," I said.

"Have you weighed her?" she asked.

"No," I said. "I did not know if that was appropriate for a god."

A small tornado spun at my feet, and a scale appeared on the ground with a single cup on either side to find balance. On one side was a long peacock feather. The other cup was empty.

"It is appropriate for all who die," Nyx said curtly. "Even a god."

I nodded and turned to Molpe. "I need you to get on the scale."

"I can't fit on there," Molpe said. "And there's no way I am as light as a feather."

"It's a very heavy feather, and you must. It will show if you are balanced or not and how clean your soul is."

"Do I have to?" she whined.

I nodded. "You must. I'm sorry."

Molpe took a breath and stepped onto the scale. As she did, her body shrunk until her whole body fit inside the cup on the scale. The scales fluctuated up and down wildly for a moment before settling, balanced, in the middle. I reached down and grabbed Molpe's hand, pulling her back into the Darkness, where she grew to her normal size.

"What does it mean?" she asked.

"You have done well in your life, child," Nyx said. "You are a pure soul."

"They said I was evil," Molpe replied. "They said we were all evil, and that's why we had to die."

"Well, the scales say different, and they are never wrong." The scales vanished. "They are proof you led a good life."

"Thank you," Molpe said, wiping away a tear. In the end, to be good was all most of us ever wanted.

"Take her to the Source," Nyx said. "Let the light have her."

"Without cleansing?" I asked. "Isn't that dangerous?"

"Yes," Nyx admitted. "But it is one soul, and she is in balance. If the light can be corrupted by one little soul, then perhaps it is not as strong as we believe."

I knew better than to argue. I simply nodded and pulled my scythe out of the pocket dimension where I kept it. I sliced upwards, and the light ripped through the dark.

"What is that?" Molpe asked.

"The Source. The light of creation. The grandest prize for all souls, to return to nothing to be made again."

"I'm scared," Molpe said. "I've never not existed before."

I smiled. "Yes, you have. We all have. It is our great gift to return to the Source and be reborn, over and over again, until the end."

"Will it hurt?" There was a squeak in her voice.

"No, my child," Nyx said. "But hurry. The light burns."

Molpe took a step forward, and her foot disappeared into the brightness. She squeezed my hand, pushed herself forward into the great unknown, and then she was gone. I wiped my hand over the light and the rip in the fabric of the universe closed.

"You did a good thing," Nyx said. "Now, leave me. The light has drained me, and I must recover."

I walked back into the Darkness, hoping she was right, and I did do the right thing.

CHAPTER 10

Julia

Location: Elysium bar, Onyti

I hadn't been with the Godschurch long, but I had been with them long enough to know they weren't really investigators, at least not at their heart. No, the Godschurch were good protectors and decent bodyguards, but they could stand a little more patience and less aggression. Investigation was about stamina and, most of the time, painstaking, mind-numbingly boring research.

Akta was a perfect example of a Godschurch soldier. She wanted the glitz of the investigation without doing any of the research, which meant lots of travel to far-off places and tracking down leads, instead of even doing a courtesy check to see if we were walking into a trap.

That was classic Akta. She relied on her pixie heritage, magic, and superior intelligence to escape a bad situation instead of using due diligence to make sure she wasn't walking into a trap in the first place.

Her heart was in the right place, at least. I appreciated her bringing me along to get me more field experience with the Godschurch. Of course, I had 10,000 years of experience in the field tracking down all sorts of bad guys, but that didn't matter to the bureaucracy-driven Godschurch. Most days, I wondered if I made a mistake joining, but both Akta and Katrina had stuck their neck out for me, and I wanted to prove their faith in me wasn't misguided.

"Do you see anybody that looks like a shady weapons dealer?"

I looked around the bar at the dozens of disreputable-looking people and aliens. Usually, non-humans stayed on their own planets, but at the Elysium, it was a free for all. Buglike Horde soldiers drank with centipedes and humans, and the humans looked like they had all been through ten miles of bad road. Most had more robotic parts than human ones.

"Literally any of them," I said, looking down at my glass of hot pink liquid, which I had no interest in drinking. I tapped the universal translator in my ear, which allowed me to listen to the different conversations around the bar. Two Yeclidian marmots were talking about a kidnapping happening in two days, while a Therilian frog was telling a story about murdering his father-in-law. I didn't hear anybody talking about an arms deal.

"Let's try to find this bartender, then," Akta spoke with her lip curled. I had convinced her to have a modicum of discretion before we went about smashing the place, but her patience was wearing thin. After ten centuries, I had come to love the slow, plodding process of an investigation.

"That one," I said, pointing to a purple blob at that other end of the bar. "She's definitely the weirdest-looking bartender here."

"Excuse me," Akta said to the gnarled-looking sea anemone with one black eye in the middle of its purple body. "Do you know Qeuntis?"

It took a moment for my universal translator to understand the creature as it searched its Rolodex for the proper language and dialect. "I might."

Akta pulled out a roll of hundred Ontyian dollars. We had it requisitioned before we left the base. "You tell me when it jogs your memory." Akta put one hundred down, then a second, and finally a third. "If it takes more than this, it would be easier to just torture it out of you."

I wasn't a fan of torture. It gave bad data and sent you down misleading rabbit holes, but Akta still saw value in it. She put down a fourth hundred, and the anemone nodded.

"Fine. Who are you, cops? You move like a cop."

Akta pulled ten more hundreds from her wad of money and slammed it on the table. "No more questions, just tell me where to find him."

The sea anemone grabbed the money with its spindly arms and placed it in its apron. "Follow me." The anemone slid through the bar and down a small hallway. It stopped at the top of a set of rickety stairs. "Go down, make your right. Tell him that Gthigor sent you."

"Thank you," Akta said, descending the stairs first. I nodded to the creature and followed. As we walked down the stairs, I couldn't shake the feeling that we were making a mistake.

"I think this is a trap."

"Everything's probably a trap. If you don't believe that, then you're an idiot."

I gripped the gun hidden under my coat as we reached the end of the stairway and turned right. There was a painted black door in front of us, covered in stickers. Akta knocked.

"What do you want?" a voice behind the door asked in a gruff voice.

"We are here to see Qeuntis. Gh—"

"No," I said, stepping between Akta and the door.

"Who sent you?" the voice said.

"I have a friend on Antigone Three," I said. In doing the paperwork for the bust, I'd learned the gun runner's name was Hanzel Yin, and it stuck with me. "He said if I'm ever in the sector, I should look you up. Hanzel Yin. Do you remember him? I'm going to be real embarrassed if you don't."

A chair pushed back in the other room, and somebody stomped up to the door. When it opened, I saw a man with a stubbly beard, a deep scowl, and a scar across his face.

"You say Hanzel Yin?" the man said in a cockney accent.

I nodded. "I did."

The man's scowl turned into a grin. "I love that sum bitch. He isn't much of a gun runner, but he makes a mean drink. Any friend of Hanzel's is a friend of mine." He hugged me close. "Come in, come in."

I eyed Akta as I slid past her into the room. She shook her head but couldn't deny that my method worked. We were inside.

"What are you here for?" Qeuntis said. "Another NOX list?"

"Another?" Akta said.

"NOX list?" I added.

"Yeah, man. He came to me about a year ago looking for a list of doxed gods for some new organization he worked for. I set up the deal—Wait, he didn't let you see that list, did he? Cuz that info is proprietary, you hear? That is my intellectual property. One-time use and all. If he showed you, I'll have to kill you and him."

"I can honestly say we didn't see it," I replied.

"Good, good," Qeuntis said, stretching his hands behind his head. "Cuz I'd hate to have to kill you fine ladies."

"Where did you steal the list from?" Akta said, cutting through his bull.

"The Godschurch, of course. Where else would I be able to put a list like that together?"

"That—" Akta wanted to pounce already, but I held up my hand to stop her. We needed to know more.

"I'm sorry, friend," I said. "I'm utterly fascinated by it, but that's not why I'm here."

"Then why else could you be here? Everything I got he's got. I know cuz he got it from me."

Akta sat down on a creaky chair across from him. "We are looking for a way to kill a god."

He laughed. "Yeah, that's what Hanzel does. He's got all sorts of Godless tech. 'Course, I can help you, too. And my stuff is better, cheaper."

I shook my head. "No, we're not looking for Godless tech. That stuff is unstable at best. Two of my men died trying to carry out a mission last month." I looked over at Akta, who frowned at me for lying, but it wasn't my fault I was a very good liar. "He told us you might have something more stable. He called it the Blue."

"Damn it, Hanzel," Qeuntis said, slamming his fists down on the table. "He's got a big mouth, you know? A real big mouth. I told him I had a buyer for that supply, and I did. It's long gone."

"We want you to get more. We'll pay any price." Akta pulled out her wad of cash. "That's just a down payment for anything you got."

Qeuntis looked around then pulled from his pocket a small vial that glowed blue. "This is all I got back. It's not enough for much. Maybe a bullet or two."

"A bullet?"

He looked at the vial. "That's the beauty of this stuff. It's in a totally solid state and stable. You can make it into everything, and a little goes a long way."

He tossed it across the table, and I nervously caught it in the air. "It's so light."

"I know. It's the next revolution in our war on the gods if anyone can figure out how to mass-produce the stuff."

"What's it made of?" Akta asked.

"No idea for sure," Qeuntis said. "I heard its concentrated souls, in the same way the Godless tech was, but it burns pure. I promise you that. I can get you a hundred grams of it in two months. Fifty million."

"Fifty million!" I screamed. "That's a hundred times more expensive than Godless tech."

"Yeah," Qeuntis said. "If you just want the standard stuff, you can take your chances. I wouldn't, though, not if I had the opportunity to get the Blue."

"We'll take it," Akta said. "And while you're at it, throw in that NOX list. If we have the tech to kill a god, we'd like to know where to concentrate our efforts."

Qeuntis leaned forward with a smile. "A woman after my own heart. That I can get you right now." He licked his lips as he picked up the money. "This'll just about pay for it."

CHAPTER 11

Katrina

Location: Godschurch Base

"I'm telling you I've run the numbers a half dozen times at least," the analyst said. She was sitting across from Rebecca when I opened the door to the Director's office without knocking. "There are fewer souls going into the Source than usual—by a lot."

Rebecca tented her fingers in front of her and pressed her head against them. "What are we talking? A point four percent drop or something. I swear you eggheads will concern yourself with the smallest minutiae."

"No, Director," the analyst said. "More like 25 percent on most days. Some days it gets as high as 50 percent."

"That is concerning," Rebecca said after a long moment.

"It is more than concerning. It's frightening. We're starting to see...odd fluctuations. There are small quakes escaping the Source and rippling out across the universe, too light to feel for us, but powerful enough for our sensors to pick up."

Rebecca furrowed her brow. "So, what are you saying is going to happen?"

The analyst bit her lip. "I'm saying if we don't figure out what is causing this drop, it could have grave repercussions across the universe, possibly destabilizing the very fabric of space and time itself."

"Then I suppose we should figure out what's going on then, right?" Rebecca said curtly, leaning backward in her chair.

"Yes, ma'am," the analyst said.

Rebecca craned her neck to me, finally acknowledging my existence. "What do you want, and do you realize I close my door for a reason?"

I walked forward. "I do; I just don't care."

"I know that," Rebecca said with a sigh. "How can I help you, Katrina?" She looked over at her analyst. "You're dismissed."

The analyst scurried out of the room, and I slid into the chair she vacated. "I talked to Cronus, and he gave me a name. Indra." I looked at Rebecca, but she was studying a report. "I've never heard it before. Is it a person? Is it a potato?"

"Did you search for it in our database?" Rebecca asked, but she must have known the answer. I never search for anything.

I slid down in my chair. "No, I came straight here. I don't like computers."

"Fair enough," Rebecca said, finally looking up at me. "And you know I'm not your personal secretary?"

I crossed my arms. "You send me all around the universe on boring peace missions, and I go. In return, all I ask is that you answer my every beck and call. I think that's fair. I mean, I could *not* go on these missions for you, and then the Godschurch would crumble."

Another sigh. "Whatever. And you're sure it's Indra?"

"Sure as shooting, that's what he said. Whether he's lying is another matter."

"Let's assume he's not lying." Rebecca typed on her computer. "All right. Here we go. Indra's the head god of his own line, which were all wiped out millions of years ago. He hasn't been seen around in a couple hundred million years, so there's not a whole lot of information on him in my database, except for the myths that people have developed about him over the years."

"How did the line die out?" I asked, leaning forward.

Rebecca shook her head. "No idea. Just says they died."

"Any last known location?"

"Well, he has his own realm, which is kind of like a Heaven or Mount Olympus, but there's no information about how to access it. Perhaps Velaska can help."

I laughed and sat back. "She's never been particularly helpful."

Rebecca glared at me. "That's not true. She was essential at the Battle of the Obelisk. She's garnered more support among the gods than you have, probably because she's a better diplomat. More importantly, she has an encyclopedic knowledge of every god in every pantheon and has had dealings with them all over the eons. I'd say she's your best bet."

"You just want to get rid of me," I said, pushing myself to stand.

Rebecca smiled. "It can be two things."

***

Velaska was as close to a countryman a god could hope to have in this crazy universe. She was the Devil on my Earth before Lucifer, who was the Devil before me. She helped me through my share of trouble in my day—my share and ten other gods, most of which she caused. She was tall, beautiful, and blonde, with big, violet eyes that you could swim in…and I hated her for stealing my girlfriend, Urania.

I had been avoiding Velaska for years, while the only person I ever loved fell deeper under her spell. One might say that I was a touch jealous, and that would be accurate, except it was more than a touch. It was a torrent. Even though I was the one who broke up with Urania, I did not want anybody else to date her, either. I just wanted her to be miserable for the rest of eternity. Was that too much to ask? And was it too much to ask for her to NOT find love in the arms of my friend? Ex-friend, now.

I had seen Velaska walk through the bullpen earlier in the day and stifled my rage to fight her. It bubbled up now that I was knocking at the door to her room. Now, I needed to talk to her. I could have asked another god, but they all pretty much universally hated me. At least Velaska had guilt to drown her hatred of me.

"What do you want?" an annoyed Urania said when the door slid open. The smell of musk wafted out of the door in a thick plume. She was barely dressed in a t-shirt and underwear, which meant she had stayed over. Of course, she had. They were lovers.

I averted my eyes. "I need to see Velaska."

"She doesn't want to see you," she said. I could see Velaska lying on the bed in the cramped room behind her. The cozy quarters of the Godschurch base didn't leave much room to hide.

"I can see her," I grumbled. "Will she just talk to me? I'm not here for a fight."

Urania scoffed, shifting her weight to her right leg. "You're always looking for a fight. That's the problem with talking to you."

"Please, let's not act like children."

Urania giggled. "That is rich coming from you." She turned back to Velaska. "You want to see her, sweetie?"

"No," Velaska said. "Absolutely not."

"I have to ask you something," I said, placing my hand on the door to prevent it from closing. "It's important!"

"Don't care."

"Let go," Urania said. "Out."

"What do you know about Indra?" I asked Velaska over Urania's shoulder. Then, I met Urania's withering stare. "Either of you."

"I've never had the pleasure," Urania said. I felt the subtext: *and I wish I never had the pleasure of meeting you, either.*

"Please, Velaska," I said. "You know this is the most I will beg, but I really do need your help."

Velaska let out a deep sigh. "Fine." She rose from the bed. Her long hair was pulled up in a ponytail behind her, and she wore yoga pants instead of her usual toga as she walked toward me. She kissed Urania lightly when they crossed each other in the middle of the room. "Who are you asking about again?"

My stomach tied in knots. I tried to shake the image of their kiss from my brain. "H-have you ever dealt with the god Indra? He's apparently—"

Velaska flicked her wrist at me dismissively. "Ancient, yes. I have dealt with him. Compared to the Titans, he's quite reasonable, considering his age."

"He's as old as the Titans?"

"Oh, yeah. He didn't agree with their uprising, even if he understood it, as he understood when the gods rose up against the Titans. He did not understand why his whole pantheon was sacrificed in the god's war against Cronus, though, and has never forgiven the Godschurch for their deaths. Honestly, he holds less of a grudge than he deserves to, given the circumstances. He's kind of a puppy dog, actually."

"The Godschurch sacrificed his pantheon?" I asked, shocked and equally not shocked because, of course, they would do that. The gods were dicks.

"In a manner of speaking. They were front-line soldiers during the war. They didn't stand a chance."

"But he's benevolent?" I asked, confused. "Are you sure? Cuz I sure wouldn't be."

"As benevolent as a god could ever be," Velaska replied. "I think he's just anti-social, honestly. After a million years, your heart grows numb to the pain of betrayal."

Was she giving me advice or stating a fact? Either way, I breezed past it. "Cronus told me that Indra could tell me why somebody was trying to kill me."

"HA!" Velaska laughed in my face. "As if anybody needs a reason. I could find a million people who would kill you for the satisfaction. Why is this god special?"

"I don't know!" I gnashed my teeth together. "That's why I have to find him and ask. Will you please help me?"

"Under one condition," Velaska said.

I didn't want to be under any god's thumb, especially Velaska's, even if she could help me. "No."

"You have to forgive me," Velaska said. "And stop this pettiness."

I shook my head. "I already said no. That's something I can't do. You stole my girlfriend!"

"Hey!" Urania said. "She didn't steal me. I'm not a sandwich. You cheated on me with Aranya, and I broke up with you. Velaska just happened to be nice to me. She didn't steal me. She treated me nicely, which is more than you ever did."

I bit my lip and looked at her. "I'm sorry. I misspoke."

"You sure did," Urania said.

Seething, I turned to Velaska. "Fine! I can try. That's the best I can do, trying, all right?"

Velaska looked over at Urania, who rolled her eyes then gave a slight nod. "I don't know why you need her to like you, but whatever. Go for it."

Velaska turned back at me. "Fine. I'll help you."

CHAPTER 12

Julia

Location: Godschurch Base

I stared, slack-jawed, when Akta and I got back to the Godschurch, and the analysts decrypted the NOX list. We immediately knew we were staring at a list of gods and goddesses, hundreds of them, and exactly where they were at any given time. The list was so advanced that it was updating in real-time while we looked at it.

"There," I said, pointing to the screen as Akta looked over my shoulder. "There's Katrina's name."

"Well, that gives a motive for sure," Akta said, holding up the blue vial that contained the weaponry we received from Qeuntis. "And this is the weapon."

"Can you put that down?" I asked. "It's explosive, and I would rather not die."

"If what Qeuntis said was true, then a drop of this could destroy this whole base," Akta placed it on the table. "So, no matter where it goes, it's still dangerous, but fine. I'll humor you."

"Thank you," I said, scrolling through the list. "It's not a very big list, unfortunately. It looks like it's little more than a couple of hundred gods."

"Is there any pattern to them?"

"Not that I can tell. Lots of Zeus's line, but there's also a god or two from Odin's and Brahma's and Osiris's. Just about every line is in here somewhere. I'm going to bring it to Edgar and see if he can make heads or tails of it."

Akta picked up the vial. "Okay, while you do nerd things, I'm going to analyze this blue stuff and see what we're dealing with."

"So, chemistry?" I asked. "That's very nerdy. Way nerdier than combing over data."

"Keep telling yourself that."

Akta disappeared into the laboratory door to the right of the command center, and I turned back to the NOX list. I started composing a message to send to Edgar, our best tech, to help me analyze the list for any clues. I was woeful with the names of gods, and most of them were little more than gibberish to me.

"Where did you get that?" I heard from behind me. I turned to see Rebecca scowling at the list on my screen. Her fiery eyes darted to me. "Answer me. Where. The hell. Did you get that?"

I stood there, mentally formulating my answer. I didn't want to get Akta in trouble, but I also didn't want to be in trouble. Rebecca's anger was boiling up and showing on her face. I didn't have a better lie, so I decided to tell the truth. "Akta took me on a mission to find a bomb maker she was tracking—we found him by the way—and we also found this list, which shows the locations of hundreds of gods."

"Move over," Rebecca said, and I pushed my chair away from the computer. "This is a gross violation of protocol. I never authorized this and—where did you get the petty cash for this mission?"

"I don't know," I asked. "That's not really the point. You can be as pissed at you want, but that doesn't change the fact that a very bad man had this list of gods and sold it to us, which means that a bunch of really bad people already have it."

"Shit," Rebecca said.

"Yeah," I said. "It's bad. I'm looking for a clue on what it means."

"It means we have a leak."

"A leak?"

Rebecca nodded. "Yeah, somebody sold this information to your bad guy from inside the Godschurch. This is a segmented list of our mainframe that allows us to track every god and where they are."

I clasped my hand to my mouth. "Holy shit. This really is ours, then? Qeuntis said it was, but I figured he was just blowing smoke to charge more."

"Yes, it's ours." Rebecca leaned into me, pointing her finger at my chest. "This is so far above your paygrade. If I weren't so desperate for agents, I would fire you. Since you seem to have stuck your nose in and found something, I will let you keep working this case, but only because I don't want anybody else knowing about this before I figure out what's happening. Now, where is Akta?"

"She's in the lab."

Rebecca typed something into the computer, and the entire screen went blank. "I'm sending this to Edgar for analysis. Then, I'm burning this computer to the ground. I hope you weren't doing anything important on it, like playing Minesweeper."

"I don't have anything of value on it," I said. I really didn't care, as long as she let me keep working the case. "There are other computers."

Rebecca was already marching past me. "Come with me."

***

"I knew it!" Akta screamed as I walked into the laboratory with Rebecca. When she saw me, Akta smiled, but at the sight of Rebecca, she scowled. "What's she doing here?

"*She* is your boss," Rebecca said. "What are you doing here, and why are you bringing a probie on a mission that I did not assign you?"

"You told me to interrogate the suspect, which I did."

"Interrogate! Not go out on a mission! Interrogate. Mission. Two very different words with two very different meanings."

"It was her collar, Director," Akta said. "I was just following up on a lead like you taught me."

"That's low, Akta. It was our collar," Rebecca hissed. "Hers and mine, which means the least you could have done was filled me in as a colleague, if not as your boss."

Akta's eyes dropped. "You're right. I'm sorry."

"At least make it worth my while," Rebecca said. "What did you find out?"

Akta spun toward the technician working with the vial. "So, a long time ago, Julia and I were dealing with an insurrection in Hell, and I came across this mystic who could turn souls into bombs. It was horrible magic—killed any soul in its path. It looked just like this, and I just found out that it's the same underlying material, only this is a hundred times more potent."

"Is that true?" Rebecca asked the technician, a baby-faced girl with big, saucer-like eyes.

"I cannot say whether her story is true, but I can say that this chemical structure closely matches the Godless green ooze which could kill a god, except that it appears to be stable."

"A stable way to kill a god," Rebecca said, turning back to us. "I'm going to tell you something that doesn't leave this conversation. There has been an alarming drop in souls coming to the Source, and now we find this. I'm wondering if they could be related."

"Not likely," I said. "Qeuntis told us that it would take a month to get one hundred milligrams of this stuff. That's barely ten souls. It's not easy to make. It wouldn't account for that massive a drop in—"

"Maybe," Rebecca replied. "But I need you both to look into this quietly."

"What about the NOX list?" I asked.

"I'll take care of that myself. As far as you know, that NOX list doesn't exist, got it?"

I raised my eyebrows. "What's a NOX list?"

She smiled. "Clever girl."

CHAPTER 13

Kimberly

Location: Godschurch Base

After leaving the Darkness, I journeyed back to the Godschurch. It only took a couple of minutes for Zalnir to open a portal and allow me access. I still found it funny that a god had to wait for access to the Godschurch at all, though I found it equally funny that I was considered a god. I'd found my access card in the pockets of my robes after I took over for the previous god of Death, whom I killed. Even though I wasn't a dues-paying member, the card was enough to get me access to the church, just not their protection.

It never made sense to me why the Godschurch insisted on maintaining the opulence of its past when it rebuilt itself after the Battle of the Obelisk. They hadn't held a service in a decade or more and had yet to replace the five bishops that oversaw the day-to-day operations of the church or even install temporary people. Rebecca chose, instead, to run the operations herself, without listening to anyone else. Nobody protested because anybody that knew about the old way of things had vanished.

The agents of the Godschurch used to be devout worshippers, back when they could afford to be picky about their agents. Rebecca had never been, and it came through in the way she ran the Godschurch, with none of the worship and reverence that once exuded from its operations. To her, the gods were simply nobles, maybe kings or queens, but not the creators of the universe.

She had no respect for the gods, which tickled me to no end because I didn't, either. The idea that I needed to be worshiped was both sickening and idiotic to me, and yet, I had never gone to a world that didn't worship me, or at least one of my forms. I was not the only god of Death, of course. There were dozens of us roaming the universe from hundreds of pantheons, and across the board, our work was that of bureaucracy. I don't know if I could have stomached being a Devil, or god of the underworld, responsible for the torture that so many had to endure before they were sent back to the Source. It was enough to convince people that the journey was worth the travel.

"Hi Zalnir," I said, waving to him as I passed. He looked back at me with contempt and confusion. Nobody talked to Zalnir. He was there to do a job, and he did it well enough. I preferred Angus, who was kindly and talkative, but he had died in the destruction of the Godschurch, like so many others.

I took the elevator down to the base of the Godschurch, where the agents and analysts worked. I found the work of the Godschurch banal and tedious. I could never imagine being an agent for them, like Julia or Akta, but both had found their purpose within the church, and so I supported their mission spiritually, if not financially.

As I passed through the corridor and into the base, I stopped to look out on the Source, where I had just sent Molpe, back to the origin of creation, which kept the universe spinning.

"Is it done?" I heard Rebecca say behind me. "Nyx told me to expect you after what happened with the siren."

I nodded. "Yes. She is back with the Source, as per Nyx's orders."

Rebecca glanced at the Source as she approached me. She was lithe and muscular, a specimen of strength and fitter than most half her age. "Good," she said. "I didn't know how to explain her death to the other gods. Honestly, I didn't even know you gods had souls."

"Everything has a soul, even the leaves and grass that we so callously trample," I replied with a sigh. "I feel them all as they die and watch them float away back to the Source."

"Everything?" Rebecca said.

"Yes," I replied. "It is my burden and my curse. Even now, thousands of souls float into the Source: animal, vegetable, and mineral."

"Then you must know that there are fewer souls coming into the Source in the past couple of months, a drop of fifty percent or more."

I nodded. "I have felt something was wrong…"

"Are your people delivering fewer people to death?" Rebecca asked.

I thought for a moment before answering. "If anything, more people cling to their lives than before. I have had to recruit thousands of new reapers."

Rebecca turned to me. "I need to know why it's happening."

"I don't work for you," I said with a growl.

"I know that," Rebecca said. "But I need your help, as a friend."

I laughed. "You are my boss's protector, and she is your benefactor or one of them, but please do not believe that we are friends just because you employ two of my friends and defend my superior."

Her face fell as if I hurt her with my words, though I doubted anything could cut her cold exterior. "Fair enough. I need your help because this concerns the whole universe. The cosmos rests on the stability of the Source, and fewer souls mean less stability, throwing everything out of whack on both sides of the divide—life and death."

I nodded. "That is a more compelling case. I'll look into it and report back, but if you ever talk to me in that tone again, as if I work for you, I will pull the soul out of your body and deliver it to the Source myself."

She laughed. "I fear I'm much too contaminated for the Source to accept me. I would taint the whole thing. Isn't that what you're trying to protect against?"

I didn't tell her that I sent Molpe into the Source without cleansing her, and I felt uneasy about it. It was my job to guard the Source against contamination and worried that I had betrayed that ideal, but I could not confide my doubt to her. She would report it to my boss. I swallowed it down and spun away from her. "I'll take my chances. Don't push me."

CHAPTER 14

Katrina

Location: Space

I hated the vacuum of space. It was slow, plodding, and insanely boring. "How much further?" I screamed at Velaska. I felt like a petulant child, and it didn't help that Velaska was treating me as such.

She sighed. "You asked me that a dozen times already, and it's barely been a day."

"Do you understand how boring this is?" I asked. "Why couldn't we just take a bridge?"

Now, Velaska giggled, mocking me. "You don't understand much about being a god, do you, even after all this time?"

"I understand this is boring."

"Being a god is boring. We think on a much different time horizon than humans. For us, a day is an hour, or maybe even a minute. When you have eternity, you don't get so caught up in the minutes and seconds."

"That's horseshit. I know you get pissed about this petty stuff. I've seen you worry about people not worshiping you or that something is taking too long."

She shrugged. "Sometimes, but then we are all hypocrites sometimes. The truth of the matter is that we are concerned with humanity all the time, which is why we try not to make more of them if we can help it. If we get caught in their petty squabbles, then every moment will feel like an eternity."

Her hypocrisy didn't seem to bother her. I had to hand it to the gods. They knew they were hypocrites, and while they didn't revel in it, they did understand and embrace their beautiful dichotomies.

"And yet, we could probably stand to have a few new gods about now, huh? I wonder how many of us have been killed just this year."

She sighed. "Far too many, as you know. Even one is too many, and if a human is made a god out of it, then even worse, for they don't know how to use their powers or comport themselves like a god."

I twisted my face up. "How does a god…comport themselves?"

"With grace and civility, of course, always."

I rolled my eyes. "You really are a pompous ass, did you know that?"

"Yes, but I also know the power I possess and what runs through my veins. I take that responsibility very seriously, while you humans never could, and gods forbid a non-human bug or reptile got their hands on our power. It could be the living end."

"Living end of what?"

"Of everything." Velaska swallowed loudly. "Do you remember what happened when the Horde even got close to killing us all? It was almost the end of everything."

"Yeah, but it wasn't because I stopped them." I pounded my chest. "Me. A little old human. I think you forget that part."

"No, I don't. I remember everything. Curse of being a god." She stopped floating forward. "Now, where is it? I know the entrance to Indra's pocket dimension is around here somewhere."

She spun around in a circle as she scratched her head and mumbled to herself. I scoffed at her. "I thought you remembered everything."

"Yes, I do, but this is buried far in my…" Her eyes lit up. "Ah yes, I remember now." She reached forward and pushed her finger through what I thought was just another twinkling star. As she did, she pulled the star apart with her fingers, revealing a white door, which she knocked on.

"King of Heaven," she said. "I come to beseech your help."

A grumble came from behind the door. "And who comes to beseech?"

"Velaska, your kingship."

"Ugh," Indra groaned from behind the door. "Not you."

"And I thought I was despised. I forgot you're also a pariah." I chuckled. "Does anyone like you?"

Velaska shot me a glare. "You do. At least at one point, you did."

"No. I just hate you less than everybody else."

"What is that, besides love?" Velaska said before turning back to the door. "We have a question for you, great king of the universe."

"Then you can ask it from there. If I deem it worthy, I will open the door."

I swam forward through the darkness of space toward the door. "I need to know why somebody would try to kill me. Cronus said—"

"Cronus!" Indra screamed. "He's back?"

Velaska held up her hand to silence me. "He is back, my king, but he is very well contained. Hundreds of god-killing weapons are trained on him as we speak."

"That is not enough to contain him. If he finds me, he will—" The voice was stilted and jarring as if every word came after a hyperventilated breath. "And you've led this one right to me, Velaska. I knew I should never have helped you all those eons ago."

"Please, you were well compensated," Velaska said, sultriness dripping off each word. "And you will be again. Both your coffers and your body. I'm sure you enjoyed the last time I gave you my body, and I will again, as a bonus for helping us in this dark time."

"Ew," I said. "Did you have sex with him?"

"Of course, he has four arms and four—well, he is very well endowed, even for a god."

I chuckled. "So you working with him was for a booty call?"

"No, that was just an ancillary benefit of working together." She turned to the door again. "It is quite important that we speak to you concerning the attempts on my friend's life."

The door swung open. A red-faced man with a long beard and four arms stared at us with literal fire in his eyes. "I will tell you this just once, the reason anybody would want to kill either of you is because you are annoying pests, and I think wiping either of you from existence would be a great service to the universe."

"Wow," Velaska said. "That's the quickest I've ever seen somebody hate Katrina."

"I hate her as an extension of hating you," Indra said. "Is this the first attempt on your life?" He spun to me. "I promise you it won't be the last. Why do you think I'm hiding from the universe? One too many attempts on my life by gods more powerful than you could ever imagine."

"I get that," I replied. "I've only known you a couple of minutes, and I want to kill you, but I'm utterly loveable, and Cro— I was told it's a mystery only you could solve."

Indra rolled his eyes. "What are you the god of?"

I shrugged. "I don't know. Just a…general god."

Indra sighed. "That's not how it works. Everybody is born of an ember of something and then assigned a task. What task were you assigned?"

"None; I used to be the Devil, though."

"Then, you are a god of the underworld?"

"Is that like a class? Cuz I did not like being a god of the underworld."

"Yes, I suppose it is a class and a very important one," Indra said. "It determines your line and where your spark came from—the Earth, the Dark, the Heart, the Light, or the End. Everything sprung from one of them, and you must know where you will return."

"I don't understand," I said. "I don't know where I'll return. Cronus made me to—"

"Cronus made you! What madness is this?" Indra's eyes went wide. "Listen, I've said too much. All I will say is this. Love is the answer. When hate fills your vision, love is the answer."

Indra slammed the door, and I banged on it with my fist. "What does that even mean?"

"Love is all you need!" Indra said, and the door vanished. "Now piss off!"

"This is not a Beatles' song, you wanker!" I looked up at Velaska. "What do you think got him all fired up?"

"No idea," Velaska replied. "He's the worst. Did I not mention that?"

"You did not."

"Well, the worst after you, that is." Velaska turned and started to fly away. "Is that all then?"

"I guess so," I said, following her. "This was the least helpful day of all time."

She scoffed. "You haven't been a god for very long."

CHAPTER 15

Kimberly

Location: Yama's Underworld

Yama had once been a human like me, which made him one of the easier gods of the underworld to get along with. In his religious tradition, he was also the god of Death, so he handled both aspects of the afterlife for over a dozen systems his pantheon had created.

They were one of the first to split with Zeus, which meant that until the Source was opened back to all gods after the Battle of the Obelisk, they had not created a civilization in millions of years. Their new attempts were not going well, and I feared they would rip a hole in the universe before learning to use the power of creation for themselves once again.

Previously, Cronus and then Zeus hoarded that power for themselves, doling it out as they saw fit, and they rarely saw fit to give a new world to one of Yama's pantheons. The advantage for Yama and his crew was that they grew closer to the humans in their sector and spent much time caring for them, seeing them as precious creations. Zeus, meanwhile, was always off on a pilgrimage to create more to worship him.

Yama's underworld had evolved greatly over the last million years. No longer was the torture done by demons, but robotic arms and pullies which cleansed souls more quickly than nearly any other underworld, and certainly any who still used the labor of demons. Due to his technological prowess, he kept the most precise data in the entirety of the cosmos, which meant he and I got along just fine.

"Kimberly!" Yama called out when I landed on the penthouse of his castle. It really wasn't much of one, and he preferred the view from a skyscraper penthouse that overlooked the craggy rocks of Hell.

"Hello, old friend," I said, wrapping him in a hug. "It has been too long."

"Yes, it has." He broke away from me, and I followed him into his office. "Is there something wrong? You only come to see me when something is wrong."

I sighed. "I wish it wasn't that way, my friend. I'm hoping you can help me."

He slid behind his desk and gestured for me to sit in one of the uncomfortable chairs across from him. "If I can, I will. What is the problem?"

"Do you still keep charts on the number of souls that are cleaned?" I asked.

He nodded. "Every month. We've nearly hit equilibrium. As one soul comes in, another goes out. We actually had it better than equilibrium, but then many of our machines went unused for lack of work, and we spent more energy turning them off and on than trying to make sure they were always working."

"So, you haven't seen a slowdown in souls coming through your underworld in the past several months?"

He shook his head, poking at his computer. "Nope. We've been steady in and out for the past…well, as far back as we tracked this data."

My eyes narrowed. "Is there any way that you could be sending fewer souls to the Source, even after they're cleaned?"

"No, we haven't changed our—" Yama looked at his computer. "That's weird. Even though we've cleaned the same number of souls, fewer have left the underworld than ever before. Looks like we're down 43 percent month over month since the start of the year. That's so weird. How does that even happen?"

"Can you look into it, my friend? I need to ask around and try to find out if this problem is widespread. If you figure anything out, please let me know."

He nodded. "Of course."

***

Connie was on the other side of the spectrum from Yama. She hated automation and loathed data. She did everything by touch and feel. She believed the best part of the underworld, the thing that made it function, was the demons' interaction with the souls of the dead. There was no replacing their touch to cleanse a soul appropriately. No amount of data could show her otherwise.

"That's the problem with automation," Connie said after I filled her in on Yama's decrease in sending souls to the Source. "You aren't incentivized for having fewer souls coming through because you paid for all those fancy machines. For me, I've been laying people off for the last two years because there are just fewer deaths than before. Most of our demons just lounge around now, doing as they please."

"That doesn't make any sense."

She shrugged. "I'm just telling you what I'm seeing. Demons are able to give personalized attention, cleaning souls faster, especially when they are properly compensated. Maybe it's the longer life expectancy up on Earth or fertility issues or something. I don't deal with any of that stuff. I just know that there are fewer souls coming in and fewer going out."

"But all the ones that are going out, they're getting to the Source? Can you confirm that?"

"I don't see how I would do that," Connie said. "Or why it would be important. Once they get cleansed, they aren't our problem anymore. If they're being lost, that's somebody else's problem."

"I gave you all sorts of programs to make sure you had all this data for me. I showed Carl how to use it and everything. It took weeks."

"Well, I haven't looked at any of them, but maybe Carl has."

I rolled my eyes. Connie was an effective Devil in some respects, but I hoped that I would not have to bring people through her Hell often. She delegated too much and didn't have a tight handle on her operation.

Luckily, Connie had a number two that Katrina had trained, and he knew every bit of Hell. Carl was in charge of the integration of our software with the soul service that Connie used, which allowed us to track the souls funneling through the afterlife and help with inefficiencies inherent in any big operation. It was part of my radical compassion movement, which worked to keep the suffering of souls to a minimum.

I leaned over the imp Carl's shoulder as he typed. "Can you show me a soul that was supposed to make it through Hell in the last couple of months?"

Carl typed on the computer, then leaned back, and pointed to the screen. "Here you go. Ezekiel Alagoas."

"And can you confirm if he was offloaded back to the Source?"

Carl nodded. "It looked like his soul was cleaned on time, and he was sent to the Source as per instructions."

I scratched my head. "Can you track the soul? This software should be able to track each soul's unique aura."

Carl typed into his keyboard, and a map popped up of the solar system. Ezekiel's soul was blinking in the bottom right as if it was still on Earth, which shouldn't happen. In fact, there should be no tracker because once Ezekiel got into the Source, his tracker would have vanished.

"Zoom in." Carl zoomed in and confirmed my worst fears. Ezekiel's soul never left Connie's Hell.

My robe buzzed, and I pulled out a tablet. It was Yama sending me a text. "I need to talk to you."

CHAPTER 16

Julia

Location: Delphizi

There were two separate leads to chase if we wanted to track down the soul bombs. Akta decided to track down Qeuntis and his supplier while I was stuck investigating the bombing of Saraswati's castle and hoping it led me somewhere good.

The first step to the investigation was talking to the deva, Lakshmi. I preferred devas to Valkyries and angels. They were not quite as devoted to their gods, even though all angel-like creatures were hopelessly devoted, and some could even be sweet, given the right circumstances. While other servants of the gods were bred mostly for war, devas had all sorts of different purposes, including hospitality, making them very pleasant conversationalists.

"You didn't do this, did you?" I asked Lakshmi in the metal interrogation room. We had stared at each other for a few minutes before I spoke, and both seemed equally comfortable with the silence.

"I already told the other one I had nothing to do with it. Doesn't it say that in your file?" She pointed down to the folder I had slammed on the table when I walked into the room.

I smirked. "Actually, that's just filled with blank paper and old newspaper clippings. Everything's been digital here for a long time. I just like the effect."

Lakshmi laughed, breaking her stony visage. "You won't fool me into thinking you aren't a Godschurch stormtrooper by being nice and having a quirk or two."

"Good. You wouldn't be much use to me if you were dumb enough to think I was on your side."

She leaned forward. "Whose side are you on?"

I leaned in to match her. "Saraswati's side. The side of justice. If you're on that side, then I am on your side, but since you're being a complete prick to everybody who tries to interrogate you, I can only believe you are not on our side."

She folded her arms, settling back into her chair. "If you are on Saraswati's side, then let me see her."

I shook my head. "It's exactly because I'm on her side that I can't let you see her."

"Why?"

"Because she doesn't want to see you, because she doesn't believe you, because she thinks you were responsible for that bomb, and even if you weren't, it was your security that was breached."

Lakshmi looked at me for a moment, tucking her long hair behind her ear. "She is right. It was my fault."

I threw up my hands in the air. "Now we're getting somewhere."

She shook her head. "Not like that. I didn't blow up the bomb. It was my job to keep her safe. Now, nobody will ever trust me again. I might as well throw myself into a pyre and burn to ash."

The art of interrogation is to get somebody to trust you, even if they don't like you. There were all sorts of ways to do that, though most of them took time to work—time the

Godschurch couldn't afford. Often, if you could just get them talking, they would talk themselves into trusting you.

"That's not true. Help me find who is responsible. Let us have justice. Prove you are on the right side of this after all, and you will be welcomed back as a hero."

"I have already told you all I know," Lakshmi said.

I shook my head. "No, you gave us a guess. You told Rebecca that Projekt Kaos was responsible for the attack, but you don't actually know that, do you?"

She gritted her teeth. "I know it as much as I know my own name."

"Then you know nothing about what you're called because nobody knows what Projekt Kaos is, even our oldest agents. And while we're tracking down your wild hunch, we're wasting valuable time."

Lakshmi shook her head. "That is all I have."

"See, I don't believe you. I am trying to track down your lead, but there are literally trillions upon trillions of planets in the cosmos. There are millions of years of history in the Godschurch archives. It could take us years to verify your story."

"What do you need from me?" Lakshmi asked.

"Anything. A direction. Guidance. Who could have done this? If we find the being that did this, then we are that much closer to getting our story straight and proving you were just negligent and not willfully treasonous."

"What does it matter? Either way, it's a death sentence."

"I don't believe that."

"You obviously do not know the gods."

"Then, if you are slated for death, you can choose to die with dignity and pride by helping us. Who are you protecting?"

"Nobody!"

I slammed my hands on the table. "Liar! I don't know who you are guarding, but it's not Saraswati! And if it's not her, then how can we believe that your intel is not just leading us down a black hole?"

"Fine!" Lakshmi said. "Fine. There is a servant in the castle. Apor."

Finally.

"Why are they so important that you're protecting them?" I asked, trying to contain my excitement. There was nothing quite like breaking a suspect.

"She is my oldest—my only—" Lakshmi appeared wounded, like the thought of Apor being behind the attack affected her ability to speak. Her face told the whole story.

I sat back down, realization hitting me. "She is your daughter."

Tears streamed down your face. "Not by blood, but by everything that matters. I have protected her since the beginning. She is the only one who could blind me this way. She is the only one with unrestricted access to the castle."

"Why would she—?"

"Because the gods treat us terribly, and she hates them." Lakshmi's calm demeanor turned into a venomous scowl. "We are their servants forever, a punishment for being born. Some of us, we grow to love our captors. Others, like Apor, she revolted and grew bitter. I knew— and I did nothing—I am a traitor." She buried her face in her hands.

I pushed up from the table. "I will let you alone with your guilt, but I have met plenty of mothers in my life. It blinds you, as you said. You tried to protect your kin, and there is some honor in that."

"You are unlike any from the Godschurch I've ever met," Lakshmi said, lowering her hands.

"That is a great compliment," I said with a smile as I walked out of the room.

***

"Have you seen Apor?" I asked a small cloud-like being with bright eyes that was cleaning the floor of Saraswati's castle. It didn't answer. It had no mouth.

"Last time I saw her," a blue being with four arms said, taking a break from laying bricks in the hot Delphizi sun. "She was in Lakshmi's office."

I nodded a thank you and walked toward the front of the castle, where the blue being was pointing. When I entered the room, I didn't find Apor, but there was a trail of blue blood running from the computer out of the room toward the back of the castle. I followed it as it weaved through the castle and into the back garden.

"Shit shit shit," a voice muttered. It was a silver-skinned woman wearing a bright red sari. One of her hands was wrapped up in it. "Gods-damn it."

I placed my hand on the gun holstered at my hip and walked closer. "Apor?"

The silver-skinned woman turned. "Who are you?"

"Your mother sent me."

Blue blood pooled at her feet. "My mother?"

"Lakshmi."

"She would lay that claim. She doesn't have any relation to me."

"She raised you. That's her story, at least. What's yours?"

"She brainwashed me to believe the gods were good and kind." She looked down at her arm. Her hand was cut off at the wrist, and it was gushing blood. "I can't stop the bleeding."

"We can get you back to the Godschurch," I said. "We can bandage it. Call your mother. Get you the help you need."

"NO!" Apor shouted. "I would rather die than see her again."

I sat down next to her. "That may be your only option."

"Death is worth it for the cause."

"Killing gods?"

"I regret nothing."

"Well, I doubt that. I'll bet you wish you weren't bleeding to death right now, and I'll bet you wish you killed the gods you meant to."

Apor laughed. "You think I meant to kill them? No, my job was only to put the wheels in motion. My soul is clear."

Apor slid off her seat and onto the ground. She had lost a lot of blood. I rushed toward her, but she held up her hand. When she did, I saw that the side of her stomach had been blown clean off along with her hand. She was dying.

"Is it, though? You have no regrets?"

"None."

"Then tell me who recruited you. Where did you get this clear conscience?"

"You think I am that easy to turn?" she said. "I am ready to die."

"Then do it with your conscience truly clear. Otherwise, we will have to assume your mother is guilty, and you know she will not survive long if that is the case."

"I don't care," Apor said. "Do you see what her security did to me? She is the reason I lie dying right now."

"No. She could not have known she was killing you when she left. She could not have known you would betray her. She thought she was protecting you. Are you willing and able to kill her in cold blood, though? After she raised you? After she loved you?"

"Your demon tongue—" Apor whispered, her breath grating. "A name. I only have a name."

"Give it to me."

"…Velaska."

CHAPTER 17

Akta

Location: Onyti

People lied, which was why I never trusted a person's words. If you needed to believe somebody, you followed their actions. I was tailing Qeuntis to find out where he went to pick up his product. He told us he had given us his last batch of the blue soul bomb, which meant he would have to make a run to get more in the near future. If I caught him at the right time, I could find his supplier.

Of course, I hated waiting. I preferred to manufacture the right time, which meant walking into the Elysium bar one more time and finding the disgusting tentacled creature that tended the bar. This time, though, I was armed with a briefcase filled with credits to make Qeuntis an offer he couldn't refuse.

"Is he down there?" I asked the barnacle tending bar. "Qeuntis, I mean."

"He's here. I'm surprised you are alive."

"If you ever try to deceive me again, you won't be." I walked down the stairs and knocked on the door in front of Qeuntis's office.

Qeuntis called out from behind the door. "Who's there?"

"You sold me some very interesting product the other day. My bosses were impressed. They want to make good on your deal."

The door opened, and Qeuntis beckoned me to enter. "Yeah, I told you it was the literal bomb, right?"

I nodded. "You did, and it is. We're planning quite a large operation against the gods, and we're going to need as much product as you can get your hands on."

"Like I said, it's going to take a mont—"

I slammed the money on the table and opened the case. I spun it to him. "This is three million dollars. We need it by tomorrow."

"There's no way!" Qeuntis shouted. "I can't get that much Blue by then. It takes ti—"

I slammed my fists on the briefcase, closing it. "I don't believe that. My bosses don't believe that. We believe in you, and if you can deliver, we'll give you ten times this, which if I can count properly is six times more than your price, just in case you have to buy back any product from other buyers. The rest is for your troubles."

"That's…a deal, I think. Yeah, a deal." Qeuntis shook his head. "You ain't a cop, are you?"

I chuckled. "I assure you I am not a cop." I dropped a small tracker into his drink before I left. The nanobots dissolved in his beer before he even noticed.

I didn't know if he believed me until I was outside and turned on my tracker. I didn't know if he would finish his drink before rushing outside, so with a large degree of caution, I placed another tracker in the briefcase and a third under his car.

I was excited to see that all three began to work in under a half-hour and that he was off in his hover car. I didn't need one of those. I unfurled my wings and flew after him, nearly undetectable in the night.

I followed the car halfway around the country until the next morning when it arrived in a desolate desert complex that looked like a nuclear bomb site. I watched Qeuntis walk across a parking lot into a large warehouse.

The smell of rotting flesh filled my nostrils, and the toxic sludge they made inside became clear to me. It was an abandoned factory that somebody commandeered to manufacture Godless weapons. Of course, they needed somewhere off the beaten path, and we would never check a planet like Onyti, as it was under the protection of Odin's line and not the Godschurch. I focused my eyes skyward and saw two soldiers with machine guns on the roof. All over the universe, humans knew how to make weapons and use them to intimidate and kill each other. It was a failing of their species. When designing humanity in their image, the gods made sure to add an extra dash of bloodlust.

I dropped some pixie dust and disappeared onto the roof. I snapped one guard's neck immediately before pulling a dagger out of my belt and slicing the vocal cords of another one. Both men dropped where they were, and I rushed through the door into the facility.

An ominous green hue surrounded me as I descended the stairs onto a catwalk overlooking a vat of green goop. This was where they made the bombs, at least the Horde ones, *but where were they making the soul bombs?*

"Are you sure you weren't followed?" a slender woman said to Qeuntis. I turned off the trackers I used to follow him in case they scanned the package or him. I touched a band around my wrist and the trackers dissolved.

"Of course, doll face. I'm the best." *Typical man.*

The woman scoffed. "You disgust me."

Qeuntis laughed. "You melt souls to make bombs that kill gods, and I disgust you?"

"Yes, which should tell you how vile I believe you to be."

"Well, I don't think you're gonna think I'm vile after you see this." Qeuntis opened the briefcase. I looked down and saw it was only half full—the shifty bastard. I would expect nothing less. "Met a girl who wants as much of the blue stuff as you can muster."

"As I said, that takes time. We're increasing production but—"

"And she said she has three times more than this if we can fulfill by tomorrow."

"Ludicrous," she said dismissively. "Nobody would pay that."

"Course they would. I've been telling you for years; we're undercharging." *Years. They've been making soul bombs for years?*

"There is no we." She poked Qeuntis in the chest. "There is an us and a you."

Qeuntis nodded. "Of course, of course. I'm sorry. I misspoke."

"Let me see what I can do." The woman disappeared down the hallway, and I followed around the dark catwalk. Under me, the halls were lined with heavily-armored troops, but as I followed her along the catwalk, it was free of any guards. They didn't seem to believe somebody could penetrate from the roof.

"We have a situation," the woman said into her headset. She listened intently as she walked. "Of course," she said. "I don't believe it either, but is it possible?" The woman passed through a door, and I stepped through a window to follow her. "That's what I thought, too. What should I tell him?" The woman stopped. "Thank you, Velaska. I will let him know."

I stifled a gasp as I stared down at the woman who had just talked to one of the Godschurch's most trusted ambassadors. I had fought with Velaska. I had bled with Velaska. And now, she was a traitor. *How could I believe that, and yet, how could I not?*

CHAPTER 18

Rebecca

Location: Godschurch Base

I frowned at Akta and Julia as they sat across from me, recounting what they had learned in their investigations. "It's not that I don't believe you. It's that I absolutely do not believe you."

"You don't have to believe me," Akta said. "That does not change the truth. The truth is the truth whether you want to believe it or not. That's the beauty of the truth."

"Please stop saying the word truth. It's giving me a migraine." I took a drink of whiskey from a glass on my desk. "I'm not discounting what you heard. I'm discounting the idea of starting a witch hunt for one of my most trusted advisors."

"What reason does a dying servant have to lie to me?" Julia said.

"And I heard the same name from the lips of a weapons dealer halfway across the universe."

"Velaska could mean anything in either context. It's a big universe, and I'm sure there are other people named Velaska out there."

Akta blinked a few times before speaking. "Those soul bombs were used in my home solar system," she said. "Developed in an underworld that Velaska used to control."

"Thousands of years ago," I snapped back. "Do you want to be held to account for things that happened thousands of years ago?"

"It's too much of a coincidence," Julia said. "And how many people do you think can get a soul bomb to a deva? Velaska has complete immunity to go anywhere at any time with no supervision."

"So do all gods!" I shouted. "So do almost all people. We are at 10 percent capacity here. Way too much slips through the cracks. Listen, I will take this under advisement, but for the time being, you are to stand down."

Akta pushed up from her chair, knocking it over. "You are being run by your emotions."

"Careful," I growled. "We are not equals."

"No," Julia said. "She's much better at this than you. Both of us are."

I pointed at the door without looking at either of them. "Get out."

Once they had left my office and closed the door, I dropped my head to my hands and tried to catch my breath. Velaska was one of my oldest friends. She brought me into the Godschurch.

Well, that wasn't exactly true. She tricked me into joining the church as a way for her to gain membership.

Oh god. She was a trickster.

After she gained membership, the Godless started to attack with more frequency. After she gained membership, the Godschurch blew up. We thought that my old partner was a spy and had given the coordinates to the base. We killed him for it. What if it wasn't him? What if it was Velaska all along?

She was a trickster god, deep down in her core. For all the things she'd been to me, to the church, at her base she was made of pure chaos. I didn't want to believe I could have let somebody so devious into my inner ranks. Maybe Akta was right. Maybe I was being ruled by emotions.

No. It was impossible. Velaska fought with me at the Battle of the Obelisk. She helped us defeat Cronus. He rests guarded at the Source partially because of her. Or was that her plan all along? After all, Cronus was not dead, nor was Rhea, and they had made it back into the universe. Perhaps she still worked to set them free...

...Or perhaps she had another plan.

I comported myself and then stood up. There was far too much conjecture and not enough solid proof. If Velaska were a traitor, then there would be a paper trail. Perhaps on the NOX list.

I walked out of my office, which led directly into the bullpen. At the far end of the room, I watched out of the window as the Source spun around and around. I could barely make out Cronus and Rhea. Even compared to Source, they were small. However, they had access to it, which was a condition of their surrender. Again, perhaps that was part of the plan.

"Edgar," I barked. He was a glasses-wearing, squirrelly guy, but he was a master at computers. The more complicated the task, the more he excelled. I had asked him personally to find out how the NOX list of gods was released and to cross-reference it to our records. "Have you found anything?"

He looked up at me sheepishly. I had ordered him not to say anything, and now I was blaring at him across the bullpen. My emotions were getting the better of me. "Are...you sure...you want to talk about this out in the open?"

I looked around and saw that nobody else was paying attention. Because of the sensitive nature of Edgar's work, I gave him a wide berth from the other office drones. "Nobody can hear us or see your screen. I made sure of that."

"I would still feel more comfortable if I had an office."

"So would everybody. Until then, tell me what you found, right here, right now."

"Well," he said, "this is a list of every known deity associated with love in the cosmos."

"Love?"

"Correct," he said.

"How did Katrina end up on this list, then?"

He shrugged. "We don't know why or how Cronus gave her the power of a god. Perhaps it was from the same source, or perhaps she was tossed on for good measure. There are several other gods from random pantheons, probably to throw people off the trail and prevent us from making the connection, but I am very good at my job. This is the only part of this list that's complete. Otherwise, it feels like a list of—"

"I don't care about the particulars. I just want to know where it came from. Do you know where it came from?"

"Well, there are only a half dozen terminals which could access it, including yours, and Katrina's, though I doubt that she would try to kill herself."

"What about Velaska?"

He looked up at me. "All gods have access to the database of their own pantheons, but you gave Velaska access to all pantheons when she started digging into the history of the Godschurch a few years ago."

He was right. Velaska had become obsessed with the origins of the Godschurch, and I granted her access to everything so she could conduct her search. Why wouldn't I? She was my most trusted advisor.

Edgar continued. "So, yes, she is one who could access everything in our database. I discounted the gods as a source of this leak, but the analysis of every other person with access did not show their time signature or ID imprint."

"Run the underlying code of the list against Velaska's signature."

He typed into his computer, and after a minute, a dialog box popped up on the computer indicating a match. "It seems that's precisely where it came from."

Damn.

***

I still didn't believe it deep in my bones, but it was impossible to deny that Velaska's name was associated heavily with the soul bombs and the NOX list. I had to bring her in for questioning. I asked Katrina to come with me, along with Julia and Akta, just in case I needed backup. I did not want to vaporize a god, but if she put up a fight, I would have to. The truth was, I wasn't sure I could shoot my friend if the time came. I knew that Akta would have no problem with it, and neither would Julia. Hell, Katrina might relish it.

"Prepare for anything."

I knocked on Velaska's door, and it slid open. She was dressed in her finest toga as if she were expecting someone.

"Hello, darling!" she said before seeing the party behind me. "This is a surprise. What is this about? What's everybody doing here? If it's for an orgy, I must decline."

I swallowed. "Goddess Velaska, you are under arrest for terrorism and sedition."

"Excuse me?" Velaska laughed. "Is this a joke? Is it my birthday? Did Urania plan a surprise party for me?"

"It's not a joke," Katrina said. "There's evidence you conspired against the Godschurch and the gods themselves, including me."

"That's preposterous," Velaska said. "I barely think of the other gods, and as for you, watching you suffer at Urania's happiness is enough joy for ten lifetimes."

"Just come with us," Akta said. "Don't make this hard on yourself."

"Absurd." She turned to me. "This isn't a joke, is it?"

I held out a pair of magic-dampening cuffs. "I'm sorry, but no."

"This is ridiculous," she said, holding out her hands. "But I'll play along, for now."

I snapped the cuffs on her just as the Godschurch began to rock and sway. A siren began to blare, and a red light flashed overhead. "Attack imminent."

"What's happening?" I asked Velaska.

"No idea," she replied, her eyebrows raised.

"Let's go." I dragged her, cuffed, toward the control room. When we got there, the entirety of the bullpen was typing furiously, but their monitors were all blackened. "What's happening?"

"We don't know!" Edgar shouted. "Something locked us all out of the system."

"Well, fix it!" I screamed.

The siren cut, and the monitors clicked over to a message. "Defensive measures engaged."

I spun to the front of the room, to the Source, where I watched all of our defensive measures fire at once. Cronus barely had time to look before he and Rhea were hit with hundreds of Godless bombs. His eyes went wide as I watched him reach out to Rhea. The pair disintegrated, holding each other's hands as they vanished.

With them dead, the sirens stopped. The monitor clicked. "Threat neutralized."

The system rocked back to life, but the damage was done. We had declared war on the Titans and killed two innocent gods. *Who would ever take us seriously again?*

CHAPTER 19

Katrina

Location: Godschurch Base

"You're a moron," I fumed as I paced back and forth in Rebecca's office. Akta, Julia, and Rebecca stood on either side of me, wondering if I would pop at any second, as I'm prone to do. "I don't like Velaska any more than the next person, but she's not a traitor."

"The evidence against her is strong," Akta said. "Even you have to admit that."

"And we follow the evidence, no matter how much we hate it," Rebecca added. "If she's innocent, she has nothing to hide."

"Bull!" I snapped. "I grew up on Earth, where innocence was only as good as your lawyer."

"I was born on that Earth, too, and this isn't that," Julia said. "We believe in justice here."

"That sounds like what the police want you to believe," I growled. "I'm going to talk to her and sort this out."

"Be my guest," Rebecca said. "Interrogation room one. With you gone, we'll actually be able to get some work done."

"You realize I could end you, right?" I said, balling my fists. "Like, in an instant."

"One thing I've learned about gods," Rebecca said with a dry chuckle, "is that you all can threaten me and talk a big game but don't have the stones to kill me. Now, get out of my office."

My lip twitched, but I didn't act on the rage tearing through my body. Instead, I ripped open the door and tossed it down in front of me. Two robots rushed past me to fix it as the analysts watched me pass as if they had never seen a pissed-off god before.

When I got to the interrogation room, Velaska was sitting properly in the hard metal chair we gave to suspects, smiling pleasantly and drinking a cup of tea. She looked every bit the regal elegance that I knew her to be.

"I didn't have anything to do with this," I said. "I just want you to know this isn't some petty jealousy thing."

"Oh, I know," Velaska replied with a curt smile. "You aren't sophisticated enough to convince Akta to move against me, let alone Rebecca."

"Akta hates you."

"Not anymore. Not since I let her out of her contract with me a millennia ago. Since then, she's had an amicable distrust of me, which any mortal should have with any god."

"Do you have any idea what's going on here?" I asked.

"Of course, my darling. Somebody is trying to set me up. If I were to betray you all, do you really think I would be so sloppy? Please give me some credit. I am nothing if not careful. If I had to guess, any moment Rebecca or one of her drones will come to tell you that it was my code that fired the rockets at Cronus. I admit I had no love for the Mad Titan, but do you think I would risk everything to kill him?"

"I don't," I said. "But I've been wrong before."

"For 10,000 years, you were the Devil. You dealt with all manner of horrible beings, out for their own selfish ends. You know more about the darkness in the hearts of people than almost anyone. Do you see that darkness in me?"

"Honestly, yes, I do. I see it in everyone. It is a curse of my previous office. I can't stop seeing the bad in everything, even if there is good out there to see."

"Yes, it is a curse of our profession. I see the good in you, too. It's there." There was a knock on the door, and Velaska turned back to her tea. "That's for you."

I stepped outside to find Rebecca waiting for me. "It was Velaska's codes that detonated the explosion that killed Cronus and Rhea."

She was right. "That's exactly what she said would happen."

"Because she's guilty."

"Maybe. This just doesn't seem like her. She's always so careful, and this feels so sloppy. I've never known her—"

"You haven't known her very long. Neither have I. She was a god for eons before either of us was born. You don't know her life before us, and I don't know if you want to. Akta does not have very nice things to say about her."

I bit my lip. "Let me talk to her for a couple more minutes."

Rebecca looked at me. "Don't take too long."

I walked back into the interrogation room. Velaska delicately put down her tea and turned to me. "What did she say?"

"Exactly what you told me she would."

She smirked. "Of course, dear, and I assume that she said that's exactly what a guilty person would say."

"More or less." I leaned against the back of the chair. "Velaska, this is really bad. I don't know how to help you."

"I don't expect you to help me. With me out of the picture, you have a clear path to Urania."

"Goddamn it, Velaska. I'm not trying to break up your relationship. It pisses me off, and I want to pop your head like a zit just about every minute of every day, but I hate myself for messing it up with her, not you. You are just a reminder…of my failure." I hated saying those words, but that didn't make them any less true.

"Interesting," she said, taking another sip of her tea.

"How can I help you?" I asked quietly.

"Follow the leads," she said.

"There are no leads. Indra's just some foolish shut-in that told me love was the answer."

"He may be a shut-in, but there is something to that word, or he wouldn't have said it. He would have just told us to get bent or some other vile phrase. But if you want to help me, figure out what is actually going on, and do it quickly, please. Meanwhile, I will enjoy this lovely tea."

"Okay." I pursed my lips and began walking toward the door.

"Oh," she said. "And get Akta to help you, and the other one who follows her around, because you are rubbish at investigation. Don't take it personally. You have many good qualities. If I want to smash something, you're my go-to."

CHAPTER 20

Kimberly

Location: Yama's Underworld

Yama led me up a craggy path toward the cliffs at the tip of Hell. He placed his hand on the edge of the cliff and asked me to do the same. "Can you feel that?"

The ground was warm to the touch but not hot as I expected for the pits of Hell. It reminded me of a heating pad that I used to place on my shoulder to relieve the pain from a hearty battle when I was alive on Earth ten millennia ago. "What am I supposed to feel?"

"This cliff is a sieve. Cleaned souls pass through this membrane on their journey to the Source. It should be ice cold, as the coolness from a clean soul mixes with the cold vacuum of space. Grab my hand."

I placed my hand in Yama's. He snapped the fingers on his other hand, and I tasted fresh tuna. We appeared in the vacuum of space, looking down upon a planet not unlike Earth, except the continents had drifted so far apart that they had merged back together, and one super city connected everything with lights speckling the surface of the planet.

Yama held what looked like a small handheld television. He pulled up the antennae and turned it on. "We should be seeing twenty souls per second pass through the membrane of Hell and head toward the Source, but right now, we're getting barely half of that, and it's going down every minute. At this rate, by the end of the week, we won't be sending any souls to the Source. Something weird is going on. I'm just not sure what it is."

I nodded silently, considering all of this. "Thank you. Keep working on it."

"I will," he assured me.

I pointed to the device. "Can I borrow that?"

He nodded and handed it to me. I spent the rest of the day traveling from underworld to underworld, testing Yama's theory, and found that his findings were consistent across every planet. Souls leaving Hell were down fifty percent from whatever the hell told me they usually cleared in a given day, and the disparity was increasing with each test.

Now I knew the problem, at least, but not what it meant. I went to see Nyx, who had been around longer than anybody, hoping for advice. I hated wandering into the Darkness because I always felt as though I was interrupting her from some great piece of work. This day was no exception, and when I stepped into the Darkness, I heard a sigh explode through the inky blackness.

"Didn't we just speak?" Nyx asked. "I told you I needed to recover from your last visit."

"Yes, goddess. I'm sorry, but I have a problem, and I don't have any answers about what is happening, just that it is happening."

"Then you should bring it to the Godschurch. That is why it was created, to help gods with problems that none but them can solve. Do not concern me with this piffle."

"I thought it was started to protect gods."

Nyx groaned. "Yes, and sometimes from themselves, but never from the truth."

"I don't think this is the kind of thing that they are equipped to deal with right now. What I need is information, and all they're offering is confusion."

Another deep sigh. "Have you thought that perhaps you ask too much of the universe?"

I shook my head. "No, my queen."

"The universe has existed for billions of years and will continue to the end, whether you meddle or not."

"But what if this is the end?"

"Now you're just being dramatic. Go away before I become perturbed and take action to harm you."

***

If she wasn't going to help me, I needed to venture to her personal library. I hated Yrowet, the homeworld of Death. The entire planet was covered in a black haze, like a gothic snow globe, and ash fell from the sky continuously. I preferred to work from the satellite offices that we had set up all over the universe. We had expanded so greatly that having a home planet seemed to be a contrivance of the past. However, deep in the chasms of Yrowet, every reaper had a desk, and Death was welcomed as a ruler instead of a burden.

I traveled through the rocky caves, sunken catacombs, and eerie tunnels of Yrowet until they broke open into its own underworld. Instead of a place for cleansing souls, it was the home of reapers, efficient bureaucrats who flew in and out.

In the center of the cave was a tall tower that housed the Library of the Night, Nyx's personal archive—the greatest collection of books in the universe. I snapped my fingers and was instantly inside of it; the walls stacked high with ancient tomes, covered in dust and riddled with gnawing paper moths. I had asked for the library to be digitized, but the imps and souls that haunted the library had barely gotten to one-tenth of one percent of the wisdom in the library. It was a big job.

The imp Hjilin tended the library since the beginning of its existence and seemed to have read every word the goddess ever wrote. He was usually dour and solemn, but when I appeared in the library proper, he was standing atop the reference desk, directing monsters around the library like a conductor on three pots of coffee.

"No, no, no. The goddess asked for them to be packed—" Hjilin was an ancient imp, even by immortal standards. His long, deep wrinkles carved a story of servitude on his face. "My, my, my goddess. I did not expect you—we haven't seen you in a long time. We thought you might have died."

"I'm not dead. I am Death," I replied. "What are you doing here?" I looked around to see that most of the catalog of books had been removed. The last time I was in the library, there were millions of books, and now there were barely hundreds. "What have you done to all the books?"

"My apologies, my queen, but Nyx has asked us to relocate some of our more…sensitive books."

"More sensitive? There's almost nothing left! Why would she do that?"

Hjilin shrugged. "I'm not sure, to be honest. The order came down some time ago, which you would have known if you bothered to check in."

"Why would she tell me to come here if—" A searing pain pressed against my head for a moment, then dissipated. "Hjilin, do you still work for me?"

"In a way," Hjilin replied. "I work for the library, and Death as a conceit, so yes, in that way, I work for you."

I stepped forward. "And you have been here for a long time, right?"

Hjilin choked on his spittle. "As long as this library has existed, I have been here to tend it."

"Do you have any idea why souls would not be able to leave the underworld, even once they are cl—" Another shock pulsed through my brain. This time the shock was so great that I dropped to my knees. A moment later, Hjilin and the rest of the imps dropped as well. "What is happening?"

"Tartarus is angry," Hjilin said through gritted teeth.

The feeling dissipated again. "Tartarus, that was the name of the underworld on my world. The original name."

"It is the original name on all underworlds, including this one. Tartarus is connected, each one with the next, and it hungers. I can feel it, even here."

"Why here?"

"This is an underworld as well, though on a dead world, which was why we repurposed it."

A third pulse, this time so powerful I thought I would tear apart at the seams. I screamed and clutched my skull.

"I'm sorry, my goddess, but he is hungry, and he cannot be satiated."

I barely had the energy to snap my fingers together. As I did, I watched Hjilin vanish into the ether before my eyes.

What was happening to the underworld?

CHAPTER 21

Akta

Location: Godschurch Base

"I don't care if you don't want to do it," Katrina grumbled. "You're going to do it."

She had cornered Julia and me in the hallway leading up to the Godschurch from the elevator, trying to intimidate us, but I was very hard to intimidate. "I don't work for you, and I certainly don't work for Velaska."

"You work for the gods, and the gods need your help," Katrina said. "I know you don't like Velaska, but she didn't do this, and you know it. Doesn't all of this seem fishy to you?"

"It really does," Julia said, nodding slowly. "Velaska is way too careful to be this sloppy."

"That's what I'm saying," Katrina said. "And since you two are agents and investigators, go investigate."

"Rebecca did say to figure out who was creating soul bombs," I said. "And if it's not Velaska, then we need another lead. What do you have for us in the way of information?"

"I don't have much," Katrina said. "I talked to Indra, a god that Cronus said would help me, but all he did was tell me that love was the answer, and I am so...I will never believe love is anything but a pollutant."

"That's not much," Julia said. "I mean, it's pretty much nothing."

Katrina scoffed. "Just do what you can, okay?"

"And what will you do?" I asked calmly.

She stepped forward and thrust out her chest. "I'll not kill you. How about that?"

Katrina bumped my shoulder on her way down the hall. I had seen her intimidate enough people that I didn't fall for it anymore. She was scared, and that was how she lashed out.

"So, what now?" Julia asked.

"Look for known contacts of Indra, do interviews. Try to find another lead since all other leads point back to Velaska."

"Maybe that's because it's Velaska, and she's guilty," Julia said. "I mean, it all adds up."

"Too well," I replied. "It adds up too well like somebody wanted us to find her."

Before Julia could respond, there was a flash of light. Once it dissipated, Kimberly appeared in front of us, struggling to stand on wobbly knees. "Help."

She collapsed on the ground and Julia ran to her. "What happened to you?"

"I don't know," Kimberly said, gasping. "But I need your help."

Julia looked up at me. I nodded. Kimberly was her protégé once upon a time, even though she was now a god, and I knew she had to help her old pupil. "I'll take care of following up on Velaska. You figure this out."

***

There was only one analyst worth my time, and that was Edgar, Rebecca's pet. The others were competent and lovely, but Edgar was actually smart and capable of synthesizing data outside of just following orders. The Godschurch wanted people to fit into a very small box, and Edgar was one of very few people I could bounce ideas off of and know it wouldn't get back to Rebecca.

"I have a new one for you, Edgar," I said with a smile as I walked up to his station. "This one is a doozy."

He spun around with a smile. "Oh, goodie. I do so love a brain teaser. Hit me."

"Interesting you say love because that's just what this is about. One of our agents talked to a god about this whole—well, all of this craziness going on—and he said that 'love is the answer.' Does that mean anything to you?"

Edgar's eyes went wide, and he turned back to his station. "Nope. Nothing."

I spun his chair back around so he was facing me. "You are a terrible liar. You know something. Tell me."

He shook his head vehemently. "I can't. I'll be fired."

I glared at him intently. "Only if you get found out, and I don't plan on saying anything to anybody. However, I can tell you factually that I will make your life miserable if you don't tell me. Now, spill."

"You're not going to let this go, will you?" After I shook my head, he sighed. "Fine, but you can't tell anybody, nobody, not even Julia."

I nodded. "Fine. She's got her own things to worry about anyway."

He sighed after looking around for snooping ears. "You know that NOX list you found?"

I nodded again. "Of course."

Edgar typed into his computer. "Well, it turns out all the gods on that list, or most of them at least were gods of love, and get this…over half of them are dead now."

"That's too coincidental not to mean something. Can you look up and tell me if Indra had any known associates?"

He typed into his computer. "Just one. An ex-wife named Sacchi, who died a long time ago... Oh wait, he's also got a mistress. Freyja, and look at this, she's the god of love in the Odinson line. God, I love it when mixed-pantheon babies happen. They are so beautiful."

"Get me Freyja's information. I need to make a house call."

***

"Can I get you some tea?" Freyja asked as I sat in her spacious apartment. Her long red hair was pulled back, exposing the amber necklace against her white skin. In the corner of her apartment, a falcon watched us warily.

"No, thank you," I said. "I appreciate you seeing me, by the way. I know the Odinson line are not fans of the Godschurch."

She came back with a cup of tea and sat down on a red velvet couch across from me. "Oh, that's silly. My family is the worst. That's why I don't even live in their space anymore. They are so uppity."

I smiled. "Some of you are okay."

She took a sip of tea. "Now, you said you wanted to talk with me about Indra? I'm afraid he's pretty quiet. I don't see him often, and he's been pulling further and further away from me over the past century. It's okay, though, there are always plenty of men to make me forget about him…and women, too, just so you know." She placed her hand on my knee. "You know."

I couldn't help but blush as I pulled back my knee from her grasp. "Good to know. He told my compatriot something interesting. He said that love was the answer."

"Well, love is the answer to a great many things," she said. "But the answer to what, specifically?"

"I don't know," I said. "He was apparently very cryptic and standoffish."

She shrugged. "That sounds like him. At least, the way he is now."

"Does it mean anything special to you?"

"Love means everything to me. It doesn't mean much to Indra, at least not now."

"What happened to him?"

She thought for a moment. "I don't know, honestly. He used to be so sweet and open. He was one of the most human-friendly gods I had ever met, but recently…recently, he started getting really weird. Talking about how chaos was coming, and it was the end. That we should prepare. I don't know. I told him that if I got up in arms every time the universe was in danger, I would never get a moment's sleep." She rubbed her silken skin. "I am very interested in my beauty sleep."

My ears perked up. "He used that word? Chaos?"

"Of course." She rolled her eyes. "He said it all the time."

I leaned forward and clasped my hands together over my knees. "Do you think he could have meant Projekt Kaos?"

"I dunno." She furrowed her brows. "What's that?"

"We're trying to figure that out." As I watched Freyja touch her lips and move her hand down to her cup, the mug began to glow a light blue. "Where did you get that tea?"

"It was delivered by one of my many admirers. Isn't it grand?" She went to take another sip, and I swatted the cup out of her hand. Her eyes went wide, and her chin jutted out. "Hey! That was a gift from a very well-endowed dwarf. How do you get off—"

"I'm sorry, goddess, but—"

I couldn't finish my sentence before Freyja's eyes started to glow. She opened her mouth to scream, but only a haunting light came out. When the light extinguished, nothing but ash remained where she once sat.

CHAPTER 22

Julia

Location: Godschurch Base

I brought Kimberly hot chocolate just like I used to when she'd had a rough night back on Earth. It was long ago for both of us, but the tradition lived on even now.

She smiled at me as she took the mug. "You know I'm not sixteen anymore."

"I know," I replied. "I'll bet that won't stop you from drinking it, though."

She shook her head as she took a sip. "Not at all. It does smell good. Sometimes, it's nice to be reminded of simpler times, when all we had on our minds was saving our people instead of the whole universe."

"If only," I said with a chuckle. "Feel any better?"

She held up her hand, which was steady as a rock. "I think so. I don't know what happened, but it felt like my soul was being wrenched from my body. I've only felt it once before."

"During Ragnarök?"

She nodded. "When I became this." She took another sip and stared off into the distance for a moment. "I didn't even know I could feel pain anymore. It made me feel…"

"Human?"

She turned to me. "Yeah, is that stupid?"

I sat down next to her. "Of course not. We were human once. Or part of us was, at least. Sometimes I think about it—Earth. Driving my car along a summer road. Going to a cookout. The simple things."

"Yeah," she said wistfully. "Eating corn dogs, reading books."

I chuckled. "I still read books."

"Like you used to? For fun?"

"No," I said, looking down. "I used to like thrillers quite a bit, but I think I've lived too many to enjoy them."

"Can I tell you a secret?" Kimberly asked.

"Of course."

She looked down into her cocoa. "Sometimes I read trashy romance novels when I go back to Earth. My favorites are still by Danielle Steele, but some of the other writers around the universe are quite good, too, even if I can't relate to them as much."

"You've gone soft," I said with a chuckle. "Isn't it amazing that no matter the planet, people still write?"

"And kill," Kimberly said before another sip of cocoa.

"Creation and destruction. There is little in between for us, is there?"

She sighed. "Not for us. Do you know what I miss most about being a human?"

I shook my head. "What?"

"The pure banality of it all." She looked up into the sky. A tear fell down her ancient face. "There were moments of great highs or lows, but usually, it was just ceaselessly boring. Predictable. When I was alive, all I wanted was action and adventure. I needed to be swept along every moment of every day, and now, what I wouldn't give for a moment of boredom."

I rubbed her back. "We always want what we can't have, right?"

Kimberly turned to me. "I don't know what is happening, but I feel it in my bones that it's bad. Like something in the heart of the universe is calling out, screaming in pain, and I have no idea what it wants."

She took one last swig of cocoa and then handed me the cup. I smiled at her. "Well, whatever it is, we get there one step at a time. First step, go to the library to investigate."

"I don't know if I can go back there."

"Then we'll wait until you're ready, but if you're right, and it's as bad as you say, then the longer we wait to act, the less time we have to stop it."

Kimberly stood, resolute. "You with your logic."

***

Kimberly jumped us to a new planet, one I had never visited before; her home. We stood on the top of a mountain in front of a cave opening. The air was thick with sorrow, and darkness covered every surface, like ashen soot that didn't wipe off no matter how hard you scrubbed. Every direction I looked was more depressing than the last.

"Cheery," I said.

"Death is less concerned with cheer than necessity," Kimberly said solemnly as she walked into the cave. I followed behind as we descended into the Darkness. "Thousands have pledged their lives to its cause not out of desire, but obligation." She turned back to me. "However, I like to think there is beauty in it, too."

"In death?" I said. "I have seen nothing but suffering in it."

I could barely make out her slow head nod as we walked further into the dark. "Suffering is a necessity, it is true, and I don't relish that part. In the end, though, you have purity, and you can return to the Source to be reborn again into something new. Perhaps a god, or a planet, or a blade of grass. Only in death do you receive salvation."

"That is kind of beautiful; I have to admit. It's a load of horseshit, but it's beautiful horseshit."

I heard her laugh lightly. "You would make a terrible reaper."

"Is that the line you use to recruit them?"

"Usually, I don't have to do much recruiting. Many are happy to join the service, escape punishment in the pits, and do their duty to the cosmos."

"So, reapers never get cleansed?"

Again, a thin shake of her head. "It is that impurity that lets us do our work. It is the Darkness that resonates with men's souls and allows us to shepherd them to the great beyond."

"So, for all your talk of salvation, you will never be saved?"

"It is not clear what happens to gods when they die, but as for reapers, they know the weight of their decision." She took a deep breath. "They get to continue their existence with the knowledge that there will never be anything better or worse than this moment." Kimberly stopped as a light grew in the distance. "This is a sacred place for us that deals in death. Please, be respectful."

"Am I usually not respectful?"

She chortled, holding back her laughter to project
solemnity. "I'm not going to answer that. Please. If not as a
friend, then as a colleague, I ask you to tolerate my work,
even if you do not condone it."

We neared, and the pinprick of light washed over us.
When the light swept over us, we were in the underworld,
both not as I remember it and exactly the same
simultaneously. I recognized every crack and crevice, but
instead of a bright, bubbling brightness, this cavern had a
gray wash across it, speckled with light from blue candles.
Kimberly opened her hand to me, and I took it. "Come."

We rose into the air and floated over dozens of tall
towers. Every dozen or so feet, the towers bulged into a
glass bulb. "What are those?"

"Offices. Every reaper has an office. Every column a
different department, a different galaxy."

"I am surprised at how much this is like any other
corporation."

"Well, humanity was modeled on us, after all. Is it that
surprising our structures resemble theirs?"

I thought for a moment. "I suppose not."

Kimberly stepped onto a platform atop the highest
tower. She walked inside, and I followed her into another
office, except this one had a bed and felt more lived-in than
any of the others we passed. She didn't have to tell me that
this was her room. I recognized all of her eccentricities, like
a bed half made and a collection of worn stuffed animals on
a shelf above it. She'd changed a lot in ten thousand years,
but some things never changed.

She led me down a set of stairs into an enormous
library whose shelves were mostly bare. Hundreds of books
lined the floor, and there were carts filled with them that
dotted the library that seemed to go on forever.

"What happened here?" I asked.

"It would seem that the fate I avoided was felt by too many here. I hope they escaped, but I feel a great chasm in my soul where thousands of reapers used to flutter. Luckily, many of my people were on assignment, but still—thousands were lost."

"Yeah, that's horrible," I replied. "But I meant in this library. What happened to all the books?"

"I don't know," Kimberly said. "This is Nyx's personal collection, culled from the beginning of the universe with the most important knowledge in the cosmos."

"It seems every ancient library thinks they are the most important place in the whole universe."

Kimberly tried to stifle her laughter, but it came out anyway. "Yes, but one of them is correct. Why not here?" I didn't have a good answer. "Start looking."

"For what?" I asked, but it was clear that she didn't know.

"An answer to why this might be happening."

"You think we'll find an answer here?"

"I don't know," Kimberly said. "But Nyx was moving these books, so it's as good a place as any to start. If you feel unnatural like your soul is being ripped out of your skull, then jump away back to the Godschurch, and I will find you."

Kimberly walked to the left down a large corridor while I went right. I didn't bother looking on the shelves for what was important. Anything important would have been removed from the shelves. It was as if somebody was trying to purge the knowledge of the library. I stepped behind a long counter where the librarians probably spent hours cataloging books.

Books were strewn everywhere, not in an orderly pile like I had generally seen from librarians in the past, but unruly ones. The books had bent spines and tattered pages. As I moved down the row, I accidentally kicked one and sent it careening down the counter floor. I knelt down to look at the cover. Scratched across the cover was one word: Kaos.

I opened it up to look at its pages, but they were all gone. Somebody didn't want us to know what was inside that book. I looked over into a small metal trash can next to the counter where I encountered the cover, and there I found a thick pile of ash. Anything remaining from the pages was gone, which meant it was important, and the fact it bore the same name as the terrorist organization we had been tracking and the people who were killing gods couldn't have been a coincidence.

CHAPTER 23

Rebecca

Location: Godschurch Base

After days of searching, Edgar found a file on an ancient server stationed on a remote planet that hadn't been backed up in eons, coded with the name "Projekt Kaos." It was so old that Edgar couldn't break the password encryption by any of the methods he knew and needed to do more research on the dead programing language used back when the Godschurch was founded. Meanwhile, I decided to do some old-fashioned agent work and start tracking down the person who created the file in the first place. I had an idea of who would know, but I was loathed to ask her.

"I was wondering when I would see you, Director," Velaska said as I walked into the interrogation room. "I was getting so lonely."

"Cut the crap, Velaska," I snapped. She knew how to get under my skin and turn a conversation to her proclivities, so I had to be on my toes. "This isn't a courtesy call. I'm here on business."

"Of course you are. You have been all business since the moment we met." She chuckled to herself. "Don't think I'm not aware of the irony of my protégé arresting me, either. It's so delicious I could eat it with a cake."

I scoffed. "I am not your protégé."

She shrugged. "Perhaps, but I was the one who brought you into the church, and I have saved you more times than I care to count. It's sixty-three times if you would like to know, though."

"Thought you didn't keep count."

"That's just what people say. I kept track in case I ever needed it." She threw her arms out wide. "And look, here I am, needing it, darling. I knew this day would come if I waited long enough, which is the way of the gods. We keep track of our favors, tallying up friends and enemies, biding our time quite a bit more than humans have the capacity to do since we have all of eternity to collect."

"You're stalling."

She smirked. "About what? You haven't asked me your question yet."

"But you know what I'm going to ask."

She fell back in her chair. "Well, if you followed the clues to their logical conclusion, then there can be only one answer. Projekt Kaos."

"Why were you working for them?" I asked, stepping toward her. "Why were you making weapons to kill gods?"

"Oh, piffle," she replied with a chuckle. "That's not the Projekt Kaos I was referring to, and you know it."

"What is it?"

She shrugged. "I don't know."

I gritted my teeth. "Then what good are you?"

She held up her finger. "Because I know who does know."

"Who?"

"The oldest god in the database. In all my research, I hit a dead end with one single name."

"And who is that?"

"That information is my leverage, now, isn't it? Why would I tell you that when I could use it in so many different ways?"

I shifted my weight and crossed my arms over my chest. "Because if you really are innocent, helping us is the best way to prove it."

She turned up an eyebrow at me. "And what guarantees do I have that you'll let me out if I am innocent? After all, I doubt you will find the true culprit, and I will make a very easy scapegoat, especially since nobody likes me."

"I like you," I said. "Urania likes you."

Velaska let out an exasperated breath. "Please, she tolerates me at best. She clings to me because I'm a less nauseating option to Katrina for the moment, but don't think I haven't seen how she looks at her. It's only a matter of time before she forgets about me…and as for you…I wish you did like me after all this time, Rebecca. I do. I truly do because I like you. I wouldn't have pushed so hard for you to be the leader of the Godschurch if I didn't."

I shook my head. I wasn't going to get caught in her web. "Now you're definitely stalling and trying to butter me up."

Velaska shook her head. "You sweet, naïve child." She snapped her fingers, and her restraints fell off. "I helped design these handcuffs. Did you really think I would not build a backdoor for myself?"

Shit. Nothing worse than a rampaging god pissed at you. I turned to the door, but as I reached for it, the lock melted into the door, and the door sealed itself to the wall. I was stuck. "I'll scream."

"If I am the evil god you say I am, do you think I care?" Velaska replied, cocking her head. "If I were the kind of monster that could do the things you accuse me of doing, would it matter if you screamed? I dare say I would enjoy it, were I that kind of god. However, since I am not that kind of god, I will leave you with a name. The last name I have been investigating. If you find it, then you will find me."

"How will I believe you?"

Velaska walked forward. "Because I'm not going to kill you, and I could. The name is Ananke."

"Is that the password?"

"How old do you think I am? I don't know the password to that file or the person who founded the Godschurch. That information is hidden by the Primordials themselves."

"The Primordials?"

"No more questions." Velaska rolled her eyes. "I'm not going to do your job for you." She let out a deep sigh. "I really do wish that you loved me a fraction as much as I loved you because I do love you, truly, and am proud of all you've accomplished. I hope you find me soon. I fear there is not much time left."

"Then help u—"

But it was no use. Velaska snapped her fingers, and she was gone.

CHAPTER 24

Katrina

Location: Godschurch Base

"She wants us to do what?" I asked, staring confused at Rebecca as I sat across from her in her office. She had just finished explaining her conversation with Velaska to me, and I couldn't believe the absolute chicanery.

"She wants us to find Ananke," Rebecca replied.

"What's an Ananke?" I asked.

Rebecca spun the monitor on her desk so that I could see it. "Ananke is one of the first gods to be protected by the Godschurch. I had Edgar track all of Velaska's keystrokes, and she had been doing a good bit of research on our origins. She has been pulling on this thread for Projekt Kaos for years."

"That doesn't do much to help her innocence."

"No," Rebecca said. "But it also makes her a great target if somebody found out and was looking for a scapegoat."

I couldn't argue with her.

"She tracked the gods all the way back as far as they could be tracked and ended up with the oldest god in the whole database."

"Ananke."

"You got it," Rebecca said. "Only one problem."

"Just one?"

"For now. There is no known location for Ananke. It just says…the cosmos."

I leaned in. "That's not helpful. The cosmos is literally infinite."

She spun her monitor back around and began typing. "I know, and I also know somebody who can help us. She's kind of the god of the cosmos, or at least plotting the cosmos."

"Do tell."

"Seriously?" Rebecca grumbled. "You dated her, for a long time, too."

It finally clicked. Urania was obsessed with the cosmos. She was the patron god of astronomers across the galaxy, and she was the most knowledgeable god on the cosmos that I had ever met.

"This is going to suck."

"You could say that about anything, any time," Rebecca replied. "And you would be equally right about this, but I don't care. Now go talk to your bitter ex-girlfriend and figure out where Ananke is, all right?"

***

"Yeah," Urania said as I stood in the hallway outside her room. "I helped her track down Ananke. That's how we met, actually. Well, not met, but that's how we started hanging out. She would look at the stars with me for hours and never once roll her eyes at me like you're doing now."

She was right. I was rolling my eyes instinctively at the utter boredom of the stars. I blinked a few times and said, "I'm sorry. You're right. That was rude. Now, will you help me?"

Urania leaned against the wall of her apartment. "You realize this is the longest conversation we've had in months. Years, even?"

My eyes widened. "That's not true. I just talked to you when I came to find Velaska."

"That wasn't a conversation. That was barking orders at me."

"And this is a conversation?"

She pressed her hand against her chest. "At least you came to see *me* this time, even if it's to help you find Velaska."

I snarled. "Asking for help is not easy for me. Being close to people is not easy for me. Opening up is not easy for me."

She dropped her eyes and her tone. "I didn't need it to be easy. I needed it not to be impossible."

"I'm sorry I'm impossible," I said, biting my lip. "You know, I pride myself in the fact that nothing hurts me, inside or outside."

"I know."

"All right, I'll tell you a secret. Maybe it will get you to want to help me."

"I'm all ears."

I sighed loudly. "The reason why I get so upset about you and I pull away is that you somehow can hurt me with just a word and make me feel…"

"Go on."

"No, this is stupid." I shook my head. "This isn't the time to air out our dirty laundry. Can you please help me find your girlfriend? I can't do it without you."

Urania smiled. "That's the first truthful thing you've said to me in a long time."

I didn't want to admit she was wrong, and she was the only one who could make me feel anything except angry. I had been so angry for so long that I honestly forgot what it was like to be me without the anger. I was indestructible, after all, and what if it was because of that anger?

Urania held out her hand, and I touched her fingers with mine. Sparks flew through me. It had been me that ended things. It had been me that cheated on her with a dead Valkyrie. It had been me that pulled away because I couldn't stand being vulnerable after being so strong for so long, and I regretted it every day.

***

We flashed outside the Godschurch in front of the Source. All the god-killer weapons had been fired at Cronus and Rhea, destroying them in an instant, so there was no chance of the weapons going off any longer.

I had traveled out to the Source dozens of times to talk with Cronus, and now I would never do it again. "What are we doing out here?" I asked.

"Do you ever wonder what is inside?" Urania asked, staring at the whiteness of the Source.

"No," I said, dismissing her. After a moment, I bit my lip. "Yes, yes I do. All the time. I wonder what it would be like to fly inside and just disappear."

Urania smiled. "Me too."

"Is that what you brought me out here to ask?"

Urania turned around. "No. I was just curious." She held up her hands, making a rectangle with the thumb and index finger of each hand. "Do like I do."

She brought the rectangle up to her right eye and closed her left. I did the same. She pointed the rectangle at a random point among the stars.

I looked back at her. "What am I looking for?"

"Pull the rectangle away from your eye slowly. As you do, watch the edges of your eye for anything strange."

I didn't like doing anything slowly, but I complied. After a long, plodding time where I pulled the box as far as I could, I came away with nothing.

"See anything?" Urania asked.

"No," I muttered. "Except a fool."

"You're not doing it right."

"I'm doing what you said!"

"No, you di—" She crinkled her nose. "Oh, I forgot to tell you. Unfocus your eyes. Yeah, you have to unfocus your eyes for it to work."

I shook my head but didn't say anything. I placed the rectangle on my eye and defocused my eye. As I pulled my hands out slowly, the stars began to blend together until they were as one, and the light from them overwhelmed my watering eyes.

"Do you see it?" Urania said.

"I don't know what I'm seeing," I replied, squinting. "It's like the Source is everywhere."

"Exactly, when you pull back the veneer of the Darkness, you see that the light is everywhere." She pushed my hand toward the Godschurch. "Now, look here."

As my hand moved across the Godschurch, I saw it shimmer with a million different colors, like a plaid rainbow that I had never seen before.

"What is that?" I said.

"The rainbow bridge," Urania said. "We believe the Godschurch itself is a portal to Ananke, and she was the original founder of it."

"So Velaska..."

"Was waiting to find the portal to Ananke in the Godschurch. That's why she never left, but she must have finally figured it out."

"How did she do it?"

"I don't know, but I know she did it because she's been searching for it for years, everywhere across the universe. It consumed her until she came here. Since then, she's been pulling on the thread, and she must have finally found it."

"We have to find a way through."

"I agree." She smiled at me, and I had to fight back the butterflies that fluttered up into my throat.

CHAPTER 25

Kimberly

Location: The Darkness

I knew she wouldn't tell me, but I had to ask Nyx why she would burn a book in her own library. I stepped into the Darkness with the cover of the Kaos book in hand. Julia brought the ashes to the Godschurch to see if anything could be done, but I had my doubts. Nyx was a powerful goddess. If she wanted something gone, it would be gone.

"You again?" Nyx grumbled. "I barely saw my son more than a couple of times in a millennium, and here I have seen you three times in as many days."

I tossed the book cover down. "What is Projekt Kaos?"

"I assure you I have no idea what you're talking about."

"Why did you attack me in the library?" I asked.

"I couldn't be bothered to do such a thing."

"Why have all my reapers disappeared?" I snarled. "There were hundreds in Yrowet, and now there are none, and no Hjilin to guard the library either."

A thunderous boom echoed through the Darkness. "If you are going to accuse me, child, know with what power you threaten! I am the seed of darkness in this universe. I am the nothing to the everything. I am the end to the beginning. I am not some cheap party magician. You will respect me, or I will show you what happens to those who get on my bad side."

Every bone in my body wanted to stand down, but I simply couldn't do it. Instead, I planted my feet firmly on the blackness under me. "You are the Darkness. Which means you are everywhere and nowhere at once. Nothing goes on in this universe without you knowing about it. Isn't that right?"

"I have my powers, but I cannot know everything. No being can. If there is something I wish to know, then it is known."

I took a deep breath. She could vaporize me at any moment and easily, but I had to press her for the truth. "Then you would know that your personal library has been disbanded and the books are being moved out. Why?"

"I will not insult you with a lie. They have been moved because too much knowledge is a burden, and I chose not to burden you with it anymore. There is information you need not know, so you must not know it."

I pointed to the book in front of me. "Is that why you burned this book specifically?"

"I am not in the habit of burning books, my dear. I'm afraid—"

"What is Projekt Kaos?"

The entirety of the Darkness shook under me. "You are playing out of your league, reaper. I have allowed you to wear my son's cloak and claim his position as your own, but do not speak to me like you are a god as he was."

"I am every bit the god he was," I said, my hands balled into fists. "Better. Because he was killed by a human, and if you kill me, then I'll have been killed by a goddess."

She laughed. "I am so much more than you will ever know."

"As am I. His power flows through my veins. I feel it passing through me, growing with every soul I shepherd into the underworld."

"Your power is contained in your scythe."

I pulled out my scythe and held it up to her. "No, it's not." I broke the staff over my knee, holding half of it in each hand. "You bound my power to the scythe to enslave me to you, but I have been free for some time. I am not your puppet, and I do not need your protection."

"You should wish you had it, though. There are things worse than me in this universe, and should I snap my fingers, it will be known that I no longer claim you."

"Why did you burn this book?" I asked again.

"Go away."

"What is Projekt Kao—"

Before I could finish, a strong jerk pulled me into the vacuum of space. A snap echoed through the darkness around me, and I knew that Nyx had abandoned me. I was on my own. But I also knew something else: She held more knowledge than she let on. Otherwise, she never would have refused to answer me.

***

"You did not tell her that!" Julia said, laughing. "You're nuts."

"I did," I replied, sitting across from her in the Godschurch cafeteria. "And she kicked me out. I think she disowned me. Good riddance, I say."

"Are you worried? She is very powerful."

"I am an immortal god of Death. I haven't been scared in millennia."

"Maybe you should be."

"Probably." I shrugged. "But I'm not."

"Fair enough," Julia said. "I don't understand though, how did you take your power back from the scythe? It held your power when you became Death."

"Thousands of years ago, I was blackmailed for my power in an attempt to overturn the rules of death by a very petty god. In order to get back my power, I had to divorce it from my scythe, which I did. It's really not that hard when you realize that all magic is bullshit."

"But wait…wasn't your power infused to the Dagger of Obsolescence?"

I shook my head. "My, you really are out of the loop, aren't you? That was so ten millennia ago."

Julia laughed again, and I found myself smiling. I missed hanging out with her. My work took me all over the universe, but now I suppose that work was done, and I had all the time in the world.

"I wish I had your confidence. I don't know how we're going to figure out what to do next."

"Yeah," I said. "I've been thinking about what Katrina learned from Urania. If this base is actually a portal right to Ananke, then I think I might know how to get to it."

"How?"

"The same way I got to the Darkness." I leaned in, speaking softly. "You just have to find the seam."

"Any more info than that? Cuz what you just said makes no sense."

I stood up and brought Julia to the window to look out on the universe. I placed my fingers into a square and held them out in front of me. "Unfocus your eyes and look through my fingers." When she did, I pulled my fingers further away from her. "Do you see the little strands of white light that burst from the stars?"

She nodded. "I do."

"Those are seams in the universe. It's like a quilt that was crocheted together, except that instead of getting an afghan at the end, you get this universe. You can pull on any of them, and it's a ticket to a little pocket dimension or a rift in space, but pull the wrong one, and you'll end up somewhere you can't escape."

"Crazy. Why doesn't everybody move that way?"

"It's not common knowledge. I only found the Darkness by accident. I'm not even sure Nyx knows how I keep finding her."

"And you can find the seam to Ananke that way?"

"I think so," I said, moving my fingers around to different places in the cafeteria. "The trick is to find the right seam." Looking through my fingers, I noticed the rainbows that made up the light in the Godschurch base all seemed to converge in the center of the room. As I moved forward, I found a long tendril of a string pulled tight between the top of the room and the bottom.

I pulled out my broken scythe and pressed the razor-sharp edge against the tendril, cutting it in half. I used my hands to push apart the seam. As I did, a wave of rainbow light flooded the room.

"Whoa," Julia said. "I should get the others."

"You can never tell them how you found this."

"I won't."

"I believe you."

CHAPTER 26

Julia

Location: Godschurch Base

"This is bonknanas," Katrina said, staring at the plaid rift in the common room. "How did this happen?"

"I can't say." I was keeping my promise to Kimberly. "But if Ananke is truly in a pocket dimension created by the Godschurch, then this is how to find her."

Rebecca stepped behind the rift, which had no depth, and furrowed her brow. "And you think we should just go inside this thing? What if we're vaporized?"

I shook my head. "I don't think you should, ma'am. You're too important, but I can."

"You're important, too," Akta said. "We're all important."

I turned to her. "I wasn't looking for sympathy. I was just saying that she is the head of the Godschurch. Katrina is a god. I'm just a cog in a vast machine, and not a high-level one, either."

"You found this, didn't you?" Akta replied. "Which means you're more than a cog."

I turned to Kimberly, who gave a slight smile. "I suppose I did."

"If anything, I should go," Akta said.

I stepped forward. "I'm going. I don't know about the rest of you."

"Katrina should go, too," Rebecca said. "We don't know how Ananke will deal with a mortal, even a dead one, and Katrina is at least a god."

Katrina wheeled on her. "So you're volunteering me for suicide missions now?"

"Exactly," Rebecca replied, deadpan. "If you weren't always volunteering for them yourself, then I would not likely do so. Besides, somebody has to bring Velaska back here to stand trial."

"I still think she's innocent," Akta said.

"Innocent people don't run," Rebecca said.

"Well, that's bullshit," I replied. "Innocent people who don't believe in the system run all the time, and the system is clearly out to get Velaska."

"Be that as it may," Rebecca said. "She's a fugitive, and I'm not confident sending a rookie agent to recover her."

"Fine," Katrina said. "I'll go, if only because I don't want Velaska getting hurt."

Akta pressed her fingers to the bridge of her nose. "Let's just go already."

I nodded and stepped forward. "You're right. No more nervous bickering. Now is the time for action."

"It's perfectly safe," Kimberly said, eyeing the rift. "At least I think it is."

"So, you're coming?" I replied.

"Gods no," she said, shaking her head. "This is not my fight."

"Yet," Rebecca said.

"Let us hope it never becomes my fight," Kimberly said. "An assault on Death is an assault on the universe itself."

I stepped toward the middle of the room, took a deep breath, and fell into the rift. When I appeared on the other side, I came upon a sight I did not expect. Instead of a desperate nothingness, or a plaid box, or anything else I'd imagined, I walked through the front door of a tea house.

A dozen small tables were situated around the room with hardwood floors and a gray stone brick chimney against the far wall. The charming aesthetic of an 18th century English tea house continued up the walls, which were trimmed with the same oak as the floor. Pastoral paintings lined the walls, and in the center of the room was a small counter. A woman wearing a white bonnet stood behind it, smiling.

"Good morning," the woman said. "If you could take a seat in the back room, I'll be with you in a moment."

"Who are you?" I asked.

She smiled. "I promise to answer all your questions once the others come."

"Others?"

"Your friends from the Godschurch. We didn't think you would ever show up." She gestured to an archway separating the front room from the back. Sitting at a long table, sipping from a tea mug, was Velaska, who smiled and waved at me.

"So, she is here," I said, turning back to the woman. "Does that make you Ananke?"

"It does," she replied. "I have been waiting for some time, and I've worked so hard to make this place feel comfortable for you. Please, come this way now so we can get started."

Not one to piss off a goddess, I walked through the tea house and into the back room, where I sat on the other end of the long table from Velaska. I took the blaster out of my belt and placed it on the table.

"Oh, I think that is unnecessary," Velaska said. "And a bit rude. Guns belong on a table no more than shoes."

"What are you doing here?" I asked.

"Same as you," Velaska replied. "Looking for answers, but Ananke was insistent we wait for the rest of you."

I looked through the archway to see Katrina walk through the rift, looking as confused as I had been when I entered. Ananke walked up to her, and they talked for a moment before Katrina disappeared back through the rift. I counted the chairs around the table, and there were seven of them, just enough for Kimberly, Rebecca, Akta, Katrina, Velaska, Ananke, and me.

Sure enough, when Katrina came through the rift again, she brought all of them with her. Ananke guided them all into the room, and they took a seat around the table, looking as bewildered as could be, which was more than understandable.

"Where are we?" Akta asked.

"A pocket dimension," Ananke said. "I am sure that you know of them. Some of you might have already been inside of one. I don't like the whole impersonal aspect of them, and since I have been here a long time, I decided to make it a bit homier than some of the other gods do."

"How long have you been here?" Rebecca said.

"And why the Godschurch?" Katrina added.

There was a ding, and Ananke held up her finger. "The scones are ready."

She disappeared out of the room for a moment, which stretched into several minutes. I had so many questions, but they crashed into each other in my brain and bottlenecked before they could escape my tongue, so I sat in silence, and the others did the same.

Ananke returned with a big smile and a tray of scones and tea, which she placed in the center of the table. "Eat, drink. You'll need your strength for what is coming."

We exchanged confused glances at each other until Velaska broke the tension by grabbing a scone. "For the god's sake. She's not trying to poison you. She's being polite, and these are some of the most delightful scones I've ever had the pleasure of eating."

"Thank you," Ananke said, turning to Kimberly. "May I see your scythe, my love, the one you broke?"

Kimberly gave Ananke a funny look, but she pulled the scythe out of thin air. It was broken into two pieces, and she placed both in the goddess's hands.

"Very good." She held the scythe tightly and muttered to herself. The scythe lit up with beautiful white light and molded back together. She handed it back to her. "There you go. Keep this. You'll need it."

When Kimberly took the scythe, Ananke reached into her pocket and pulled out a glass stopped with a cork. "This too. Keep it with you. You'll know when to use it."

"Thank…you?" Kimberly said. "I'm so confused."

"Do you have any of the clotted cream left?" Velaska asked, staring at her cranberry scone.

Ananke snapped her fingers, and another tray appeared on the table, with glass jars filled with jam, lemon curd, and, of course, clotted cream. "Apologies, but I don't have time for more quaint theatrics. We have a lot to get through."

"Then, let us begin," Rebecca said.

CHAPTER 27

Katrina

Location: Ananke's Tea Shop

I grabbed a blueberry scone from the middle of the table and took a bite. Velaska was right. It was a freaking amazing scone, and for a moment, I tried to focus on it, avoiding the ridiculousness of sitting in the middle of the Godschurch, in a pocket dimension created by Ananke, eating a frigging scone and drinking tea.

Ananke looked at all of us before smiling. "Since you have made it to me, I can assume that you've done your homework on the history of the universe, yes?"

I shook my head. "I don't know anything. We just followed Velaska here to bring her back for trial."

"And I'm here to learn about Projekt Kaos," Rebecca said. "And how it relates to the death of so many gods."

"And Akta and I are just here," Julia added, "to track down a lead on a case."

"Oh, dear," Ananke said. "That is disappointing. And here I thought I had planned for every eventuality. By the time you reached me, you were supposed to be enlightened already."

Velaska raised her hand. "That was my fault. I was trying to construct a case that I could present to Rebecca and Katrina. The others, well, they don't mean much to me, but at least some of these guys were supposed to be up to speed, but then Cronus...well, I was arrested for the death of a Titan."

"The death of many gods, actually," Akta said. "Though I believe the death of Cronus and Rhea did push Rebecca over the edge."

"I don't know why I'm here," Kimberly said, pressing her hands into the table. "I just want to make that clear."

"You are here," Ananke said, looking at each of us in turn. "All of you, because you each play a part in the end of the universe."

"Excuse me," I said, scone still stuffed in my mouth. "Did you say the end of the universe?"

"I did," Ananke nodded. "Before the Titans existed, before time existed, even, there was a single god: Chaos. The Big Bang, I believe you humans call it, moves backward in time into her mind, and while she rests, the universe exists. When she awakens, the universe vanishes in the blink of an eye."

"I thought Cronus created the universe?" I said.

"And I thought Zeus did," Akta said.

"Of course, men would say that, but the universe was made, built, and conceived by Chaos, a goddess—the most powerful of all the goddesses, actually. We all live at her pleasure."

"So, she's the 'Chaos' in Projekt Kaos?" Rebecca asked.

"Exactly, and here we come to the crux of the story. In the beginning, primordial beings rose from the nothing to populate the universe. They were the first gods, more powerful than any others would ever be."

"Primordial beings?" Kimberly asked.

"Primitive understanding of the concepts of the universe would be based upon Darkness, Love, Earth, and the Underworld, which would allow for the beings of creation to be cleansed and returned to the Source of Chaos's creation powers."

"What about light?" Velaska asked. "How can there be a being of darkness and not light?"

"Chaos is the light in the universe. She is creation. She is light. From her, everything springs, and the same was true with the primordial gods. Every god from every pantheon, along with every living thing in the universe, sprang forth from these primordial beings when they were broken apart. The earth mother, Gaia, is infused in every single blade of grass and in every god that carries out her charge. The same is true with the other gods."

"How does this relate to Projekt Kaos?" Rebecca said.

Ananke smiled. "Impatience is not a virtue."

"I am not virtuous," Rebecca replied.

"I can vouch for that," I said with a grin.

"Projekt Kaos was a failsafe in case the universe became too…unpleasant," Ananke explained. "Many gods have become…distasteful of the universe and the chaos that exists inside it. They long for it to end and have been working to destroy it for a long time."

"So, Projekt Kaos is about trying to destroy the universe?" Kimberly asked.

Ananke nodded her head. "Yes, the primordial gods are working to return, so they can wake Chaos, destroy the universe, and end this failed experiment. Each has its own conditions for returning. Eros will return first if the prophecy is to be believed."

"What must happen for him to return?" Julia asked.

"He must kill every god of his line and rebuild himself from the ashes. I believe you have a list of gods and don't understand its purpose?"

Rebecca nodded. "A list of the gods of love."

"That is the line of Eros. When every god of love is gone, then Eros will return. He is the most persuasive of all the Primordials. With him returned, there will be no stopping the others from returning as well: Gaia, Tartarus, Nyx, and Erebus.

"Wait a minute," Rebecca said. "I thought there were four Primordials. You just listed five."

"Nyx and Erebus were once one but separated into two at the dawn of creation. For our purposes, they are of the same line."

"Fine, whatever," Rebecca said, blinking several times as understanding sank in. "If the Primordials return, that would mean the death of every god in every pantheon."

Ananke nodded. "And the destruction of every world in the universe. Infinite souls will call out at the same time and vanish from the universe without returning to the Source. Then, the Primordials will destroy every planet, every underworld, and every human in the universe to power their return. With so much destruction, the Source will become unstable, and that instability will allow them to enter the Source and wake Chaos. You must stop it."

There was silence around the table as all of us absorbed this information. Finally, I spoke. "How?"

"Stop Eros from returning. Bring stability to the underworld, so Tartarus is not awoken. Protect the gods of the earth, bring them under my protection."

"Does that mean—?"

"Yes," Ananke nodded. "I am the one who created the Godschurch so that we could protect this exact scenario from happening. Everything we have ever done has come to this. If we fail, so will the universe."

I stood up. "We won't fail. Don't worry about that."

Ananke smiled and stood as well. "I gathered each of you because you have a role to play and must do your part, or the universe will crumble."

"What part?" Akta said.

Ananke shook her head. "I cannot tell you without tipping the scale of the outcomes. As we rest in the mind of Chaos, we default to chaos, and order disrupts her. If I told you your part, it could cause a domino effect that would destroy everything. We sit now on the head of a pin. Any false move could destroy everything. Be very careful."

"We won't let you down," Julia said. I tried not to chuckle. As if we had a choice.

Ananke turned to me. "You do not believe, but you will in the end, or we will fall."

"If this is going to rely on me believing, then I think we're in big trouble."

Ananke kept her gaze on me. "I believe in you."

"Don't get ahead of yourself," Velaska said, pushing up from the table. "This lot is capable of saving the world, and I've watched them save the universe before, but I've also watched some of the pettiest squabbles between them."

"I still believe in them and you," Ananke said.

Rebecca rose. "I suppose this means that Velaska was not responsible for the bombings or the death of Cronus."

Ananke shook her head. "She has tried to be helpful."

"I could have told you that," Velaska said. "And did."

"I'm sorry, then," Rebecca said. "You have to understand, the evidence—"

Velaska held up her hand. "It's okay. It's fine. Can we just try to save the universe now?"

"Yes," I added, brushing past them toward the exit. "Let's."

BOOK 2

CHAPTER 28

I wasn't about to blindly believe an all-powerful deity that lived in a tea shop to tell us the next steps for the Godschurch or that the world was going to end. Luckily, after we returned to the Godschurch, it was a simple matter to unlock the Projekt Kaos files, what with knowing the name of the primordial god of love, Eros. It turned out love really was the answer.

The files contained inside the folder confirmed everything that Ananke said to us in her shop beyond the rift. Billions of years ago, Chaos fell into a deep sleep and created the four pillars of her universe: Darkness, Earth, Love, and the Underworld.

Over time, the primordial gods broke apart, had children, and created all the Titans and the gods in every pantheon. When they reproduced, a part of themselves was embedded into their newly created offspring.

Some, like Eros, gave so much that he disappeared into the very concept of love itself. Tartarus, by contrast, and Gaia, gave themselves not just to the gods but also to the planets, spreading themselves thinner with each iteration; with Tartarus, it meant that every time a new underworld was formed, his essence formed the basis for making it function, and with Gaia, she gave a piece of herself to every planet in the universe, even those that held no intelligent life.

At the end of the universe, each primordial god would be reconstructed, and together they could enter the Source and wake Chaos, ending this dream and our universe in the process.

It was, to steal a phrase from Katrina, "bonknanas," even for a person who dealt with gods for a living.

I was studying the text of the document when Edgar entered, knocking rapidly on my door as he passed it. "What is it, Edgar?"

"I'm sorry, Director, but you need to see this." He handed me a tablet. On it showed the NOX list of all the love gods. As I watched, more and more of them flipped over from living to deceased. "In the last couple of hours, 84 percent of them have died. At this rate, every god on this list will be dead in a matter of hours."

"What's happening?" I asked. "How are they dying so fast?"

"I don't know, ma'am. It's like somebody flipped a switch, and they all started dying in earnest."

"I thought we put extra guards on all these gods?"

"We tried," Edgar said sheepishly. "None of them accepted our protection. None except for one. Cupid, who's in the Zeus—"

"I know what pantheon he's in. Send Julia and Akta to protect him. Get as many agents over to him as possible."

"Yes, ma'am," Edgar said, scuttling to his feet.

"And Edgar," I called after him. "Send in Kimberly."

He nodded on his way out of the room. A few seconds later, Kimberly walked inside. "I am not an errand boy to be summoned."

"I am aware of that," I replied. "But I need your help."

"And how can I help the director of the Godschurch?"

"You are the only god I know who can talk to Nyx. If Ananke is to be believed, then one of the Primordials is your boss."

Kimberly nodded. "Nyx doesn't like me very much right now. She kind of…fired me."

"I can't force you to do anything, but since Ananke told us all that we had a part to play, I have to believe that this is yours. You have to figure out where Erebus is and make sure he doesn't get summoned."

"I think I can do that if I have to."

"Thank you." I watched Kimberly walk toward the door. I had to admit, having direction helped me have some bearing in the world. "Can you send in Katrina and Velaska while you're out there?"

"I am not your messenger."

"Then please do it as a favor." Katrina grunted as she passed Kimberly on her way into my office. It looked as though I didn't need Kimberly to track her down after all. "Never mind. Looks like she found me herself." Kimberly turned out of sight as Katrina walked toward me. "I have a mission for you."

"Please don't make me go track down Tartarus. That's my only ask of you."

"I absolutely can't not ask you that. You were once the Devil, which gives you incredible insight into how the underworld works."

"What about Velaska?" Katrina said. "She was a Devil for longer than me."

"Yes," I said. "You can take her with you."

"Fabulous," Katrina snapped, stomping away. "It'll be just like old times."

"Wait," I said. She stopped in her tracks but didn't turn around. "I know the two of you are not on the best terms, but please remember that Ananke told us all, including Velaska, that we have a part to play in all of this, and since we have no idea what that part is, all I can do is put you where I think you'll do the most good, or have the biggest impact."

She turned her head to the side and nodded slowly, listening to me. "No, I get it. That doesn't mean I can't hate it."

I smiled. "A sign of maturity is understanding that you can hate something and do it anyway."

"I have never been accused of maturity before." Katrina walked out of my office, and I leaned back in my chair, letting out an exasperated sigh as I did. I enjoyed control, but it came with a heavy burden. I hoped I was sending my agents where they were needed most and could do the most to stop the end of the universe.

I had no idea, though, about my own role to play, besides making sure the resources of the Godschurch were being used appropriately to protect the gods. I would have to figure that out later.

If all the gods of love were being targeted, it was only a matter of time before the other gods would become targets, which meant I had to keep them safe. That meant bringing them to the only place I could guarantee their protection: the Godschurch itself.

CHAPTER 29

Julia

Location: Niroja

Akta left to protect Cupid immediately, but there was
something that didn't make sense about any of what
Ananke told us, and when my gut smelled something fishy,
I knew that it was an instinct I needed to follow.

After the mass killing off of love gods, there were only
four of them left, and only Cupid was under Godschurch
protection. The other three were Siebog, Turan, and Rati;
their pantheons each controlled disparate areas of the
universe, and all had bad blood for the Godschurch. I
couldn't stand on ceremony, though, and stay away from
them until I got diplomatic permission to enter their
domains. I had made my life and afterlife on following my
gut, and if I had a role to play in saving the universe, then I
was going to rely on my gut to tell me what to do.

Siebog lived in a mining village on the small moon of
Niroja, circling the dead planet Ftune far outside the
jurisdiction of the Godschurch. The Godschurch didn't
have much jurisdiction these days anywhere in the
universe, though.

"I don't want to talk to you," Siebog said when I caught
up with him in a fresh air market, though fresh air wasn't
something that the mining colony had in abundance. Soot
and rust from the mine covered everything. "I'm fully
aware of the Godschurch's warning that I was in trouble,
but frankly, I think that you all cause more trouble than you

solve." His bright blue eyes shone past his bushy beard. "I mean, you're putting my life in danger right now."

I brushed the soot from my face. "Aren't you the least bit concerned that we knew how to find you, and that could mean somebody else could? Somebody with more sinister intentions than ours."

Siebog laughed heartily. "You work for a huge organization that has information on every god in the universe. I think you're the ones with the sinister intentions."

"Just answer me this question, have you received any packages in the past couple of days?"

He shook his head. "I've already made clear that I'm not going to help you."

"Then don't help me, help the other gods who are in trouble just like you. Almost every other love god in the cosmos has been killed. Once they finish with you all, they'll turn their eyes to the gods of the underworld, and the ones from Earth, and every single other—"

Siebog held up his hand. "I can tell you're going to make an impassioned speech, but I don't want to hear it. I did my part to protect myself. I moved to this small village. I am mining the ground. I am tilling the soil. I have not hurt any other god or person in many eons. I am making penance for anything that I've done in my life." Siebog grabbed a hard hat from a bench and placed it on his head. "We've increased production inside the mine 10,000 times since I joined, and there hasn't been one death. Isn't that a good thing?"

"Nobody cares about that. They want you dead to bring back Eros, the god of—"

"Yes, I read the memo." A horn sounded and ripped through the air. "That sound means the end of my break. I have to get back to work."

I sighed as I watched Siebog head into the mine at the end of the market. I shook my head because he was a damned fool. I barely had a chance to finish my thought and curse him before a bright blue light flashed through the air, and the mine collapsed, pluming dust into the air.

I didn't have to check my list, but I did anyway and watched as Siebog's name ticked from alive to dead, and a big red line went through his name.

***

Turan would have been much harder to track down if I didn't have her exact location from the NOX list. However, using it allowed me to discern that she locked herself in a bunker dozens of feet below ground, with a hundred guards or more protecting her. A good start, I thought, to protect herself, but still not enough. Using the exact coordinates the NOX list gave me, I teleported into the well-protected room that held Turan.

"Ahh!" Turan shouted, holding a scabbard. "Go away. I will not die this day."

"Relax," I said, holding up my hands. "I'm not here to hurt you. I'm here to—"

"I don't care," Turan said. "You will leave now, pixie."

"I'm from the Godschurch."

"Even worse!" Turan swiped at me, and I dodged her attack. "I know of it and its evil ways, subjugating gods until it was time to pick us off one at a time. They are the worst evil in the cosmos, and now look at what they have subjected me to. Living like a prisoner on my own homeworld."

"You're wrong," I said. "I've seen the work they do. The Godschurch has saved many gods."

"Yes, as long as they pay up."

I shook my head. "Not anymore. We've opened it up to all gods, for free, until at least we can stop the end of the universe. If you come with me, I will show you."

"No," she said. "Now go."

"Fine. Then at least answer one question for me. Have you received any packages in the last couple of days?"

She shook her head. "No. I would refuse them if they came."

"Any change in diet or staff?"

"I—" Turan's face twitched, and she grabbed her stomach. "I don't feel so good."

I knew what would happen before it did. Her mouth opened, and a blue light escaped into the room. Turan melted in front of me, and I watched her fade into nothingness.

Nobody knew I was there, which meant I could hide and see who was behind the attack. I cloaked myself in the darkness of the room and waited. Sometime later, a bellman with a sword came into the room and smiled at the ground.

He reached into his pocket and pulled out a tablet. He typed onto it and then sent a picture through it. Once he was done, I stepped out of the shadows and held up my gun.

"Don't move."

In one motion, the man slid his sword from the scabbard, but he didn't get a chance to use it. I kicked him across the face and sent him tumbling across the room, then picked up his sword to examine it.

"Who do you work for?"

I couldn't see the pill he was chewing until it was too late. He began to convulse, and his mouth foamed until he was dead. I looked down at my tablet and saw that Turan had been crossed off, but as I was watching, I also saw that Rati had died as well, leaving only Cupid in the line of the love gods.

I picked up the bellman's tablet and used his finger to open it. The email he sent was masked, but even if I could decode a planet, I would be on the right track. That's when I read the email and realized I didn't have to track it. I knew exactly who was behind it. The email read: "Turan is dead. You are all that is left of the line of Eros."

It was Cupid, all along, right under our noses.

***

I raced to Cupid's apartment as fast as I could, but by the time I arrived, it was already a bloodbath. All the soldiers who guarded Cupid were dead. As I stepped through the carnage, I felt a hand on my shoulder. I whipped around to find Akta.

"Do not," she said. "He has snapped."

I shook my head. "No. He's the one responsible for all of this. I have to find out why."

"Very well," she said with a nod. "Go. I'll follow you."

"Be careful; he's the last of the love gods. If he dies, Eros is reborn."

I drew my weapon, and Akta followed behind me. When I entered Cupid's room, he was holding a vial of blue soul bomb, crying. He was small and pudgy, the innocence about him that belying the brutal killer that had destroyed so many gods.

I pointed the gun at his head. "Why did you do it?"

He lifted his face. "The universe needs to be reborn. Have you not felt it? The horror. The death. The destruction. It's all wrong."

"You're not saving anybody by bringing about its destroyer."

Cupid smiled. "You know so little."

Before I could fire my gun, Cupid swallowed the soul bomb and began to shriek. It was over. We were too late. He opened his mouth, and the blue washed over the room. A bright white light escaped him and then imploded back inside his body.

A quake shot through the room and dropped me to my knees. When I rose, a magnificent winged god stood in front of me. Gone was the pudginess of Cupid, his innocence replaced with the rugged masculinity of a god who could have only been Eros.

"Don't move!" I screamed. "You are under arrest by order of the Godschurch."

Eros looked at me and scoffed. "Cute."

Then, with the snap of his fingers, he vanished, leaving us with nothing except a mission that was an abject failure. We had let the god of love return to the universe and then let him escape us. The cosmos was one step closer to destruction.

CHAPTER 30

Kimberly

Location: The Darkness

Darkness was there at the beginning, and Nyx was the Darkness, created by none other than Chaos herself, world bringer and universe creator. I knew that Nyx was old, older than anything I could imagine, but that she went back to the beginning of the whole universe put our relationship on a different plane. I had seen so much in my 10,000 years, and it was nothing but a blink of an eye to the things that Nyx had seen in billions of years. It gave me an insight into the deference with which she treated me, always keeping me at arm's length.

I heard the grumbling the moment I walked into the Darkness, but Nyx did not address me. I had been walking through the nothingness for quite a while longer than I ever had before when the grumbling grew louder.

"Hello?" I finally asked. "Nyx?"

I knew she could hear me, even if she didn't respond. Her grumbling spoke for her. It said to leave her alone; leave the Darkness. Basically, piss off. I had infuriated her with the way I disrespected her the last time we met, and now it was my duty to grovel for her help.

Julia taught me that sometimes groveling was necessary. She grew up black in small-town America during the 1970s, where overt racism was alive, and well, so she knew all about deference for the sake of your life when dealing with an overpowering force. Nyx was certainly that. I hoped that she would have guidance for me, and I was willing to grovel to get it.

"I am very sorry for the way I treated you during our last encounter. It was wrong of me to accuse you, an immortal deity of unknown power, to have ulterior motives. I am young compared to you and have a lot to learn from your grace."

The grumbling stopped, and in the Darkness, I heard Nyx clear her throat. "Well now, darling, that wasn't so hard, was it?"

"No," I replied, cowing my eyes to the ground. "I forgot my place. It won't happen again."

"I don't believe you," Nyx said, adding a soft chuckle. "You humans have a way of forgetting your place in the cosmos, trying to take your destiny into your own hands. It's awful. Not to mention the smell."

"Yes, your worship." I bit my lip. She was testing me, and I knew it, but if I was to find out what side she was on in the upcoming battle, I needed her to speak to me. "Perhaps when I am as old as you, I will have learned patience and wisdom."

"Where did you go?" Nyx asked. "I can usually feel you on your journeys throughout the galaxy, but for one brief moment, it seemed as if you blinked out of existence. I thought I would have to find a new Death, but then, quickly as you left, you came back."

I wasn't about to lie to her. She likely knew the truth anyway. "Yes, your majesty. I left this plane and met with a god whom I believe you know."

"Possible. I know many gods. Which was this?"

"Her name was Ananke." I felt the air leave the area around me as if the entirety of the Darkness heaved in exasperation and surprise.

"That gossipy bitch. I'm surprised that she dared show her face in this universe again after what she did." There was an edge to Nyx's voice that I'd never heard before. It frightened me.

"What she did? From what she says, she created the Godschurch."

"Ha!" Nyx said. "More like worked against us as we set about a system to protect gods." Something didn't make sense. There was fear in Nyx's words, a trembling. "No, she is not your friend, and you should not listen to her. It took all of our energy to contain her."

"Why would she work against you?" I asked.

"She didn't think we should break ourselves apart and give ourselves to the gods. She thought we should be enough for the universe. When we started to make planets, the Titans, the gods, and human settlements, she was furious that we would dare give our spark to a lower being. She thought that by giving our spark away, we dirtied Chaos's gift."

I furrowed my brow. "But you did not agree because you birthed children."

"I did," she cooed. "Children and other deities bound to the Darkness with me."

"And yet, you never gave enough of yourself away to lose your form."

"No," she replied. "I suppose I didn't."

I looked up into the sky. "All the others did. There is no Gaia, or Eros, or Tartarus, but there is still a Nyx."

"They were foolish," Nyx said. "But more importantly, there is a finite supply of earth, and love, and places to store the dead, but the Darkness is infinite. With the collapse of any star, the Darkness fills in, which means I can never dilute myself like the others could. Even if I could, my work is too important. I cannot risk being unable to oversee it." She stopped for a moment. "You, child, look like you have something you want to ask me but are afraid."

"I do have a question, and it is true that I fear your answer." Not just her reprisal or repudiation, but fear that she would choose the wrong side, and I would have to side against my old boss.

"You have never feared asking me a question before. Come, ask it, and hear my answer. I swear to speak the truth."

"I fear the truth," I said. "But I will ask anyway. Are you ready for the universe to end?"

Nyx's hearty laughter echoed across the entire Darkness and shook the floor under me. When she had comported herself, she spoke. "No, child. I am eternal here, and if the universe were to end, then that eternity would be over."

"Is an eternity too long?" I asked. "I have been alive 10,000 years, and there are many days I wish for an end to the monotony."

She chuckled. "That is very human of you. In time, the feeling fades, and you will grow accustomed to forever, as I have."

"If you are truly on the side of the universe, then I need your help. Ananke said—"

"Yes, I know what Ananke said. She has tried to bring about the end of the universe for ages, and I have felt Eros on the wind. He has returned, yes?"

"He has."

"And he seeks to bring about the end?" Nyx asked.

"I don't know what he wants."

"It is not your place to know or to ask. Your job is that of death, and you have neglected your responsibility. You're too caught up with your old mentor to see the forest for the trees. The dead rise all over the universe. Without the reapers to pick them up, the universe will bend to chaos. We would not want that, right?"

"No," I said. "We would not want that."

"We are the order in the chaos. The Darkness is what keeps the light in check."

"What should I do?"

"Stop worrying yourself with this petty squabble of the Godschurch and go about your duty, as you always have. For all the pain you bring, you are a good, noble worker. Lose yourself in the work. I pay the Godschurch to protect your work. Let them do their job. Call a quorum with the ones that didn't die on Yrowet and find new reapers."

"I was told I have a part to play in this end."

"Yes, by a liar. She will do anything in her power to bring about the inevitable. It's best not to do anything and deny any prophecy she gave you."

"Thank you," I said, turning away from her. I didn't know what to think about our interaction. Part of it was comforting, and at the same time, it was terribly unsettling. I wasn't sure if I was on the side of good or evil most days, but I left the Darkness having even less understanding of what I should do or whose side I was on.

CHAPTER 31

Akta

Location: Godschurch Base

After the death of Cupid and the return of Eros, the Godschurch went on the defensive, pulling all the gods we protected into the base and assigning them to different agents to protect them. We opened the church to any god in any pantheon. From our intelligence on Eros, we knew the Primordials had to kill every god of their line to reconstitute, which meant we only had to keep one god alive out of a few hundred, but we didn't want any of them to die.

Rebecca was furious at me for failing to stop the return of Eros, and it showed when she assigned me to the minor god Kalma. It wasn't even clear that Kalma's line had a sector of the universe they controlled, as her kin mostly integrated into other pantheons. In the end, I told myself, that made her no less in need of protection.

She was pale and wisp-like. We had found her wandering a gravesite on the remains of a small burnt-out star housing a small agricultural community that harvested food for several systems controlled by the Svarogian gods. They were creepy and vengeful. I hated going into their systems because it was like walking into a horror story. I did my time in Hell, and I would prefer to spend my time in the vacuum of space rather than being reminded of it.

I decided that the last place somebody would look for a god of Death who liked creeping around graveyards was on a lush planet, so I took her to the Entara system. There was a planet there called Therisin that circled three suns but was far enough from them to avoid being scorched by their light.

Darkness rarely fell on the planet, and I could tell within the first hour that Kalma wasn't happy with the constant light. Her maudlin face turned down with disgust as we stood in the clearing surrounded by a large forest on all sides.

"This is boring," Kalma said, kicking a rock. "When can we go home?"

I squeezed the daggers in my hands and gritted my teeth. She was an annoying god, and every word out of her mouth made me cringe.

"I'm sorry you are uncomfortable, your worship. We are trying to save your life."

"I mean…that's fine and all," Kalma replied, "but what if we…didn't do that. I mean, death is a natural form of life. The end of the universe is as normal as the beginning of it. The universe has to end sometime."

"It won't end today."

"That is what they say every time, and while they've always been right so far, you only have to be wrong once. We all have a 99.99999 percent survival rate, and if we say that we will live today, we will almost always be right until we aren't."

"That is a morbid thought."

"No, it's not." She shrugged. "It's a factual one. People think I am a pessimist, but I am just a realist, a pragmatist, even. You said that the god who dreamed this whole universe is Chaos, right?"

"I did. So?"

"It's funny because we spend so much time fighting chaos, trying to bring order to everything, even our own deaths, and it turns out Chaos has been working against us this whole time, bringing the universe back to entropy; back to herself. That is irony."

"Entropy," I scoffed. "I will never believe there is nothing that can be done to change our fates."

"I know," she said with a smile. "That is why you humans are so interesting. Your lives are so fleeting, but you constantly rail against the inevitable. I respect that."

"I'm not a human."

Kalma looked around at our surroundings, bored. "Mortals of any type look the same to me. Dog, horse, pixie, human, you are all mortal, and all decay into nothing."

I turned away from her. "This is a really cheery conversation."

"I'm sorry." She looked at me with cold, dead eyes. "My job is not to make you more comfortable. My job is, apparently, to stay alive, while your job is to save me, even though I am not sure I even want to be saved. Of course, I was not given a choice, just as you weren't given a choice."

"Your pantheon pays for our protection."

"And they are welcome to rail against the inevitable, but I should get a choice in it. I have lived a long time. Perhaps I am ready to die."

I spun back to her. "And are you ready to bring the whole universe down with you?"

Kalma flicked a small rock disinterestedly. "I am but a small fleck on the universe. If it chooses to end, then perhaps that is its right, as it is mine to choose the manner of my death."

I wanted to respond, but, at that moment, the sky turned black. One, then two, and finally three stars vanished from the sky. The earth around me rumbled, and out of the tree line, a creeping darkness came upon us.

"Stay behind me," I said, my voice cracking.

"You have terror in your voice." Her own words were calm.

"Just do as I say!" I growled. I shoved the daggers back into their sheaths and pulled out a pinch of pixie dust. As the Darkness swept over the clearing, I slammed the dust on the ground and disappeared.

I knew the planet well, which was why I'd chosen it. I used it as a place to let loose my thoughts when I had downtime and often spent it in Ghavi, the planet's most decadent city. We reappeared on the top of the tallest building there, and I watched from our vantage point as darkness swept over the planet. Underneath me, the screams of millions of people cried out in fear and confusion.

"We have to get off this planet." I threw a pinch of pixie dust and vanished, reappearing in front of the Godschurch portal. I pounded on the door. "Come on!"

The dark slammed upon us like a tsunami. It rose high into the air, and Kalma stepped forward. "Go! I will save you." She closed her eyes, and a dark glow washed over her, enveloping her.

"No!" I shouted. I tried to get to her, but the Darkness shut me out, pushing against me like violent sea waves. "Get off of her!"

The Darkness threw me out, and, as I was tossed into the door of the Godschurch, it opened for me. Another rush of light sent the Darkness shrieking away. I used that moment to grab Kalma and pull her into the light of the

Godschurch. As we disappeared, I saw the disappointment in her face that today would not be the day she would die.

CHAPTER 32

Julia

Location: Hestia's Forest, Borestack

"We really should go," I said to Hestia. Her long hair was filled with flowers, and she wore a long, green dress as she tended her garden. Rabbits hopped through her legs, and assorted animals from foxes to deer roamed around her forest without a care in the world.

"Oh, my dear," Hestia said softly. "I'm not going anywhere. If I went, who would look after the forest?"

"There are millions of forests that survive without your personal touch," I replied.

"Yes, but they have found equilibrium. This one has not yet." She looked up at the red sky. "I'm not sure it ever will, and if the forest does not maintain equilibrium, the entirety of the mortals on this planet will die, and billions of lives will be on my head, not to mention the other animals and plants that call this place home. They look to me as their mother to take care of them."

She stroked a deer who had come to drink water out of her hand. She was a real-life gods-damn Disney princess.

"And if you die, nobody will look after them at all."

Hestia shrugged. "Perhaps that is true, but I know what happens if I stay here. I prefer to think about the things I can control. I have stayed away from the wars of gods for eons."

She wasn't wrong. She never took sides in any battle, always taking the side of nature and the plants she nurtured.

She was a steward for them, unlike any steward I had ever met before. In a certain way, I was impressed by her resolve to guard the planet, even if her stubbornness was frustrating. Gods always thought themselves invincible when they were anything but.

"I can assure you that the threat is real."

"Yes, and you heard it firsthand from Ananke, who asked you to personally look after me."

"Not you specifically, but to stop the end of the universe, and you are an earth goddess, which means Eros will come for you soon."

"I have made my peace with Gaia. I believe I am a good steward for her planets and that she will look favorably on me should we ever meet again."

"That's just the thing. You can't meet again because, in order for her to exist, you have to die."

"I don't think that's true. She lives in every planet. In the core of every planet, there is a piece of her essence. In order to kill me, she would have to destroy every planet in the cosmos, and nothing could be that cruel."

"Eros can," I said, my eyebrows raised. "That is his aim. To destroy every planet and bring Gaia back, destabilize the Source, and wake up Chaos."

She thought for a moment, then shook her head. "No, I don't believe it. Gaia would never allow such cruelty."

"She has no part of this. It's all Eros, and she can't stop a planet from being consumed any more than you can stop yourself from dying without the Godschurch's help."

Hestia scoffed. It was her turn to raise her eyebrows. "It seems the Godschurch has caused more deaths of gods than it has protected. I'm not sure I would be any safer with you than without you, frankly."

"That's not fair," I said, bolting upright. "The reason gods die under our protection is because they are targeted already. Otherwise, they would never call upon us."

"Have I been targeted?" Hestia asked, flatly and with earnest seriousness. "Personally, have I personally been threatened?"

"Not specifically, but your kind—"

"Then going with you will do me no good."

"I'm not saying that."

She turned to me. "Please, enlighten me. How do you plan to protect me from this threat?"

"I don't—" I threw my hands out in front of me, desperate for her to listen. "By guarding you."

"Is this the same way you protected others?"

I pulled back. "Y-y-y-yes."

"And did they die?"

I dropped my eyes. "Yes."

"Then I reassert that you can protect me here or go. It's your choice, but I am not leaving this planet until it has found stability."

"What if Eros comes for it?"

She threw some seeds on the ground. "Let him come. There are trillions of planets in this sector alone. I doubt he will be able to find me."

"That is where you are wrong, sister." I turned to locate the voice. Eros stood nearby, rippling muscles and holding a quiver of arrows, looking at us. "I could smell you a million miles away."

"Stay back!" I said, holding up my gun. I fit it with god-killer bullets before I left the base, but I still wasn't sure they could take down a Primordial.

"It's time," Eros said. "I need your help before the Darkn—"

I moved in front of Hestia. "I will shoot you."

Before I could think, Eros pulled an arrow and unleashed it on me. I spun to avoid it and fired three bullets at him that sunk into the trees around him. When I looked over at Hestia, I saw that she had been shot by the arrow Eros had fired and was bleeding profusely from the chest wound.

I had failed, again.

"This was your fault!" Eros screamed. "I had no intentions of—"

"I will kill you," I shouted, losing control of my head. "I will kill you!" I fired a half dozen bullets into the trees as Eros rushed away.

"You will need me before the end." He snapped his fingers, and he was gone.

I turned to help Hestia, but it was too late. She was convulsing and bleeding out, grasping the ground under her, and smiling.

"You were right," she said with a whisper.

"I know, but that's not really a comfort now."

"There is a planet—" she started. "The first—Gaia's heart—don't let them—"

I didn't understand what she was saying or what she wanted me to do. Everything was cryptic and confusing, but I kept Hestia's words with me as the earth enveloped her.

"It's so beautiful," she said as the light left her eyes and she vanished into the earth which she loved so much.

CHAPTER 33

Katrina

Location: Cupid's Apartment

"Find anything?" I said, kneeling in the apartment where Cupid had just died and evolved into Eros like a frigging Pokemon. "Cuz I got nothing over here."

Velaska hadn't moved from the door since we snapped into the apartment. Groups of cleaners were working around the room to scrub it for contaminants and remove the bodies. "Nothing."

I turned to her. "Well, it's hard to look for clues at the door."

She smirked. "You don't know what I see."

"And what do you see?"

She shook her head. "A monster. An absolute monster. And you thought that I was just like him."

I held up my hand. "Whoa. I never thought you did any of that stuff. I might hate you, but I don't think you're evil. Just a dick."

She smiled a fake smile. "I guess that's something."

We were all going to die, probably, and I didn't want anything left unsaid if we died together. I had held something back from Velaska, the reason for my seething hatred of her, and it was bursting to come out.

"I don't trust easy, you know?" I said, pacing around the room. "And I trusted you. I was more pissed you broke that trust than anything."

"So I hurt your pride? That's what really mattered to you?" Velaska chuckled. "Oh god. You are so self-centered."

"How?" I asked, both wounded and offended.

"Because…Urania, man. She's not a piece of meat." She stepped toward me. "She has feelings, and you treated her like she was nothing. Clearly, nothing is as important as Katrina and her precious pride."

I faltered, trying to come up with a response. "I…know that she's not an object. I was just saying…" *She was right.*

"'Just saying' it doesn't matter that I stole your girlfriend, who you treated terribly, by the way, but the thing that really mattered was I hurt your pride. You've got a hell of an ego. You fit right in with the gods."

"I didn't come here to be attacked!" I shouted.

"Yes, you did!" Velaska replied. "You thought it was going to be a physical attack and not a mental one. You're always ready for a fight as long as you can punch something, but not if you actually have to examine yourself."

I clenched my fists. "I'm ready for one right now."

Velaska rolled her eyes. "I'll pass. How about we just get back to the business at hand, and you take up your feelings with Urania yourself."

"I don't have feelings for her!" That was a lie. A big one, but I wasn't going to give Velaska the satisfaction.

"Bullshit!" Velaska shouted, walking through the bedroom door. "But I don't care. I just wish she didn't have feelings for you, too."

I stepped back as if I was hit by a punch. "She…does?"

"Yes!" Velaska shouted. "You two spend more time talking about each other than anything else in the whole universe. I have to hear it every day. It's frustrating, but please…this is a crime scene, and we're bickering like two children. Can we take this somewhere else?"

I threw my arms in the air. "I would love to take it somewhere, but this is a complete dead end, and I have absolutely no idea where to find Eros!"

A voice thundered through the room. "I can help you with that."

I dropped to the ground. Through my pain-wracked eyes, I saw Velaska for a moment before she suddenly vanished. I looked down at my hands, trying to get a hold of myself, but I couldn't. All I could do was scream. In a blink, everything went black, and a snapping sound rang through my ears.

***

When I came back to reality, I was on the top of a comet floating through space. Velaska knelt across the face of the comet, being examined by Eros. I cracked my knuckles. Fighting was something I knew all too well, and I needed to let off some steam. "Oh, hell yes."

I reared back and punched Eros as hard as I could in the side. He flew across the comet, and I picked Velaska up.

"Bet now you're happy I'm always looking for a fight," I said.

"Yes, sometimes it can be very convenient," she said, brushing herself off. "And here he comes."

I spun around and decked Eros across the mouth with a right cross and sent him skidding across the comet.

"You made a mistake showing yourself to us," I said with a smile. I smashed my hands together, and fire shot out of them toward Eros, covering him in fire. "I am gonna pull you apart."

"Stop!" Eros said, flinging a shockwave across the comet and rocking the ground until I lost my balance. I fell to the ground, and by the time I looked back up, Eros was on top of me. "You smell like Hell, Devil."

I struggled against him as he grabbed me around the throat. "I'm not the Devil anymore."

"I'm sorry I have to do this, but killing two Devils at one time will move us forward in ways you cannot imagine."

"I don't think so!" Velaska smashed Eros with a piece of meteor that sent him rolling off of me.

I pushed myself up. "Thank you."

"I have some fight in me," Velaska said with a smile.

"Don't get up," I said to him. "You're under arrest, by order of the Godschurch."

Eros laughed. "That pitiful organization has no idea what is coming for them."

I stomped my foot. "Yes, we do, and we're not going to let you win."

"Oh, I know," Eros stood, grabbing an arrow from the quiver on his back and nocking it in his bow. "But you have no choice. The gods of the underworld must die."

He fired arrows as fast as I could move. I grabbed Velaska and jumped into a crater as they flew over my head.

"What are you talking about?" I said. "We're not gods of the underworld!"

"Yeah!" Velaska added. "I just ruled it for a while."

"I can smell Tartarus on you. You are from his line, and his line must be returned."

I stood up to confront him. "Are you an idiot? Velaska is not a god of the underworld. Have you ever seen her, even a little bit? She's clearly a trickster god."

Velaska propped herself up on her elbows. "It's true! I have nothing to do with the underworld except being tricked into the job for a time. And Katrina, who knows what she is. She was given her powers from Cronus and never even ruled the Underworld with them."

"Yeah," I replied. "I'm a mutt."

Eros's eyes narrowed. "You are not gods of the underworld?"

"No!" I shouted. "When will you get that through your stupid head!"

Eros dropped his bow. "I believe you. Neither of you speaks like gods of the underworld. You'll forgive me for my rudeness." He breathed deeply. "Do you feel it? It is done. The underworlds have been cleared, and Tartarus has been reborn."

I did feel something, a hollowness in the universe like all the joy was swept out of me for a moment, and I was an empty vessel. A shiver rose through my spine.

"What just happened?" I asked, barely able to stand.

"His body has returned, and I will find it."

With a snap of his fingers, he was gone, leaving Velaska and me behind, both very confused.

CHAPTER 34

Rebecca

Location: Godschurch Base

Saraswati was true to her word and gathered as many of the Brahman line gods as she could find. Unfortunately, our meeting wasn't going well. Instead of listening to me, they had been arguing and calling each other names for the past hour while I tried to explain to them why the Godschurch was important to protecting their line.

"All I can say," Saraswati said, "for the fiftieth time, is that the Godschurch saved my life."

"Oh? How many have died on their watch?" Yama, the god of their underworld, said. "I know a dozen gods who have fallen due to their incompetence."

"That's not fair," I replied gruffly. "We're doing the best we can on limited staff. If we had the budget for—"

"That's exactly why we shouldn't trust you," Ganesha screamed, his long trunk swinging frantically as he flung his arms in the air. "You don't have adequate staff to give us protection."

"That's why I'm proposing the Godschurch become a sanctuary for all gods. No payment required until after we get through the next couple of weeks. The Godschurch will be open to all gods, and we will protect you twenty-four hours a day."

"Like we are refugees?" Brahma scoffed. All three of his mighty heads shook. "We are not refugees."

Akta beckoned me from the other side of the glass-enclosed conference room, and I held up my hands to the assembled gods. "If you could just give me a minute."

I ducked out of the room, happy for a break from the onslaught of negativity. Akta's face was pale like she had seen a ghost. I saw Kalma over her shoulder, still alive and looking out the great window observatory toward the Source.

"Why are you back?" I asked. "I told you to take Kalma and keep her safe."

"I tried. I took her into the middle of nowhere, on a backwater planet I've never seen a god within a hundred parsecs of, but…something happened."

Her eyes dropped, and so did my heart right into my stomach. "What happened?"

"The Darkness," she said. "It was sentient. It was fighting me to absorb the planet, Director. I barely got out with both of our lives."

"You're sure it was the Darkness?"

"Yes, it swallowed up the suns like they were nothing."

I stepped down into the bullpen and walked toward the biggest monitor we had. "Pull up a map of the universe," I barked at nobody in particular.

The analysts glanced at each other and seemed to come to a silent consensus as to who would deal with me. One of them, with thick black glasses, pulled up the map of the universe. There was more black space than I remembered around the edges of the map. I pointed to it. "What's all this?"

There was typing on the keyboard, and a brown-haired recruit spoke up. "It must be a glitch. It's saying that those stars—all those planets—are just gone, but that can't be right. It's impossible."

I spun around to Edgar. "Is it impossible?"

Edgar typed into his system. "No, ma'am. It seems every minute there are hundreds of planets and stars being swallowed by something that we've never seen before."

"How long until it makes its way to us?"

"At this rate?" Edgar said, pausing for a second. "A week at most, less if it speeds up, which it will likely do the closer it gets to the center of the universe."

"Brilliant," I said, noticing Kimberly appear near the observation deck. I ran up to her. "Come on; we need to see your boss."

"About what?"

"About her part in the end of the world."

***

I had never been inside the Darkness before, and I was sure I didn't like it. It was nothing but vast blackness and the cold.

"She's not going to like this," Kimberly mumbled to me. "She doesn't like being interrupted, especially by mortals."

"I don't care."

A voice boomed. "What won't I like?"

"Nyx," Kimberly said, bowing her head. "This is—"

"I know the director of the Godschurch, Kimberly. To what do I owe the pleasure?"

"My agent told me the Darkness is swallowing up planets. I didn't believe her, but all our data says the same thing. I know that Eros is working to raise Gaia and Tartarus, and I have to ask, are you behind this too?"

"Insolent cur!" Nyx said. "You dare—first Kimberly, and now you—I have never been so insulted in all my years! And when I say all my years, I mean ALL the years!"

I swallowed my fear. I did not like talking to gods on the plane where they had control. Even though I talked to gods on the regular, I was all too aware that they could destroy me in a moment, and none more easily than Nyx, if she truly was a Primordial. "If it's not you, then something else is using the Darkness. I can't imagine that would happen without your knowledge."

"Quite," Nyx said curtly. "I'm afraid I was not completely honest with you, Kimberly."

"About what?"

"A great many things," Nyx replied. "Death, dreams, nightmares, and every kind of darkness god was formed from the Darkness, but I was not always the Darkness—at least, not on my own. I had a brother, Erebus. We loved each other and wanted to spread around the galaxy. He believed we should break apart and conceive the gods around the universe. I did not agree, so he offered himself as the spark for you and your kind, Kimberly. Thanatos was built from that spark, so was everything else that oozed from the Darkness. I have been tracking the death of gods myself, trying to keep it under wraps, but it seems like my brother found a way to return even without his spark, cocooning himself where even I could not see him."

"How could he do that?" I asked.

"The Darkness is infinite, which means our gifts might be infinite. I believe these are remnants of my brother, not the whole of my brother himself. Either way, I cannot stop them. If he finds a way to kill you, Kimberly, then you will see Erebus in his true form, and I fear he has been corrupted by Eros."

"What should we do?" Kimberly asked.

"Your reapers need to work with the Godschurch to protect the gods and you." Her voice was sad in a way I had never heard before. "Turn your attention away from humanity, for a time at least."

"What about the souls stuck in limbo that need us to guide them?"

Suddenly, a shudder went through Kimberly, and she fell to the ground, screaming. I knelt to her. "What's happening?"

"Tartarus has cleared the underworlds of souls and is using their energy to rebuild his ancient body. He has the power now to reconstruct himself."

"No," Kimberly said on weakened hands. "It's impossible. He couldn't—He didn't—"

"He did," Nyx said, a mixture of contempt and pain swirled on the air. A guttural grumble rose in her voice, then. "Trillions upon trillions of demons, gods, and souls gone in an instant."

"No," I said, barely able to eek out a sound. "Wiped them all out in an instant?"

"That is the power of the Primordials. It knows no bounds."

"He's a…monster."

"Yes," Nyx said. "A monster with more than enough power to rise again. You must stop him and my brother from destroying every planet and raising Gaia."

"Thank you for your help," I said. "We will do everything we can to keep Kimberly safe."

"See that you do," Nyx said solemnly. "For the sake of the whole universe."

CHAPTER 35

Kimberly

Location: Godschurch Base

I pulled Rebecca back beyond the pale and into the Godschurch base, my heart weighing heavily with what Nyx had told us. How was I important to preventing Erebus from returning?

I looked down at my hands. They were shaking, and my stomach was hollow. A quadrillion souls were gone in an instant, and I had no idea how to prevent Tartarus from rising, or Erebus from raising Gaia, or how to stop that kind of power if it was unleashed upon the world.

"My reapers are not fighters," I said, shaking my head. "I do not see how we could help you."

"I understand," Rebecca replied. "But every single body helps when it comes to the fight. If they can swing a scythe, they can shoot a gun, and we need every one of them if we hope to stop Erebus and protect you."

Something felt off, and it had for days. I was being led in circles, like a dog chasing its own tail, but when I latched onto it, I howled out in pain at what I found. Reapers were peaceful. Their job was a solemn one, and many of those attracted to their numbers were pacifists. Most did not like even the scythe they were assigned and chose not to use it.

"There is something bigger going on here," I mumbled.

"Bigger than the end of the universe?" Rebecca replied. "Listen, none of this is ideal, but you have thousands of reapers under you, right?"

"I do."

"And their job is to shepherd souls into the great beyond?"

"You are telling me something I already know."

"That's not my goal. My goal is to show you that your people probably would like to stop some of the death they see every day."

"You're wrong," I replied. "My reapers understand that life and death are intertwined."

Rebecca pressed her fingers to her temples. "I can't force you to help us. Even Nyx can't force you. The reapers are yours to control."

"I don't control them. Thanatos played at that. My reapers choose to work for me and choose to follow me of their own volition."

Rebecca placed her hand on my shoulder. "Then, give them a choice. Let those that choose not to help continue with their work, but at least give them a chance to save the universe."

I nodded. "You make a compelling case. They should be given a choice to pick up arms to defend their home, even though I do not like it."

"I don't like it, either. None of us like to send people into harm's way. Unfortunately, sometimes that is the job of a leader."

***

Yrowet felt colder than when I last journeyed to it. Perhaps the chill running through my bones came from the choice I had to offer, or the loss of so many uncleansed souls had hollowed me out.

My reapers trusted me with their afterlives. I had spent ten thousand years building that trust, and it all came to a head here at the end. I knew that if I asked it of them, many would say yes without a second thought. They had faith in me to protect them, to look out for their best interests.

I closed my eyes and opened my mind to call out the reapers all over the universe. "Come to me."

I had been taught that death was a part of life and that we should not fight it. Was the death of the universe no different? Did the death of the cosmos not have its own beauty? How were my actions any different than those of the souls we shepherded into the great beyond?

I had helped millions let loose their mortal coil and understand the beauty of the great beyond. Was I a hypocrite for fighting against my own death or the death of my universe? More so, was Nyx not a hypocrite for asking me to fight for my life? She, after all, taught me that every death is sacred.

As I pondered those questions, thousands of flashes of light appeared on the horizon, and in their wake, reapers floated on the sky. Thousands, tens of thousands, enough to wage a battle even against the grandest foe in the universe, should I ask for it.

I waited until the flashes dissipated before I spoke. "We have been attacked," I began, "by an unseen force. You must have felt it, an emptiness in your very core. Every soul in the underworld was swallowed to feed an ancient evil. Our brothers and sisters all over the universe are in danger. We are not an army, but we have the numbers of one. We are fierce and determined. We know duty and sacrifice. Every one of you has sacrificed to be here. I have taught you to keep every death sacred and that every death has meaning. I have asked you to shepherd many to their afterlives and tell them of the nobility of death."

I swallowed. The words came hard and tasted harsh against my tongue, but I had to continue. "You might have felt the weight of death weighing more heavily on you now than usual. That is because the entire universe is at risk. Countless trillions of lives have been wiped out by a dark force called Erebus, brother to Nyx. He is eating every world and hopes to bring on the death of the whole universe."

I had to lie to them. It was the only way. I broke my trust with them in every word I uttered. "This is an affront to death. All death is sacred, but these deaths are unnatural. The death of the whole universe is against the order that we vowed to protect, so I ask you, on this day, to take up arms with me and the Godschurch, to protect the universe, and make sure that our order remains intact."

There was a gasp and chatter among the reapers. I waited a moment for it to calm down. "I will not force you. If this is against your natural inclinations, I will not force you to fight, but if you will fight with me, then and only then do we have a chance to save the universe."

"If you choose to join me, stay, and if not, then you may return to your work. It is more precious than ever, and even more will need our help in the coming days. However, know that if you leave, there will likely be few days left to comfort the dead before the whole universe collapses upon itself. Go now, if you choose. If you stay, you have cast your lot with me and the Godschurch."

I expected hundreds, thousands to abandon me, but as I looked upon my sweet reapers, I did not see one deserter, not one flash of descent. They all cast their lot in with me, and I sealed their fate. I just hoped their deaths would be honorable, and they would find peace after they were gone.

CHAPTER 36

Julia

Location: Tweenus 10

"You realize you can't force me to go," Veles said, walking beside me along an urban street, his dragon head turning fewer heads than his loincloth. "I am a god. I don't answer to mortals."

"I can't stop you from being stubborn, but at least don't be a fool." I spun around. "Tweenus is on the edge of the universe, which means that until we can stop Erebus, this is a really bad place to be. At least come closer to the center of the universe until we work something out and stop Erebus."

"Explain to me how all of us gathering in the Godschurch, a tiny space station in the middle of everything, is a better solution than having us split up all around the universe?"

I didn't have a good reason. I was just following orders. Frankly, having gods all over the galaxy makes it harder for Eros to track them down but also harder for us to guard. Having them on the base made them sitting ducks, but in theory, we could protect them better.

I spun around. "The love gods were spread out across the universe, and Eros still found them, didn't he?"

Veles scratched his chin. "I suppose so, but the Godschurch has done as much bad as they have done good. I don't know why I should start trusting you now."

He made a fair point. "If the universe doesn't end, then we can talk about paying for our sins. Right now, we're running low on options." I stopped in the middle of the sidewalk as people crashed around me. "But you're right; I can't make you go. You're under our protection, but we protect at your pleasure. Perhaps you would be better protected here, by yourself, or perhaps you would be better with us. I don't know, but we can't spare the manpower to protect every god right now. There's power in numbers—not just ours, but your gods as well. You are very powerful, and together, we believe you stand a better chance against Eros than on your own."

Veles thought for a moment as his options flashed in front of him before nodding to me. "Very well, I suppose I will go with you then."

I was surprised, but I tried to keep a straight face so that he couldn't see my shock. "A wise choice."

He shrugged. "I suppose we won't know that until later, will we?"

***

I brought Veles down the elevator into the Godschurch. When the doors slid open, the distinct and pungent smell of gods and humans attacked my nostrils. They crowded the hallways and bullpen. There was barely room to walk. The room was more packed than I had ever seen it. Several gods milled around upstairs, but nothing like down in the base itself.

When Rebecca saw me with Veles, she made a beeline for us. My stomach dropped, wondering what I had done wrong this time. Rebecca had been riding my ass since I joined the Godschurch months ago, and I wasn't in the mood for another tongue lashing.

"Oh good," she said. "You got him. Hello, Veles. I'm glad you could make it."

"And I am grateful to be here." Veles nodded. "Good to see you again, Director."

"I wish it were under better circumstances," she replied. "Please, go inside and make yourself comfortable. I think I saw some others from your line in the medical bay."

He rolled his eyes as he passed. "Ugh, I have no interest in seeing family, but thank you."

When he was gone, Rebecca turned back to me. "I'm glad you were able to find him without incident. I'm afraid we're not having as much luck with the others."

"How many are inside?" I asked. "How many did we convince to join us here?"

"Less than a hundred. I wish there was more we could do besides just waiting for them to die."

As we talked, Kimberly flashed into the room. "Director," she said, "we have them. My reapers are at your disposal."

"Good," Rebecca said. "Thank you."

"Do not thank me. I have condemned many of my people to death. I just hope it will be worth it."

"Position them around the Godschurch and upstairs. I know that he will come, but I don't know when. I just hope Ananke can help us. Katrina is talking with her now."

"May the gods be with us."

CHAPTER 37

Katrina

Location: Ananke's Tea Shop

I hated tea. Not the actual experience of drinking tea, which was fine, especially black tea, but the idea that tea was supposed to calm you down, or that it was somehow more elegant than coffee, and thus was worthy of a fancy tea shop. It's a bunch of leaves dipped in hot water. Quit being so pretentious about it.

Of course, Velaska loved the pomp and circumstance. She delighted in every moment as Ananke slowly poured the tea out to her and served her tiny bites of food on extra small plates. After we returned from our near-death experience with Eros, we had a bunch of questions for Ananke. As with most things involving gods, she stood on ceremony and circuitry and had no interest in speaking before her time. Like there was all the time in the galaxy. Even the end of the universe couldn't stop her from taking her sweet ass time.

Ananke set the pot down with a simpering smile. "The temperature of the tea is essential to the experience of it."

Velaska, Urania, and I sat around a table too small for us as Ananke bustled around, finding all the fixings for high tea. Velaska insisted that Urania come with us, as the death of the stars was something that Urania cared very deeply about. I was fairly certain she did it just to stick under my craw, just one more fork in me, and I was pretty close to losing it.

"Can we move this along?" I said, trying my best to keep my aggression under check.

"Oh, please," Velaska said. "We have time."

"No," I replied. "We actually, really, don't. We have a Primordial out to destroy literally the universe and another one eating every planet in the cosmos. Every second we waste is another one we don't have."

Ananke smiled at me. "That's not true. Time moves differently in here, so it's more like every four seconds we have in here is like a moment in your world. We have more time than you realize."

"Of course," I grumbled. "As if an eternity wasn't already excruciatingly long enough."

She placed a plate on a tiered serving tray. "It takes a long time to perfect tea, and scones especially. I needed as much time as I could have until the end."

"Did you already know the end was coming?" Urania asked.

Ananke chuckled. "Well, for every beginning, there is an end. Even if we save the universe this time, it will have to end at some point. There are only so many world-saving moments in our lives."

"I feel like I've had too many," I sighed.

"You have had your fair share, but they all led you here, into the inevitability of having tea here with me, as Erebus eats the universe and Eros works to destroy it." She turned the tray to us and placed it on the table, then slid out of her chair and sat down. Pulling a miniature sandwich down from its tray, she bit into it. "I always like the cucumber the best."

"I. Don't. Care." Between each word, I clapped my hands in front of her. "Can we get on with it?"

"You'll have to excuse her," Velaska said. "She is, after all, only human."

"I'm literally not only human. I'm a god, too."

"But you are a human, too," Velaska said.

"Oh," Ananke replied, wiping a crumb from the corner of her mouth. "I was wondering where the bad manners came from."

"I liked it, once, loved her even," Urania said, taking a small sandwich for herself. "But I admit that it's quite exhausting."

I scoffed at them. "You are all pretentious assholes, do you know that?"

Ananke sipped her tea, smiling sweetly at me. "You are impetuous and rash." She turned to Urania. "But perhaps that uncertainty and impetuousness are what allows her to keep winning. After all, the gods are so predictable. They always revert to their natures."

"So perhaps Katrina is the key?" Velaska asked, raising a thoughtful eyebrow.

"Perhaps." Ananke shrugged, looking into her teacup. "Perhaps not. Everything is odds, don't you know?"

"I don't know," I replied. "It's incredibly frustrating. I wish you would just tell us what to do."

"I promise if I knew what to do, I would tell you, assuming I wouldn't destroy the universe in the process."

"Please," Urania said. "There must be something that you can tell us about Gaia and Tartarus. Why did they choose to become planets and Hells anyway? It seems like a crazy thing to do."

Ananke smiled. "It was a bit crazy, admittedly, but you have to understand that when we came into being, there was nothing except a big, black void and several billion stars in the sky. Chaos couldn't help us. She merely dreamed this place up and gave us a playground to operate in. It was up to us to make the universe function through our own compulsions."

"What does that mean?" Velaska asked.

"Each of the Primordials was compelled to do certain things. Erebus and Nyx clung to the Darkness, which they nurtured and used to weave space to the ends of the cosmos. It was easy enough for them to find their purpose, but what was Gaia to do, she who had a compelling urge towards plants and animals, things that didn't exist, or Eros who was compelled to spread emotions, or Tartarus who was compelled to cleanse souls, of which there were none? There was no rule book for their spark. Over time, they experimented and found their essence and function."

"That's why Tartarus took all the souls out of the underworld?"

"Yes." She stirred her tea. "That was dreadful. Gaia gave him the space in her planets, and Tartarus laid the seed for each underworld, but his gift, what fueled him, was the souls. He needed them to resurrect his body."

"And what about you?" Urania asked. "What is your part in all this?"

"I am inconsequential, unfortunately. I merely make sure all the chips are on the table, and the game continues. The others, though…Gaia eventually created a world, and it made her whole. From that, she created humanity and all the plants, and the human emotions made Eros feel whole. When they died, Tartarus found ways to cleanse their souls, and he was momentarily satiated. They needed to create a scale, though, to truly be whole, which meant doing it millions upon millions of times. I fought with them because that meant the balance would be in jeopardy, but I was outvoted.

"One planet led to millions, and they stretched themselves too thin, with every new world creating more problems to manage. Enter the Titans and the gods. With every new god, the Primordials split themselves thinner. Now we find ourselves at this moment."

"Is there no way to kill Gaia, Erebus, or Tartarus before they come back?" Urania asked.

"Oh my, yes," Ananke said, drinking her tea. "Did I not mention that? You just have to find their hearts."

"Their hearts?" Urania said.

"Every being has a heart, and that includes Gaia, Erebus, and Tartarus. If you can find their hearts and destroy them, you can kill them and end this whole thing quickly."

"What about Tartarus? You said he was resurrected?"

"Only his body, not his heart, which was lost to the ages. Yes, if you find their hearts, they will die, just like anything else."

I pushed back my chair. "Why didn't you tell me this before?"

"You…never asked," Ananke replied, blinking.

"How could we know to ask that?" I stood up. "Just because you're lonely doesn't mean you can jerk us around for company!"

"Katrina," Velaska said with disdain, "there is still more tea."

"You're welcome to mine." I spun around and walked back through the portal into the cafeteria of the

Godschurch. When I did, I heard screaming from the bullpen.

The base was under attack. In the center of it all was Erebus's darkness and the reapers fighting bravely with the Godschurch troops for their lives and the lives of the gods they protected.

CHAPTER 38

Rebecca

Location: Godschurch Base

"I'm afraid they don't have a good track record with protecting gods, despite their efforts to convince us otherwise." Vishnu crossed his four blue arms over his chest. I had been sitting across from the entire Brahman contingent for hours, and it was like talking to a brick wall. Even Saraswati's pleas fell on deaf ears.

"We're only trying to help," I said. "Please, if you just—"

Brahma twisted his three heads and sneered at me. "Do not ask us favors. We are appreciative of your efforts, but we have made up our own minds. We will return to Rintiri, my home, and should Eros come for us, we will be ready for him."

"I beg you to reconsider."

"We do not take kindly to groveling," Brahma said. "This has been a hard decision, but it is one we have made together. Simply put, we don't trust you."

Before I could respond, a giant shockwave rocked through the Godschurch, and the base vibrated violently. Everybody inside began to scream as the Godschurch rocked back and forth.

The glass panes of the conference room snapped and screeched. A second later, it exploded through the room, and the Darkness fell inside.

"Lock down the whole base!" I screamed.

The red lights flashed as the alarm sounded, but it was too late. The Darkness was already inside the base. Erebus was here for the gods. Metal encasements locked into place around the perimeter of the room.

"What's going on in—" Katrina stopped when she saw the Darkness oozing through the room. "Oh no."

"Flood the room!" I had a trick up my sleeve. If Erebus loved the Darkness, we would see how he handled the light.

A dozen analysts typed commands into their computers, and the room flooded with light, brighter than I could bear. I squeezed my eyes shut and reached into my pocket for my sunglasses. I had distributed a pair to everybody in the base, and one by one, my agents put them on and pulled out their blasters, ready for a fight. A screech careened off of the walls as the Darkness fell back with nowhere to hide.

"Bring everybody into the center of the room!" I shouted.

"What about the agents and gods who are in other places?" Katrina asked.

"Shit," I said, but Erebus was too quick. The shattering of glass came from outside the room, and I didn't have to be a genius to know that he was trying to get into the Godschurch from the windows outside the bullpen. Luckily, the defenses were up, which would make it hard, or at least harder. He was a Primordial, and his powers incalculable. "Turn on all the lights, now!" Blast the whole base! And open this gods-damned door."

The door from the bullpen into the rest of the base opened, and I followed the lights down the halls. They were nearly blinding me. As I passed the cafeteria, Velaska and Urania stepped out of the rift from Ananke's shop.

"What the hell?" Urania said when she saw the bright lights. "What's happening here?"

"Erebus has come for the gods," I replied. "Get back into the rift and protect Ananke!"

I rushed through the Godschurch base, screaming at everybody to get out of their rooms and into the bullpen where we could protect them. At least I hoped we could. When I reached the end of the hallway, I spun around like a cattle dog and pushed everybody toward the bullpen.

"Hurry—"

A cold chill crashed into the room and traveled up my spine. There was a flash, and Eros stood in front of me. I pulled out my gun and fired three rounds, but he easily dodged them.

"Go!" I pushed the horde of people through the hallways. As I did, I fired backward into Eros. He pushed my bullets away, and they ricocheted off the walls. I didn't care if it punctured the outside and depressurized the base at that moment. The Godschurch was invaded. If we didn't kill Eros, we would be dead anyway.

"Stop!" Eros shouted, firing arrows into the walls right above my head.

I fired backward, and he blocked another round, except this time the bullet hit the floodlights, and in their destruction, the hall went dark. With the Darkness came Erebus.

"Oh no."

One by one, the lights smashed and broke. The Darkness encircled us as we pushed through into the bullpen.

"Close the door!" The door slammed closed, but a second later, a huge crater burst through it from Eros's fist. One more punch and the door flung off its hinges across the room.

"Listen—" Eros said.

"Open fire!"

Dozens of reapers and agents opened fire on Eros, but that only caused more lights in the room to explode, and in their shadow, the Darkness took root and filled through the room. I watched as it swallowed up dozens of agents, reapers, and gods. Eros confidently strode across the room. Urania and Velaska entered with a blinding flash of light.

"Give me your hands, all of you!" Urania shouted after another flash brought her into the room. "Rebecca, help me!"

"What are we doing?" I asked.

"Ananke's dimension. It's the only place that's safe right now."

I grabbed onto Velaska's hand. "Everybody. Grab on!"

"You don't—" Eros started, but it was too late. Velaska jumped the dozens of us remaining into the void. I saw plaid, and when the blinding light dissipated, several dozen of us were inside Ananke's tea shop.

Ananke came from behind the counter. "I was hoping it would not come to this."

"Eros is coming," I said.

"No," Ananke replied. "He cannot come here. Not without my permission."

I nodded. It had been a long time since I had used my Fae powers, but I closed my eyes and jumped back into the cafeteria just like Akta had taught me. As I did, the screams through the abyss were deafening. "Everybody. SCATTER!"

I looked back over at Eros, who shook his head. He was not involved in the fighting. If I didn't know any better, I would have thought he was helping a reaper hold off the Darkness, but it couldn't be true.

I fired again toward the primordial god of love, and Eros simply vanished into the ether to avoid the bullets. I felt a pull on my leg, and when I looked down, the Darkness was wrapped around my right shin.

"No!" I fired my gun into the ground, and the spark of light forced Erebus to loosen his hold on me. I took one last look around the Darkness and realized I had failed. Everything was ruined, and the Primordials had everything they needed to come back into the world.

I closed my eyes and jumped out of the room and the site of my greatest shame. I had presided over the death of the Godschurch not once but twice. Now I would preside over the end of everything unless I could find a way to stop it.

CHAPTER 39

Katrina

Location: Godschurch Base

"How many are dead?" I asked as we surveyed the bullpen, which was now basically empty of gods and agents, save for the ones Urania pulled into Ananke's dimension with her. "Is dead even the right thing to call them? They seem to all have just vanished."

I spun around to Rebecca, who was standing over Edgar's desk. The talented programmer was one of only a few people remaining from the attack. When Eros vanished, the Darkness departed as well, leaving us to pick up the pieces.

"We're going through the numbers to be sure," she said. "But the locators show that every earth god and underworld god we looked after is gone, which was over 93 percent of the remaining ones. On top of that, looks like all but a few of the others are dead as well. This is going poorly. I can't believe how much I screwed up." She looked at me. "How did we screw up so bad by telling them to come here?"

"Hey!" I shouted. Then I softened. "You didn't screw up. You made a decision."

"And it led to the death of dozens of gods and put the universe at greater risk of collapsing upon itself."

"I am not denying that," I replied. "But they would have died anyway. Somehow Eros can find them even without a NOX list—wait—no… Do you think that that's why they came? Did they come for a list of the locations of every god in the cosmos?"

Edgar typed into his computer. "It does look like the list was accessed, which would make sense. The rate of death for the gods has accelerated since the attack."

"Of course." I slammed my fist into my hand.

"They couldn't have known we would bring gods into the church, but they damn sure knew we kept tabs on all the gods in the universe." Rebecca sighed. "I really am that stupid."

"Hey, we were all that stupid, okay? It's not just you."

"Yeah, but only one of us is the director of this place." She smacked herself in the head. "Only one of us has the responsibility for what the Godschurch does at the end of the day, and that's me."

"Well, boss," I said with a smirk. "What do we do now?"

Rebecca thought for a second. "Ananke told you that each of the Primordials has a heart, right?"

I nodded. "That's right, but there must be hundreds of underworlds and millions of planets. There's no way to search them all."

"We don't have to find them all," Edgar said, typing rapidly. "Just the first one and the last one."

"Explain, please," Rebecca said. "And please try to do it without the technobabble. My brain can't take it."

"Logically, if the god had a heart, it would most likely be kept on the first planet they created or the last one. I mean, I suppose it could be on the five hundred and thirteenth, but the probability is far less likely, so if we peg down the first planet and last planet that was created before

Gaia and Tartarus confined themselves to the planets, we'll at least have a starting point."

I blinked a few times. "I only understood about 10 percent of what just came out of your mouth."

"Same," Rebecca added.

"He's saying," Velaska said, walking into the room, "that we need to go to the first planet and underworld that were created, which I assume he can figure out."

"I can!" Edgar said. "In fact, I already have a program working on it based on carbon da—"

Velaska held up her hand. "Don't care how, just tell us where to go."

Kimberly floated across the room. Somehow, she had survived the attack. It was as if Erebus wasn't even looking for her. "Meanwhile, I'll go into the Darkness and find Erebus's cold, black heart."

"What makes you think it's there?"

"He loves the Darkness, and it is infinite, giving him infinite places to hide in the only place he feels safe."

"Makes sense." Rebecca nodded. "I'll send Akta and Julia to the first planet to look for Gaia's heart."

"They survived, too?" I said. "What are the odds?"

"Maybe it's just our luck, or maybe the odds are on our side for once. It doesn't matter," Rebecca said flatly. "Either way, while Kimberly, Akta, and Julia are busy, Katrina, you, and Velaska go to the first Underworld and look for the heart. By the time you're done there, Edgar will have figured out where to go next."

"I will?" Edgar said. "I mean that could take days—"

"And you're going to do it in hours," Rebecca said in a commanding tone. "Because we don't have another option. Now, turn around. Grownups are talking."

Edgar spun around in his chair and faced his computer. "Yes, ma'am."

I slapped my hands together. "What are we waiting for? Let's do it."

***

Edgar's program found the first Underworld ever created, and both Velaska and I snapped into it. Before long, we were looking out upon an empty chasm, not unlike the one both Velaska and I ran at some point in our lives. I was surprised that even though it was clearly millions of years old, it still looked as ancient and decrepit as my Hell did when I took it over 10,000 years ago.

More surprising, though, was that it was completely empty. Carts were overturned, pits were still steaming, but there were no demons, or souls, or creatures of any kind.

"I don't like this," I said.

Velaska smiled at me. "It kind of feels like home to me. I mean, I didn't rule it long, but there was a simplicity to Hell that I miss in times like these."

"I never took you as someone who cared about simplicity. I figured you were somebody that thrived in chaos."

"Given the fact that Chaos is likely to kill us soon, that is extra funny." She looked at me for a smile, but I had nothing for her.

"It wasn't my intention," I replied. "Any idea what this heart will look like?"

Velaska looked around. "I'm assuming it will be a big, glowing kind of heart-type thing. I don't know, but we both know underworlds, so let's look for anything out of place."

"What makes you think it will be glowing?"

"Television, I suppose. I sure hope we recognize it." She hopped over a crack in a chasm. "Otherwise, we will be very, very screwed."

"I think you are very, very screwed anyway." I spun around to the voice and saw Eros standing behind me with an arrow pointing toward my heart. "I won't let you stop me."

"You don't have much of a choice," I snarled. If I was going to die in battle, I was going to make it a glorious one.

CHAPTER 40

Akta

Location: Invera

The first planet Gaia ever created didn't have a door to the Godschurch on it, as it wasn't habitable. Even if it had once been, the people that lived there were either long since dead from an unimaginable catastrophe or transcended somehow beyond the physical plane. Or maybe they just abandoned the planet. No matter the reason, there was no civilization on Primera.

The closest habitable planet, light-years away, was Invera. Every light year less we had to jump meant that there were fewer calculations that could go drastically wrong. Jumping between planets was a dangerous game, and many had been left cold and drifting among the stars for miscalculating even by a fraction of a percent.

"Do you have the coordinates?" Julia asked as we walked out of the Godschurch into the bustling street of Invera's biggest city, Hanzig.

I had been to the planet once before and had friends hiding out in the recesses of the underworld there. I called them when I knew I was coming, asking them to help me with a problem that I couldn't tell Julia about, and they agreed to meet us at the coordinates I gave them as soon as they could. Julia wouldn't like my plan, but she would accept it, if only begrudgingly, when I sprung it on her at the jump site. That didn't matter yet. We had to make it to the jump site first, which was several hours' drive outside the city.

"I do, and the rotational charts from here to Primera for this time of year. Assuming Edgar is correct, we should be able to jump from about a hundred miles south of here and hit the deepest cave on the planet straight on."

"And if he's wrong, we're floating or burning alive in the core of a planet," I replied. "So, let's hope that he is right. I checked his math three times, and it looks good to me."

"Fingers crossed."

I hailed a cab that took us most of the way to the jump site. I could have gotten there myself in less time, but I never liked jumping around on random planets, especially if I could just as easily drive. Time was of the essence, but so was safety, and we needed all our energy for the mission ahead.

"You don't seem like yourself," Julia said as we drove. I had given the cab driver a thousand bucks to shut up and pay attention to nothing but the road.

"I'm fine." Of course, that wasn't true. It seemed like every few years, it was some other intergalactic catastrophe or another since I joined the Godschurch, but this one felt different. This one felt bigger than we could manage. I feared we would not be able to survive this disaster.

Julia could tell that I was lying. In the past ten thousand years, we had worked together many times. She could see through to the very core of me. Though our methods were very different, it was as if we shared a brain when we were on a mission together. I didn't like hiding things from her, but I needed her calm for as long as possible.

Two hours later, we were walking through the desert toward the jump site. Julia looked down at the map. "It's just up ahead. Come on."

I held back. It was time to drop my bombshell on her.

Julia saw me stop after a moment and looked back, confused. "What are you doing? Come on."

I shook my head. "What if it's wrong?"

"Excuse me?"

I scratched my head. "What if the math is wrong, by even a fraction of an inch?"

"Your math has never been wrong before," Julia said.

"This wasn't my math. I just checked it."

"Three times!" Julia shouted. "I trust you."

"I don't."

I looked up into the sky. If my friend was as punctual now as he had always been, then his ship would show up any second. Sure enough, I squinted into the sun and saw a large metal ship lowering itself down from the sky.

"It's too important to risk it, and what if the heart isn't there? Then we'll have to get back here somehow, and that's a whole different can of beans, with a different set of calculations."

"And you've done those, too."

"I have," I said as the ship began to kick sand up into the air. "I've done all the calculations, and this only works if we split up."

"What?" Julia shouted. "You can't be serious."

I nodded. "I'm serious as a heart attack. You go with the ship. I'll take the jump, and worse comes to worst, you'll be safe in the ship."

She scrambled toward me. "And what if you need me on the planet while I'm flying there? This is stupid."

I shook my head. "It's not stupid. It's practical. We have two chances if we split up, which means our odds double—well, actually they go up ten times, but that's— listen, I've thought about it from every angle, and this is our best option."

"And you decided you shouldn't tell me about it until you could sandbag me, is that right?"

I nodded. "That's right. I knew you wouldn't like it. It's my math. I'm willing to take the risk."

"Like hell you are!" Julia stomped toward me. "If you want to take the coward's way out and go with the ship, then fine. We don't have time to hedge our bets. I'm jumping because I trust you."

"I don't, not when it's this important."

Julia looked up at the sky and then back at me. "That's where you and I are different then. I'll never stop trusting you." She closed her eyes and flashed away without another word.

"Julia!" I shouted, but it was too late. She was gone. I looked over at the ship. Just because Julia jumped didn't change the fact that we needed to split up to have the best odds of having success. I had to take the ship and hope that she would be there when I got to the planet.

CHAPTER 41

Julia

Location: Primera

I flashed into a meadow at the bottom of a deep crater. The sky was torched with orange as the sun set over the lip of the chasm. To my left, there was a cavern leading deeper into the planet, exactly like Akta said there would be. Her directions were perfect, as always.

Who the hell was Akta to treat me like a child? I was just as responsible for saving the world during Ragnarök as she was, and I'd been just as helpful as she was during this whole end of the universe situation. Not to mention the literally hundreds of other times I'd saved the world.

Relax, Julia. She was just trying to protect you.

"Well, I don't need protecting. I need a partn—wait, who just said that?"

You know who I am.

"Gaia?"

Yes, child. Anything said on any planet in the universe resonates through me. I feel every ounce of pain and every moment of joy and have since the beginning.

"This is very weird. Can you, like, show yourself?"

Of course.

The moss around the meadow began to shift, and the trees spiraled as they deconstructed themselves into the form of a woman with short hair and trousers held up by sunflower suspenders. Her eyes were made of daisies, and her smile of flower petals scoured from the canyon floor. The scent of lilacs wafted off of her.

"Is this better?"

I stared for a moment. "Maybe a little."

"Good," Gaia replied. "If you don't like this form, I can take another."

I shook my head. "No, this is good. I think I like it. I suppose you are here to convince me not to kill you?"

"Cutting through the word games, are you?"

"Well, if you can hear everything said on every planet, then you already know what I'm here to do. So, are you here to talk to me or fight me?"

Gaia laughed. "No. I'm not a fighter. I've seen enough in my years. I'm honestly ready to die if it should be your wish. My question, though, is what will replace me when I am gone?"

"Excuse me?"

"I am the earth. I am the trees. I am everything you see. If you kill me, what will replace me? Will it be you?"

"No. I don't have much of a green thumb. Technology, I guess?"

"Has it advanced so much in the outer cosmos? Because in a billion years, humanity has not been able to recreate all that I do, try as they might."

"You're right." I shrugged. "I honestly don't know what will replace you, but I can't let you destroy the universe, either."

"I'm afraid you will have no choice but to take my place, and it is a thankless job."

"I don't want it."

"Me either. I embraced it, though I didn't ask to be born." Gaia leaned against a boulder. "So, if you kill me, you have doomed yourself to my life. If you let me live, you have doomed the universe. Not the greatest options, are they?"

"You're taking this surprisingly well, me trying to kill you."

Gaia laughed. It was subtle and sweet. "You are not the first to try. You are not the first who has come here, either. Just the first in a long time."

"You're way too calm," I said, furrowing my brow. "Even if you're not pissed at me, Erebus is destroying your planets, your life's work. Doesn't that piss you off, after all you did to create them?"

"It's not ideal, but frankly, humanity has wasted the gifts I have given them. Every time I think it will be different, but the only places where my continence thrives is where humanity no longer exists. I fear that they are a blight on the universe, and at least his destruction goes a long way to wiping them from the cosmos."

"I'm part human," I said softly, walking toward her.

"I know, and that part of you is a blight on the universe. The gods made a mistake creating you. Of course, by the time I realized our mistake, I was long since molded into the very earth I love. Besides, few came to ask my counsel about such matters and wouldn't have listened even if I told them."

"You would have told them that humanity was a bad idea."

"Molding mortal gods who could barely think beyond their immediate needs? Yes, I would have told them humanity was a mistake. I hoped after their experiment failed several times, they would stop straining my power to make new worlds, but they never did. They are arrogant and foolhardy, just like their creations. I was so weak for so long that I couldn't even constitute myself until just now."

"So you feel more powerful with the worlds being consumed and destroyed?"

Gaia breathed deeply. "Yes, I feel more myself with each planet that is destroyed. I weep for the worlds that have been lost, though not for the humans that inhabited them. A million civilizations and they didn't respect me on any of them. Did you know that?"

"There were people that respected you on my planet."

"Yes, and what became of them? Slaughtered? Enslaved? Forced off their land—my land?"

"I—" I didn't know how to finish that sentence, so I simply let it fade onto the wind.

"You don't have to answer, for I know the response already. It has been the same on every planet, and the gods have never tried to fix their mistake. I doubt they could, honestly, for they don't even see it in themselves." She looked off into the sunset. "Don't you see? It's time to wake from this nightmare and begin again, better this time."

I shook my head. "No. I'm sorry, I don't see that. There is a lot of bad in humanity, but there's a lot of good, too. With the gods as well. I won't let the universe vanish if there is even a sliver of good on it, and I believe there is more than a sliver. I can't just step aside and let the universe die in darkness."

"It was made in darkness. Why should it die any differently?"

"Because we have seen the light, and we can't go back."

Gaia shook her head. "Very well. As I said, I won't stop you. I am too old for that, but I will tell you that you're in the wrong place. I used too much of my head on this planet. My heart is on my favorite planet. The one that I love above all others."

"That sounds like something a god would say if they were trying to trick me."

She laughed. "I could kill you in an instant if I wanted, and yet I don't lift a finger. Why would I send you on a wild goose chase when death would be so much easier?"

I shook my head. "I don't know. The gods do a lot of things out of boredom."

She held out her hand. "Come, I will take you there."

"Can I trust you?"

"No," Gaia said. "But you should try anyway."

I hesitantly placed my hand into hers. She closed her eyes, and I tasted the earth as we vanished from the planet's surface.

CHAPTER 42

Kimberly

Location: The Darkness

There was a cold sterility to the Darkness. The void had never been a warm and inviting place, but it felt hollower and lonelier than it ever had before. I had lost hundreds, thousands of my men in Erebus's attack, and it weighed heavily on me. I had to defeat Erebus, for their souls, and mine, to ever find peace.

I gripped the scythe so tightly my knuckles turned white. Ananke's craftsmanship in reforming it was exquisite. I had learned long ago that the scythe could kill a god though I had rarely used it to that end, except when I needed to defend myself. What I didn't know was that the Darkness could kill a god as well. It could kill anything by enveloping it and bringing it into its cocoon. I watched it kill my friends and colleagues, watched them fall screaming into the abyss as it swallowed them whole.

The power of the Darkness made Nyx even more formidable. She was more powerful than Gaia, who created life, or Tartarus, who cleansed the dead, or even Eros. I had come to respect Nyx, but now I feared her. I watched Erebus swallow up gods like they were lambs to a slaughter and knew her power was just as terrible.

"My brother is destroying the universe, isn't he?" Nyx said solemnly, her glowing eyes appearing from nowhere.

"You should know," I replied. "Don't you know everything?"

"I once knew what happened in the Darkness, but my brother has blocked me from it. I feel naked and alone for the first time in an eternity."

"How is he able to survive when I am alive?"

"The Darkness is infinite, my love," Nyx said. "He gave himself away, but the Darkness consumed more and more, and so he returned again and again, like the tides in an ocean. A planet is finite. Even a trillion billion planets in the universe have a limit, but the Darkness is infinite, which means that we must stop him at the source of his power."

"The heart of Erebus," I said.

She blinked, indicating agreement. "Yes, I have protected it since the beginning, unable to give it up. He is my kin after all, and he birthed my children."

I scrunched up my nose thinking about it.

"That kind of thing is not taboo among our kind. We were all that was in existence at the beginning, and we were outcasts, even from the other Primordials, given our comfort with the abyss."

"Well, it's taboo among mine."

"If you judge me, I suppose I could leave it to you to find the heart of darkness. I'm sure you will find it in the next thousand years, given all of the infinite void to search for it, if you are uncomfortable."

"I can do two things at once."

"That's not good enough."

"Fine," I sighed. "I understand that life is messy and complex, but I need your help, so I suppose I can hold back my feelings on this matter, even though...gross."

"Very well," Nyx grumbled. "But try to hold back your feelings on all matters, not just this one. It is not an easy thing, killing a god. Not as easy as comforting death. No, to kill a god takes a special breed, more so to kill a Primordial."

"I can do it," I said. "Lead the way."

A gust of wind pushed me forward. Nyx led the way. Several times I lost her in the blackness and only found her again minutes later, sometimes hundreds of yards ahead of me, and I had to rush to catch up.

"We are passing through the Milky Way galaxy now, where you used to call home."

"How do you know?" I said.

"After an eternity living inside the Darkness, you get a feel for a place. So many important gods came from your home planet that I have kept an eye on it for quite some time, especially when my son—" She stopped. "All of the universe is contained inside the Darkness, just as the Source contains all the light. Every shadow cast from even the smallest insect can be found inside the Darkness."

"Is it lonely?" I realized I had never asked her that before in all my years in her service. She was stuck here, by herself, an observer of the universe but not a participant in it.

"Yes," Nyx said. "Quite. Which is why, as annoying as your visits are, I appreciate you joining me in the void. Nobody ever visits me here. I'm not sure anybody ever could, except my dear brother, gods rest his soul."

What did that mean? Gods rest his soul? *He was destroying the universe as we spoke, wasn't he?* How could she have pity on him? Something didn't add up, and I couldn't put my finger on it. Everything, every instinct of my bones, said to pull away, but the universe was pushing me toward an inevitable point in the horizon, and against my better instincts, I kept moving.

Nyx's eyes turned back to me. A purple smile rose across her face. "Here we are."

Suddenly the black veil pulled back, and an enormous purple chrysalis bloomed in the center of my vision. It rose from the ground until it was my height and bathed me in its violet glow.

"Does this light not hurt you?"

"It does," Nyx nodded her head lovingly. "It is worth it, though, to be close to my brother. I have kept this hidden for a million years, waiting for the right moment to—" She swallowed and took a moment to compose herself. "I welcome the pain. It keeps me close to him."

"And you would have me destroy it?" I asked solemnly, looking for confirmation that she wouldn't stop me.

"He is destroying the universe, is he not? It is either him or us."

"Why don't you do it?" I asked.

"I cannot. Darkness cannot hurt darkness, only light can do that, and your scythe is the light to destroy my brother once and for all. Ananke told you that you had a part to play in all of this, did she not?"

"She did…how did you know that?"

"As you so astutely pointed out, I know everything that I choose to know. Besides, I know her quite well, having been through eternity with her. Now, pick up your scythe and do the work you were born to do. Untether the Darkness and send my brother to his final demise."

I stepped forward toward the chrysalis. It was a shame to destroy something so beautiful, but I had a duty to the Godschurch, to the universe.

I back swung my scythe and flung it forward with all of my might. I only caught Nyx's devilish smile when it was too late to stop the momentum, and as the scythe cracked the tip of the violet heart, I knew I had made a horrible mistake.

CHAPTER 43

Rebecca

Location: Godschurch Base

Five hundred and thirteen gods. Dead. Because of me. Because I was foolhardy. Because I was brazen. Because I thought that I could protect them when I couldn't. Now, there were less than a handful of gods left in the whole universe, and they were all the ones that didn't listen to me. The Norse gods, and the Egyptian ones, what few remained of their ranks, who banded together long ago for their own protection.

"Start a general broadcast to every gods channel," I said to Edgar. I was grateful he didn't die in the attack.

"Yes, ma'am," Edgar said. He hesitated. "Are you sure about this? We are running out of juice. We'll have to go onto emergency power soon."

"I am."

"All right then." He finished typing. "The channel is open."

I cleared my throat. "Earlier today, Erebus attacked the Godschurch. While we tried to protect everybody inside as much as possible…it was a massacre. Over fifty of your brothers and sisters were killed in the attack, along with 90 percent of our already depleted staff. Since then, over five hundred more gods have died due to information Erebus stole from our servers."

I took a deep breath. "There is nobody else to blame for this terrible occurrence other than myself. As such, I will be stepping down as director of the Godschurch once a suitable replacement can be found, if we can even find a suitable replacement if we even survive. I hope they will be more capable than me, though I fear that I have already done irreparable damage to you all, and for that, I apologize. You were right not to trust me, but the Godschurch is still a symbol of protection for all of you, and I hope you will continue to use it as a resource.

"Additionally, I will tell you that Erebus is not done with the gods yet or the universe. He works to send us all into darkness, destroy every world you gods created, resurrect Gaia, and destroy the universe…and we have no idea how to stop him. If you have any suggestions, please find me on the Godschurch base. I will not rest until we have found a solution. We have faced the worst before, and we have always come through for each other, and I'm sure we will do it again." I bent down to Edgar. "Cut it off."

"Yes, ma'am." Edgar typed a command. "We're off."

"Thank you," I said.

"For what it's worth," Edgar said, "I think you did a good job in an impossible situation."

"Thank you." I gave an exhausted smile. "You're wrong but thank you."

As I turned to my office, the door to the bullpen slid open, and Urania walked through frantically. "Oh my god. I just heard the broadcast from Ananke's tea shop. What the hell possessed you to broadcast something so foolish?"

I wrapped my arms around her tightly, gripping onto the back of her toga to steady myself. "I…just couldn't…I don't…I'm just a stupid, little human, okay? Why do you have humans running the Godschurch?" I was crying. "It's too much for us. We're not infallible."

She hugged me back, gingerly patting my shoulder. "I'm sorry. I'm so sorry."

I pushed back from her. "It was a bloodbath, and now Erebus has killed nearly all the gods."

"What are we doing to stop it?"

I shook my head. "I don't know. We have a plan, but it's desperate and reckless."

Urania smiled. "Well, if we are talking reckless plans, I think I have one."

I furrowed my brow. "I'm listening."

"Come with me."

CHAPTER 44

Akta

Location: Primera

Tybalt landed on the edge of the crater where I'd sent Julia. I hoped she made it safely and was deep into the bowels of the planet by now. If so, she had a chance to destroy Gaia's heart quickly without needing me. When I stepped out of the ship and onto the planet, I knew she hadn't. I couldn't explain how; I just knew. I pulled the daggers out of my belt. If she was in trouble, I needed to rush to catch up.

Tybalt pulled on his shirt as he stepped down the ramp of the ship to meet me. "You sure you don't want me to come with you?"

I nodded. "Thank you, my friend, but this is something I must do alone."

"Fair enough. I'll hover in low planet orbit for a while to wait for you unless I get another call. If you need me, just reach out."

"I will."

Tybalt walked back up the ramp, and it lifted up to lock with the rest of the ship. I watched as the jets fired and the ship rose into the air. The dirt swirled around me, kicking at my face. When the ship was out of sight, I turned my attention to the cave. It was the deepest on the whole planet, according to Edgar's scans, and should lead me as close to the center of the planet as I could reasonably get without burning alive. If the heart was on this planet, it would be in that cave.

"Another one?" a sweet voice said as I stepped into a mossy meadow surrounding the cave.

Edgar had picked up strange geological phenomena outside the cave, which made it the most likely candidate for where Gaia would store her heart, but it also meant the potential for godly interference was strong. I was prepared for something weird to happen on my trip down into the cave. Her heart would be well protected, as was mine. She had lived since the beginning of time without dying, which meant that she was both powerful and savvy.

The voice spoke again. "Why, this must be my lucky day."

The leather grips of my daggers dug into my hand. "Who said that? Show yourself."

"Gladly," the voice said. I watched as the moss slid across the ground and the trees unspooled, forming the outline of a woman. It didn't take a genius to deduce what manner of being I looked at when she finished forming herself. "Gaia."

She smiled, her lips formed by rocks. "In the flesh, or as close as I can get these days."

"I thought your consciousness was disbursed between millions of planets."

"And who told you that?"

"Ananke."

"Of course," Gaia said, with an amused tinge to her voice. "She has her uses, but relaying reliable information isn't one of them. I am nowhere and everywhere at once. I can feel a trillion feet on the grounds of my planets and still be here with you at the same time. In fact, as we speak, I am having a similar conversation with another like you far across the universe."

"Julia," I growled. "What have you done with her?"

Gaia shrugged. "Nothing. She's perfectly fine. She came to this place in error, trying to destroy my heart, which I am sure you seek as well."

"I do."

"A pity. I do not get many visitors. It is a shame that the two of you I've seen in centuries have such avarice against me."

"It's not against you," I replied. "It's against the universe ending."

Gaia stroked her hair, made out of tangled vines from her garden. "And what has the universe done for you, pixie?"

"Excuse me?" I said, shocked. "It has given me everything."

"A long life, yes, but is it truly better than nothingness? You have been a servant for a million years."

"Not quite that long."

"How long will you be in the service of the gods before it is enough and you can find rest?"

"I like being of service."

"Do you or is that a lie you have told yourself to trick yourself into submission?"

I thought for a moment before delivering my answer. It was one I had considered many times over the years. "There was a time that might have been true, and I have certainly been raw about my station more than once. However, service for my own ends and those of others merged into one positive experience for me. I cannot tell the difference, honestly and truly."

"You are as good at deceit as your jailer, Velaska. I could make you free, you know. Free to roam the universe. Free to live your own life."

"She gave me my freedom long ago." I shook my head. "I see all the universe I want, but thank you all the same."

I began to walk toward the cave, but Gaia blocked my path. "Regrettable, but it is your choice. Very well. If you come with me, I will show you the way to your friend."

"What about the cave?" I asked.

"It is not where I keep my heart," Gaia replied. "There is another planet that keeps it for me, which is what I told the other one like you. A friend of yours?"

"A descendant of mine, yes, but also a friend." I puzzled over Gaia's words. "And she just went with you?"

"Of course," Gaia said, feigning meekness. "Why would she have any reason not to believe me?"

I scoffed. "And she just believed that you would be okay with your own doom?"

"I'm not sure if that is what she believed," Gaia replied. "She believed the truth of the situation, which is that I do not keep heart here."

I shook my head. "Julia is wonderful, but she does not deal with many gods. Most of her experience is with third-rate scumbags, and the gods are first-rate. I have dealt with your kind for a long time, and I have never met one that goes willingly to death."

"You accuse me of trying to end the universe; what is that but a kind of death? Either way, I cease to exist."

"I have not discerned why you want to wake Chaos, but I do know that I have never met a suicidal god in all my time. You're hiding something. Otherwise, why would you come to me and speak such dulcet words?"

"Because you are fascinating." Gaia smiled at me as she moved closer, her rocky hand grazing my cheek softly. "You must know that."

I pushed past her. "Leave me be."

Gaia grabbed my hand. "Don't go in there."

I saw the fear in the daisies she used for eyes as I looked deep into them.

"I see your fear, and I can taste your lies."

I took one of my daggers and stabbed her through the chest with it. The surprise forced her to stumble backward for a moment before her expression changed from fear to vengeance.

"You will regret that."

I palmed a handful of pixie dust as I rose into the air. "You'll have to catch me first."

I spun around and flew as fast as I could toward the cave, with Gaia fast on my heels and the fate of the universe on my back.

CHAPTER 45

Katrina

Location: The First Underworld

"Don't get in my way," Eros spat venomously. He stood across from me on the great plane of Hell. "I don't want to hurt you."

"You have a funny way of showing it," I shouted, a fireball growing in my hands. "By killing hundreds of gods."

I shot the fireball across Hell toward him. Eros fired an arrow through it, splitting the ball in two, the cleaved pieces passing harmlessly on either side of him.

"I have fought more powerful than you," Eros said. "And twice as hot-headed. Leave me alone to do my work, and I will not kill you."

"Yes, you will!" Velaska shouted. "You'll destroy the whole universe if we let you."

"You know so little." Eros rose into the air. "Do not follow me."

"What are you after anyway?" I called out to him. "Tartarus has already taken every soul in Hell."

"I search for him," Eros said with a smile. "His body, reformed, calls to me."

Eros shot through the air like a rocket in the opposite direction from us, kicking up a storm of dust and debris behind him in the process. I lifted myself into the air, and Velaska joined me.

"We can't let him escape," I said, taking off after him.

"Agreed," Velaska said. "We can't let him find that body."

We raced across the planes of Hell, following Eros, close on his heels. As we neared him, I shot a torrent of fire at him, and he spun to dodge the flames. He turned and let loose three arrows at us. I strafed to avoid them, and Velaska mimicked my movements. She was not an experienced fighter, but she knew a wealth of defensive magic. She threw a shield up so that the next barrage of arrows bounced off of it and fell to the ground harmlessly.

"You are infuriating!" Eros shouted back at us. He must have spotted something along the edges of Hell that drew his attention because he scrambled to a stop and dove for the ground. I looked down at the spot he beelined for, a little cave that bore a strong similarity to the rest of them. It looked unimpressive to me but evidently held great interest for Eros. There had to be something in there that could help him raise Tartarus.

"Let's go!" I shouted.

By the time we reached the ground, Eros had disappeared into the cave.

"Wow," Velaska said, holding up her hands in front of her. "This cave is pulsating a powerful kind of magic. I've never felt anything this strong before."

"The heart?"

"We don't know that," Velaska said. "But there's certainly enough magic."

"It has to be. He's trying to do something to wake Tartarus."

I rushed for the cave entrance, but Velaska grabbed my hand. "You shouldn't go in there, into some enclosed space, without a plan. Eros is incredibly powerful. He will kill you."

"We'll snap away before he can."

"He's faster than us," Velaska said. "Last time, he almost killed you."

I shook her off. "But he didn't. We might not have another chance to save the universe if Eros gets what he's going for and gets away. Who knows how we'll find him then?"

"We need more help."

I stomped toward the entrance. "No, YOU need more help. What's wrong with you? You just said we can't let him get away."

"That's before he went into a crazy powerful cave warded with ancient magic. We might have been able to take him in the sky, but in a tight space, he will be much more formidable. We have no idea what's in there! At least now we have him trapped. We can close him in and go get help from the Godschurch."

"No," I said. "If he can find a way to wake Tartarus, then it won't matter if we have a thousand agents or a million. I'm going in. Don't try to stop me."

She sighed and started walking toward me. "Fine. But this is stupid."

"I know." I shrugged. "But we've survived stupid before."

She bit her lip. "That doesn't mean much. We all survive…until we don't." Velaska could really be a wet blanket.

"Then we'll be in no worse shape than we would be if the universe ended right now."

With that, I disappeared into the darkness of the cave. Velaska walked lockstep with me into the unknown. Together, we had only one chance to save the world.

No, to save the universe.

CHAPTER 46

Rebecca

Location: Godschurch Base

"Do you really think this will work?" I asked as I stood in the astronomy tower high above the Godschurch. We had built and developed it to look at the stars for predictions on supernovas and other phenomena around the universe; all of that stuff could affect the life and times of the gods.

"About fifty-fifty, honestly," Urania said, turning to me from her telescope. She had outfitted it with the hands of Apollo, which she had creepily kept in a jar for so long that the hands barely held their form. "We used it years ago to pull all the planets back from other dimensions. Oddly, that's probably how Eros is able to bring back Gaia now. Had we left those planets beyond the stars, then Erebus couldn't have eaten them, and Gaia would never be whole. Weird how one good thing leads to a hundred worse ones, isn't it?"

"Absolutely," I said dryly. She smiled for a moment. "Maybe we should send the planets back beyond the void, then."

"I don't know how to do that. Even if I did, I wouldn't have time to learn how to do it at scale."

She looked at me, and her smile dissipated when she saw that I didn't share her excitement. "You don't think it's fascinating?"

"No," I said. "I was on one of those planets that fell into a black hole, and I spent what felt like an eternity on the other side of the void. I am very thankful you saved us…but the memories of it still keep me up at night."

"Oh…yeah. I forgot about that."

"And besides, that's not the only time we used it. If you recall, we used the same strategy at the Battle of the Obelisk."

"Holy crap. We did, huh? Yeah, crazy what you forget and what you remember, isn't it?"

"Not the best memory, huh?"

"I guess not, at least not about that stuff. Numbers I never forget, though." Urania turned down her eyes. "I'm sorry, I know I geek out. These things are very exciting for me. I mean, we actually reversed a black hole and saved billions of people—probably trillions. Maybe trillions upon trillions, depending on how many people survived from each of those planets." Again, she faltered when she looked at me. "I'll stop."

"How is that going to help us now?" I asked, trying to pull the conversation into a more productive direction. "It's not like we're saving planets this time."

"Well," Urania said, "the telescope magnified Apollo's powers with light and the sun. I figure if it could do that to pull the stars back into place, then we can use them to create a beam of light powerful enough to kill Erebus, or at least stop him in his tracks."

"Don't we need Apollo for that?"

"I think just his hands have enough power left in them to work for a little test, but yes, we'll need him, or some sort of sun god, or maybe a god of light, in order to make it work on a massive scale."

"How massive are we talking?"

"I figure we would have to create a barrier several billion miles across to stop Erebus. The further he comes in from the edges of the universe, the less diameter we'll have to give him."

"That sounds like a lot of work." The mere thought of the logistics of a billion-mile barrier nearly split my brain in half. "We really only have to stop him from eating one planet if we don't want Gaia to return."

"But we'll be sending untold trillions of people to their deaths. What good is the universe if there's nobody to enjoy it?"

I looked down at the Source. "Once, the gods built planets and created things. You can do it again, as long as there is a universe to save."

"Not good enough." She shook her head. "There are so few of us left, and I can't abide more death. Not if I can stop it."

I spun around and snapped at her. "Then it will be harder, won't it? You're being naïve."

I was too mean, I knew, but we needed action, and setting up a billion-mile perimeter felt impractical. More than impractical. It felt impossible.

"I'm sorry," I said. "I'm on edge, and I have no idea what to do next."

"That's understandable. Let's just test this theory, and then we'll have to find Apollo if it works, assuming he's alive."

***

We agreed on a collection of a hundred telescopes circling a series of barrier planets a million miles around the Source, protecting trillions of lives…if they worked. Edgar gave us the coordinates of a desolate planet in Erebus's path so that we could test the efficacy of the telescopes. Would they be able to protect us against Erebus? Urania and I set up the telescope on an island at the equator and then waited for the Darkness to arrive.

"How long will it take you to make more of these?" I asked. "Assuming this works."

"I'm a god," she said. "I can make them quickly once I know the specs work. The hardest part will be convincing Apollo to help us. He was barely coherent last time I saw him."

I shook my head slowly. "I thought he would turn it around after the Battle for the Obelisk. I honestly did."

"My brother is complicated," Urania said. "He loves Hera above all others. Seeing his surrogate mother again made him happier than I had ever seen him, but he is broken, and Hera does not abide brokenness from anyone. She tried to love him unconditionally, but his broken body disgusted her, and that destroyed Apollo."

"Woof, that is a complicated relationship. No wonder he's so screwed up."

I looked up and watched as the stars dimmed away, the sky turning to blackness as if the rest of the universe didn't exist. Erebus had arrived.

"I hope this works," I said.

"If not," she replied, "get ready to jump."

"Either way, I'll be ready. One telescope isn't going to stop him for long."

Urania handed me a pair of sunglasses, and I put them on without breaking my gaze from the sky. She flicked a switch at the base of the telescope. The telescope vibrated heavily, and then a beam of light, brighter than anything I'd ever seen, shot out of the telescope into the air.

Erebus shrieked and retreated. In the light, I saw purple eyes glaring back at me. They were not new to me, I realized. I had seen those eyes in the Darkness before, but they were not Erebus's. They belonged to another.

"Nyx," I whispered under my breath. We had been deceived by the god of the night. Erebus was not our enemy. It had been Nyx all along. *I was so stupid.* How many times would I be tricked by the gods before I realized they couldn't be trusted?

"It's working!" Urania said, pointing to the sky. The stars returned to the sky and broke up the Darkness. It was working, or at least it worked for a moment until the telescope jittered and failed. When the light cut out, the hole in the cosmos collapsed, and we had a very pissed Nyx bearing down on us.

"Let's go!" I shouted, taking Urania's hand. She grabbed the telescope and snapped her fingers, disappearing just as the Darkness smashed down on the planet, swallowing it whole.

My heart pounded against my chest in exhilaration. We had found something that could stop Nyx from destroying the universe. My excitement quickly turned to fear when I realized that Kimberly was alone in the dark, on a mission to destroy Erebus's heart and that she was in extreme danger.

CHAPTER 47

Kimberly

Location: The Darkness

Black ooze dripped out of Erebus's heart as it flashed and sparked like a broken transformer. I picked my scythe out from the gooey chrysalis. The ooze ate through the metal, creeping slowly from the tip of the scythe to the hilt.

"Ew." I tried to wipe the goop from the blade with my robe but only succeeded in getting the sticky tar all over me.

"It will eat through everything soon," Nyx said. "You should get rid of it as soon as possible before it consumes you, too."

I threw down the scythe, and it disappeared. The tar crept up my robe and tightened around my legs, forcing me to drop to my knees. I pressed my hands into the inky black ground and tried to regain my breath. When I tried to pick them up, they were stuck to the blackness, and I was unable to lift them.

"What is happening?" I said.

Nyx's bright purple eyes appeared in the air before me, and she materialized bit by bit. First, a shimmering bronze face, then long, flowing, white hair. The Darkness wrapped around her in an elegant ball gown that caught just enough of the fading purple light of Erebus's heart for me to see.

"Help me."

I had killed gods before and accepted their power four separate times, though only Thanatos's remained, so I knew the transfer of power well. Erebus's black essence swirled and rose through the air, sparkling like a thousand purple fireflies at once, and then, the disparate flickers coalesced and molded into a dagger and shot toward me.

I closed my eyes and opened my arms wide to prepare to receive the Primordial's power, but the shock of it entering my body never came. I opened my eyes to see a sheet of black ooze blocking me from the heart. Purple lightning sparked for a moment, and then it settled into calm. Nyx had absorbed the power instead of me.

"Thank you, my love. I could never kill him, partially because of the pact we made never to harm each other…but also, he was the love of my life, even if he was the scourge of my plans. I have ingested his energy and am more powerful than ever."

I looked up at her. "You…manipulated…me."

"I am the goddess of the night. What did you expect?"

"Erebus was never the enemy, was he?"

Nyx cackled. "Nobody is an enemy or friend, my dear. If you are asking if he was the one destroying the universe, then no, I'm afraid I did lie to you about that. And yet you believed me. It takes two to build a lie. The liar and the one who believes them. Neither is without blame."

"Are you kidding me? You can't fault me for believing you. You're my boss. You're supposed to protect me!"

Nyx knelt so that we were face to face as the tarry Darkness rose to my navel. "Of course, I can blame you. And your friends will, too. It won't matter for long, though. Now that my brother is dead, my power has no limit."

"Why kill him?" I asked, the blackness slinking up my arms to my shoulder. "Why force me to murder your own blood?"

"He was a detriment to my plan. He might have been disbursed, but the heart still ate at me, burrowing into my brain and telling me to spare the cosmos. He always loved this universe. So much that he gave himself to you, and your kin, and the universe itself. I was able to absorb Thanatos's brothers and sisters back into myself, but I could not kill you, as the mortal piece of you fought against it. Then, I realized I could use you, Kimberly, to kill him, hoisting him by his own petard. His aura mocked me. His light weakened me. With him gone, I am as powerful as Chaos and can face her as an equal."

"You're insane."

Another cackle from Nyx. "You really are pathetic. You have no idea what it means to be eternal. I have seen everything. My life…I have watched the Titans, the gods, the humans… everything that has ever existed not appreciate the universe for what it is. I have been forced to watch, to suffer, while what Chaos gave you was squandered, and you dare tell me I am the crazy one? No, my dear, you are all crazy. Chaos made a mistake creating this dream, and she will learn that when I journey into the Source to confront her. I will rip the power of creation from her head and take the crown for myself."

"She created you. She created all of this, and you are so vain to think you know better than her?"

Nyx pulled me up by the chin. "Why not? You are so vain to think you know better than me, and I created you."

"No, you created Thanatos, and I killed him, just like I'll kill you." There was ice water in my veins as the

Darkness pulled me down to the ground. "I vow to kill you."

"I appreciate your spunk, but once I absorb you, my victory will be total. I thank you for your sacrifice. I truly couldn't have done it without you."

I was about to die, and, with my death, Nyx would have the power to control the whole universe. I should have known she was the one all along. There were so many signs that it was her who was manipulating me. It was too late. My stomach and elbows disappeared into dark inky tar, followed by my chest.

I strained to keep my neck free. I could still use my limbs under the black sludge even if it was draining to move. My fingers grazed the handle of my scythe, and I reached out for it. It was in my hand, but I couldn't move it through the murky black. There would be no redemption for me.

As my chin disappeared into the ooze, a bright white light, as brilliant as any I had ever seen, cut through the sludge like a lightsaber. The charred smell of a burnt body rushed into my nostrils as the sludge flinched in pain.

Nyx shrieked out, and the tar lost its grip on me for a second as it recoiled in horror from the light. Suddenly, I could move. I pulled myself up until I was standing toe to toe with Nyx.

"No!" she shouted.

I swung at her with all my might. I thought I might kill her, but at the last moment, she regained her composure and caught my scythe by the handle.

She tried to shake me free, but I latched on tightly until she threw the scythe away and me along with it. I watched her eyes glow with a menacing vengeance. The brilliant beam of light ceased, and the sludge collapsed on itself once more.

"That's better," Nyx said. "Now, to deal with you."

I had to warn the others…even if it was the last thing I did before Nyx ended my existence.

I cut through the veil with my scythe and disappeared back into the universe. I didn't know what the light was that caused Nyx so much pain, but it had saved my life, if only for the moment. It was a real-life deus ex machina, and I would be forever in the debt of whoever or whatever had given it to me.

CHAPTER 48

Katrina

Location: The First Underworld

"Do you have a plan yet?" Velaska whispered to me as we walked deeper into the cave. Her voice echoed through the tight corridors. At any moment, I expected Eros to pop out from behind a passageway and embed an arrow into my skull, which kept my eyes forward and head on a swivel. "I know you like pulling things out of your ass, but I'm hoping there's something in there rattling around that's more than just—"

"Kill him," I said definitively.

"I was afraid of that. No, of course, you don't have a plan. Look who I am talking to."

"I rely on instincts."

"Instincts only get you so far."

I turned to her but didn't stop moving forward. "They helped me kill Lucifer, become the Devil, and ascend to godhood. I think I've done pretty well for a little girl from Oregon, don't you? I've saved the universe, what, at least twice?"

She grumbled. "I suppose you do have a point. It's going to get somebody killed one day."

I took a deep breath. "It's already gotten a lot of people killed, but it's saved a lot of people, too."

The words tasted bitter on my tongue. I didn't like to admit that I was directly responsible for the death of so many gods and people. I'd even killed a bunch of them myself. I comforted myself by saying that I saved more than I killed, but that was little relief the longer I lived and the more I watched those I loved die because of my actions. Still, I was the god I was, and I worked hard to be okay with that. Skittering noises echoed down the hallway in front of me, and I pushed Velaska down. Two shimmering gold arrows flew over my head.

"I told you to stay away." It was Eros, at the end of a long dirt hallway. My hands filled with fire, and I shot the flames at him. Before they could reach him, he ducked down a corridor and vanished.

"Are you okay?" I asked.

Velaska brushed herself off as she rose to her feet. "Just fine, darling."

"Good," I said. "We must be frustrating him."

She smirked. "You have a way of doing that to people."

The walls, which had been nothing but flat clay along the way, had changed. Now there were large holes carved into them on either side of us, with skeletons in each of them.

"A catacomb," Velaska said. "So, it is true."

"What's true?" I asked, looking at one of the skeletons in one of the holes. "What does it mean?"

Velaska studied the bodies, too. "People didn't use to be sent back to the Source. Originally, they were buried here, while Tartarus learned how to cleanse them." Velaska moved to another hole. "And this was an angel or a Valkyrie. Or maybe a deva. Do you see the wings?"

I knelt to get a better look and saw the bones of wings behind its ribcage. "Crazy."

"There was talk of it, but never did I imagine it was true."

I stood up. "Come on. Let's go. We still have a Primordial to track down and a universe to save."

The catacomb branched again and again. I followed the path I saw Eros duck down after our spat. He was a god, but he still walked on the ground for some reason. His footprints were fresh on the floor. Perhaps he wanted us to track him for some reason. Either he was leading us into a trap, or he didn't think enough of us to bother hiding himself. Either way, I had a nasty feeling in the pit of my stomach.

The catacombs twisted deeper into the depths of the underworld. They slanted downward, and the temperature dropped as we trudged further into the belly of the planet. Eventually, the catacombs broke into a large room with a stone altar at its center. Eros was standing in front of it.

"You will soon be with me again, my friend," he said quietly, dipping his head down low. "I had hoped you would not follow me," he grumbled and turned to look at me. "I gave you every opportunity to go back, but I will not be stopped. The universe depends on it."

Faster than I could track, he pulled up his bow and let loose an arrow from his quiver. It glowed gold as it cut through the air, highlighting the room in a faint glow. Velaska stepped in front of me to cast a protection spell, and I tried to grab her, but it was too late.

"Shie—"

The shield rose, but it didn't matter. The arrow cut right through it and embedded deep in Velaska's chest. She convulsed as she dropped to the ground, dark red blood covering her white toga.

"Velaska!" I shouted, kneeling next to her. "No, no, no, no, no."

Her eyes went wide. "I don't—I don't feel good."

"You're going to be okay," I said, leaning her against me. "You're going to be okay."

"Don't lie to her," Eros grumbled. "There are few things in the universe that can kill a god, but that arrow is one of them. My aim is true. Your friend will be dead in a moment, and once the life leaves her eyes, you will be next."

I snapped my fingers, trying to leave the catacombs and get back to the Godschurch, but nothing happened. "Why isn't it working?" I shouted. "Come on! Let me out of here!"

"You can't teleport into this room, or from it, without a piece of him," Eros said, his bow drawn. "Tartarus made sure of it for his own safety. He reconstructed his body using the souls of the underworld, and now, it is time to bring him back and end this."

Velaska's breathing was shallow. Her skin was pastier than even her natural white glow. "I told you…"

"Told me what?" I said to her.

"I told you…you were going to get somebody killed."

Her eyes shuttered back and forth for a moment, and then she let out a gasp and fell back, limp. The light went out of her eyes, and I wailed. I had so few friends in the universe, and she was one of them, even when I hated her.

"I'm going to kill you," I hissed, rising to my feet.

"No, my dear," Eros said. "I'm afraid it's the other way around."

He let loose the arrow from his quiver, and it was as if time stood still. I grabbed the arrow out of the air and snapped it in half, taking the tip for myself. As the world cleared and time sped up, a look of terror passed through Eros's eyes.

"You son of a bitch!" I said, swinging the arrow tip at him. "She did nothing to you!"

Eros dodged the arrow and kicked me back into the wall, then scampered to the far wall to avoid my continued attack. "You are trying to stop me from saving the universe. That is something!"

I pushed myself to my feet. Dirt plumed around me. "What are you talking about? You're the one trying to destroy the universe, and we're here to stop you!" I rushed forward. Eros spun to avoid me, and I slammed into the other side of the room.

"Well, that's just not true," Eros said, cocking his head to the side. "Who told you that?"

"What does it matter?" I growled. "Soon, you'll be dead."

I slashed at him, and he leaped away. "If you kill me, the universe will certainly end. Tell me! I need to know who betrayed the universe."

"Ananke," I replied.

"How did you—"

"We know she created the Godschurch to protect the universe from you." I sliced the air again, but Eros dodged me. His muscles were no longer tense, though. It was as if he had no intention of attacking.

"My dear, that is not true. I helped create the Godschurch as a prison for Ananke and a way to protect the universe from her lies. We all created it to contain her.

Tartarus, Gaia, Nyx, Erebus, and I, back when were all on the same side."

"And which side was that?"

"The universe's," he said, his arms raised to indicate the space around him.

"Lies!" I screamed, rushing him. He spun around and punched me in the back hard enough to sting but not hard enough to do lasting damage. "Fight me!"

Eros sighed. "I don't have time for this."

He pulled six arrows out of his quiver and leaped back to get some distance between us. This time he loosed all six of the arrows at once. I expected to be riddled with arrows, but instead of becoming a pin cushion, the arrows latched onto my shirt and pants, pinning me to the wall of the cave. No matter how hard I struggled, I couldn't escape them.

"Now, I hope that shows I'm not the enemy here," Eros said.

"You killed my friend. You will always be my enemy."

Eros looked back at the body of Velaska. "If what you say is true, then I regret my actions and the death of your friend. I did not know you had seen Ananke or that she corrupted you against me. I went to the Godschurch that day to make sure she was still entombed, and the fight got the better of me. I wanted to save the gods you had collected, but the Darkness is more powerful than me." He dropped his head. "They were all more powerful than me. It was always Tartarus they feared, which is why I am here. His body rests in this tomb, under that altar, and along with it, the location I need to find his heart and make the resurrection complete."

"I don't believe you."

"I don't care." Eros walked to the altar and pushed the top of it to the floor. "Hello, old friend."

He reached down and pulled a scroll from the ground. The scroll was wrapped with an amulet, which he placed over his neck. "Now, I can transport in and out of here, but I still need to know where to go."

He unfurled the scroll and read it intently for a moment. Satisfied, he snapped his fingers, disappearing from the space, leaving me with two dead bodies. No matter how hard I struggled, I couldn't escape. The frustration mixed with my grief, and I started to cry once again.

CHAPTER 49

Julia

Location: Rebargan

Gaia and I teleported into an enormous cavern. Something creaked and groaned in the darkness ahead of us. Gaia closed her eyes, and thousands of glittering fireflies spread out from her body around the cavern, giving it an ambient light. The darkness was bad, but it was even worse to have the small light give shape to the jagged rocks, making them look almost alive as the bugs fluttered through the cave.

"Where are we?" I asked as I followed Gaia. Everywhere she stepped, her footsteps formed a trail of moss and grass.

"Rebargan was the site of…" She turned back to me. "I'm not sure I should tell you."

I shuffled toward her. "No, please, I need to know. Anything you tell me could be important to the future and saving the universe."

She smiled. "You are very polite for somebody that has come to kill me."

"It's not personal," I replied. "We need to save the universe."

"Ah, yes." Gaia smiled, her voice quiet and resigned to her fate. "You are very adamant that the universe needs saving and that I seek to destroy it."

"Don't you?"

Gaia shrugged. "I certainly don't think I owe you an explanation as to my plans, little one."

"Please, if we've got it wrong, then what you say could save your life."

"If I wanted my life saved, I would not have brought you here."

"Fair enough, but you should tell me anyway."

"And you would believe me, wouldn't you?" Gaia said, giving me a searching look. "If I told you I didn't wish the universe to end, you would believe that?"

"I don't know," I said. "I would certainly take it under advisement."

She studied me for another long moment. "You have a kind heart, not like most of your ilk."

"Which ilk is that?"

"Choose. Pixies. Humans. Godschurch agents. None of them have much honor to them or kindness."

I shook my head. "I don't think that's true. I think people are up their own ass, but everyone I've ever met has compassion for someone or something. It's just that they compartmentalize that compassion and lack the empathy necessary to generalize their love. If people had as much love for everyone as they had for their pet or their favorite video game, then the world, and the universe, would be a better place."

"I suppose it would," Gaia said. "I never had much use for humans. They were a cancer on most of my worlds, maybe a parasite. Either term is apt. I found myself caring more about the animals and vegetables and let the gods worry about humanity."

"Is that why you want to destroy the universe?"

Gaia chuckled. "No. Well, yes, I suppose. It is certainly one reason why I don't care whether it ends. There are so many reasons, though, and so many things I got wrong at the beginning. So much I've learned. I would like the chance to start over with all the knowledge I've gained. I don't think of the end of the universe as a destruction but as a rebirth."

I stepped over a large rock as we continued through the cave. "But you can't do that. If you end the universe, your life ends right along with it."

"You mortals…you think you have such a grasp on the world, but really, you know nothing. Nothing is certain. I am wise enough to know that. I also don't know what will happen, but I am willing to see the end and take my chances that I will come out ahead somehow."

"And yet you lead me to your heart, so that I may destroy it, and kill you. How could you end up better if you don't exist?"

"So naïve." She looked up at the stalactite stone daggers pointing down at us from the tip of the cavern. "If I cannot see the next universe, then I might as well leave this one." Gaia looked around the cavern. "Especially since it led me back to this place."

"What is this place?" I asked again. "You never told me."

"You are too inquisitive for your own good," Gaia said, not breaking her gait. "Very well, pixie. You have done me a great service in listening to me, so I will tell you. This is the site of my biggest regret. It is here that I lost the love of my life, Tartarus."

"Tartarus? The underworld guy?" I asked, surprised.

She nodded. As we walked forward, a red light rose past the crest of the next hill. "We differed on how we would deal with humanity. I believed we should wipe them out for the good of the universe, but he said that it was his duty to clean them and return them to the Source. For that to happen, humanity needed to exist. Otherwise, the Source would destabilize."

"We fought for ages in this cavern." She turned around. "This place was the prototype for the underworlds that I gave him, and where he would imbue his essence. He abandoned me in this place and broke my heart in half, even after I gave him everything. I thought it appropriate to leave my heart here."

"But didn't he become a part of you? All of his underworlds existed inside of you, didn't they?"

Gaia smiled a wistful smile. "I had never thought of that, but yes, I suppose that's true."

We crested over the ridge, and at the bottom of a canyon was a red, glowing chrysalis. Gaia grabbed my hand, and we flew down to the bottom of the ridge until we stood so close to it that the light reflected off both of us.

"We are here," Gaia said.

I looked over at her somberly. "I'm sorry I have to do this."

"Don't apologize," Gaia said. "I have lived long and lived well. Do what you must."

"How do I destroy it?" I asked.

Gaia pointed to the left, beyond the chrysalis. A pair of vines extended from Gaia's hand and picked up a discarded sword. The vines pulled it toward me and laid it in my hands. The hilt was covered in soot, and the blade had dulled with age, but the runes inlaid on the blade and handle showed just how beautiful it had once been.

"I have thought of this place often, ready to end it, but I could never bring myself to do it. You see, you do me a favor, really. If I cannot have my love Tartarus, and he will never have me again, then it is better to end it now."

I gripped the hilt and raised the sword over the heart, hesitating. Gaia was kind—kinder than any other god I had met. However, it was my duty to kill her, and we all had to do what we had to do.

"I'm sorry."

I moved to strike the blade down on the chrysalis when a whistle shot through the air. An arrow hit the blade and knocked it out of my hands.

"Wait!" Eros screamed, running toward us. "You shall not kill my friend this day, hag."

"She asked me to kill her!" I said, pointing to Gaia. "Also, rude!"

"Not you, human," Eros scoffed. "I see you are under the spell of this witch. Don't listen to a word she says."

"You tried to kill me!" I shouted. "I watched you and Erebus murder hundreds of gods in the church! Don't tell me not to listen to her. You're the bad one, here."

"You have no idea what you are doing. If you destroy that heart, any chance we have of saving the universe dies with it."

"Shut up, Eros!" Gaia screeched. "You know nothing. You gave yourself to the gods and haven't even been conscious for the past million years. I have seen everything."

A thorny vine slung from Gaia's hands and flung across the chasm. Eros fired an arrow from his bow, and it broke the vine in half, slicing it down the middle and causing Gaia to shriek.

"Step away from the heart of Tartarus!" Eros said.

I spun to Gaia. "Tartarus? You said this was your heart."

"Yes, I did…" Gaia smiled a wicked smile. "Didn't I? I suppose you could call that a lie. A pity. I hoped I could keep this civil. Oh well."

I rolled out of the way as one of Gaia's vines darted toward me. As I spun to avoid a second strike, I found the sword. I rolled forward to avoid a third strike. When I landed, the sword was under me, and I picked it up. Gaia fired another vine at me, and I sliced it at the root and cut it from her arm. Again, she shrieked.

"Was anything you told me the truth?" I asked.

"I'm honestly not sure," Gaia said, never losing her wicked smirk. "Does it really matter? You'll be dead soon, along with everything else in the universe."

"Here in the barren darkness, she is rather powerless, but she will soon pull power from the planet's core and regain her strength." Eros rushed forward and kicked Gaia, who tumbled away from the heart. "Come with me."

What other choice did I have? Stay with a liar or go with a killer. I grabbed Eros's hand. He pressed his free hand onto the heart, and the two of us vanished along with the heart of Tartarus, leaving Gaia to scream into the depths of the canyon alone.

CHAPTER 50

Katrina

Location: Tartarus's Tomb

I didn't know I could cry as much as I did. I missed Velaska terribly and mourned her life, but my tears weren't just for her. They were for every single person, god, and monster I had watched die at my hands and those who inadvertently died because of my actions. I thought I did so much good, but every piece of good I put into the world boomeranged back with just as much bad. I wept for every deed I ever performed, both good and bad.

But I also cried for Velaska, my friend and the only being that put up with me, even when we hated each other. She indulged my eccentricities and encouraged me to be better, at least when we didn't outright loathe each other. She hated the part of me that was human, but she never understood how much I hated that part of me, too.

She was right. I never learned.

Ten thousand years of mistakes, death, destruction, and here I was again, fighting for the right to exist. That was honestly all I'd ever wanted: the right to exist peacefully. When something came to threaten that dignity, I fought tooth and nail. If I could just be left alone and not forced to justify my existence...

I balled up my fists and tried one more time to escape the arrows that bound me to the wall of Tartarus's tomb. No matter how I struggled, the arrows simply dug in deeper.

Footsteps moved toward me in the dark.

"Hey! I'm in here!" I screamed, pushing as hard as I could against the arrows.

Into the archway stepped Eros, holding a glowing red egg in the palm of his hand. "I know. I put you there."

"You!" I screamed, wriggling unsuccessfully to break free. "Let me out of here!"

"In a moment," he said, walking further into the room. "Sorry it took so long. I would have been quicker, but I had to figure out how to shrink this heart down to fit into Tartarus's body. Eventually, I got it."

Behind him, of all people, was Julia, holding a dusty sword in her hand. "Oh my god!" Julia said, running to Velaska, whose blood pooled on the dirt beneath her. "She's dead."

"I'm afraid so," Eros said. "An unavoidable misstep."

Julia touched the arrow sticking out of Velaska's chest. "Did you do this?"

Eros nodded. "A regrettable mistake, but I had no idea we had the same aims at the time, so I acted in what I thought was the best interest of the universe."

Julia looked pensively down at Velaska for a moment before closing the goddess's beautiful purple eyes. Julia turned to me, gesturing at the arrows. "And you did that?"

Eros scoffed. "Obviously. Now, I have a lot of work to do." He nodded in my direction. "Can you get that one down from the wall—assuming she can behave?"

Julia smirked. "I've never seen her behave, for even one second, in all the time I've known her."

Eros moved toward Tartarus's tomb. "I was afraid of that. In that case, please leave her bound until I am done.

After that, we'll be on our way. A lot to do and very little time to do it."

"Sure," Julia said, though she jogged over to speak with me. "Are you okay?"

"No, I'm bound to a frigging wall!" I screamed. "And you're working with a psychopath! What are you doing here? Why are you with him?"

"Eros found me and stopped me from destroying Tartarus's heart."

I stared down at her from my perch on the wall. "Tartarus's heart? That's what Velaska and I were looking for! You found it?"

"We did."

"Wait. I thought you were looking for Gaia's heart."

"I was, and I thought I found it, but Gaia led me astray. I thought she had brought me to her own heart, but she really led me to Tartarus's and wanted me to destroy it."

"What? That doesn't make sense."

"I'll explain later. Just know it was shenanigans on an epic scale."

"That does sound like the gods, using humans as pawns in their games. C'mon, let me out of here. We can still destroy the heart before Eros brings Tartarus back."

Julia shook her head. "No, we can't. We need Tartarus. He's on our side. So is Eros. They're the good guys. Nyx and Gaia are the bad ones…oh, and Ananke's not great either."

"No," Eros said. "She isn't. That's why we had to bind her to the Godschurch."

"Bind Ananke?" I had no idea what was going on. "What is he talking about, Julia?"

"He can explain it better than I could," Julia said. "Can you please—"

"No time." Eros started chanting under his breath. "A little busy here trying to restore balance to the universe."

"Right," Julia said, watching him for a few moments before turning back to me. "Ananke is evil, too. She's wanted the universe to burn since the beginning. Gaia and Nyx have been trying for the last billion years or so, but until you and Urania brought back the planets from the other universe, they couldn't restore Gaia."

"Thank you for that, by the way," Eros grumbled.

"It was a genius bit of fuckery," I added, not able to stop myself from speaking my piece.

"Now that the planets are all back, they've been biding their time, waiting for the perfect moment," Julia said. "This is it. Nyx made her move, and Eros came back to try and stop her."

"Sounds inconceivable," I said, twisting my mouth as I considered the plan. "But so does everything when you're dealing with the gods."

"Ain't that the truth," Julia mumbled. "Sometimes, I miss the simplicity of Hell."

"Me too," I replied with a deep sigh.

The red egg glowed brightly enough to light the whole room, and when Eros had finished murmuring incantations, he stuffed the shimmering heart down into the tomb.

"Arise, Tartarus!" Eros said, lifting his arms high over his head. "Arise!"

"I hope you're right about this," I said out of the corner of my mouth. I didn't take my eyes off Eros. "Otherwise, we're screwed."

Julia frowned. "Gaia seems to hate Tartarus, and if she's one of the bad guys, then I guess we should go with the old 'enemy of my enemy is my friend' saying, at least for the time being."

"That assumes Gaia is the bad guy."

"I met her," Julia said. "She comes across as sweet, but she's as bad a guy as they come."

The ground began to rumble. A massive paw slammed through the side of the tomb, and another broke the altar into a thousand pieces.

Tartarus sat up. He was massive, armored in thick black steel with fire filling his helmet. As he pushed himself to stand, genuine fear filled my lungs. If this was the end of a video game, he would have been the final form of the ultimate boss, but according to Julia, we were supposed to trust him, even work with him.

"I have returned." His voice was deep and guttural, like he had smoked three cartons a day for a million years. He hugged Eros, who disappeared into the black armor for a moment as Tartarus brought him close to his bosom. "It is good to see you."

Eros pushed himself away and looked at his friend. "It's good to see you, too, my friend. I wish it were under better circumstances."

Tartarus pounded Eros's shoulders. "Were it so, then we would not ever see each other again."

The cave surrounding us began to quake, and the wall behind me rumbled underneath my feet, causing the arrows to rub against my shoulders and leg, opening up jagged, tiny cuts across my body. These arrows were sharp enough to slice through even my god-hard skin.

"What's happening?" I screamed.

Eros looked around the room frantically. "With Tartarus free, the underworld is unstable. It won't keep its form for long."

"Who is this? Who are these people?" Tartarus asked.

"Nuisances, but potentially useful ones," Eros said curtly. "The pixie over there found the sword we need to destroy Gaia, and the hanging one somehow beat me in battle and followed me here."

"You have lost a step," Tartarus said before laughing a cringe-inducing laugh.

"If so, we'll need them even more."

Tartarus nodded. "Do you know where she keeps her heart?"

"I think I do," Julia said. "It only makes sense if it's on Primera, which means Akta is in trouble. She doesn't have the sword or any way to kill a god. We must get to her."

"If she's taking on Gaia alone, she will need our help." Eros pointed to me. "Can you get her down?"

Tartarus nodded and approached me. With one movement, he pulled the arrows from the wall, and they fell to the ground. He placed me on my feet as Eros completed the circle around us.

"So what?" I said. "I'm just supposed to trust you now?"

"Absolutely not," Eros said. "But we need your help anyway. You seem like the kind who is always looking for a fight. Ever fight a Primordial before?"

"Just once," I said, failing to suppress a smile. "And I kicked his ass."

"Ha!" Eros said. "I like you, but you exaggerate. I believe we fought twice, with me winning our second encounter. If anything, it was a draw. Gaia, though, is a whole different level of battle. She and Nyx are the two most powerful beings in the universe."

"I fear her not," Tartarus growled. "I am ready for battle."

"You don't have your war hammer, friend," Eros said. "You hope to withstand Gaia without it?"

"He doesn't need to withstand her for long," Julia said, holding up the sword. "Just long enough for me to stab her in the heart with this."

"HA!" Tartarus said, laughing that horrible laugh again. "I like this one, and I can do that assuredly."

I nodded. "I suppose I can help. At least then I can keep an eye on you."

"Wonderful," Eros put his hand in the middle of the circle. "Then we have an accord. Shall we?"

I placed my hand on his and Julia above mine. Tartarus's mandibled hand sat on top of us all, ten times bigger than all of ours combined.

"Julia," Eros said. "Think of Akta in your mind's eye, and I will find her anywhere in the universe."

"That's a neat trick," I said. "If it works."

"It will work," Eros snapped.

Julia closed her eyes, and after a few seconds, she smiled. "Ah yes. There she is. And none too soon."

Eros snapped his free fingers, and we were gone into the ether.

CHAPTER 51

Akta

Location: Primera

I turned hard left down another dark tunnel to avoid one of Gaia's vines as it raced toward me. She was chasing me into the depths of her planet and seemed to be gaining energy with each passing moment while I was losing it. I had a nearly infinite supply of stamina, but hers was even greater than mine.

There was a snap, and suddenly Gaia was in front of me, building a gigantic spider web across the entire tunnel. I had some pixie dust left, and I smashed some down onto the ground and disappeared, rematerializing on the other side of the web. That was the game we played, and she didn't seem to learn that I could evade any obstacle she put up. Of course, the caves inside her planet were circuitous labyrinths with dozens of twists and turns, and I had no idea if I was going the right way. Still, we had a rhythm. She would set up a blockade, and I used my pixie dust to avoid it.

I was dangerously low on the stuff, though. I could still flash away without it, but it was far less reliable and not as powerful. I feared what would happen if I ran out and what would happen if I actually reached Gaia's heart, as I had no way of destroying the primordial being.

Another snap echoed through the chasm, this time followed by a bright flash. When it dissipated, I saw not Gaia but Julia, holding a sword, and Katrina, flanked by

Eros and another large being that towered above the others with a flaming face and thick, black armor.

"Go!" Tartarus growled as he slammed his hands together. With one swing, he burned Gaia's vines. A thunderous crash echoed behind me, and I turned back to see Gaia and the flaming-faced stranger engaged in hand-to-hand combat. I didn't stop to watch who was winning.

Eros, Julia, and Katrina rose into the air to follow me as I passed by them.

"What is he doing here?" I asked frantically. "Who is that flaming guy? Why are you working with Eros? What is going on?"

"He's on our side, I guess," Katrina said. "At least, for now, that's how it seems."

"Oh, that's nice. Then why did he kill all those gods?"

"That was a misunderstanding," Julia replied, fluttering her wings faster to catch up to me.
So he says."

"Quite the misunderstanding!" I said, glaring back at Eros.

He let loose a bevy of arrows on the vines, pinning them to the walls of the endless cavern. "What she means is that I didn't actually kill anyone. I tried to help, but Nyx is more powerful than I am. There was nothing I could do to protect those that fell in the battle."

"Did I ask you to talk?" I snapped. "No offense, but offense. You're a murderer."

"My apologies. I was just trying to explain." He went back to firing arrows behind him as we sped forward. "I'll just stay over here and let them do that."

"No," I replied. "I'm sorry. I suppose the fact that Katrina and Julia trust you is enough for me, for now."

"Whoa!" Katrina said. "I did NOT say I trusted him, but I trust him more than I trust Gaia, and we have to fight one big bad at a time."

"Fair enough," I replied. "Who is the other one, the one with the flaming face?"

"Tartarus," Julia said.

"Oh great, so now we have that to deal with him, too?" Enraged, I picked up my pace. "Awesome."

"Turn here!" Eros said to us as we reached an intersection of three tunnels. "Head down to the biggest artery on the left, and it will lead us to the heart!"

"Are you sure? I've been flying these tunnels for hours, and every turn looks the same."

"I'm certain!" he said. "If you trust nothing else, trust that I want Gaia to die."

"That I believe," I replied. "Fine. We'll go your way."

We turned together as a unit and sped up. "Why aren't you killing her, then?" I asked. "If you're so powerful."

A sheet of rock crashed in front of us, and Julia grabbed us, flashing us to the other side before I could use my pixie dust.

"I can't." Eros turned to me as we continued through the tunnel. "The Primordials took an oath when the universe was young. We cannot kill each other."

"So that's why she needed me to kill Tartarus?" Julia asked.

"Yes," Eros replied. "If you killed Tartarus, you would have absorbed his powers, and then she could have killed you and absorbed yours."

"So, she was right, then—at least about that—" Julia looked down at the sword. "Will I become Gaia if I destroy her with this sword?"

"Yes, you will. And the minute you do it, you will be a target for Nyx, but it will be three against one, and we might have a fighting chance with the Primordials against her power, even if it is nearly limitless."

"Three against two, right?" Katrina said. "Her and Ananke."

"Ananke won't join the fight. She will manipulate it from the sidelines." Eros sneered. "We don't have to worry about Ananke. Not yet."

The tunnel broke open into a large cavern. There was a loud bass thumping throughout it, pounding in rhythm like a heartbeat. The room pulsated green in time with the thumping that rattled my bones.

"This is it," Eros said. "This is Gaia's heart."

"Where?" I asked.

"Look up."

I looked to the ceiling and saw an enormous green chrysalis protected by a stone rib cage.

"It's so much bigger than Tartarus's," Julia said with a small gasp.

"Yes," Eros replied. "But it is still just as fragile." He pointed up to the center of the cavern where the stone ribs came together. A bright green light shone through it, unprotected by the stone around it. "There is a weak point at the top of the cave. If you run her through with the sword there, then you will kill her."

"And then what happens?" I asked. "To the world? To all worlds, without Gaia?"

Eros shook his head. "I don't know, but I don't imagine it will be good. Worlds, though, can be rebuilt. Gods can be remade. Humanity can be rebuilt. The universe cannot."

Julia squeezed the hilt of her sword with both hands. "I'm ready, I think."

I nodded. "I'll go with her."

"Hurry," Eros said. "She will not die easily. I feel her closing in on us even now."

As he spoke those words, a torrent of water crashed through the artery. A group of killer whales swam out in front of it. I grabbed Julia's hand as Katrina shot fire and Eros let loose a stream of arrows.

We rose ourselves as fast as we could toward the top of the cavern. Hundreds of vines sprung from the walls and rocketed their way toward us. I pulled the daggers out of my belt and swiped at them. There were too many, and it was impossible to get through them all. I looked down at my pouch—one last pinch of my pixie dust.

"Here!" I threw the dust at Julia.

"I don't need it! I have—"

"Eat it!" I screamed.

Pixies knew that ingesting pixie dust boosted their powers for a short time, even if it had dire and addictive consequences. Saving the universe was worth the potential risk. A vine squeezed around my leg and pulled me down. "You need to be more precise than usual. Use it to amp yourself up!"

Julia gave me a contemplative look, then pulled the last of my pixie dust from the pouch and caked it on her lips. Her eyes went pink, and she smiled. I watched a jolt of energy rush through her. She flashed away, once, twice, three times in an instant, jumping higher and higher into the cavern to avoid the vines as she moved.

More vines, meanwhile, wrapped around me so that I couldn't move. Just before they reached my eyes, I saw Julia flash to the top of the cavern and, without hesitation, stab the sword through the heart.

A deep, guttural scream quaked the cavern, and the vines fell away from my eyes. The green light from around the room pooled in a single stream of light that shot down at Julia, filling her with a green aura in every crevice of her body and pushing her down to the rock floor far below.

In an instant, the green light stopped. Julia let out a scream and fell through the air toward the ground. I fluttered my wings and caught her.

"I got you," I whispered, but she couldn't hear me. She was unconscious. I came down to the bottom of the cavern.

"It worked," Eros said.

"Yes," I replied. "I hope you are on my side."

"If I weren't, I would have already snapped both of your necks." The ground shook, and the ceiling of the cavern began to fall upon us in huge boulders. The cave was breaking apart. As we gathered ourselves, Eros whistled into the bowels of the cavern. A moment later, Tartarus appeared in front of us.

"It worked?" Tartarus asked.

Eros smiled. "It worked. She's gone."

"We should get out of here," Katrina said, grabbing on to Julia and me. Eros placed a hand on her, and Katrina snapped her fingers. We vanished just as a massive piece of the cavern ceiling fell upon the place where we stood.

CHAPTER 52

Rebecca

Location: Neblus

"Why should I help you?" Apollo said with a smirk. I was used to cocky gods, but there was something about him I found more grating than even the usual fare as if his lack of hands and battle scars forced him to overcompensate with over-the-top arrogant dickishness.

"Because the whole universe is in peril," I replied.

Apollo held up his golden hands. Katrina chopped off the originals decades ago, and he had been trying to live with the golden ones to varying degrees of effectiveness.

"What do I care?" Apollo said. "The universe deserves to die."

I placed my hands on the desk. "You can't believe that."

Apollo leaned forward. "Why shouldn't I? I mean, I once had everything, and now I have nothing, so it makes sense for this universe to be everything and then be nothing. There's a poetry to it."

"That's selfish," I said.

"And what you're asking isn't?" He rested his golden hands on his chest.

"No!" I glared at him. "I'm asking you to save the universe. That's the opposite of selfish."

He blew me off with a dismissive flick of his gilded hand. "Been there. Done that. And all I got was this stupid t-shirt." He pointed to a holy, ripped, white shirt that he was wearing. "Yes, I do think this is the shirt I was wearing last time I saved the universe. You were there. You said it would be great, that I would be a hero, but it was horrible. I've never been more miserable."

I snorted. "And how will you ever be able to throw that back in my face if the universe is destroyed?"

Apollo thought for a moment before a small smirk came across his face. "You're right, you know. And my pettiness knows no bounds."

I smiled. "I'm aware." Now I had to lie. "And then there's the matter of your hands."

"What about them?"

"We have them. If you help us, then I will expend every bit of energy at my disposal to reattach them for you."

Apollo touched his prosthetic hands to his face. Then pulled them away. "If I were whole, maybe mother would love me again."

"I'm sure she would."

A smile cracked across his face. "Okay. I will help you, but if you are lying to me, my wrath will be like nothing else you've ever seen."

We couldn't reattach his hands any more now than we could a decade ago, I knew. That was one of those details I would worry about if we saved the universe, and that was a big if. Besides, it was hard to be frightened of a man such as he had become.

***

I couldn't believe it. Urania's blockade was working. A hundred planets with a hundred telescopes creating a perimeter from the Darkness around a bottleneck in the galaxy, all powered by Apollo and connected by Urania.

"Power levels are holding steady," Urania said. "We could do this forever, frankly, as long as Apollo doesn't crap out."

"I will NOT crap out!" Apollo said, shaking. "Can we not do this forever, though?"

"We're working on it," I said. I could tell he was tiring quickly, no matter what his cocky mouth said. "Hopefully, we can find a way to stop Nyx instead of just containing her. Until then, keep pushing."

He was fat, slovenly, certainly not the god he had been in the legends others tell of him. At least during the Battle of the Obelisk, there had been a spark left in him, a shred of hope. I couldn't see any of that in him now. He was hollow and simply going through the motions.

Still, going through the motions was working for now, and it was giving us a chance. That was all I could hope for, even if we were simply doing triage on the wound. If we could get the field stable and contain Nyx, we could find a way to go on the offensive. I very much wanted to go on the offensive.

The ground began to shake underneath us. "What's happening? Are you doing this, Apollo?"

"No!" Apollo said. "I have no control over the earth."

"What's happening, Urania?" I asked, frantic.

"I don't know!" she said. "It's not coming from us, and it's all over the whole planet like it's breaking apart. I can't hold the telescope up for long. If even one of them goes, then the whole network will shatter."

"Do what you can! I'll check on the other telescopes!"

I had a horrible feeling like perhaps Julia had found a way to kill Gaia, and that caused the worlds to crack and warp, unable to sustain life without their life source. Perhaps they were going through their death rumbles before they fell into nothingness. It was an eventuality I hadn't even considered, instead assuming both Julia and Akta dead or at the very least mutilated since I hadn't heard from them. I should not have underestimated them. They had a habit of getting out of impossible situations.

I closed my eyes and flashed three light-years away to the location of the nearest telescope. When I landed on the planet, a crack in its crust sucked the telescope into the abyss. The light let out a final sputter and then fell dark.

"Get back to the Godschurch!" I screamed to the group working the telescope. They had only narrowly avoided sharing the telescope's fate.

I flashed to the rest of the telescopes one after another. On every planet, there were massive, calamitous earthquakes destroying Urania's work, and the interconnected mesh that held Nyx at bay was collapsing. There was only one safe place left in the whole galaxy: the Godschurch. We would have to regroup there.

I returned to Urania just as the telescope fell and Apollo's light died. I looked up into the sky to see Nyx's darkness blot out the sun. There was no stopping her now. All we could do was prepare for a final stand at the Source.

"What do we do?" Urania called over the rumbling and crashing sounds.

"Get Apollo back to the Godschurch!" I screamed. "Construct a new perimeter around the Source! It's all we have left!"

Darkness ate away at the sky. It was coming, and it was pissed. I teleported to the Godschurch. When I got there, I looked at the disheveled, disheartened faces of my fallen warriors. We had tried so hard, and we had failed in every conceivable way. As my eyes tracked around the room, a sudden flash obscured my vision, and in its wake stood Eros with a tall, fiery being clad in black armor next to him. In front of them was Katrina, and Atka, who cradled an unconscious Julia in her hands.

"You did it?"

"We did it," Akta said. "But at what cost?"

"At the cost of everything. And it's not over yet."

BOOK 3

CHAPTER 53

Julia

Location: Godschurch Base

I didn't know how long I'd been asleep, but I woke up in a dark place that I only vaguely recognized. A monitor beeped above me, and when I turned to look at it, the movement tugged at several tubes stuck into my arm.

"Don't move too fast," I heard Katrina's voice from the foot of my bed. She and Kimberly sat vigil over me, and they stood up in tandem. "Take it easy."

"Where am I?" I asked.

"Sickbay on the Godschurch," Kimberly said. "Rebecca thought it was best for Katrina and me to welcome you back since we're both mortals who became gods."

"A god?" I asked. "What are you talking about?"

Katrina walked closer. "Don't you remember? You stabbed Gaia's heart. She died, and her power transferred to you."

I looked down at my hands, my feet. They looked the same as they ever did but a faint tingle pulsed through them. It felt more like my hands were numb than imbued with the powers of a Primordial. "I don't feel much different. If anything, I feel worse, actually."

My throat was parched, and I coughed at the dryness of it. Kimberly handed me a glass of water from my bedside table. "Drink something. Be careful with the cup, though. You don't know your own strength."

I reached over and gingerly grabbed the water, downing it all in one gulp. "Thank you."

"I'll get you more," Katrina said, taking the cup and walking toward the fountain in the middle of the room.

"This is crazy," Kimberly said with a smile. "Who would have thought both of us would be gods, and one of us would be a primordial deity?"

"I never wanted to be a god," I said, shaking my head until the pain from my neck forced me to stop.

"Me either. I just wanted to save the universe."

"Oof." I rubbed the back of my neck. "You said a mouthful. You know, I thought that being a god would mean fewer aches and pains, not more."

Kimberly nodded. "It does, but there's…let's call it a complication."

"What complication?" I asked.

Katrina handed me another glass of water. "The Primordials are more powerful than any god, and with each planet Nyx destroys, your powers grow more concentrated. Your body isn't powerful enough to handle your godhood. With each passing hour, your power will intensify until it destroys you. It…sucks."

"Then get it out of me!" I said sternly. "I don't even want it."

"It doesn't work like that," Eros said, walking into the sickbay. "You can't just give your power up without dying. We think you might be able to keep it under control if you use it."

"Use it?" I said.

"Like releasing the pressure valve on a tea kettle," Kimberly said. "While the steam is bottled inside, it builds up the pressure, but if you release it, then maybe we can stop you from exploding into a million pieces."

"Yes, I would very much like that," I replied, trying not to show the fear bubbling inside of me. "What do I need to do?"

Eros nodded. "You're the most powerful of us all, aside from Nyx, and I think you can hold your own against her."

"By myself?" I asked. "That's crazy."

"I don't think so." Eros shook his head. "Gaia is a force of nature. You just have to make sure not to die. If she kills you, then your power will be hers."

"Because she killed me," I replied, understanding washing over me. "I assume you have more of a plan than punch Nyx really hard."

"We have a plan," Katrina said. "But it's damn foolish, and we'll need to outfit the Godschurch with better weapons to pull it off. I'll need one, too. Earth has been destroyed. Our Earth, which means the Sword of Damocles and the other god-killing weapons I hid there are gone."

"We'll need an armory of god-killing weapons," I said. "Nobody has those kinds of weapons, do they?"

Katrina nodded. "I know somebody who can help, assuming Hephaestus's planet hasn't been destroyed, but we still have to find Tartarus's hammer if we want to stand a chance against Nyx."

Eros pressed his finger against his mouth, deep in thought. "His flaming war hammer will not slow down a Primordial, and I fear even the greatest blacksmith in the cosmos could not forge another one."

I frowned. "So, I'm going to hold her off until you all can get together an army, and then you'll come to help me?"

Eros nodded. "Something like that, yes."

"I thought you couldn't kill Nyx," I said. "What does it matter what kind of rutting hammer Tartarus has?"

"We can't kill her," Eros said. "But we can still beat her within an inch of her life, and the hammer is one of the few weapons in the whole cosmos that Nyx fears."

"I have to admit," I said. "It sounds like you're sending me on a suicide mission."

"Not if you are as powerful as we imagine you are. If that is the case, you stand a chance of winning before we're ready. Even if you can only slow her down, it will still give us time to find weapons to fight off Nyx and join you."

"And what do I have to fight her with?" I asked. "My hands. It's not like I can just throw trees at her."

Rebecca appeared at the door. "I think I have something that will work in a pinch." She held up a blaster. "Urania retrofitted these with the same light cannon tech that hurt Nyx before. It won't kill her, but it will cause her a lot of pain, which is almost as good. Just stay away from her as best you can and hit her with this over and over, wearing her down until you find a clear shot to take her down."

I took the gun from Rebecca. "I'm going up against a Primordial with a pea shooter. Awesome."

"Are you in?" Eros said.

I shrugged. "I guess it's as good as any other damned thing. Sure."

"Then we have a plan," Eros said, before his face turned down. "There is one more thing. Nyx cannot be allowed to kill you. If you die by her hand, even indirectly, she will take your power and be unstoppable. If you should falter, then I will leave a single arrow, enough to kill even you, with Rebecca. If you feel you cannot move on, you must come back here and let Rebecca kill you."

"I take no pleasure in it," Rebecca said.

I rose to my feet and grabbed the gun from Rebecca's hand. "Then I will have to be sure not to let her take my power."

"All right, then," Rebecca said. "Eros, you and Katrina go with Kimberly to meet with Hephaestus. Let's hope he's not dead. Tartarus, you go with Akta to find your hammer. She's the best tracker we have left. I'll stay here and try to keep Nyx away from the Source, and Julia will fight Nyx from the other side of the barricade. This plan is insane, but it's the best one we have. The gods speed to you all."

CHAPTER 54

Kimberly

Location: Godschurch Base

I rushed out of the Godschurch's sick bay after Rebecca while the rest of the gods were hashing out their plan. "Excuse me? Director?"

She spun to me. "Yes?"

I hesitated before finally saying, "I think it's a bad idea to send me with Katrina and Eros."

"Why?"

"There is almost no chance that Tartarus's hammer isn't on a planet that has been swallowed by Nyx, and if that's true, then you'll need me to get inside the Darkness and find it."

"It makes sense. On last count, she had eaten up over 80 percent of the universe. Do you really think that the planets could be inside of Nyx and not completely evaporated?"

I shrugged. "I don't know, but whether they are, or they aren't, I'm the only one who can enter the Darkness and find it, and we need that hammer to defeat Nyx and defend the Source. Let me go with Tartarus and send Akta somewhere else."

"I don't know."

I chuckled. "I'm sorry, Director. I said that as if you had a choice. I was trying to be polite, but you see, I don't have to ask you anything. I am a god, not one of your little agents."

"Fine," Rebecca said, her hand to her forehead. "I'll figure something else for Akta to do."

"Perhaps you could give her one of your little light guns to fight with."

"Watch it," Rebecca grumbled.

"No," I replied. I reached into my robe and pulled out the corked, empty vial that Ananke had given me, except now it was filled with black ooze. "I thought you might want this. It was stuck to my scythe when I last escaped the blackness. Perhaps you can find a way to fight Nyx with it."

Rebecca grasped the vial with her hand. "Thank you. Your scythe? Is it—"

I pulled it out of the pocket dimension and showed it to Rebecca. It was crisp and clean. "When I got out of the Darkness, the ooze fell off of it. It was the damnedest thing. I'm guessing it had to do with Ananke fixing it, which is one reason I'm not 100 percent convinced that she's not on our side."

"One thing I know about gods," Rebecca said, "is that they are only on their own side." She held up the vial. "Thank you again for this."

"You're welcome." I turned back to the sickbay and saw that Tartarus wasn't there. I searched through the interrogation room and cells before turning to the rest of the base. I thoroughly searched every room with no luck, leaving only one place for him to go: Ananke's coffee shop.

I walked through the plaid rift. When I stepped into the shop, it was like entering a war zone. Chairs flipped over, tables snapped in two, blast holes in each of the walls, fire raging uncontrollably across the floor. The glass in the counter had been smashed through and the metal underneath had been smashed to Hell.

"Where are you?" a guttural voice cried out. "Where are you, Ananke?" Tartarus didn't bother to use the door to the kitchen when he smashed through it back to the shop. "I will destroy you!"

"Easy, champ!" I shouted at him, stamping out the fire. "What's wrong?"

"The god of certainty is gone. She must have left when she learned her chances of surviving a battle with me were minimal."

"What does it matter?" I replied. "We have stuff to do without her."

"She is working with Nyx to bring about the end of the universe. In a matter of hours, the dark goddess will be upon this place. If we can't subdue Ananke, she will help Nyx break through our defenses and corrupt the Source."

"We'll find her, then. I happen to know the best tracker in the universe, according to Rebecca."

I led Tartarus back to the Godschurch. He grumbled the whole way, stomping back into the bullpen where I found Akta sitting at a desk engraving her name into it with one of her daggers.

"This is boring," Akta said to Edgar. "They don't tell you how boring agent work is most of the time. Since I'm not a god, I don't have anything to do. Isn't that ridiculous? I'm their best agent—probably their only agent left—and they're keeping me on the sidelines."

When she saw me, she shot upright. "How is Julia?"

"I don't know, honestly. She's got a damned fool's plan and a lot of power. Let's hope that's enough, but we need something else from you."

Akta squinted. "Can you order me to do things?"

"I'm a god, this is the Godschurch, and you technically work for me. So, yes. Maybe. I don't really care. Either way, I need your help."

"Well, at least it will get me out of my own head," Akta replied. "What do you need?"

"Ananke has escaped, and I need you to track her down."

"All right." She nodded. "Yes, ma'am. Sounds fun."

"And take Urania," I added. "There's no one on this base that knows the cosmos as well as her."

"Alright," Akta said, confused. "I guess that makes sense."

"Good," I turned to Tartarus. "Let's go. Where was the last place you had the hammer?"

"I left it in the care of Anubis should the frost giants ever return, or Surt ever rear his ugly head again."

"Oh…shit," I said.

"What is it?"

"Nothing," I replied. "It's just I kind of destroyed a hammer like that when Surt returned, and the Four Horsemen were being real dicks about it."

"Let us hope for the universe's sake that it wasn't mine," Tartarus said. "Was this hammer twenty feet long and made out of black obsidian, carved with the runes of those that I felled in battle over the eons?"

"Oh, no. This one was way lamer than that."

"Then I believe we are fine."

"Let's hope," I said. "Have you looked through the archives for the hammer yet? The Godschurch keeps records and an armory of all the most powerful weapons in the universe."

"What…is an armory?" Tartarus asked.

I smiled. "Come with me. You're going to love it."

CHAPTER 55

Katrina

Location: Godschurch Base

"Are you ready?" I asked Eros, who was still standing next to Julia's now empty bed. "Time is wasting."

He nodded, placing a single golden tipped arrow on the edge of Julia's bed. It was the same type of arrow he had shot through Velaska's heart. If necessary, Rebecca would use it to kill Julia.

"I hope it doesn't come to this," Eros said, sadly. "We have seen too much death."

I didn't want to think about it. "Well, the sooner we go, the sooner we can get back and try to save the universe."

Hephaestus had settled last on a small planet called Gilpour, close to the Source, that processed iron ore, giving him a basically unlimited supply of raw resources for his forge. However, with so few gods left, there weren't many to use them.

The Godschurch doorway let us out in the middle of a sleepy little town on the far side of Gilpour. Unfortunately, Hephaestus was halfway across the country. We took to the air to make better time and set out across the rocky terrain. The world was covered in a thick layer of soot from the refineries that pumped around the clock. Five systems' worth of ore was processed through this planet and then offloaded around the galaxy, which meant there was a ton of pollution everywhere.

"It's hard to believe we're working so hard to save them, isn't it?" Eros asked. "Humans, I mean."

"No," I replied. "I used to be one of them, you know, so I understand their appeal."

"I did not know that, actually, but even so, you have lived long. Have you not shed your love of them and grown contempt in its place?"

"Oh, I always had contempt for them, but I had a lot of love too, especially because I am flawed in every way, just like them." I shook my head. "I used to be a Devil, and the one thing I always tried to be was equitable with humanity. Even then, I didn't want them to suffer. So, no, I never did lose my love for them."

"You are blessed. Most gods grow to hate their creation."

"I didn't create humans or a planet, so they were never toys to me. I just tried to stay under the radar, which is maybe why I can still love them. They aren't playthings to me. They are living, breathing beings, and they deserve our protection, just like any parent has an obligation to their child."

"Many humans don't feel that way about their offspring. They abandon their children and treat them terribly often even if they keep them."

I smirked. "Those ones I hate." I looked down at the beacon on my tablet and realized we were almost there. "Land here."

We touched down in front of an enormous factory I immediately recognized as one the Horde used to create their god-killing weapons. However, the stench was not the goop made of souls, but something else—a tinge metallic, like the rest of the planet, but purer.

Inside, several hundred angels, imps, and devas worked the assembly line, creating weapons in a manner that did not feel much like Hephaestus to me. As long as I'd known him, he had made all of his weaponry by hand.

"Katrina?" A big, gruff-looking man with a beard and thick muscles called out from the center of the floor. "By the gods, it is you!"

It was unmistakably Hephaestus, hairy as a grizzly bear and bulky as a great ape. He pulled me into a crushing hug.

"Good to see you, too," I grunted. "Can you put me down?"

He dropped me onto the ground. "Of course. I know how little you like affection. I got carried away because it has been too long since we have seen each other. I hoped to see you one more time before the end."

I straightened out my clothes and hair he'd mussed up with his hug. "What are you doing here, buddy? This is not how I remember you working."

"Innovation, my friend. I took all of my know-how and industrialized the whole operation. The Horde gave us the tech to kill a god, but it was sloppy, unrefined." He walked over to his assembly line and pulled a sword off the line. "I have been working to integrate their tech in all my weapons so that even the lowliest imp could kill a god in a more civilized manner."

"Why would an imp want to kill a god?" Eros asked.

Hephaestus pointed the sword at him. "Who is this knave?"

I held up my hands. "Whoa, killer. He's a friend. We've come to ask you a favor."

"Of course you have."

"We need weapons."

"Weapons we have," Hephaestus said. "I have more than I could ever use, especially now."

I looked around at the factory floor, and an idea came to me. We had so few agents left, and Hephaestus employed dozens of workers. "And an army."

"Ha!" Hephaestus said. "That would be a little bit harder. Come and drink with me, and we will see what we can do."

"We don't have much time, but I always have a spare moment for a drink with an old friend." I nodded. "After that, you will help us?"

He smiled. "Only if you can hold your liquor better than you used to."

CHAPTER 56

Akta

Location: Godschurch Base

"What are we looking for?" Urania asked me as we stepped through the rift into Ananke's tea shop.

I didn't know. I hated being a detective. That was more Julia's bag. I just knew it was important to be methodical and look for clues when you had no idea where to begin. I doubted Tartarus would have spent time checking for clues. He seemed more of the steamroller type, which meant there was a good chance he missed something—or destroyed something.

"Anything that will help find where Ananke is right now," I said, as much to myself as to Urania. "Nothing is too unimportant to check. I know she's a goddess, but that doesn't mean she's perfect."

"No, it certainly doesn't," Urania said.

I turned over the table nearest the door, picked up containers, scanned napkins, kicked open the overturned counter, opened every drawer, and even looked through every recipe in the kitchen but found nothing. I walked into the kitchen and found Urania on her hands and knees, searching every piece of broken ceramic for a clue. "Any luck?" I asked.

"Nothing." She sighed before falling back on her butt. "This is hopeless."

"No, it's not. We just haven't looked everywhere. Did you ever think Ananke wants to be found, just not by Tartarus?"

"I hadn't…that seems ludicrous."

"Maybe," I said, scratching my chin. "But she's been here pushing us around and nudging us in the right direction this whole time. Why would she give up now?"

"Hrm. You make a good point."

"Where would Ananke leave a clue if she didn't want anybody else to find it?"

As I thought about it, my eyes trailed across the shop to the brick fireplace in the far wall. It was an odd thing to have in a pocket dimension, though everything about the tea shop was peculiar. It was one of the only places I had yet to check.

A black cauldron rested on a wrought-iron hearth inside the fireplace. I walked over, knelt down and felt it. The metal was cold to the touch, and even the wood and parchment that had burnt to ash underneath had lost its last embers. Out of habit, and Julia's nagging voice telling me to check everywhere no matter how stupid, I placed my hand into the flue and felt around. I patted the near wall and those on either side of me and found nothing, but when I pressed my hand against the far wall, I felt a piece of paper.

"No way," I said.

I pulled it down and unfolded it. The letter was signed by Ananke.

Very good, Akta. I see that you have learned much in your time at the Godschurch. Yes, I know you are looking for me and that you will eventually find me, so I thought we would cut the charade, yes?

*You are with Urania. Have her point her telescope, the
one in the observatory, of course, to 12 degrees right
ascension, 36 degrees declination. Find the brightest
star in the sky. I will be watching.*

***

"Have you got it calibrated yet?" I asked Urania from the
other side of the astronomy tower from where she was
working. "We don't have much time."

"Just about. Adjusting a telescope takes time, and this
one is brand new since the other one…"

"Was destroyed when we killed Gaia. Yes, I know.
How dare we succeed."

"Exactly. How dare you." She chuckled to herself. A
couple of seconds passed while Urania looked through the
eyeglass. "There we go. I believe I have found what we are
looking for."

Urania beckoned me forward, and I looked through the
eyepiece. As I did, the whiteness of the star grew until it
filled my vision. I felt my stomach lurch, and I was
suddenly outside of the astronomy tower, floating in space
for a moment, then shooting forward faster than I thought
possible. After a minute of speeding through the universe, I
crashed into the front door of an old tea shop on the
crumbling remains of an ancient planet.

"Ah, well there you are. Took you a while, though only
a fraction of the time you would have taken had I not
intervened." Ananke was smiling at me, pristine and
dressed in shimmering white.

"You're crazy," I said, pulling out my knives. "I won't
let you destroy the universe."

"Ha!" she said. "If I wanted the universe gone, I would have gone into the Source and woken Chaos when I left my pocket dimension, wouldn't I?"

I thought for a moment. She wasn't wrong. "I suppose so."

"So, the fact that I am here, having a lovely, though quite stale, cuppa, must mean I don't want it destroyed, correct?"

"It makes logical sense. Then why would Eros say that you did?" I asked. "He said he built the church to stop you."

"Oh, he did." Ananke set down her teacup. "He and the others did not like that I was playing both halves against the center, as it were."

"Speak English."

"Don't you see? Gaia and Nyx want to destroy the universe, but so do Eros and Tartarus, just for different reasons, or should I say, for the same reason. Control of the future."

"What do you mean?"

"Whoever wakes Chaos will be endowed with the power of creation. A new universe will dance in their mind, and they will have the ability to mold it in any way they see fit. They all, each one, want that power, which is why I came up with a compromise to stave off the inevitable."

"What did you do?"

"Each would give themselves to the cosmos, play their part, seed their young, and allow the universe to flourish."

"You are the one that forced them to dissipate their auras."

She smiled sweetly at me before taking another sip of stale tea. "Not forced, dear, just lovingly convinced. I also got them to agree not to hurt each other while they watched the universe play out. Then, in the end, they could fight it out again for control."

"This is the end?"

"Heavens no, but it seems that Eros got bored and leaped into action, which forced Nyx and Gaia into action, or perhaps it was vice versa. It's hard to know who started it, but they all played their part to get us to this point, which forced my hand to activate you all. I thought we had more time."

"Except that Gaia is on our team now. Julia has—"

She swiped her hand at me dismissively. "Oh dear, is that what you believe? Gaia is far too powerful to be contained in a human soul. She is manipulating our dear Julia so that she can rise again and enter the Source with Nyx at the opportune moment."

"So that is their game, to enter the Source."

"Their game is the end game."

"What will happen at the end?"

Ananke picked up her tea. "That all depends on Katrina."

"Katrina? Why?"

Ananke flicked her tongue at the acrid tea. "I'm afraid I've said too much, and now, you must go. Feel free to tell Rebecca where you found me. I promise I won't be here when you come, and you'll waste precious time on me while the real threat is out there."

I started to speak, but she snapped her fingers, and I was gone.

CHAPTER 57

Rebecca

Location: Godschurch Base

I walked into the lab with my stomach lodged in my throat. We were running out of options for how to fight Nyx, who had destroyed over 85 percent of the universe already, and there was less and less of it to fight for with each passing moment.

"Please tell me you have something," I said to the beleaguered and overworked lab techs barely able to stand at attention when I walked into the room.

I felt bad for them. They had been working around the clock to analyze the Darkness goop from Kimberly's scythe. One of the techs, Haga, a slight man with thick glasses, turned to me. "It simultaneously matches every substance we ever tested against it and is like nothing we have ever seen before."

"Explain that again, more slowly."

"It's formed out of the same stuff as the whole universe. There is a little bit of every building block material contained inside this Darkness, but watch this…" He took a dropper of the Darkness and squeezed it in a petri dish. We watched as the single drop overtook everything inside of it. "It is only contained by the constraints of its container. A single drop of the Darkness could destroy this Godschurch easily."

"How do we stop it?" I asked without taking my eyes off the petri dish.

"I think we have an answer, maybe." A woman with a stocky build and flyaway hair walked over with a blaster. Her name was Giselle, I remembered. "Well, as you so astutely determined, a ray from the sun damages it." She fired a small beam of light at the Darkness. "You see that while it's active, the Darkness cannot grow anymore. However, when you turn it off...watch." She demonstrated. "It grows once again, almost immediately."

"Yup, you're right. I already knew that. So, we have no way to stop the Darkness for good."

"Not necessarily," Haga said. "Sunlight is not the purest form of light in the universe. The Source is."

Haga turned on another light, this one pure white, and again the Darkness stopped growing. However, when he turned off the light, the Darkness no longer came back.

My eyes widened. "This is brilliant. If we have it go into the Source, it's dead."

Giselle shook her head. "No, that won't be good enough. If the Darkness comes in contact with the light of the Source, there is a 50 percent chance that it will corrupt the Source for good."

"Then we need to weaponize it," I said.

"We have started that process. We gave a prototype to Kimberly to try if she manages to get into the Darkness. However, the light is so pure that it vaporizes everything we put it up against if it's any bigger than the light beam we just used. You need somebody who can tap into the Source themselves."

"Who?"

Haga shook his head. "Somebody more powerful and pure than Apollo. Somebody who can connect directly with the Source."

"Thank you. Keep working."

I walked out of the lab and into the bullpen. Everybody had deep bags under their eyes that weren't there before the last few days forced us to work brutal hours to make up for the productivity of our lost brothers. Nobody complained because it was better to be overworked than dead, but that math was changing as the exhaustion set in around the base.

"Edgar!" I called. "I need your help."

He spun around. He could barely keep his head up as he looked at me. "Of course you do. What can I do for you?"

"Can you pull up a database of the gods that are left alive?" I asked.

"Sure thing." He typed on his computer. The main viewer in front of him lit up, and a list of gods appeared. "Filtering out all the gods that have died by our hand, their worlds being destroyed, or were killed by Projekt Kaos, that leaves…seventeen gods."

"SEVENTEEN! In the whole universe. There were thousands just a couple of days ago."

"I-I-I—yes. It looks that way." He typed into his computer again. "I'm double checking my math, ma'am, but my calculations are always impeccable, as you know. It wouldn't be off by more than a few—nope. Flawless. Man, if there was a time I wished I was wrong, it's right now."

I stepped closer to the monitor and squinted at the list of names. "Wait…" One name caught my attention. Indra. It showed his location was unknown. "How does that happen? How can we not know where he is? This system is supposed to know everything."

"I have supposed that there could be a pocket dimension or something. But as you can see, most of the gods here must have their own pocket dimension cuz all of their locations are unknown. Except for Kimberly, Katrina, and Urania, of course."

That was it. He was a god of the light, and he was hiding out…because he knew someday that we would need him. That's why he was so weird to Katrina and why he refused to help. He knew one day we would have no choice but to call on him to save the world…I couldn't believe it, but my mouth actually formed a smile. We finally might have caught a break. Perhaps Cronus was trying to help us after all.

CHAPTER 58

Julia

Location: Primera

The earth screamed out to me when I placed my feet upon the planet. The ground gave a bitter tremble as I reached down and placed my hand on it. It was in incredible pain.

"Be still," I whispered to it, and as if by command, it stopped shaking, calming itself under my touch. "That's good. I'm here."

The earth was joyful as I stood atop it, like an excited puppy greeting its master after they came back from a long trip. Grass grew again under my feet, and a meadow burst forth from my fingertips.

It was beautiful magic. I had never seen such wonderous use of the god's gift. Usually, I was investigating a war or stopping a terrorist attack, and yet, here, in this moment, the power was used for creation in its purest form, love.

I always felt the gods worked too much from a place of vanity, even down to the humans and monsters they made in their image. Watching the grass, flowers, and trees grow from Gaia's gifts brought me to tears.

"So," a booming screech came from above me. I looked up to see two glowing purple eyes in the Darkness. "She truly is dead, then. A pity."

It was time. I stood up and pressed my feet firmly on the ground. "She is, and I have her power now."

"A bit scrawny, aren't you?"

"I promise, Nyx, you won't feel that way when I'm done with you." I cracked my knuckles. I felt the power flow through me, and I instinctively knew how to command it. "I will not let you past me."

"A fight?" Nyx said with a scoff. "You can't be serious. I am the Darkness. I am everything and nothing at once."

"And I have the power of the earth. I won't let you destroy this planet."

"You have already done quite the job of destroying it. Outside of the meadow you stand in, the rest of the planet, every planet I've come across this day has been destroyed, cracked in half from negligence—your negligence." Nyx took a deep breath. "There are another hundred more planets gone from the universe. Do you feel them?"

I winced, dropping to my knees. A shudder ran through me as if the power I was trying to contain was fighting for control of me. I had to struggle against it. I couldn't let Nyx win. I couldn't let her unite with Gaia.

I pushed myself up to stand and sent two enormous oaks up from seed to stab at the Darkness.

"Ha!" Nyx said. "As if that could hurt me."

I smiled. "That was just the distraction."

I pulled the light gun out of the holster on my hip and fired at her. Far from the cackle she had been emitting for the last thirty seconds, the sound that came from her when I fired my blaster was more of a shriek. A small hole grew in the Darkness, and behind it, I could see the stars.

"Enough!" Nyx said. The trees were ripped from their roots, rose into the air, and then fell onto me. My first instinct was to run, but that came from my former self. Now, I had the power over everything in the earth. All I had to do was raise my arms, and the trees fell gently on either side of my body.

I closed my eyes and felt the heat boil inside of me. When I released it, every geyser and volcano on the planet shot into the air, causing another shriek from Nyx. It was working. I was growing strong, and every time I used my powers, the pain ripping through my body settled.

"Not bad," Nyx said. "But I have battled Gaia at the height of her powers, and she always succumbed to me. Only the light stands a chance, and I have grown too powerful to be stopped by it."

I fired my blaster into the air again, and Nyx's eyes disappeared into the Darkness. "Funny," I said. "Seems like it still hurts you."

I fell to the ground again with another wave of pain. The power growing inside of me pulsated through my body and made my blood hot. I looked down to see boils growing on my skin.

"A thousand more," Nyx grumbled. "You will soon break apart, and her power will be mine, or she will rise up and unite with me."

"No!" I screamed.

I slammed my hands on the ground, and water formed from my fingers. A lake grew around me, and I used it to cool myself down. For a moment, it worked, but then another surge grew in me, and I screamed from the pain. The water around me began to bubble until I could no longer stand it and burst through the lake into the air.

"You poor fool," Nyx said. "You were just a pawn in all of this. I almost feel bad for you, had you not chosen your side."

The pain was almost too much to bear. "I choose the side of the light. I choose the side of humanity. I choose the side of good."

Nyx chuckled again. "My love, there is no good or evil. There is only power. If only you understood that during your life."

My knees buckled under me. "I understand people like you think that's all there is, but I believe there is more."

"And yet power is why you will be ripped apart. Not the power of a god, or a Titan, not the watered-down power of those you serve, but true power, the power of existence itself, and now…you feel it as it rips you apart."

I couldn't stand it anymore. She was about to kill me. I felt myself losing consciousness. I closed my eyes and teleported myself to the Godschurch. I screamed out at the sparsely populated bullpen.

"Rebecca! Rebecca!"

She rushed out from her office. "Julia!"

"Do it!" I screamed. "We don't have much time. Use the arrow!" I pointed to the golden-tipped arrow sitting atop Edgar's desk. "Do it now, or there's nothing I can— AHHHH!!"

Another jolt of pain, and I vomited. The pain was too terrible for me to even think. I fell over, crying into my own sick. Rebecca didn't hesitate. She was a stone-cold killer. She rushed to the arrow and nocked it in the bow Eros left for her.

"I'm sorry." Rebecca pulled back and loosed the arrow.

My arm worked without me. It reached over and snatched the arrow out of the air.

"Fool," my mouth said without me making the words. "You dare try to kill me. I am the earth. I am the ground. I am Gaia."

The light went from my eyes, and I found myself falling away. Gaia was in control now, and the Godschurch would certainly fall. The powers I had felt surging through my body were incredible, and I barely knew how to control them. Gaia, on the other hand, knew how. And now she was in control of my body in the last place in the universe which was protected from Nyx. With a mere flick of her wrist, Gaia could change that, let Nyx in, and corrupt the Source.

CHAPTER 59

Kimberly

Location: Godschurch Base

"I'm bored!" Tartarus said, standing behind the grate of the weapons locker. He didn't fit through the door, so I was forced to look for the hammer myself while he waited by the entrance. "I dislike standing around and waiting."

I raised my eyebrow. "Well, if you weren't so big and bulky, then you could help me."

Tartarus growled. "I am the way I was built."

There was usually an agent working the records desk. It was one of the worst jobs in the whole Godschurch, or so Julia told me. She was often assigned to it when she misbehaved, so frequently. Since Nyx's attack, though, there was little help anywhere as the church was stretched thin. My own reapers were pulling most of the security duty on the remaining gods, but they were not fighters. They were bureaucrats if anything. They did not kill. They dealt with the dead.

I found the electronic records log, finally, and Julia's password allowed me access. She hadn't changed her password in ten thousand years, which had to be some kind of security hazard. *Scooby-Doo* hadn't been a show for millennia, so I suppose it was effective…unless you happened to watch it at her house with her after a night of patrolling, back when you were both alive.

"Did your hammer have a special name?" I asked.

"No," Tartarus said. "When it was created, it was the only one in existence. I simply called it 'my hammer'."

Since the hammer wasn't in the weapons room, it had to either be checked out, or the Godschurch didn't have a record of it, which I had trouble believing. I typed in "Tartarus" as it seemed to be the most likely way it was categorized.

Sure enough, the name came up. "It looks like Anubis deposited your hammer in the Godschurch a million generations ago. It was checked out by a god named Sucellus after he lost his hammer at the Battle of the Obelisk, and he's been using it since then."

"Where is this Sucellus?" Tartarus asked, fist in his palm.

***

"He's dead," Edgar told me, completing a rotation in his chair on his way back to his desk. "They're all dead. All but these seventeen." Edgar squinted at the screen. "Sorry, fourteen."

"Where was the last place he lived before he died?" I asked.

He typed into his computer. "Fwyvern…and it's been destroyed by Nyx. Thus, why he is listed as dead."

"Give me a location. I'm going after it," I said.

"And I'm going with you," Tartarus added.

"It's dangerous in there, and Nyx will be after us before long, especially if I show up with an enormous black-armored, fire-faced Primordial."

"Then let her come, and I will face her."

I held up my hands in defeat. "Whatever floats your boat."

Edgar gave me the coordinates, and I teleported both myself and Tartarus to the place where the planet should be. When we arrived, there was nothing but dark. I used my scythe to cut open the veil separating us from the Darkness, then pushed it open and stepped inside. The air was danker on the other side of the veil and more humid. It smelt of burnt toast and overripe bananas, like a garbage dump.

I felt the planet under me. It was there, just covered in sludge. Black, inky ooze covered everything and pulsated to close the wound I had left by penetrating the veil. In short order, it would consume Tartarus and me. Luckily, Haga had given me a new toy to use. I just hoped it worked.

"Let's cross our fingers that she's too distracted to feel this."

I pulled out the small laser that Haga made from the light of the Source and used it to cut away at the tar, making a hole big enough for us to navigate through. I stepped into it, slowly and painstakingly slicing my way through the disgusting ooze inch by inch. The sludge undulated around me as I bore into it. Then, the ooze ceased in front of me and was replaced by the window of a building.

"Break this!" I shouted at Tartarus.

Tartarus pulled back and smashed through the window, and we ducked inside as our path through the ooze collapsed behind us. The sludge hadn't penetrated inside the tall building as it had the rest of the planet. The façade of the building was slowly eroding, though. Like stomach acid, the goop was eating away at the planet. It was slow work, as the planet was massive. Perhaps, if we could defeat Nyx quickly, we could save it.

"Wait here," I said to Tartarus.

I opened my notebook and reviewed the coordinates where Sucellus had been when he died. Hopefully, my calculations were correct.

"Please be a house."

I closed my eyes and teleported there. Luckily, when I reappeared, I was inside a house. Black ooze pressed against the glass windows in its living room, the pressure causing it to wheeze and creak. The house was massive, sleek, and modern, but a slow drip of black ooze onto the floor meant it would soon be eaten through.

"Hey!" a voice shouted behind me. "What are you doing here? Thief!"

"I'm not a thief," I said, turning to see a fat, bearded man eating a bowl of cereal. "Wait, are you Sucellus?"

"I go by Steven now, but yes, that's me." He shoveled a spoonful of cereal into his mouth. "What's it to you, thief?"

"What are you doing eating a bowl of cereal?"

He took another spoonful into his mouth and chewed. "Well, I'm hungry, and it's not like I'm going anywhere any time soon. This might be my last meal, so I'm going to enjoy it. I haven't had carbs in months."

"Whatever. Do you still have the hammer you took from the Godschurch?"

He shook his head. "By the gods, you couldn't possibly be here to repossess it. The world ended! Get over it."

"Would you shut up and just answer my question? If you do have it, maybe I can fix all of this before the Darkness swallows you. Maybe your world doesn't have to end. Maybe the universe doesn't have to end."

Sucellus shrugged and took another bite of cereal. "Over there."

I hurried across the room to a glass trophy case. In the center of it was a massive hammer, twice as big as me, made of black obsidian and covered in complex runes all the way down the hilt. I smashed through the glass and picked up the ax from the mandibles that held it in place. It was lighter than I imagined.

"Hey!" Sucellus shouted. "That's private property."

"With all due respect, shut up."

I snapped away, back to the building from whence I came. When I reappeared, I heard Tartarus's thunderous scream echo through the building.

"Get off me, witch!" Tartarus screamed. He was being dragged down into the tar just like I had been once.

"Tartarus!" I shouted.

"You!" Nyx called out. "I wondered who was piercing through the veil. I knew Tartarus was too dumb to do it himself."

"Use the hammer!" Tartarus said.

He didn't have to tell me twice. I gripped the hammer tightly and slammed it onto the ground. The thunderous shock rippled through the Darkness and released him. I reached out to pull him to his feet and pushed him through the Darkness back to the universe. We snapped away to the Godschurch.

Rebecca was in the middle of the bullpen, staring at me with horror.

"They're not dead," I screamed, standing up. "They're not gone. The planets. They're still in the Darkness. If we can kill Nyx, maybe we can get them back." Rebecca didn't reply. She just pointed at something behind me.

I turned to see Julia's eyes, glowing green, with a sinister expression on her face. "Well, that is very good news. Too bad the universe will soon be ended, and none of this will matter."

CHAPTER 60

Rebecca

Location: Godschurch Base

"Get them into Ananke's pocket dimension!" I screamed as Gaia and Tartarus took sides on either side of the bullpen. If they fought, it could blow up the whole Godschurch in a matter of seconds, and I knew the Primordials wouldn't care about our puny lives.

"I'll get Julia—Gaia!" Kimberly said.

She bum-rushed Gaia and grabbed her by the leg, and then disappeared with her with the snap of her fingers. Meanwhile, I pulled Tartarus and flashed to the tea shop.

When I arrived a moment later in Ananke's pocket dimension with Tartarus, Kimberly was ducking for her life from a boulder that Gaia flung at her. Tartarus immediately broke from my grip and barreled toward Gaia.

"Come on," I shouted, pulling Kimberly to the edge of the portal. "Let them fight it out." I pulled her through the portal and back to the Godschurch cafeteria. "Close it up."

"Are you sure?"

"Yes!" I replied. "We can open it again when we have a solution. By then, hopefully, Tartarus would have won."

"That's Julia!" Kimberly screamed, gesturing at the plaid portal leading back to the tea shop. "She's my friend! I can't just—"

"Not anymore, she's not. Now she's a vengeful primordial deity," I said. "Spare me the sanctimony. Close it up."

"I don't work for you," she growled.

"You know I'm right. Quit letting your emotions control your decisions. Lock them inside before we can't anymore."

"Fine," Kimberly grumbled. She didn't say another word. She simply sewed up the rift to the pocket dimension, and the plaid light vanished, leaving both Tartarus and Gaia inside battling to the death. When she was finished, she turned to me. "What now?"

"We need to find Indra and hope that he has a way out of this."

"Indra? Again with him?"

"We're running out of hope, and there's only a dozen or so gods left. If he doesn't have a way to weaponize the Source, then I fear nobody does. At least, nobody who is left. All the other remaining gods are lowly deities, none powerful enough to understand the power of the Source."

"Good luck," Kimberly said.

"Come with me. He won't entreat with me alone. I'm just a human, but with another god…"

"I. do not. Work for you!" she said through gritted teeth.

"I'm not asking for you as an agent, but as a friend."

"We aren't friends."

"Then as somebody that doesn't want the universe to end."

"Fine."

***

Bang. Bang. Bang.

It was easier than we expected to find Indra's pocket dimension. It moved to avoid the Darkness, but with Nyx destroying more of the universe every minute, the search area became smaller, and so we were able to track the anomaly.

"I'm not coming out, Nyx!" Indra screamed from inside the dimension. "Quit asking."

"This isn't Nyx. It's Rebecca, director of the Godschurch, and—"

"Kimberly, goddess of Death," Kimberly added before I could introduce her.

"Kimberly?" Indra said. "That's not a very scary name for what should be a frightening goddess."

"We've changed our image. Death isn't supposed to be scary, now."

Indra snorted behind the door. "Well, if you are here to kill me, you can forget it. I'm not coming out."

"We're not trying to do either of those things. We need to talk to you about stopping Nyx."

The door popped open, and two dark red arms reached out and yanked us both inside the door. Indra's pocket dimension was nice, serene even. We stood outside a cabin next to a crystal-clear lake. Sitting on a large pillow and smoking a hookah, Indra, red-bodied with four arms and gold necklaces resting on his hairy chest, sat looking at us.

"What do you know of my destiny with Nyx?"

I looked at Kimberly. "Nothing. We just need some help, you know, stopping the universe from ending."

Indra blew a cloud of cherry-smelling hookah out of his nose. "I believe you. Ananke told me I would be asked twice for help before the end, and the second time, I would see Death. She is never wrong."

"And what did she say after that?" I asked.

"She said that I would make a choice. Die to protect the universe, or watch it descend into chaos."

"Cryptic. That sounds like her."

"I have chosen to let it descend into chaos. Thus the pocket dimension, where I can live in peace. You're welcome to stay. My last girlfriend didn't work out, and I could use some companionship."

Kimberly narrowed her eyes. "I'm sorry, but I don't consort with cowards."

He snorted hookah into his nose, forcing him to choke. "Cowards? I am no coward! I'm the most intelligent being in the universe for not getting involved with this garbage. What do you know about bravery anyway?"

"I know all about bravery because I know death. I have seen the brave face their deaths like cowards and the meek face it like heroes, but they all faced it, one way or another."

"I'm immortal. '*Im*' meaning NOT, and 'mortal,' meaning something that dies. I am NOT something that dies. I am not supposed to have to deal with death. That's the whole gods-damned point."

"Most of the other gods are dead already. Only a handful in the universe are still alive," Kimberly said. "If we can find a way to fight Nyx and pull the planets she's consumed out of the Darkness, we might be able to save them before they're digested."

Indra stood up. "Nyx is the worst goddess that has ever existed. She is evil and wants nothing but destruction. She has always wanted it to end. Now she will get her wish."

"And yet the universe has continued for epochs," I replied. "What's been keeping her in check?"

Indra took another puff of his hookah and blew it out. When he did, the smoke formed into a scale. "Balance. The gods have always loved balance. For life, there was death. For day, there was night. For light, there was dark. While the universe was in balance, Nyx could not make her move, trapped by the balance she revered. Something must have happened to tip the universe out of balance. Any idea what that might have been?"

Rebecca looked at me. "I mean, the Horde killing gods. Cronus returning. The Godless. Could be a lot of things."

He spun his hookah in his hand. "Interesting. Killing gods could have certainly tipped the universe into chaos. The gods are like counterweights on each other, and their deaths, especially at an incredible rate, could tip the balance." He stopped spinning the hookah and clamped it in his hand. "All the more reason why I must keep my finger on the scale and not die."

"Then Nyx will reach the Source, corrupt it, and end the universe, and you along with it."

"What difference does it make?" Indra said. "Either way, I die."

"But whether you die a hero or a coward," Kimberly said, "is up to you."

He sneered. "I don't care how people see me. Death is death, and what is there after death for a god?"

I stepped forward. "Even a god returns to the Source to be reborn again, so long as they are not corrupted. Come on, you've lived a long time. Don't you ever get curious about the great beyond and what's waiting for you out there?"

"No." He blew another puff of smoke from his hookah. "I do hate Nyx, though, more than anything, and it would almost be worth dying to see the look on her face knowing that I was the reason she died." Indra looked at me. "My weapon is a piece of me. The vajra is my essence, made of the light directly from the Source. It is as pure a light as has ever existed. With it, you can kill Nyx if you can get her into her goddess form."

I held out my hand. "Then give us the weapon, and we will leave you here."

"It doesn't work like that. I imbue my godhood into the weapon. To defeat Nyx, I will have to give you everything I have." Indra sighed. "I will die."

Kimberly knelt. "And then you will go into the beyond."

"Is it beautiful?"

Kimberly smiled. "As beautiful as anything you will ever see. It is worth death to stare at it for just one moment."

Indra nodded. He pulled out a golden club, inlaid with markings, with a ribbed spherical head on either side. He placed it into my hands, and I was struck with how small it was.

"You will be there with me?" Indra said.

Kimberly looked into his face. "I will guide you the whole way to the great beyond, like an old friend."

"That sounds nice." Indra smiled and placed his hand on the vajra. "Then let us begin. Do not let my death be in vain."

"I won't."

CHAPTER 61

Katrina

Location: Hephaestus's Armory

"This is beautiful," I said, holding the flaming sword in my hand. "It's just like the Sword of Damocles that I used to wield, but lighter somehow."

"I thought you would like it," Hephaestus said. "I'm afraid it's got far fewer folds than I would like since we're on a time crunch, but I had to forge it by hand for old time's sake. These old bones are not what they used to be. I have more arrows for Eros. Plus, there are enough extra weapons to outfit an army."

"Good," I replied. "We're going to need them."

"What is happening out there, Katrina? I have holed myself up for good reason, away from the gods, but is it true that the universe is at an end?"

I grinned. "Not if I have anything to say about it." I stopped myself for a moment. "You know, with your help, we stand a chance. You've done a big thing for the universe today. Why don't you ask all your angels and devas to join with me and fight the Darkness? It's coming for us all, anyway."

Hephaestus took his hammer into his hands. "It is my great honor to fight for my universe once again."

Hephaestus, Eros, and I brought the swords and other weapons outside and gave them to his workers. They were a ruddy lot, but they would have to do because we were running out of options. We needed every possible hand left.

Eros stood atop the pile of weapons. "I know you haven't fought in a long time, and many of you likely worked here to avoid the fight, but it is coming to your doorstep any moment. Fighting is the only choice we have left."

I looked up into the sky after we finished arming Hephaestus's people, and the few remaining stars vanished, cloaked in sackcloth as Nyx's darkness came for the planet. I turned to my newly-minted troops. "We will make our stand at the Source. One last stand for the universe."

***

I dropped a pile of weapons in the middle of the Godschurch. "Everybody take one and get ready to fight. Nyx can't be more than an hour away."

Edgar picked up a sword. "I'm not much of a fighter. None of us are."

Eros placed his hand on Edgar's shoulder. "I know, but there's not much choice. We must be strong and hearty to protect the universe from Nyx and Gaia."

I pushed Eros's hand off Edgar's shoulder and spun the computer analyst around so that he was facing me. "Call us every agent, deva, angel, and Valkyrie left in the universe. We have one shot at stopping her, and this is where we're most protected, so it will be where we take our stand."

As Edgar walked back to his desk, a light flashed, and both Kimberly and Rebecca flickered into the bullpen. Rebecca fell onto the cache of weapons with a loud crash.

"What is all of this?" she asked, pulling herself out of the pile.

"It's time to end this once and for all." I turned to Kimberly. "Are there any reapers left?"

"Some, but they have lost the will to fight," she replied.

"Get them back here. We're going to need them all to defend the Source." I turned to Rebecca. "How did you do?"

She held a two-sided mace in her hand. She twisted it in her hand, and brilliant white light came out of it. "It is Indra's vajra. This should be able to injure Nyx permanently if she breaks through the barrier."

"Ha!" Hephaestus shouted. "I know that weapon. I studied under its maker. It is imbued with the power of the god's essence, which comes straight from the Source."

I looked down at the cache of weapons. "Any chance you could take the power from this weapon and imbue it into all of these ones?" I pointed outside to the Source. "Or with that, so we stand a chance against Nyx."

"I believe I can," Hephaestus said. "But it will destroy the vajra."

"If it must be done." Rebecca tossed the vajra to Hephaestus. "Then get to it."

Eros scratched his head. "And where is Tartarus?"

"He's battling Gaia in Ananke's dimension," Rebecca said.

"Alone!" Eros said. "I must go to him."

Rebecca pressed her hand into Eros's chest, trying to stop him. "They're trapped in there. It was the safest option for us. Otherwise, we would have had two Primordials ripping this place apart."

"And all you risked was my friend?" Eros said. "I will not stand by while he fights that shrew. As two against one, and with the weapons we have brought, we could end Gaia once and for all."

"He's right," I said. "If we take on Gaia together, we can bring her down."

"That's still Julia," Kimberly said. "We can't kill her."

Rebecca gave Kimberly a hard look. "I know how you feel, but she made a choice, and you know she wouldn't want the universe to end by her hand, would she?"

Kimberly shook her head. "No. She wouldn't."

"Then we have to stop her." Rebecca turned to Eros. "We'll go in there once everybody is armed and ready for a fight."

"Very well," Eros said. "If he dies, it will be on your head."

"I have enough god's deaths on my conscience. Trust me, I have no desire for more blood to soil my hands."

***

There were few angels, Valkyrie, devas, or reapers left in the cosmos, but we were able to cobble together a little more than a hundred of them, mixed with a couple dozen demons, and stationed them floating outside the Godschurch with blasters and swords.

What remained of our own agents waited inside the Godschurch, dressed in spacesuits and carrying light blasters, while the whole Godschurch was being protected with Urania's telescopes, arranged in a 365-degree barrier around us and the Source. With any luck, they would shield us from Nyx, who was moments away.

I took a last look at the few stars that remained, knowing that any minute they would be blotted out. I just hoped that we would be able to defeat Nyx before she corrupted the Source. I hoped we could rescue the universe yet again.

"Were you ever going to tell me that you killed my girlfriend?" Urania said as she walked up to me.

"I didn't kill your girlfriend. I was just there when it happened," I replied.

"Was it your stupid plan that got her killed?" Urania's hands were shaking with frustration.

"Yes, it was."

"Then who killed her doesn't matter. You were supposed to look out for her, and instead, she's dead, and I blame you." She crossed her arms over her chest. "You were just going to let me go to my death thinking she was alive or hating you for not telling me about it."

I spun to face her. "You were always going to go to your death hating me. I figured I didn't have to see the hate in your eyes when I told you."

"I don't hate you, Katrina. I just think you can be a dick sometimes." Urania tried to smile, unsuccessfully. Then her face turned down. "Did she suffer?"

I shook my head. "It was a good death, as far as deaths go. I was there at the end. Eros was kind in that she didn't suffer."

"And you trust him, even though he killed my love?"

I shook my head more vehemently. "Absolutely not, but I trust Gaia and Nyx less. At least Eros and Tartarus have tried to save the universe. It's not much, but it's something."

She sighed. "I miss her."

"I miss her, too." I wrapped Urania in a hug. I longed for her so much, and if I didn't see her ever again, I wanted her to know it. Still, I couldn't make the words escape my lips. Instead, I just gave a smile and wiped the tears from her eyes. "Let's hope we get the chance to miss her for a long time yet."

"Hey!" I heard from behind me. I turned to see Kimberly. "It's time. Let's go."

I let go of Urania. It was the hardest moment of my eternal life. "Be careful."

Urania smiled back at me. "I would tell you to do the same, but I know that's impossible."

There was more to say, but I walked off without saying goodbye. If I did, the tears welling in my eyes would cascade down my face, and I didn't want that while I was about to face my death and the potential destruction of everything I held dear.

I met Rebecca, Eros, and the others in the cafeteria, and we gathered in a semi-circle, prepared for a fight. Kimberly walked to the center and pulled a plaid seam out of midair.

"Ready?" she said.

I pulled out my flaming sword. The others did the same, and the glow of our weapons gave the room a golden hue.

"Ready," I replied.

Kimberly nodded and cut open the seam. As she did, a bright light filled the room, but it was not the plaid one from the seam. It shone from behind us for a flash of a moment. When the light dissipated, Akta was standing behind us.

"Wait!" she shouted. "Eros is not fighting to save the universe. He wants to destroy it as badly as Nyx and Gaia, but just for his own ends!"

The rest of us looked over at Eros, and a creepy smile rose on his face. "Damn. You figured it out. Luckily, it's too late to stop me now."

As I took a slice at Eros, Tartarus bowled me over on his way out of the pocket dimension. He was melded together with Gaia in an epic struggle that rolled them across the cafeteria. As they struggled with each other, their weight smashed through the window and fell off the edge of the Godschurch, where they continued their fight amidst the stars. Eros leaped out after them to join the fray, firing at reapers and angels alike as he went.

We watched the Primordials battle each other, and what stars remained in the universe blacked out, leaving nothing but the Source for light.

Nyx was here.

Gaia, Tartarus, and Eros made their way to the Source, fighting for who would rightly end the universe.

It had begun. The last battle we might ever undertake.

Now was the time to risk everything for the sake of the universe.

This was our last stand.

CHAPTER 62

Akta

Location: Godschurch Base

"Don't let them get to the Source!" Katrina screamed as she tumbled out of the Godschurch through the window Tartarus and Gaia had broken through. She fell into space after them.

I opened my wings and flew out as well. Aside from the brightness coming from the Source and the light from the telescopes protecting us from the Darkness, there was no light out in space. I was used to seeing millions of stars reflected back upon me, but now there was nothing except overwhelming gloom.

"Do not allow Nyx to breach the telescopes!" Kimberly shouted to her band of reapers, who fired light guns through the barrier. Her people were not very good shots, but they didn't need to be very good. All they needed to do was hit the air, and they hit Nyx. Meanwhile, any errant shots created obstacles between the other Primordials and the Source.

"Akta!" Rebecca shouted, pointing past me. "Gaia is nearing the telescopes. You can't let her break them apart, or Nyx will be able to enter the Source."

"I'm on it." I nodded and flew toward Gaia, who wore the face of my Julia, as she kicked and fought against Tartarus and Eros. She was on her way toward the telescopes that bound Nyx away from the Source. I preferred my daggers, but I had exchanged them for a bow and blaster, which were more effective at long range. Plus, they could kill a god, which my daggers could not.

Eros took his bow and fired it at Gaia as she struck Tartarus with a thick bramble of thorny vines. My heart jumped into my throat as I watched the arrows embed into her back and heard Julia's voice scream out in agony. I wanted to help my friend. I gasped, watching her reach back and pull them out of her back as if it were no more painful than a simple splinter.

"What sorcery is this?" Eros shouted. "That should have killed you easily!"

"Thank you for these!" She cackled before flinging the arrows at the telescopes around her.

"Fire!" I shouted at an angel next to me. He turned and shot at the arrows, hitting one before it felled the telescope. I fired at another arrow before it hit the target.

There was still one more arrow, and it found its intended mark. A piece of the barrier fell, and that was all that Nyx needed to seep inside.

CHAPTER 63

Julia

Location: Space

"Stop!" I screamed inside my own head as loud as I could. I had no control over my body, but I still tried to pull my arms and legs away and take back my own agency. Tartarus reared back and punched me square in the gut. I felt every agonizing blow rippling through my body.

I could think straight, but I couldn't think hard enough to gain back control. Thousands of years ago, Kimberly had been bombarded by the mind of Death, but she was able to gain control of it and keep control as Conquest, Famine, and War each tried to take control of her consciousness as well. I always thought her a freak of nature to be able to withstand that kind of mental onslaught, and now I knew the depths of the struggle she overcame. She had a will I could never match.

I felt Gaia's power surge through me every time I tried to move independently of her, like a shock collar reminding me that I didn't have the capacity to stop her. I had no energy to fight.

"Let me go!" I screamed into the abyss of my own mind.

A searing pain shot into me, and a moment later, Gaia pulled three arrows out of her back. Blood gushed out of the holes they left. My body couldn't take much more abuse. Perhaps Gaia was immortal, but I was not, and I felt myself falling apart.

Gaia raised her hand and flung the arrows toward the telescopes protecting us from Nyx. "NO!"

I tried to grab them back with my arm, but I couldn't do anything. They were gone. I heard Akta shout out, and one of the arrows blew up in midair before another one was hit by Akta's deadly accurate aim, but the last one found its target, and with that, the entirety of the grid began to fail. Nyx seeped in through the hole in our barrier.

"Ah," Gaia said, deflecting Tartarus's strike as she watched the ooze soak in through the gap in our shield. "You have come back, sister, to honor our agreement."

"Agreement?" I asked her, even though I had no expectation that she would speak to me. "What agreement?"

"Quiet, mortal," Gaia hissed as she flew toward the opening in our shield. As she did, a tall, statuesque woman materialized. She had flowing black hair and was wearing a long black cape.

"I am here," Nyx said with a grunt. "Let us finish this as it began and send this universe into nothingness."

"Only to remake it in our images," Gaia said.

"What are you talking about?" I screamed inside my own head.

Gaia sighed. "Will you please shut up?"

A shock ran through me, so painful that I could only whimper. I lost all hope of control at that moment. My body was flying more quickly than I ever had before. My poor eyes could not keep up with the movement as we neared the Source.

CHAPTER 64

Kimberly

Location: Space

"Form up!" I screamed. "Do not let them through your ranks! Reapers around the edges, angels and devas in the middle! Valkyries, around them!"

I didn't know what I was doing. I wasn't a general. I just knew we had to prevent the Primordials from entering the Source, and I was doing the best I could by collecting a small squad around the entrance to the Source. We barely masked a small portion of its surface. Aside from Rebecca, I was the only Godschurch associate left with any experience leading people, even if until now I had been a peacetime bureaucrat.

"Aim your fire at the Darkness coming toward us!" I pointed to a group of reapers stationed in front of the Source. "When one group runs out of ammo, switch with the group behind you!" I pointed to a group of angels. "When they get close enough, you all charge forward and attack them hand to hand."

I couldn't swing a sword any better than I could reap a field, but guns had a simple point and click interface which anybody could use, and I fired at the Primordials.

"Next line!" I shouted. "Open fire!"

We fired our guns, but they could have been water pistols. We fired fruitlessly all the same.

When the Primordials charged closer, I yelled into the air, "ATTACK!" The troops flew out valiantly, but we were no match for them, and the Primordials easily barreled through them.

All we could do was brace for impact and hope our line would hold. "Grab onto each other!"

The shockwave as they tore through our line sent a ripple through my body so powerful that I could do nothing but scream and fall into the blackness of the universe, my eyes squeezed shut.

CHAPTER 65

Rebecca

Location: Space

There wasn't enough time to prepare. There was never enough time to prepare, and here we were, on our last stand, and without any plan at all except trying not to kill each other.

"The universe is doomed," I heard in the light, and then a crack echoed through my ears. Everything went white, and I reappeared in a silver room. Ananke sat in front of me with her legs crossed. "This is the end game. You must worry about getting to Chaos first."

"What are you talking about? We're not Primordials. We can't stop them when they get into the Source."

"Who told you that?" she asked.

I thought for a moment. "Well…nobody. I just assumed because—"

"The lack of souls has destabilized the Source. Now anyone can enter."

"I—"

"Do you know who I am? Who I truly am?"

I furrowed my brow at her. "I know you're Ananke, and that's all you've ever told us. You are very cryptic."

"Yes, I suppose I am." She smiled. "In my own dimension, I was best friends with Chaos. We were not very powerful gods, and we did not like what was happening in our own dimension, much like the

Primordials here do not like it. We thought we could do it so much better, naïve as we were."

"Okay. Then how did you get here, tripping on a power fantasy?"

"Very much like the Primordials here are trying to get to Chaos. We traversed the universe, entered the Source, and woke the sleeping one, who was then called Azathoth. For our impudence, we were given the chance to remake the universe in our image. Her job was to keep the cosmos on a pin, and mine to make sure it didn't fall off into the abyss."

"You did a terrible job. Both of you."

"Yes, quite. Unfortunately, what I didn't know was that my friend's mind was fractured and disorganized, and thus her thoughts were full of darkness. She created the Primordials and chose the matter I had to work with: Darkness, Night, Love, Earth, and Death. Not the cheeriest way to build a universe. She breathed life into a universe born in chaos, as she was chaos personified. I did not like it, but it was her universe to create. She chose to sleep, and I chose to be awake to shepherd the universe that she created, and when this incarnation falls into the abyss, only those two, the Dreamer and the Shaper, will remain."

"That is why—"

"Yes," Ananke said. "That is why Eros and Tartarus work together and why Gaia and Nyx do the same. They have a compact. There can be only two."

"Why are you telling me this now?"

"Katrina, Akta, Kimberly, and you. You four can still stop them. You cannot stop them from reaching the end stage, but you can find Chaos before them and make your own pact with each other."

"But only two of us will remain. Is that right?"

Ananke nodded. "But at least it won't be two of them, and you will be able to craft a universe that is better than theirs. This universe is over, and my work is done, but it is not over for you four. You must hurry. If Nyx can corrupt the Source enough with her darkness, you will not be able to get in, and all hope will be lost."

"I understand."

"Good."

Ananke stood and pushed me back into the light, and when my eyes focused, I was once again in the battle for the Source. I returned just as Kimberly's troops were knocked away by Tartarus, and I watched him and Eros disappear into the Source, followed by Nyx and Gaia.

CHAPTER 66

Katrina

Location: Space

"Come on!" I screamed, throwing my hands up in the air as I watched Nyx disappear into the Source, leaving behind a fast-moving trail of Darkness that was sure to kill the light if we didn't stop it soon. "We barely held them back at all. This is bullshit! All of that for nothing! Gods-damn it!"

Then, there was a flash of light, and Rebecca was flying toward me. "Come on!"

"Where did you come from?" I shouted as she flew past. "Did you see what just—"

"I was just with Ananke! She told me everything. Now hurry up. We have to get inside the Source while we still have a chance!" She called over her shoulder. "Otherwise, the whole universe is doomed."

I took off behind her. "How is the—you know what, screw it. At least it's an ethos. I'm in!"

"Grab Akta!" she shouted. "We need her!"

"Why?" I asked.

"Just do it! Stop asking questions."

I craned my neck around the battlefield until I saw Akta hovering in place, looking around at the carnage. I flew down to intercept her. "Come on. We're following Rebecca."

"Where?"

"I think we're going into the Source."

"Why?" she asked. "All is lost."

"Cuz...cuz I don't know. Cuz Rebecca said to and doing something is better than watching the universe die."

The pixie nodded. "Fair. All right, lead the way."

I led her to where Rebecca was picking Kimberly up from a near-comatose state and slinging her over her shoulder.

"What's this about?" I asked as we neared the Source, which was being covered with inky blackness. "We're really not doing this, are we?"

"Ananke told me there's still a chance to save the universe...in a way," Rebecca replied.

"What way is that?" I asked. The Darkness was swirling wildly, consuming the Source.

"I'll tell you when we're inside."

"You're not usually one to go off halfcocked without a plan," I said, raising an eyebrow.

"Ananke has a plan," Rebecca said. "Or at least the inkling of one."

"I don't like her," Akta muttered. "Why should we trust her?"

"It doesn't matter at this point. She gave me a glimmer of hope when all hope was lost, and that's all we have right now."

I nodded. "Then let's go."

We flew forward as the Darkness consumed the light. I placed my hand on the Source and felt its enormous power. I looked at Akta, then over at Rebecca and Kimberly. If I was going to do something stupid, I could have found a worse team. I pressed my hand forward, and it disappeared into the Source. The rest of my body pulled forward until I was subsumed by it.

CHAPTER 67

Julia

Location: The Source

We pushed through the white ooze of the Source and emerged with a loud pop on the other side of the great divide between life and death. I was surprised at what I saw—not a great and vast whiteness but a bustling metropolis extending as far as I could see. It rivaled the great cities of the universe, complete with flying cars, towering buildings, and people, bathed in white light, walking about like they were taking a pleasant stroll on any planet in the cosmos.

"Where are Eros and Tartarus?" Gaia asked as she turned to Nyx, who was busy filling her darkness into the crevices. "They came in before us."

Nyx placed her hand on the membrane that protected the Source from the universe, trying to catch her breath. "Gone."

"We should go as well," Gaia said.

"No, if we don't close the seal, then more can come through," Nyx said. "I need time to perfect the seal so we can go about our work."

"You're already fading. And if we don't go now," Gaia insisted, "then they will find Chaos before us."

"A five-minute head start is nothing. The Source is infinite. Without a guide or a clue, you can be lost in here for a million years and never find Chaos. Luckily, I have both. The advantage of being the only one of you who didn't fall for Ananke's trick and lose their consciousness to the universe means I had an eternity to plan for this moment. Eros and Tartarus have no chance."

"Let us hope you are right. Either way, let us away. You have done enough, and you need your strength to fight the light of the Source."

Nyx turned away, breathing heavily. "Very well. If you don't care about stopping any other interlopers from joining us, then neither do I."

"If they come after us, we will deal with them," Gaia said, turning away from the entrance.

As Nyx moved across the street, she left a black mark on the ground, which was slowly absorbed into the light, but even after a block was still faintly visible. It was a dark stain on the perfect white of the Source as if her very presence was vile and tainted.

I watched as if I were viewing a movie; Gaia used my body as her own as if it had always been hers. I had long since stopped fighting against her. She was more powerful than me, but that didn't mean I couldn't pick my moment to attack and pepper her with questions to discover her weakness.

"So what happens if you find Chaos first?" I asked, whispering into Gaia's mind.

"You really will not shut up, will you?" She grumbled. "Do you want to be shocked again?"

"It's my body. I have a right to know."

"You forfeited your rights the moment you killed me, or don't you remember that?"

"I do, and it was impulsive of me, probably. However, you wanted to destroy the universe, so I don't feel bad about it."

"And you failed, either way." Gaia chuckled. "At least you are honest. All right, whelp. I will tell you. Should we find Chaos, then I will wake her up and take over the dream. Nyx will join me as my proxy, and together we will remake the universe in our image, without the capriciousness of humanity. It will be a paradise: pure and logical, with order and beauty on every surface."

"And you're sure you can trust Nyx?"

"No, my pet," Gaia said. "But she is the closest thing to a friend I have ever had. The Darkness kept me comforted through many eons."

"I hope she doesn't screw you over." I thought for a moment. "No, wait. I hope she does, and you both fail miserably."

"She will be in for a reckoning if she does."

We walked for an hour, passing hundreds of stores and thousands of people. It was like I was back in New York City in the years before my death. There was an electricity in the air as the people spoke to each other about some mundane thing or another as if they weren't glowing beings made of light energy. When different groups of people we'd passed saw the trail of blackness building up behind us, they gasped and turned their attention to us for a moment, whispering under their breaths.

"Don't you listen to their gawking," Gaia said. "You are as Chaos made you."

"And we will make it right next time," Nyx said, grumbling under her breath.

"We will."

"And nobody will hate me because it will be perfect."

"Absolutely."

Finally, we stopped in front of a tailor shop, and Nyx walked inside. I couldn't believe anything needed tailoring in the Source but supposed I didn't know much about the place. Until now, I thought it was just a white light spinning in the middle of the universe, not a bustling city full of millions of shops and buildings.

A tall woman with bushy hair looked up from her work and smiled at us when we entered. "I've been waiting for you a long time," she said, standing up and wrapping Nyx in a hug.

"I am grateful to see you," Nyx said with a sullen, exhausted nod. She had lost a great deal of energy. "When it came to our agreement…I did not know if you would honor it or even if you could."

The woman nodded. "I did exactly as you said. For your part, thank you for returning my family to me. I am eternally grateful."

"And how are they?" Nyx asked.

She sighed. "Passed on into the white thousands of years ago, but I had more work to do. Or did. Now, I hope to pass on to join them."

"Pass on?" I asked. "I thought the Source was passing on."

Gaia turned from Nyx. "It takes time for people to untether themselves from their bodies once they come here. The underworld purifies their sins, so they can come to this place, but they must make peace with their lives themselves and fold into the Source when they do. Until then, they are left here to come to terms with their lives."

I shook my head. "Just when you think you know the end, you realize there really is no end."

"That's right, poppet," Gaia said. "Even folding into the Source is simply a new beginning when you reenter the universe as something else, possibly a tadpole, or a blade of grass, or even a god."

"Except for me," I said. "I'll be asleep with you for an eternity, I assume."

"God, I hope not." Gaia shuddered. "And if so, you better shut up. But even if so, all of this will be remade into a new universe. As you said, there is no end, just new beginnings and old endings."

The woman walked behind her counter, opened the till, and pulled out a ticket. She handed it to Nyx. "I believe this is the place you seek."

"How certain are you?"

"As certain as a hundred millennia can make me. Even with so much time, I could only sweep a fraction of this place. It's enormous."

Nyx held up the ticket. "Thank you." She turned to Gaia, and by extension, me. "Come, we have a date with Chaos."

CHAPTER 68

Kimberly

Location: The Source

"Ow," I said, squinting against the white light. "Where are we?"

"The Source," Akta said, helping me up, my head throbbing. I was confronted with nothing that I expected. I expected to see a lot of nothing, like the Darkness. Instead, I was met with a sprawling city expanding into the distance, every bit the splendor of any metropolis I had ever seen in my long life.

"I don't believe you," I replied with a grumble. "I think I'm in Hell. Yup, this would be my Hell."

"Well, it really doesn't matter where you think we are," Katrina said. "Cuz we are where we are, and where we are is the Source."

"Lovely," I said, sitting up.

"Aaaaand," Rebecca added, "we have no idea how to track down the Primordials."

"There's a good reason for that," Katrina said. "It's because last time I went straight into a white light, it was a vast expanse of nothing, not a giant, frigging city."

"And why are we here?" I asked, still dazed from the battle. I looked back to see the entrance to the Source covered in inky blackness. "That can't be good."

Rebecca pushed on the inkblot covering the entrance, and it didn't give an inch. "It just means there's no going back. We can only go forward."

Akta pounded her fists together. "Forward to find Eros, Tartarus, Nyx, and Gaia, and end their lives."

I spun away from the entrance. Hundreds of people stared at the Darkness in horror. It was a right metropolis, like any other I've come across in my travels. *What was going on?*

"I say we split up," Katrina said, holding her sword close. "My sword will kill a Primordial. Kimberly, we know your scythe will kill one. Akta, do you have your bow?"

"No," she said, "I lost it in the battle."

"Then you come with me," Katrina said. "What about you, Rebecca?"

She held up a gun. "I just have this blaster."

"Then you take Rebecca, Kimberly. I'll take Akta, and if we find those gods, we kill them."

"What about Chaos?" Akta asked. They were straight-up talking over me now, both literally and figuratively. "I thought we were supposed to find her. Isn't that the end goal?"

"Not if we don't want the universe to end," Katrina said. "If we kill the Primordials first, then we won't have to destroy the universe, and everybody can stay alive. Let's make finding Chaos our absolute last resort."

"Where do you think they went?" I asked, coming out of my fog and starting to grasp the magnitude of the situation.

Akta bent down. "Here, embedded in the ground, there is a very hazy remnant of a footprint, and since everybody here is pure light, I can only assume that this is Nyx. Perhaps if we follow it, we'll find her."

"Good," Katrina said. "Akta and I will go this way." She turned to me. "You and Rebecca go...some other way."

"And what?" I snapped. "Just guess?"

"Your reapers brought lots of these people to the Source, I suspect, so why don't you ask the people in front of you if they saw a love god today or a towering, twenty-foot-high Titan with its face on fire. Maybe they'll decide to help." Katrina pushed through the crowd with Akta and followed after her.

"It's not a bad idea," Rebecca said. "Do you recognize any of these people?"

It was impossible to pick out a single, specific face in the millions upon millions I had shepherded to the end. They all looked the same to me, and they all stared at me with a combination of horror and wonder. I squinted closer, trying to pin down a face, and that's when I saw her. Her eyes were as wide as when I brought her to the Source the first time. Molpe, the siren, was smiling at me.

"Hello, friend," I said, walking toward her.

"I knew it was you," Molpe said, flying into the air. "I knew I would see you again."

I shook my head. "I'm not back for you. I need your help. Did you see—"

Molpe held up her hand. "I saw a mad man and a robot-looking man with fire in his face. That's why I came here. I can bring you to them, or at least where I saw them last."

"Then lead the way," I replied.

CHAPTER 69

Akta

Location: The Source

"They went into this shop," I said, kneeling in front of a shadow footprint embedded into the sidewalk. It was barely perceptible to the naked eye. I remembered when we believed that Nyx would corrupt the Source. Now I wondered if she would be cleansed by the Source before she could even reach Chaos.

I stood up and turned into a tailor shop. Behind the counter, a woman with bushy hair was screaming. "Let me go! I'm ready to go! Why won't you let me go?"

"Um, hello?" Katrina said, walking up to the counter.

The woman spun and nearly jumped out of her skin. "You're...not glowing."

"We're not," I agreed. "We're looking for somebody that came in here."

"And don't play games," Katrina said, grumbling. "Like you don't know who we're talking about. They'd be the only two beings since you entered the Source that didn't glow like you do."

"Of course, I remember. You're looking for Nyx. She cursed me, you know!"

"Who?"

"Nyx, the bitch. She told me that if I helped her find Chaos, she would return my babies to me without having them tortured by Tartarus. I promised to help her, and here I am, a million generations later, and I can't find peace. Everybody I love has folded back into the Source, except me."

"Maybe you aren't cursed. Maybe you're still here because your work is not done," I said, walking up to her. "Did you ever think of that?"

"How could that be?" she said. "My heart feels so hollow."

"Yeah," Katrina said. "How?"

"Think about it," I replied. "You helped Nyx, who is looking to destroy everything, but you can still help us save the universe. Tell me what you told her. Tell me where she's going. You can still do the right thing, and maybe, if you do, you'll find peace."

"And if you're wrong?" the woman said. "What if it doesn't help?"

I smiled. "Then, at least you did the right thing. There is honor in that, and honor is its own reward. If you can't find peace, at least you can look at yourself, live with yourself, knowing you did the right thing, for as long as this universe exists."

She nodded. "Okay. I'll help you."

Katrina leaned into me. "I'm shocked that worked."

"I'm not."

I believed that being good was its own reward, and I would go to the end believing that, even if this was the end.

CHAPTER 70

Rebecca

Location: The Source

"They are not subtle, are they?" I said, staring down a street where several shop windows were smashed through, and light poles had turned over through brutal force. Dozens of glowing people screamed as they rushed past us. "Do you think they want us to find them?"

"I don't think they have any reason to believe we are even in here," Kimberly said.

"You should be able to find them if you just follow the carnage," Molpe said, smiling at me.

"Thank you," I said. "I hope you found peace."

The siren nodded. "As much as I ever thought was possible, and more. Thank you."

Molpe walked away as we turned up the street, Kimberly clutching her scythe tightly and me holding my gun. "I should have been the one to go find Nyx since I have a gun that can hurt her."

"Well, I should have been the one to look for Nyx because I want to stab her through the neck with my scythe for deceiving me. Neither of us is getting what we want, so let's just do what we can to end this, okay?"

I shook my head. "Why do I even listen to Katrina? She's just so forceful I forget that I literally outrank her and that I can outthink her if she pulls back the intensity for even one second."

"She has a way about her," Kimberly said, then stopped abruptly. "Do you hear that?"

I tilted my ear to the sky. A guttural scream bounced through the air. "Tartarus."

I took off in a sprint, and Kimberly followed behind me. We turned the corner just in time to see Tartarus grab a hovering car out of the air and toss it into a building across the street.

"Come out and face me, Chaos!" he screamed. "Or I will destroy everything you love!"

Eros pressed his fingers to the bridge of his nose. "That's not how it works. That's not how any of this works! Why won't you listen to me?"

Tartarus pressed his bulbous gauntlet into Eros's face. "You told me it would be easy. This city is a maze, a labyrinth that goes on forever, and we have no idea where Chaos could be. This is your fault! They're going to get to her first, and then we'll be vaporized!"

"That's not very nice, pointing fingers. I admit this isn't ideal, but we'll find her, or at least somebody that knows her. How many people could there possibly be in here?"

Tartarus threw his arms in the air. "Trillions upon trillions, from every planet in the cosmos. Literally an incalculable amount."

Eros shook his head. "I doubt that Gaia and Nyx are having any better luck."

Tartarus stormed toward him again. "And how do you know? I knew we needed a better plan. Ugh. Why do I listen to you?"

"Because I got us this far!" Eros shouted. "Without me, you'd have no plan! You'd have no ambition. You'd just be a...a...lumbering brute."

Without another word, Tartarus smashed his hands into Eros's body, slamming him into the ground like a jackhammer. "Never speak that way to me again."

When Tartarus slowed down his pummeling, Eros rolled from under the gauntlets and rose into the air. He took his bow and fired three arrows into Tartarus's armor at the joints of his right arm. "Do you really think I don't know your secrets, old friend?"

Tartarus went to raise his hand, and Eros fired four arrows into the elbow and shoulder joints of his left arm, pinning it against a glittering white wall behind him. Eros turned his attention to the legs, and when Tartarus tried to step forward, he again fired arrows in rapid succession into the joints of his hips and knees, locking him in place against the wall.

"Trickery!" Tartarus screamed. "I should have known better than to expect anything else from such a weak god. Chaos should never have made you."

"I don't know about that," Eros said, nocking another arrow. "Love, after all, will set you free."

Eros fired another arrow, this time right through Tartarus's helmet, which flew through the air, embedding the helmet into the glittering white wall behind it. Fire shot up from the place where the helmet used to be, but Eros wasn't done. He nocked another arrow and fired it through the arms and legs of the armor, and they all dropped off as easily as the helmet. There was nothing underneath them, and when they were gone, the chest cavity fell to the ground.

After a moment, the front plate fell off, and a small, old man with a potbelly jumped up. "You really suck, Eros! Did you know that? Do you know how long I worked on that armor? A million years! You ever work on anything for a million years? No, because you're an asshole who got by with his good looks!"

I looked over at Kimberly. "This seems like a good time to make our move."

"I agree."

I stepped out from behind the building and fired two bullets from my gun at Tartarus. He fell back, screaming.

"You!" Eros said, but already Kimberly was on top of him, slicing at him with her scythe. Eros flew into the air and fired a bevy of arrows at her. I rushed to knock her out of the way before they could hit her.

As Eros turned to fire at us again, a huge sword flew out of the ground toward him. Eros barely turned away to avoid it and fired again down to Tartarus, where the sword came from. Tartarus ducked behind his breastplate, which covered his whole naked body.

"I don't need you!" Eros screamed.

"Yes!" Tartarus said. "You absolutely do! Who will control your universe for you?"

"I'll do both!" Eros screamed and flew away.

Tartarus ran after him, but his stubby legs couldn't keep up. Eventually, he stopped, tired to the point of exhaustion, and we walked up to him.

"It's over," I said to him.

"You don't know anything," Tartarus said, panting. "It was over for us the moment we stepped into the Source. Without a plan, we will all succumb to it soon enough. The Source will cleanse us." He could barely take another step. "You will be doing me a great favor to kill me in battle."

"This is not a battle," Kimberly said. "But I will gladly send you to your maker."

"This is as close to my maker as I can be. By killing me, you prevent me from being used by her again, and I am so tired of being used."

He opened his arms to Kimberly, who looked over to me. "Do it."

She nodded and sliced her scythe across his neck, severing it from his tiny body. He fell, dead before he hit the ground. The essence of his power rose into the air. I expected it to flood into Kimberly, but instead, it popped and crackled like a firecracker as the light absorbed it back into itself. It seemed like Chaos had another use for him after all.

"One down," I said. "One to go."

CHAPTER 71

Julia

Location: The Source

"I'm so tired," Nyx said, stumbling down on the sidewalk, unable to stand any longer.

Gaia kneeled beside her. "Come on. We're close. Don't make me carry you."

"It's too much," Nyx said, barely able to speak, her breath labored. "The light. Is too much. I thought. I was more…I thought I could…too powerful…"

She fell over onto the ground. Gaia tried to pick her up, but Nyx was like a million pounds of dead weight stuck like a magnet to the ground.

"Remember…" she said. "Remember…when they said I would corrupt her…and here…she has cleansed me…without…ever…seeing…me."

"You are too stubborn to die," Gaia said, her voice cracking and a tear forming on the edge of her eye. It would have been sad if it weren't for her genocidal nature.

"She…is more…stubborn…than even I…" Nyx's lips moved, but the words didn't come. After her voice vanished, her body faded from the Source, and nothing of her remained except a shadow on the ground, embedded into the light.

"Shit!" Gaia said. "Shit! Shit! Shit! What am I going to do now?"

"Well," I replied. "You could stop this, you know. You don't have to end the universe."

"You don't understand," Gaia replied. "Without darkness, there can be no light. There will be no balance in this universe. Even if I wanted to give up, we doomed everything the moment we stepped into the Source and took the Darkness with us. I have no choice but to continue, even if I must do it alone."

As she bowed her head, a bolt shot across from her. She turned to see Eros standing on the other side of the street from her, hovering in the air.

"Gaia?" Eros said. "Where is Nyx?"

"Gone," Gaia said. "Where is Tartarus?"

"Who cares?" Eros said. "I have decided to go on alone."

"And I have no choice but to do so," Gaia added.

"You know," he said, floating toward us, "perhaps there is a way we could both get what we want. I know of your deal with Nyx. You were to be her herald, yes?"

"I was."

"As Tartarus was to be mine. We could have the beginnings of a beautiful partnership, and we have very little choice but to take it."

"We hate each other."

"Which is why this is perfect. We never have to see each other…There must be two, and you know it. Unless you have a better plan…"

Gaia thought for a moment. "Very well. I suppose there is reason to have an accord, as long as you agree to let me run the universe my way."

"I do, though I will not make it easy on you. I have many ideas I want to explore."

They shook hands, binding themselves to each other, and a jolt of energy passed through me.

Eros cocked his head. "I don't suppose you know how to find Chaos."

Gaia looked down and noticed a piece of paper on the ground. She knelt and picked it up. It was the piece of paper the tailor gave Nyx. The last remnant of Darkness left in the universe.

Gaia's lips curled into a smile. "In fact, I happen to know exactly where to find her."

CHAPTER 72

Katrina

Location: Chaos's House

"This is it," I said, looking up at a small townhouse squished between two high rises. I expected there to be guards stationed all around the property, or maybe a glowing white dog—you know, some sort of protection for the most powerful being in the universe, but there was none. When I pushed the door, it swung open easily.

"Hello?" Akta said. No answer.

"Do you think they're here already?" I asked.

"No," she said. "If they were, this would all be over."

There was a set of stairs on the left, and I made my way up, each step creaking loudly. I rose into the air to prevent the noise.

"Remember, we're not going to wake her. We're here to kill the Primordials and save the universe."

"It's too late for that, my love," I heard in my head. "You must end it."

"What?" I said, stopping on the steps. "I'm not—!"

Akta put her finger to her lips to remind me that there was a sleeping woman somewhere in the house who, if awoken, could end the universe. I quieted again. "I'm not ending the universe. This was a rescue mission."

"No, there is no choice but to destroy the universe," the voice said in my head. "You have tainted the Source. The Darkness sealed it shut and destroyed the exit, meaning the universe will descend further into disaster until it disintegrates. You must destroy the universe to save it."

"I don't want to," I said. "There has to be another way."

"I promise you; there is no other way." The voice was soothing, even as its words shredded through me. Somehow, I knew they were correct, even though I hated them.

"How?" I asked, tears streaming down my face.

"I will walk you through it," I heard in my brain. "Come up the stairs. You are so close."

"Are you Chaos?" I asked quietly.

"Yes," the voice whispered. "I have watched you for eons. You have fought against my will harder than any other in the whole universe, my love. You are my greatest creation. Together, we sowed so much chaos."

"I never wanted that," I sobbed. "I just wanted peace."

"There is no greater peace than eternal slumber," Chaos said sweetly. "Come get your eternal reward."

I reached the top of the stairs. "What will happen to you?"

"I will be remade with everything else, like clay for you to use for the next universe, and when somebody wakes you, the same will be said for you." The voice stopped for a moment. "I am in the room at the end of the hallway."

The walls were covered in photos of a little girl, dark-skinned and smiling, and two men behind her, one dark-skinned and one light smiling just as brightly. "Who are they?"

"The parents I wish I had. The life I wish I had."

I pushed open the door and saw the same girl lying on a bed, asleep. The room was covered in black paint, with stars everywhere. On her bed lay a comforter made of stars that moved in time with her breathing.

"When you are ready, place your hand on my forehead and say, 'beautiful girl, I wake you from your slumber,' and then it will be done."

"Did you plan this? All of this?" I asked. "Did you plan for me to be here at the end?"

"No, Ananke is the one with the plans. I prefer to trust my gut. I did hope it would be you, though. I wish I could see what you will dream."

I stepped forward and looked back at Akta, who was still in the hallway. "There's somebody coming."

"You must hurry," Chaos said to me.

"Come here," I said to Akta.

"She should grab your hand," Chaos whispered.

I held out my hand to the pixie. "Grab it."

As she did, I heard the door open and two pairs of feet stomping up the stairs. Gaia stood panting at the top of the stairs, dressed in Julia's body. Eros was behind her, glaring. "What are you—"

I looked down at Chaos and then closed my eyes. I wasn't ready for this. I wasn't ready for any of this, and yet, here I was. Here I am. I placed my hand on her forehead. "Beautiful girl, I wake you from your slumber."

A gasp, and then everything went black, and I fell into the abyss.

CHAPTER 73

Kimberly

Location: The Source

I looked up into the sky, and everything fell away. The light. The dark.

My stomach sank.

The breath left my lungs.

I looked down at my hands, and they fell apart. I looked over at Rebecca, and saw the fear in her eyes, and watched as it was replaced with peace as she disintegrated into a billion pieces.

Maybe this was our happy ending.

Perhaps the next universe would be kinder than this one.

I could only hope.

CHAPTER 74

Katrina

Location: Nothing

Nothing. Not blackness. Not darkness. Simply nothingness in its pure form. Chaos floated in front of me, her eyes sparkling white, her hair floating like she was submerged underwater.

"Where are we?" I asked. There was an emptiness in my soul. In my everything. I ached with longing and missing something—no, not something, everything.

"The Absence," Chaos said.

"The Absence?" I said. "What's that?"

"It is the absence of everything," she said. "Once I finish speaking to you, I will transfer the power of all creation to you, and then I will…be done."

"You will leave me, too?" I asked, nervous.

She shook her head. "I will be within you always, as will the essence of every living thing that will ever exist. They will fold back into you and leave again for the rest of eternity."

I shook my head. "I'm not ready."

"You are," Chaos said. "You will do wonderfully."

"You're wrong," I replied, crying. "I mess up everything I touch. I don't know what I'm doing."

She laughed. "Perhaps that is for the best. I thought I knew what I was doing, but my universe was worse than the one I left, all because of my hubris. Ananke was no better. We were so sure of everything that we ended up causing…well, chaos. When your name is synonymous with disorder and mayhem, perhaps you have made a mistake."

"The universe really was awful, wasn't it?" I asked, looking up at her.

She shook her head slowly. "It didn't start out that way. It started out as a beautiful dream, but it spun out of control. The Primordials birthed the Titans and first gods, who birthed their pantheons, who birthed humanity, and at every stage, a little bit more disorder crept in, until…until it all ended."

"Are you sad it ended?" I asked.

"No," she replied. "I am happy that I can finally have a new dream."

"That sounds nice, I suppose."

"Give it several billion years of being stuck in one dream, and it will sound even better." She cleared her throat. "Okay, there are words I need to say. Words I have been holding in my mind for billions of years. Are you ready?"

I shook my head. "No, but tell me them anyway."

"Very well." She smiled. "You are the catalyst. People called it the Big Bang, the First Shock, the Initial Explosion, and much more, but you set the parameters of the universe. Then, you cannot interact with anything. The universe simply exists in your mind as you slumber."

"How do I do it?"

"Take everything good, everything that you believe is right with the universe, everything you think will make the universe better, and hold it in your mind, and then, when I touch you, let it explode out of you, okay?"

I choked back tears. "What if there is no good in me?"

"There is nothing but good in you, my love. Just dig deeper." She smiled softly at me. "Let me know when you are ready."

Would I ever be ready? I was privy to so much horror in my life, so much evil, so much hatred. I was fueled by hatred, but I could not bring any of that with me into the new universe. I did not want it to be filled with the evil that corrupted so many in my time.

Zeus, Hera, Odin, Surt, Asmodeus…there were so many others that their names slipped through my mind. No, I could not think of them. They were the bad in the universe. *Where was the good?*

Think, Katrina. There must be good out there. Yes, there was good. You could almost touch it.

Connie. She was willful. She would never take no for an answer, but she was also ceaselessly kind. And she was filled with love…love for Dennis…love for demons…love for everything.

Dennis. He…he came back for us during the Apocalypse so many epochs ago. Even in Heaven, he came back for us and led us through Hell. He didn't have to do that. He could have forgotten us in Paradise, but he didn't. He didn't. He was loyal.

Lucifer. He never lost faith in me. He tried so hard even in the worst possible conditions; even when people thought he was evil incarnate, he tried to help me.

Rebecca. She was willful. She was proud. She had a sense of duty more than any person I had ever met.

Julia. She was all justice. She always knew the right thing to do. She was guided by a north star of hope.

Kimberly. She gave of herself freely. She had great compassion for the dead. She saw everything and everybody as greater than the sum of their parts.

Velaska. Underneath her hard exterior, she loved deeply. She was the best friend I ever had.

Urania. My poor Urania. I would miss her most of all. I loved her with more depth than I could muster. The thought of her made me weep. I would never see her again. I would never see any of them again.

I opened my eyes and looked at Chaos, who was breathing calmly. "I can never see them again, those I lost."

"They are all a part of you now. You carry them with you."

"What if I wanted to bring them into this universe? What if I wanted to make them again?"

Chaos smiled. "There were none I cared about except Ananke, which is why I made the Primordials hollow shells. It was my greatest mistake. If you choose it, you can create them again, but be sure to make them whole. Reach into yourself and pull them out."

I smiled. "Then I am ready."

Chaos took a deep breath and touched my chest. The raw power knocked me backward and caused me to suck wind deeply. The entirety of the universe, the history of the universe, passed through me. Not just one universe, but every universe back to the beginning. The film of it rushed through me at blazing fast speeds, and yet I could see every moment. I watched every transition and every universe rise and fall.

I did not know how my universe would be better, but by the time the stream of images reached the end of Chaos's universe, I was ready to create. Opening my arms, a million galaxies shot out of me. Every bit of myself exploded across infinity. I took one more gasp and fell backward as solar systems and supernovas expanded in my mind.

The new universe cascaded out before me, and I saw Akta floating in front of the Source. As she materialized, so did Julia, and Rebecca, and Velaska, and Lucifer, and Connie, and Urania, and Dennis, and Kimberly. Together, they would lead the universe, and I hoped they could make it more beautiful than I could ever imagine.

But they would have to do it without me because my part of the story was done. I fell back into the comforting bosom of the Source and hoped I would have a pleasant dream.

***

If you loved this, you can start the universe all over again with *Magic*. Keep reading after the author's note for a sneak peek of that book.

AUTHOR'S NOTE

I can't tell you how hard it was to write the last words and end the universe of the Godsverse Chronicles. I read those final words several times before you read them, and they were some of the hardest to get through of any in my whole career. They hit me hard right in the feels, still even several drafts later.

Katrina was a difficult character to write, but she was also the one thing that held the Godsverse together. She was the sun that everybody else circled around, so it made all the sense in the world to make her the bearer of a new universe. In nearly every book, even when her power wasn't increasing, her presence sucked the wind out of a room and turned all attention to her.

When I started thinking about this book, I considered all the things I loved about mythology, and one of my favorite mythological figures is Azathoth from Lovecraft's pantheon, the idiot god who rests the whole universe in his mind. I thought it would be so cool if there were another god like that from Greek/Roman mythology.

That's when I learned about the Greek goddess, Chaos. There are lots of different stories about Chaos, but in several, she is the god that created the universe, and the universe rests in her mind, which is the EXACT thing that I wanted. The minute I learned of her past and that I could use the title *Chaos,* I knew I had a book.

On top of that, Katrina is Chaos personified, and that the universe defaults to chaos most of the time was a perfect analogy for the entirety of the Godsverse. It was then that I knew that this would be the end of the universe.

I'm not saying it's the last book in the Godsverse because there are all sorts of stories that can be told in the past, or inside Katrina's new universe, with the characters we've already seen or new ones. Imagine this group of Primordials, made up of Julia, Akta, Rebecca, Kimberly, and Connie, that NEW main characters have to interact with. Imagine going backward and telling new stories from the last 10,000 years with the current cast of characters.

I don't know if that will happen because, for me, this is the last book in this universe for a long time, but it might not be the last time I write in it. The Godsverse has an incredible pull on me.

I didn't necessarily intend to destroy the universe when I set out to conceive this twelfth book in the Godsverse, but I love how it turned out.

I cried when I wrote those last words because it was a bittersweet ending for Katrina. All she ever wanted was to rest and be left alone, and that is how her story ends, destroying the whole universe and creating a new one.

I hope you enjoyed it as much as I enjoyed writing it.

***

Keep reading for a sneak preview of *Magic*.

MAGIC

Book 1 of The Godsverse Chronicles

By:
Russell Nohelty

Edited by:
Leah Lederman

Proofread by:
Katrina Roets & Toni Cox

Cover by:
Psycat Covers

Planet chart and timeline design by:
Andrea Rosales

CHAPTER 1

Orcs smelled like moldy cheese.

Even if I couldn't see under their thinly-veiled illusion charms to their true faces, I would be able to smell them from across a room because they reeked of cheese. Every race had its own smell. Demons smelled like charred meat. Not pleasantly charred meat, but the kind that you left in the oven for an hour too long and caused a visceral, uncontrollable wretch in your gut.

Elves smelled like lavender and not in a pleasant way. More like that "why did you fill a room with lavender and then close all the windows for a week, so the lavender plumed out all at one time and kicked me in the face" kind of way. Dwarves smelled like stale grog, even if they hadn't been drinking.

Humans smelled the worst of all. They smelled of death, like a corpse trying desperately to mask their rotting flesh with perfumes and cologne.

My sensitive nose was only one of the many curses my parents heaped on me. I was also cursed with second sight, which allowed me to see through any illusion charm to the true nature of something, even if I didn't want to see it. They also bestowed on me a hatred of everything on either side of the divide, angels, and demons alike, though that was more a function of nurture and not nature.

It's amazing I turned out as stable as I did, given the truckload of garbage heaped on me as a kid. On second thought, though, perhaps working in the underbelly of Los Angeles, trafficking in magical weapons and trinkets wasn't the best way to prove that I turned out well-adjusted.

Most people who don't know any better call it the black market, but to me, it was just the market. If you needed a hard-to-find weapon to kill a lasa, or a spell to impress a girl, or just a charm to make you smarter to pass an upcoming test, I was your girl.

I wasn't a drug runner, or an arms dealer, or an assassin, but those were the types that filled my Rolodex. I preferred to think of myself as a facilitator. Somebody who could introduce you to the right monster at the right time for the right job at the right price.

Sure, you could search for what you need yourself, and you might even find it, but you'd more likely get your face busted, ripped off, or killed, than if you'd hired me. I wasn't cheap. I was absurdly expensive, actually, but I got the job done, and I kept you out of the fray. *How much would you pay for that kind of peace of mind?*

My clients paid a lot for it, and I made a good living working with bad people. I knew they did bad things, but they never did it in front of me. To me, they were perfectly pleasant, sweet even, sometimes to a sickening extent. Maybe it's because I wasn't bad to look at or because I could slice their throat with the flick of my wrist. Either way, I never had issues with my clients or my suppliers.

Or, I rarely did.

My latest client was a complete pain in the ass. He buzzed my beeper every two hours asking for updates on the location of the precious dagger he had contracted me to find. Usually, it could take me months to track down a specific piece, but he was paying me three million dollars to find it in a week, forcing me to push my contacts to push their contacts, and well, in the end, everyone was on edge, and I hadn't slept in three days. I hadn't slept in a month before that, honestly, because I didn't sleep much. The past week was because of stress, and I didn't like stress. Though

I operated in a very dangerous profession, I went out of my way to only work with and for people who reduced my stress, or at least didn't add to it.

This was the exception to the rule. I had no idea who my client was, which was completely against protocol. However, three million was too much to turn down, even for me. Even after I had greased every palm in Los Angeles, I would still be left with two million, free and clear, for a week's work.

It had been a hellish week, but I had finally tracked down the dagger to an orc named Blezor. Of course, he was only an orc to those in the know. To almost everyone else, he was just an eccentric art dealer. A smaller group of misfits knew he laundered drug money through his art collections, but even those people knew him as a human.

It was a special kind of person that knew who we were, which was how we all lived in plain sight for thousands of years. We were your bank tellers, your grocery store clerks, and your doctors. If you've ever had a strange interaction with somebody that didn't seem quite human, that was probably one of us.

I preferred to do my work through proxies rather than get my hands dirty, but when the money was right, and the timetable was tight, I didn't have any other options. I took it upon myself to make a move on Blezor. Orc males run hot, and it was particularly easy to seduce them. I wasn't the most sexual person in the world, but for three million dollars, I was willing to bed just about anything. I had no problem being a whore, especially a rich one. We're all whores for something.

Blezor wasn't a bad lay. He wasn't great, but his problems lay with being a selfish lover and not in the stamina or aptitude departments. The whole time I couldn't get over the fact that he smelt like rancid Limburger cheese, and when he was done, his musk had oozed all over me. At least he tired himself to sleep.

After I screwed him into a sex coma, I slid his arm off my naked stomach and rose slowly. I dressed in the leather pants and crop top which I had worn to get his attention. I reached into the pocket of my leather trench coat and pulled out my sunglasses. I never took them off if I could help it, but Blezor insisted, and…again, three million dollars, so I relented.

I slung my black leather coat around my narrow shoulders and walked out of the bedroom. Blezor was all too happy to regale me with stories about his collection of art and weapons, including the gnarled, sinewy, black dagger I was after, mounted behind a glass case in the study set off from the main foyer.

I pulled my willow bark wand from the interior pocket of my coat. "*Toddi gwydr.*"

Most witches and wizards used standard Latin to cast spells, though they were effective in any language, especially if it held specific significance to you and your wand. My mother had given me my wand, one of the few things she ever gifted me. She'd made it herself with the core of a unicorn hair she plucked herself from her beloved Welsh countryside.

Of course, you didn't need a wand to cast spells, at least not when you were as powerful as I was; it just helped focus your power for more delicate or powerful spells that you needed to be concentrated in a specific area. I wasn't interested in blowing the case to kingdom come, so I needed the deft touch only a wand could bring.

A thin stream of orange light came from the end of the wand, and I used it to cut the glass case protecting the knife. When I had cut a circle big enough for my hand to fit through, the glass popped off into my hand.

"*Dyblygu*," I whispered to the wand, and it made a perfect replica of the dagger in the display, hovering above it. I jammed my hand into the display and picked up the dagger, placing the duplicate behind it to complete the illusion.

When I pulled the dagger free, I replaced the piece of glass and melted it back in place. It wasn't perfect, but it would do in a pinch. Hopefully, Blezor wouldn't be able to tell it disappeared until I was long gone.

"What are you doing?" I heard a gruff voice grumble. I turned to see Blezor scowling at me. "Are you stealing from me?"

Well, this wasn't good.

"Oh, this?" I said, stepping backward. "I can see how you would think that, but… *FFLACH*!"

I closed my eyes, and a flash of white light escaped the end of the wand. Blezor screamed, and I barreled over him, rushing for the exit.

Outside, I flung open the door to Lily, my 1968 Plymouth Barracuda, tossing my wand and the dagger into the passenger's seat. It would be a pain to fix this mess now that he'd caught me stealing, red-handed. There wasn't time to worry about that. I looked down at my watch. I had less than an hour to get to the meeting spot and make the exchange. *Cutting it close, Ollie. Real close.*

I gunned the engine and sped off into the night, wheels squealing as Blezor rushed out into the driveway. He screamed something at me that I couldn't hear over the blare of Lily's engine, which was probably for the best. Whatever he had to say couldn't have been pleasant, and I didn't need that kind of negativity in my life.

CHAPTER 2

The docks in San Pedro had one thing going for them—it was easy to keep everything in front of you and avoid being ambushed from behind if you planned it right. After some deft maneuvering and a dash of lead foot, I arrived at the dock from Burbank twenty minutes before my scheduled meeting, allowing me to position myself perfectly for a quick escape if I needed it. I had never worked with this client before, and the people who hired me had a higher propensity than most to be bottom feeders. Even if most of the bottom feeders I knew had ethics, it paid to take precautions.

I kept the car running while I rummaged through the mountain of weaponry and armor in the trunk, looking for a sheath big enough to hold the curved dagger. *Three million dollars for a stupid dagger.* I couldn't believe it, but I wasn't complaining either. I slid the now sheathed dagger into my coat, slammed the trunk closed, and exited the dock.

Lily and I had been through a lot together, and I loved her more than anything else in my life. She was the only thing that never let me down and had saved me more times than I cared to admit. Even when you are careful, in this line of work, you got into plenty of hairy situations. It paid to have somebody to watch your back—my somebody just happened to be a car.

A 1985 Oldsmobile Cutlass pulled to a stop a dozen yards from me. I pulled down my sunglasses to get a better look at it. It must have been barely off the lot because even in the darkness, it shimmered. I hated the boxy look of 80s cars, which was why I had no desire to get rid of my '68

Barracuda, even though it was almost twenty years old. They didn't make cars like Lily anymore.

Neither of the demons who exited the car was my client. I had never even spoken to him except over the phone, and none of my contacts knew anything about the smooth-voiced stranger, which put me on edge. Still, he had already given me five hundred grand in cash as a down payment, which gave me all the confidence I needed to take the job.

The driver was Balaam, a six-eyed demon with an underbite disguised as a black, square-jawed ex-wrestler. The other demon was Moloch, whose horns were tall enough to give him trouble getting in and out of cars. Moloch fancied himself charming, but he was as vile as any demon. They were both bulky and muscular and always chose to remain shirtless, perhaps to show off how ripped they were. I had lived long enough to know that muscles don't mean much in the grand scheme. A small girl like me was stronger than both of them combined, and I looked like a swift breeze would blow me over.

"Ollie," Balaam said. The duffle bag slung over his shoulder could have only been my money, even if it looked too small for three million. I knew that money was a lot slimmer than they made it seem in the movies.

"Boys," I said with a confident smile.

"Do you have it?" Moloch said.

I walked toward the demons, hand tight on the dagger's hilt under my coat. "Of course. It was a real pain finding it."

"That's why it cost three million dollars, right?" Balaam said, gruffly, as if it was his money he was spending and not his boss's. "We didn't think you'd show."

"I always show." I pulled the dagger out of the sheath as I removed it from my jacket. I felt the power of it in my hands then, which I hadn't quite appreciated before. My heart began beating faster, and I took a deep breath.

"Impressive," Moloch cooed.

"I should have charged you double," I told them, holding out the dagger for them to see.

"We would have paid it, too." Moloch beckoned me forward. "Now, give it to me."

I shook my head and slid back a step. "That's not how this works. You slide the money over, and then I hand you the merchandise. We talked about this."

"Afraid we can't do that," Balaam said. "Just do as he says."

Something's wrong. Sure enough, a moment later, they pulled out their guns, massive hand cannons with barrels nearly as big as my head. The kind of thing impotent and feckless men used to compensate for their inadequacies.

Moloch looked down the barrel of his gun. "Now, hand it over."

I couldn't help it. A big grin rose on my face. I was most at home in a fight. Subterfuge wasn't my jam, even though it was almost always called for in my line of work. I preferred to punch my fist through something squishy when given the chance.

"You don't want to do this," I said. "All you're gonna get is dead, and then I'll have the knife and the money."

Balaam's trigger finger twitched. "I'm sorry about this. You seem like a fine person, but we have orders."

"So did the Nazis, and they still fried. This is your last chance."

"Enough!" Moloch screamed.

"Yes, I agree," I replied. "I have given you enough chances."

I leaped high into the air as their hand cannons fired, sending several bullets into Lily's chassis. They would pay for that. I flipped around and landed behind the demons, where my smile dropped into a snarl.

"Now you've done it," I growled. "*Chwyth iâ!*"

A massive ice blast flew from my hands. It smashed into the two demons and sent them crashing into my car— my beautiful car.

"Lily! Dammit!" She was an innocent in all of this, but with the duffel bag Balaam dropped at my feet when I blasted him, I had the money to fix her up. "Now, look what you made me do!" I knelt and picked up the bag. "I'll take this as compensation for not killing you. It'll cost you another three million to get the dagger."

A shadow filled my vision, but not from the demons. This one was coming from the air in the form of a monster truck. "YOU BITCH!"

I spun out of the way, and an enormous monster truck, purple and red with tires at least six feet around, landed between the demons and me. Blezor popped his head out of the driver's side door, shaking his fist at me. "I loved you!"

"We barely knew each other!" I almost laughed. "I'm good, but I'm not that good!"

"I'll kill you!" Blezor screamed. "How could you steal from me?"

"It wasn't personal!" I shouted back. "It's just business."

"That's bull! Everything is personal!"

I had to get clear of these psychopaths. I couldn't reach Lily, but the demon's car sat idling behind me. I slid over the hood and ripped open the driver's side door. The car hummed under me as I slammed the gear in reverse. The tires screeched, and I took off backward across the dock.

Bullets pinged against the hood as Blezor fired an Uzi at me. *That little prick!* I looked into my rearview mirror to see a half dozen cars and trucks turn on their lights at the entrance to the dock. The way out was completely blocked by a string of Blezor's men.

Oh, poor Blezor. You really didn't know me at all, did you? No wonder we didn't last.

I slammed my foot down on the brake and spun the car until I was straight on with the blockade. Blezor was gaining with his monster truck.

"*Tonnau sioc!*" I shouted, and a shockwave echoed out from the car as I gunned it forward. Two cars in the center of the blockade flipped and crashed upon two other cars, giving me the perfect window to freedom. I slid through them and out into the night, Blezor hot on my heels.

CHAPTER 3

Blezor chased after me in his monster truck while two other cars that didn't care a lick about the rules of the road fired guns at my trunk. They were gaining on me! *Stupid car.* Lily would have dusted them easily. This awful Cutlass dragged like it was pulling a boat anchor behind it.

"Come on, come on, come on!" I urged as I felt around the passenger seat and in the grooves around the seat as well. "Wand, need a wand."

I didn't mind throwing magic around on the dock without a wand because there weren't a lot of buildings or pedestrians around, but after I turned onto the street, there were other cars and people that would be severely demolished if I let magic fly wildly everywhere. On top of all that, I was amped up and full of adrenaline, so my power would be even greater and harder to control. I definitely needed a focusing agent. *We couldn't all be as careless as Blezor's cronies.*

"Please, come on," I said to myself.

Then, a pen presented itself in my field of vision. "Will this work?" I heard from the back seat. I glanced back to find a demon girl in the back seat with big, green eyes and a disarming smile. "Hello?"

"Uhhh," I replied. "Who are you?"

"Anjelica, with a J. That's not a mistake. That's just how it's spelled." Her finger pointed to the windshield. "You should really keep your eyes on the road."

I had drifted into oncoming traffic, and a Mack truck was bearing down on me, blaring its horn. I screamed and swerved back into my lane. When I was steady again, I looked at the girl through the rearview mirror.

"Who are you, and what are you doing in this car? Are you working for those demon toadies? Do I need to kill you?"

"Um…okay. Like I said, I'm Anjelica, with a J and a C. I was kidnapped by those demon toadies, so I'm not working for them. In fact, I kind of hate them." She stopped for a second. "And for the last question, why would anyone say yes?"

"Touché," I said. "If you were kidnapped, then why aren't you tied up?"

"I was. I gnawed through it like a beaver and then burrowed through the back seat. If you look next to me, you'll see that there's a big frigging hole in it. Why would I rip a big hole in a car if I wasn't trying to escape?"

She was right. There was a roughly demon-girl-sized hole in the back seat. "I suppose I believe you."

"Good," Anjelica said, holding up the pen. "Because it's the truth. Now, you're looking for a wand. Will this work?"

I grabbed it from her. "In a pinch. Can you drive?"

"Kind of? I mean, I passed driver's ed but—"

"Then take the wheel."

I didn't wait for Anjelica to leap forward and snatch the wheel before I rolled down the window and aimed the improvised wand at the cars chasing me.

"*Nodwydd!*"

A thousand little needles shot from the end of the pen and popped the tire of the blue car in the lead, sending it careening into the white car that pursued me. Both cars crashed into the end median in a fiery crash. The monster truck drove right over them like it was nothing, crushing whoever was inside into a little flat pancake.

I fell back into the car and took the wheel again from Anjelica. "Thanks."

She grinned. "We definitely didn't learn that in driver's ed."

Bullets ricocheted off the car again. Blezor was firing a submachine gun out of his driver's side window.

"We have to lose him."

I spun the wheel of the car and hit the brakes, turning the car into a sideways skid before gunning it up the street. A monster truck could never take that turn, and I watched Blezor speed through the intersection. Halfway up the street, I spun up into an alley.

I pointed the pen out of the window. "*Trawsnewid!*" A green spark shot out and created a portal in front of us big enough for the car to drive through. "Hang on!" I shouted.

"What are you doing?" Anjelica asked, her eyes darting from the portal and back to me.

"Trust me," I said.

"No!" she yelped, covering her face.

The car glided through the portal. When it emerged on the other side, it was no longer a car, but an ice cream truck with a big ice cream cone on the top of it, playing Christmas melodies, as they often did for some unknown reason. *Seriously, there were all sorts of public domain music; why Christmas music?*

I slowed the truck to a stop at the end of the alleyway then looked in the back for Anjelica. She kicked her way out of a metal chest, holding a chocolate ice cream cone.

"This is so weird, and I am so cold."

"Just get down, okay?" I said, turning onto the street. "He should be going the other way on this road right about now."

Sure enough, I watched Blezor's monster truck race the other way down the road, missing us completely. We had avoided him, at least for the moment, and now I could figure out what the story was with my little stowaway.

"Phew," I said as I threw my car in park and caught my breath.

Anjelica peeled open the ice cream cone and nibbled at it. Her audacity made me chuckle. "You really thought of everything with this transformation."

"How is it?"

"Good." She smacked her lips and shrugged. "Not great, but good."

"That's what you get with a five-second spell cast under duress." I turned to her. "Now that the insanity's over, who are you again?"

She must have been starving because I heard her stomach grumble from the other side of the truck. "Can we do this over food? I haven't eaten all day."

"You are literally eating an ice cream cone."

Anjelica rolled her eyes. "Ice cream isn't food. It just slides down."

"I didn't know that."

"It's basic science. So, can we get some real food? Like a dozen hamburgers?"

"Sure, kid."

CHAPTER 4

When I was younger, I wanted to be a dancer. I spent nearly every afternoon taking classes until my feet bled and my muscles ached. When I wasn't in class, I was teaching them or helping somebody teach. I was good, too. So good that it got to the point where I really thought I had a chance at a scholarship to Julliard or perhaps the Sorbonne, in France, thousands of miles away from my nagging mother, where I could start over.

I was not much older than Anjelica when that dream began to fizzle and eventually faded from my life. My mother had stopped paying for my lessons, but I was determined to continue, so I got a job to pay for them myself. That's what led me to the lucrative and dangerous world of organized crime. It wasn't my life then, just something I did on the side. Steal something here, sell it to a fence there. It was just a taste, then.

It was only after I came home with gobs of money, enough to pay for lessons for the rest of my life, that Mom told me the truth: I wasn't human. I couldn't apply for the scholarship because it wouldn't be fair; I would always be stronger and faster than anyone else in any class. I tried to tell her that I was a great dancer because I worked harder than everyone else, but she insisted it had nothing to do with my skill and everything to do with my breeding.

She refused to sign the permission slip for my scholarship audition and swore that if I got in, she would not co-sign a loan for me. I couldn't do anything because I was underage. I swore that I would make enough money to pay my own way, but there were few jobs I could take that paid enough to get by, let alone get ahead.

Thievery, however, always paid, no matter who or when you were, and with my naturally lithe body, innate stability, superior strength, and small frame, I was a natural thief. I worked on my own terms, in my own time, and as long as I got the goods, I got paid. Sure, sometimes bad men tried to stiff me, but I was more than happy to knock teeth out if necessary.

I was sixteen then. By the time I lifted my head to look around, I was twenty-five. Even with all the money I'd earned, it didn't matter. My body was too old for professional dance. That's a younger woman's game. I never dance anymore, and while I take most of the blame for that, it all started with my mother telling me no when I was Anjelica's age. It wasn't fair that something that happened in your youth could derail your whole life, and being kidnapped was not a small little thing. It had the potential to knock her out cold, and I couldn't let that happen.

"Feel better?" I asked, taking a sip of coffee as Anjelica stuffed another bite of burger into her mouth. Either she didn't have any shame, or she was already comfortable with me because there was mustard, ketchup, and grease all over her little demonic face.

"Mm-hmm," Anjelica replied, wiping her mouth with the one-ply paper napkin until it ripped apart in her hand. She used the sleeve of her shirt instead. "So much better. You build up an appetite, locked in a trunk all day. It was so hot. I feel like I dropped ten pounds from sweat alone." She took a sip of her milkshake. "Are you going to eat anything?"

I shook my head. "I don't eat. Coffee is fine with me."

Anjelica cocked her head. "What do you mean 'I don't eat'? Everyone eats."

"I'm not everyone." I didn't feel like explaining to her that I didn't have to eat unless I wanted to indulge. Another gift and curse from my dear, old parents.

"Ominous." Anjelica crammed a half dozen fries into her mouth. "You should try eating. It's awesome." She dipped another fry into her milkshake. "Mmmmm…sweet and salty. The ultimate flavor combination."

"That's disgusting," I said, wrinkling my nose in disgust. "Can we get back to you, please?"

"If we have to."

"We have to," I said. "Any idea why those monsters kidnapped you?"

"I know exactly why."

"Would you care to enlighten me?"

"All right." Anjelica looked around, then leaned forward to whisper. "But what I have to tell you is gonna shock you. It will blow your mind." Her eyes were wide. "You sure you can handle it?"

"Yeah, I'm good." I chuckled. If this girl knew even a hundredth of what I'd seen. "Hit me with it."

"It's really big news." Anjelica looked around again. "You sure this place is safe and stuff?"

I nodded. "I'm sure. I know the owner. Anything you say here will stay in our confidence."

She sighed before nodding slowly. "All right. Don't be scared—for I am—" She was so close to me I could taste the fries on her breath. "—a demon."

I leaned away from the table. "Oh, is that it? Cuz I already knew that."

Anjelica cocked her head, disgusted. "What do you mean you knew that? Nobody knows that. I didn't even know until those demon pricks told me earlier tonight."

I pointed to my glasses. "I see everything. The owner's a troll. The waitress is a changeling, and the barback, she's a gorgon, a real pretty one at that." I took another sip of coffee. "And you, you're a demon."

"You knew I was a demon, and you didn't say anything?" She glanced around the room one more time, this time with curiosity. "If all that is true, then this place is so gnarly."

"I don't come here for the weak coffee. I come for the company. It has a very monster-y clientele, and I dig that." I took another sip of coffee. "I'm surprised you didn't know you were a demon until somebody told you. It's not even a very good masking spell."

"Well, I didn't even know to look for it until tonight, did I?"

"I guess not, and it would take somebody like me to see through it."

"What are you?" she asked, cocking her head to the side.

I waved my hand. "This isn't about me. It's about you. Being a demon doesn't explain why you were kidnapped, so spill."

Anjelica pouted. "You suck. Did you know that?"

"I saved your life, didn't I?"

"I guess you did."

"And I'm buying all this food for you, right?"

"Well, yeah. That's true."

Now it was my turn to lean in, close to her face. "Look, I want to help you. If you want my help, I need to know everything."

"Fine." Anjelica sighed. "Just know this is no fun."

"More fun than being in a trunk." I smirked. "I can put you back, though, if you would prefer."

Anjelica stuffed another bite of her hamburger in her face and washed it down with more of the milkshake. "Fine, fine. So, I'm not just a demon."

"Obviously."

"I am…" she paused for dramatic effect, "the antichrist."

I paused, considering this. "Well, that is considerably more interesting, and it makes much more sense why you were kidnapped."

"Glad it could hold your attention, finally."

I slid the knife out of my jacket and placed it on the table. "Must be why they needed this."

"Holy sh—" She nearly spat out her milkshake. "That is a big knife!"

I nodded. "Big and powerful. I can feel the dark energy flowing through it. Any idea why they would take you today of all days?"

"I dunno."

"Think," I said. "It's important."

She threw her hands in the air. "Oh, you want me to think? Really helpful. Like I wasn't already. All they said was I'm the antichrist, and I had to die tonight."

I finished my cup of coffee. "Well, that's good news."

She sighed and slammed her hands on the table. "How did you hear good news in the sack of dung that is my life?"

"Because if we can keep you alive until morning, you should be safe."

"Okay," Anjelica said. "That's good because I would very much like this not to be my last meal."

I shrugged. "You could do worse."

"Oh, it's delicious, but I definitely want my last meal to be sushi. No doubt in my mind."

"I'll keep my fingers crossed for you on that one."

Anjelica looked up from her food. "Are you really gonna help me?"

I offered a tight smile. "As much as I can. Those pricks tried to kill me tonight, too, ya know. The least I could do is keep you alive to thwart whatever plans they had."

"Thanks."

"Don't thank me yet. You've never had to spend a whole night with someone like me." I held up my hand to ask for the check. "Now, finish that up. We have work to do."

***

If you enjoyed this preview, make sure to pick up *Magic* today!

ALSO BY RUSSELL NOHELTY

NOVELS
My Father Didn't Kill Himself
Sorry for Existing
Gumshoes: The Case of Madison's Father
Invasion
The Vessel
The Void Calls Us Home
Worst Thing in the Universe
Anna and the Dark Place
The Marked Ones
The Dragon Scourge
The Dragon Champion
The Dragon Goddess
The Obsidian Spindle Saga

COMICS and OTHER ILLUSTRATED WORK
The Little Bird and the Little Worm
Ichabod Jones: Monster Hunter
Gherkin Boy
How NOT to Invade Earth

www.russellnohelty.com

1000 BC – BETRAYED [HELL PT 1]
/PIXIE DUST

500 BC – FALLEN [HELL PT 2]

200 BC – HELLFIRE [HELL PT 3]

1974 AD – MYSTERY SPOT [RUIN PT 1]

1976 AD – INTO HELL [RUIN PT 2]

1984 AD – LAST STAND [RUIN PT 3]

1985 AD – CHANGE

1985 AD – MAGIC/BLACK MARKET HEROINE

1985 AD – EVIL

1989 AD – DEATH'S KISS
[DARKNESS PT 1]

2000 AD – TIME

2015 AD – HEAVEN

2018 AD – DEATH'S RETURN [DARKNESS PT 2]

2020 AD – KATRINA HATES THE DEAD
[DEATH PT 1]

2176 AD – CONQUEST

2177 AD – DEATH'S KISS
[DARKNESS PT 3]

12,018 AD – KATRINA HATES THE GODS
[DEATH PT 2]

12,028 AD – KATRINA HATES THE UNIVERSE
[DEATH PT 3]

12,046 AD – EVERY PLANET HAS A GODSCHURCH
[DOOM PT 1]

12,047 AD – THERE'S EVERY REASON TO FEAR
[DOOM PT. 2]

12,049 AD – THE END TASTES LIKE PANCAKES
[DOOM PT 3]

12,176 AD – CHAOS